D1585649

Quintin
Jardine

BLOOD RED

headline

Copyright © 2010 Portador Ltd

The right of Quintin Jardine to be identified as the Author
of the Work has been asserted by him in accordance with the
Copyright, Designs and Patents Act 1988.

First published in 2010
by HEADLINE PUBLISHING GROUP

First published in paperback in 2010
by HEADLINE PUBLISHING GROUP

1

Cataloguing in Publication Data is available from the British Library

978 0 7553 4026 2 (B format)
978 0 7553 5769 7 (A format)

Typeset in Electra by Avon DataSet Ltd,
Bidford-on-Avon, Warwickshire

Printed in the UK by CPI Mackays, Chatham, ME5 8TD

Headline's policy is to use papers that are natural, renewable and
recyclable products and made from wood grown in sustainable forests.
The logging and manufacturing processes are expected to conform
to the environmental regulations of the country of origin.

HEADLINE PUBLISHING GROUP
An Hachette UK Company
338 Euston Road
London NW1 3BH

www.headline.co.uk
www.hachette.co.uk

Quintin Jardine gave up the life of a political spin doctor for the more morally acceptable world of murder and mayhem. Happily married, he hides from critics and creditors in secret locations in Scotland and Spain, but can be tracked down through his website: www.quintinjardine.com.

Praise for Quintin Jardine's novels:

'A triumph. I am first in the queue for the next one' *Scotland on Sunday*

'Remarkably assured . . . a *tour de force*' *New York Times*

'The perfect mix for a highly charged, fast-moving crime thriller' *Glasgow Herald*

'[Quintin Jardine] sells more crime fiction in Scotland than John Grisham and people queue around the block to buy his latest book' *The Australian*

'There is a whole world here, the tense narratives all come to the boil at the same time in a spectacular climax' *Shots* magazine

'Engrossing, believable characters . . . captures Edinburgh beautifully . . . it all adds up to a very good read' *Edinburgh Evening News*

'A complex story combined with robust characterisation; a murder/mystery novel of our time that will keep you hooked to the very last page' *The Scots Magazine*

This book is for the talented bundle of fun that is Kirsti Louise Abernethy, who pulls an immaculate focus, and once helped to splash paint all over Glasgow. She and I have many things in common, but this is the most important: we both love her mum.

In memory of Joaquim Alay Calmó, 1946 – 2009

I'm not visited by too many bad dreams, far fewer than my fair share, given some of the things I've done in my time. But for the last few months, there's been one; it stops my breath, until I sit bolt upright in bed, wide eyed and slicked with sweat, knowing that sleep is over for the night and weak enough to wish that there was someone beside me, someone to be awakened by my distress, someone to hold me and tell me to be calm, that everything's all right . . . even though I know that it isn't, and that it might never be again.

In my dream I can see the body fall, arms and legs flailing in a vain attempt at flight. I'm observing this from below, but I don't consider for a second that I'm in any danger myself. I don't attempt to move out of the way. I stand there in frozen fascination, for there is something I want to know, something I need to know.

To trot out the old cliché, it's not the fall that does for you, it's what happens immediately afterwards. Yes, sure, except . . . There's a school of thought that claims that the victim will have fainted before coming to a very abrupt stop. I'm here to tell you, that isn't true: for in my nightmare, as that doomed, plummeting human comes towards me, about to be killed by gravity, the very force that is keeping me and all the rest of us safe, I can see the face, eyes bulging, teeth bared, and I can hear the silent scream. I can see it, and I can recognise it and I scream myself, out loud, because it's . . .

And that's when I wake up, the name dying on my lips, the body shattering on the rocks as illusion fades into reality, and I yearn for the comfort I may never truly have again.

One

Nobody calls me Prim any more, not since I got to this place. To tell you the truth, I've always preferred to be called by my proper given name, Primavera, but I've been too polite to object to the abbreviation. Where I live now, in the tiny community that I've chosen as my home for the rest of my life, no one would ever dream of shortening such a beautiful word, and that suits me just fine. It was always an inappropriate nickname anyway; I have many qualities, the same mix of good and bad as most people, but primness has never been one of them.

I never really believed, in my heart of hearts, that I'd settle down, not until four years ago. Through my teens, and my twenties, as my barely committed search for Mr Right grew more and more haphazard, until it dwindled to nothing, my life became that of a nomad, moving from place to place and job to job, without any sense that I would ever find either vocation or location, on a long-term basis.

When, finally, my path and that of the man of my dreams did cross, it hardly brought stability. Instead my wandering continued, the background to a series of adventures and betrayals, in which I was not always the innocent party, until I found a home for a few months in Cornton Vale, Her Majesty's less than charming prison for Scotland's female offenders. The regime in the place didn't straighten me up, but the experience toughened me. Also, it left me with an unspoken determination to regain custody of my lovely son Tom. His birth should have triggered the change in me; in truth I'm more than a little ashamed that it didn't. But no; instead, it took a near-death experience in a plane crash to do that and to make me understand that what I had to do from then on was to dedicate my life to my boy.

And that's what I am doing. He and I are a two-person unit, living comfortably in the picture-postcard village of St Martí d'Empúries, on Spain's Catalan coast, in a rambling old house overlooking the Golfe de Roses. Tom's eight now; old enough for sensible conversation yet young enough still to be excited by things like the arrival of the Three Kings, the climax of the Spanish Christmas celebrations. Sometimes I wish he'd just stay that way, that the two of us could be sealed into a time bubble and go on as we are, for ever. I suppose most mums feel that at some point. No harm in dreaming, is there?

I settled here looking, unashamedly, for a quiet life. Have I found it? So far, fat chance! I did manage peaceful for a couple of years in St Martí, before I ran into all that bother with my cousin Frank. That was hairy, but it passed off and things were smooth again for a year or so, so smooth that I began to think

I had cracked it. There were no clouds on our horizon; but out here it can rain when you least expect it . . . or is that just on my life?

Two

There are four men in my life of whom I could say 'Yes, I love him' . . . not that I've ever been into such public declarations.

One is my dad, the eccentric David Phillips, master craftsman and totally atypical Scottish gentleman. He's been there for me all my life, even if we've actually seen very little of each other for the last fifteen years. I feel the pain of guilt from time to time when I think about that, but my father is as wedded to Auchterarder as now I am to St Martí d'Empúries. He'll die there, as I hope I'll die here . . . although not for a hell of a long time yet.

My son, he's another; top of them all, in truth. Tom Blackstone is only eight years old, but in terms of the emotional support he gives me, he's going on eighteen. We were a one-parent family from the start, Tom and I, not out of any choice I ever made, but, if you believe in such concepts, by the justice of Fate, paying me back for all the wrong choices I went for through the chaotic decade that was my thirties. He and I live in our big, ancient stone house, in our tiny Catalan village. His passport may say that he's British, but his being is multicultural, with roots in Spain, in Scotland, in Monaco, where his half-siblings live, and in America, where his cousins are and where he spent some of his earliest time. In looks he's like his father, naturally, although in the last year or so, I've seen more of myself in him; the colour of his eyes, the dimple in his chin. His friends are mostly Spanish kids, although there are a few junior Brits among their number, the children of people who've moved south to become involved in the tourist industry, or in some cases in search of a more civilised environment. For now, he goes to school in L'Escala, the 'parent' town of St Martí, where he's taught in Catalan, the language that was banned during the Franco years. (The old general must have been a little paranoid about Catalunya; he even banned its national dance, the sardana.) When he's older, he'll . . . he'll make that choice himself. Most mothers believe that their children are special, but I don't. I believe that my son is very special indeed, and that at some time in the future he'll do something great, something truly exceptional. He's my Galahad, the perfect youth formed out of the imperfections of his parents. A romantic notion? Maybe, but be sure that I won't allow him to go out into the world as one of those innocents who are easy prey to the wicked.

Tom's father? Yes, of course he's on my list. Oz Blackstone, a lad about Edinburgh when we met, with no ambitions other than to get his leg over and to maintain a single-figure golf handicap. Sometimes I wonder how his life would have turned out if our paths hadn't brought us face to face; I don't have too many possibilities to consider. He'd have married the love of his life, as he did anyway, but they'd have stayed in Edinburgh rather than move to Glasgow. Jan wouldn't have had the 'accident', and today they'd be smug, boringly blissful forty-somethings, with a raft of strangely identical children . . . or she would be, to be accurate. But we did collide, he and I, an explosive reaction took place between us, and Oz, without a single scrap of planning, was launched on a career that took him to great fame, great fortune, and three marriages, the brief second, during which our boy was conceived, being to me. Oz was good at everything he did, except marriage. The world thought that his third was idyllic, but the truth is that even then, when he had a happy, stable home background, he and I could never keep our hands off each other for long. He'd have denied it of course, but if you'd known him you'd have realised that his life was full of secrets, most of them deep and dark.

No? Hey, I believed for a couple of years that he tried to kill me. It's only recently that I've been persuaded that I was wrong, but the very fact that I could accept that possibility should tell you everything about him. If the true story of his career was ever written it would be a global bestseller, but I'm the only person left alive who could do that, and trust me, it ain't going to happen. The only thing about Oz that's clear and undeniable is this: he's dead. Doesn't stop me loving him, though. This is how I see it: we were apart for spells during the ten years or so from our first meeting, and only together full-time for two or three of them; so this is just another separation, only longer.

What? Sorry, I was drifting for a moment or two. The fourth man I love? His name is Gerard Hernanz Rivera, he's thirty-nine years old, about three years younger than me, big, dark-haired, an outdoor type with strong legs, well muscled from mountain-biking, and broad shoulders from swimming, his two principal hobbies. He's well read, amusing, courteous, multilingual, and he's the ideal dinner companion. 'How is he over breakfast?' I hear you ask. He's exactly the same, but I have to add the qualification that the only breakfasts I've ever shared with Gerard have been in the cafés in St Martí, or occasionally those facing the town beach in L'Escala. This is not to say that I wouldn't like to serve him croissants and coffee on my bedroom terrace, watching the sun make its presence felt, but that was a non-starter from the beginning, the blocker being Gerard's job as our parish priest, of the Roman Catholic variety. But why . . . pray . . . should that stop me loving him? He's a truly lovable man, possessed of all the qualities I mentioned, and the fact is that half the women in his parish fancied him from the moment he moved here. I know this, because I've seen the look in their eyes on those occasions when he's been my partner at local events. He probably noticed it too, but he didn't mind, because he understood from the beginning of our friendly relationship that I had respect for his calling. There was just one time, when we had dinner together for my birthday, on the back terrace in Can Roura, that I could see an uncertainty in him. I'd had more to drink than usual, and maybe I'd looked at him in a way that made him feel uncomfortable. Whatever it was, I told him, 'Gerard,

I'll make you a promise here and now; I'll never be a danger to your vocation. I'll be there for you when you're lonely, as you must be from time to time, given that God does not do stimulating conversation. I'll chum you to the movies. I'll share a bottle with you whenever vanity gets the better of you and you feel like showing off your undoubted knowledge of the fine wines of Spain. I'll be your informal confessor, as you've been mine. But I will never, ever, try to entice you into my bed. I don't need any of that stuff right now, and if I ever find that I do, I'll make alternative arrangements, of which you will know nothing. This is not to say that I'm not physically attracted to you, but I value your friendship and your company way too much to ever put it at risk.'

He raised an eyebrow as he looked back at me. 'I have one brother,' he began, 'in Granada, although he is everywhere. His name is Santiago, Saint James in English . . . although he is no saint . . . called Santi for short. But I have no sisters. Perhaps, Primavera, you would like to fill that gap.'

And that's how it was. He became the brother I never had, and vice versa. And if there were still a few cynical crones who muttered behind our backs, then, as Gerard would never say, far less do . . . fuck 'em.

Three

I was really looking forward to last summer. Unforeseen events had cast a shadow over the year before, and it had taken me a while to get over them, emotionally, if not physically. One of the positives of the experience had been its demonstration of the strength of the friendships that Tom and I had in the village. The resident population, within its ancient walls and in the area that surrounds them, is just a little short of a hundred, but there are none I don't know, and none I don't like.

When you're shown such goodwill, it has to be returned, and so, in the aftermath of the blip in my tranquillity, I decided to do everything I could to involve myself in the village life and events. But that resolution isn't as grand as it sounds, since for half of the year the people are devoted full-time to serving, and making money from, the hordes of tourists who descend on L'Escala and on the campsites along the beaches to the north of St Martí, and for the other half they're devoted full-time to doing not very much.

I looked around, and asked around for ways to help; after

much head-scratching, Cisco, who runs Meson del Conde, the restaurant that faces the church across Plaça Major, pointed out that one thing the village lacked was a proper information centre for visitors. I jumped on that one. My house is bang next door to the church, and I have a small garden . . . and dog-pound . . . in front. With the cooperation of the town's tourist office . . . no Catalan can resist something for nothing . . . I had a small booth built, set into the fence on top of the wall, with a frame to hold all sorts of leaflets, and a bell that people who wanted more specific advice could use to call me, or Tom (who's comfortable with adults, knows as much about the area as I do, and who's well big enough to see over the top of the booth), or even Father Gerard if he happened to be around.

My new facility was a success; it opened at Easter and within a couple of months I'd been asked to sell tickets for the pleasure boats that cruise along the coast, and tokens for the *carrilet*, the tractor-drawn train that runs between St Martí and the beach at Montgo, on the far side of L'Escala. I'd even been approached by a golf course twenty kilometres away and asked if I'd handle bookings for them. (I turned them down; I was there to help visitors to my village, not send them away.)

The venture gave me something positive to do, and made me feel good about myself. But it didn't use up all of my time. The peak tourist season lasts for only six weeks or so, from mid-July to the end of August: I knew I would be busy then, but for the rest of the mid-year months, most of the business is done at weekends. I was still in the market for things to do, and that's when Ben told me about his wine fair.

Benedict Simmers is an English guy who pitched up in St Martí pretty much as soon as he finished university, so he told me, and never left. He did a few tourist-related jobs, involving, mostly, parties of school kids, before he got 'repped out' as he puts it, and went into the wine trade. He sold online for a while, until he saw an opportunity, and opened a bodega, a wine shop at the foot of the street that leads up to Plaça Major.

He's Tom's friend as much as mine, thanks to the dogs. We have an intellectually challenged Labrador called Charlie, and Ben has two of the same breed. As I understand it, Cher, the older of his pair, is Charlie's aunt, which makes Mustard, her whelp, his cousin. When he's not at school, Tom often helps Ben when the shop is busy, by walking all three of them. This is no problem for him; he seems to speak Labrador as fluently as all his other languages, for they all obey him instantly, even Mustard, who's lawless with everyone else.

He was doing that, one Saturday in May, and I was in the shop restocking my wine cellar, according to Gerard's guidance and recommendations . . . he'd been drinking a fair bit of it, so I decided that he might as well help me choose . . . when I saw what looked like a poster displayed on the shop's computer monitor.

'*Arrels de vi*,' I read aloud. 'Means "The roots of wine" in English, doesn't it?'

I should explain that the St Martí community, even Tom and I sometimes, when there's nobody else around, speaks a variety of tongues in its daily discourse, but most commonly Catalan, the language on the screen.

'That's right,' Ben replied.

'What is it?'

'It's the name of my wine fair ... the fair I'm planning, that is.'

'What's a wine fair?' I asked.

He and Gerard gazed at me, their expressions dangerously close to patronising. 'A wine fair,' the priest replied, 'is a gathering of producers, brought together to display and offer their latest and finest vintages, for an educated public to taste and, hopefully, to buy.'

I looked at the Englishman. 'Where are you going to hold it?'

Ben waved a hand towards the door. 'The plan is that it'll be out there, in Plaça Petita.'

I walked over to the entrance and looked at the small square, gently sloping, but terraced. Four pathways lead into it, two of them rising from the car parks that lie below the village. 'Will it be big enough?'

He nodded. 'Should be. I reckon it'll take at least a dozen stands, and that's as many as I'd want ... for a first effort, at any rate.'

'Who'll be here?'

'I don't know yet. I'm approaching all the Emporda wine-makers. So far the response has been good.'

Catalunya contains a number of *comercs*, or regions; Emporda is ours, and it's split into two subdivisions, upper and lower. 'When are you going to have it?' I asked.

He pointed to a date at the foot of the poster on the screen.

'First week in September, soon as the August chaos is over . . . that's if I can get everything put together. I've still got a hell of a lot to do.'

'Need any help?'

He grinned. 'Nice of you to offer, but I have to sell the concept to the exhibitors myself.'

'There's more to it than that, surely. There's marketing, publicity; I could use the information centre to plug it, and to sell advance tickets.'

'Advance tickets? I plan to sell on the day, that's all.'

I frowned at him. 'Ben,' I said, 'I don't know a hell of a lot about business, but I do know that if you've covered your overheads before the show opens, everything else is profit.'

'I hear what you're saying,' he conceded. 'If you'd do that, I suppose it would be a big help.'

'I will, and you could sell tickets through the hotels as well,' I added.

'That would be good too. I know most of them. Then there are the restaurants I supply; I'm sure they'll advertise it, at the very least.'

I was well warmed up. 'I could talk to the people I know in the tourist department in L'Escala; to see if they'd help. They have a website.'

Ben grimaced. 'You might have a problem with them. There's one big fly in the ointment; I need the mayor's co-operation. I called her yesterday and . . . let's just say she didn't make any encouraging noises.'

'Why do you need her onside?'

'Because Plaça Petita is public land, and the mayor has the power to decide whether it can be used or not.'

'What about the local traders' association? You're a member. Can't they put pressure on her?'

'I've talked to the leaders; they're scared of upsetting her. A lot of them rely on town hall approvals to run their businesses. Getting on the wrong side of the mayor is never a good idea in L'Escala. Besides . . .' He paused.

'What?'

'I'm not sure, but I think there might be a little bit of prejudice.'

'Are you saying they're agin it because you're British?'

'Could be.'

Beside me, Gerard sighed. By that time, he'd come to know my rising hackles when he saw them.

'The hell with that,' I declared. 'Most of their businesses only survive because of the money that the Brits, the French, the Belgians and the rest of Europe spend in this town. And as for the mayor, L'Escala educates its children and runs its social facilities thanks to the taxes paid by expat property owners. You concentrate on bringing in the wine producers and leave her to me.'

Ben frowned. 'Are you sure? I can't afford to pay you, Prim. This will be a shoestring operation.'

'I don't want paying,' I told him. 'But I'd better have some sort of authority when I go to see her.'

And that is how I became operations manager of Arrels de Vi, the St Martí d'Empúries wine fair.

Four

If I ever suspect in future that I'm getting too big for my boots, I'll remember my visit to the Casa de la Vila, the town hall of the Ajuntament of L'Escala, climbing the stairs to the reception desk on the first floor, and confronting authority, face to face.

Dolores Fumado Ortega, the mayor's chief of staff, as she had introduced herself, was a short, stocky woman of an age that wasn't easy to guess, but had to be fifty-something, maybe edging towards the next Big One. She was dressed in a grey seam-strained skirt, and a white blouse outlining the industrial-strength bra that was necessary to restrain her formidable bosom. Her hair was on the dark side of blond, but with a blue sheen, professionally shaped and lacquered. The ladies of L'Escala have a wide choice of hairdresser; I suspected that she paid daily visits to hers.

She had greeted me coolly, in a way that made it clear that whoever I was, she was more important, and the temperature seemed to be falling by the minute. She peered at me over the top of gold-framed, light-reactive glasses, her eyes offering nothing. 'It is quite impossible,' she declared. 'The mayor's diary is full. She couldn't possibly see you now.'

I smiled, taking the meek and mild route. 'I'll wait.'

'There is no point, senora.' (There is no proper equivalent of Mrs in Catalan or Castellano.) 'She has meetings all day and will have no free time.'

'I'll come back tomorrow, if you'd like to schedule me in.'

She sighed, telling me that I was trying her patience. 'That will not be possible either.'

'The day after?'

She shook her head. 'The mayor is busy with the affairs of the town, with important matters.'

I tried smiling again. 'Everything is important to someone,' I ventured. 'The wine fair is important to us.'

'But not to the mayor.' She had grown so frosty that she reminded me of a dumpy version of the witch in Narnia.

The truth is, the meek never will inherit the earth, so I changed tack. 'When's the next municipal election?' I snapped. I could feel my eyes narrow as I spoke.

'In two years. How is that relevant?'

'How? Time for a reality check, Senora Fumado. I did some research before I came here. At this moment the mayor is at the head of a coalition. Her party has six seats out of thirteen; she's sat on her arse in that office ten feet away from us thanks to the support of the single independent councillor that the people returned last time, her sister's father-in-law, as I understand it. She's hanging in there by little more than one polished fingernail. Two years from now she's going to need all the goodwill she can get.' Dolores began to move, as if to walk away from me, then stopped, as if she'd realised that wasn't going to shut me up. 'What she won't need,' I told her loudly, 'is a determined, well-resourced person who speaks English, French, Catalan and Spanish lobbying against her, and maybe even fielding a multinational slate of expatriate residents. It may be an inconvenient truth, but truth it is, that I, and people like me, British, Belgian, French, Dutch and the rest, have a vote in the local elections and can stand as candidates. How many of us voted last time? Damn few. But how many of us are there in this town, just waiting to be stirred up? You don't need much to find the answer. Just pick up the local telephone directory and flick through it.'

I'd cracked her; I could see that. I stood there waiting for a response. But when it came, it was from behind me.

'You'll waken the sleeping giant, Mrs Blackstone?' said a female voice, in English. 'In that case you'd better come in.'

I turned, and saw a tall woman, in her mid-thirties, gazing at me with a half-smile on her face. She couldn't have looked less like her executive assistant if they'd both worked at it. Her eyes were big and brown, long lashed, the compelling feature of her oval face. Her hair was dark, and fell to her shoulders in loose curls. She wore a white T-shirt emblazoned with the name and logo of the town's anchovy museum . . . no, I'm not kidding; L'Escala has an anchovy museum . . . and tucked into blue denim cut-offs in a way that emphasised the swell of her breasts, the narrowness of her waist and the curve of her hips. As I looked at her my first thought was,

21

'How come this woman didn't pick up every male vote in town?'

'I am Justine Michels Fumado, the mayor,' she said, slipping into Catalan. 'I can tell you don't react well to the word "no". Not many people get past my guardian. Congratulations.'

As she showed me into a small wood-panelled office, with a door leading out to a balcony that looked down on to the square below and across to the church, I pondered her name. 'Fumado,' I repeated.

She knew what I was asking. 'Yes.' She confirmed my quickly formed suspicion. 'That dragon outside is my mother. She's one of the old-time L'Escala families; half a dozen of them still own much of the town. When I moved into this office six years ago, she insisted on moving in next door. I was only twenty-nine then, and she thought I'd need protection. As you've found out, she still thinks so.' She smiled. 'She's useful, from time to time, against those less formidable than you. In the summer L'Escala fills up with people who turn up to discover that they have problems with their apartments or villas. They don't know the local system, so all they can think to do is march into the town hall and complain to the mayor.'

'I'll take that as a compliment to us both.' I paused. 'And your first surname? Michels: that's not Catalan.'

She pointed to a photograph, in a silver frame on a small cabinet. I looked and saw her eyes gaze out at me, from the face of a tall, handsome, silver-haired man. 'My father was Belgian; he came to Catalunya forty years ago, to sell furnishings; my mother met him in his store in Figueras and snapped him up. His brother, my uncle, used to joke that he went to lay her carpets, but she laid him. Papa died two years ago, but I probably have him to thank for still being in this office. He was the unofficial leader of the Belgian community; they're probably the original foreign arrivals in this town, and they're my solid supporters, regardless of their usual politics. So, Senora Blackstone, you might have trouble lining up all the expats against me ... although I suspect that with your name, you could recruit the British, if you were determined to try.'

'My name?'

'I know who you are,' she told me as she settled into the leather chair behind her desk, and as I sat opposite her. 'I've known since you moved to St Martí, or back then, I should say, since you've spent time here before. Eyebrows were raised when an outsider was able to buy the house you did in the village, and there was talk; indeed there still is gossip about you. I'd be a pretty poor mayor if none of it had reached my ears. You are rumoured to be sleeping with the priest, Father Gerard, but I know him too, and I know, from someone very close to him, that isn't true. You are the former wife of Oz Blackstone, the famous actor, who lived here with you once himself, but you are not his widow. Your son is his. Your sister is the actress Dawn Phillips, and your brother-in-law is the film director Miles Grayson.' She smiled. 'You can afford to send professional people to make your point. So why are you breaking my door down yourself?'

'Because I don't employ people like that. I'm a hands-on

person, and I've been brought in by Ben Simmers to help organise his wine fair.'

'Ahh!' The mayor's head fell back as she sighed; as she gazed at the ceiling I could see that her chin showed no sign of sagging. 'That's what it is.'

'That's what it is,' I repeated. 'Ben reckons we need your permission to hold it in Plaça Petita. Is he right about that?'

'Oh, he's correct. The people of St Martí like to think that they're autonomous, but they're not. That is and always has been public land, and the town council of L'Escala decides what happens there. As leader of the council, the executive power is in my hands.'

'So? Can we do it, Madam Mayor?'

'Justine, call me Justine. I don't know; I still have to reach a decision.'

'I'm Primavera. What's difficult about a simple "yes"?'

'Nothing, but this one isn't simple.'

'In what way?'

'I have opposition to it within the town council. There is one member who's determined that it won't happen. And no ordinary member either; it's my coalition partner, the man whose vote keeps my group in power.'

'Your sister's father-in-law?'

'That's him. José-Luis Planas Ros. He's powerful within the council, because of his unique position, and also within the trading community in L'Escala. He owns the big furniture shop in the old town, a couple of bars, an estate agency, and a pizzeria on the seafront. When Ben approached the shopkeepers' association, word got to him; he opposed it and the sheep fell into line.'

'Even though Ben's a member of that group?'

'Even though.'

'What's this guy's problem with Ben? Is it because he's English? Because I warn you, if it is, I'll follow through on the threat I made to your mother. I wouldn't have to field my own slate either; if I deliver enough British votes to your main opposition . . .'

Justine Michels threw up her hands. 'I know, I know. That could swing the election. But I promise you, Mr Simmers' nationality has nothing to do with it . . . at least not directly. I think this problem would still exist, even if he was Catalan.'

'Then what is it?'

The mayor opened her mouth as if to reply, then fell silent, for almost half a minute. 'I think,' she said, eventually, 'that it would be better for you to ask your friend.'

'I will, don't you worry. And I'll be asking Senor Planas as well.'

'You'll be wasting your time if you try to lean on him. Come what may, he gets re-elected to the council every four years as an independent. The expatriate vote doesn't bother him.'

'I'll bother him, though.'

She smiled, sympathetically. 'You going to make him an offer he can't refuse?'

'I'm going to reason with him.'

She laughed. 'That's a line from the same movie.'

'I know; it's my favourite.' I had to chuckle myself, as I

recalled *The Godfather*, and the man who woke up to find his thoroughbred's head on his duvet. 'Does he have a horse?' I asked.

'Not even that would shake José-Luis. He's old school, and the problem you'd have with him is typical of his generation.'

'As in me being a woman?'

She nodded.

'How do you handle him?'

'He tolerates me and gives me his grudging support because of my sister.' She paused. 'No, because of my brother-in-law, Angel. Most of the time, he doesn't interfere with the administration. He has a portfolio, environmental services; he gets on with that and he's good at it. But occasionally, if he gets agitated about something, he can be difficult. This is one of those times.'

'And you won't overrule him and give us permission.'

'Primavera, I would do it in a second, but it's very difficult for me. As you know, I have two years left in power, and to be honest next time I may struggle to stay in this chair. This town has a modern history of turnabout in its local politics, and I can sense the swing against my party. There are many things my colleagues and I want to do, or at least get under way, before the next election. If I cross Planas, he could make it very difficult for us to fulfil these ambitions. One small local event, set against an improved social housing pro-gramme, against new classrooms for the school, against traffic improvements . . . Christ, we still have dirt roads in some parts of this town . . .'

'But is Planas so important? Wouldn't some of the other councillors support your programme?'

'Not all of it. Social housing, road improvements; they'd have to go. Planas, misogynistic old goat that he is, supports the whole platform. I haven't said "no" to your fair, not yet, but the real decision is his, and he knows it.'

I threw up my hands in surrender. 'OK, I understand.'

'I'm sorry, truly.'

'I believe you.'

'Don't you have an alternative to Plaça Petita?'

I smiled, wryly. 'No, short of holding it in the church . . . and if we did that, then nobody would ever believe that I wasn't screwing the priest. You are right, we need a Plan B, against rain, if nothing else. But I'm not giving up on Plan A without tackling this man myself.'

'But you'll talk to Benedict first, yes?'

'Yes, I will. I can't imagine what he's done to get this man so firmly against him.'

'You can't?'

Five

Everybody blushes. It's a physical thing, the effect of increased blood flow through the facial capillaries caused most commonly by embarrassment. It has nothing to do with race, but you'd think that when someone is as heavily tanned as Benedict Simmers, it would be impossible to see it.

Not so. But I'll get there.

The wine shop was open when I got back to St Martí; it was a lovely day and midweek or not, the village was starting to get busy. I headed through the square towards Plaça Petita, but slowed my approach when I saw a shape half in, half out of the doorway and realised that Ben had customers. One doesn't get in the way of a potential sale, after all. It was only when I got closer that I realised who the people were.

Ben's mum, Ingrid Simmers as was, is a part-time resident of L'Escala. She is also one of his best customers. She and his dad are divorced; she's Ingrid Reid now, and the bulk I had seen filling the door frame was that of her second husband, Matthew, a retired PR guru. They split their time pretty much equally between their two homes, the other one being in East

Lothian, in Scotland's golfing country. Oz and I once went to the beach there; got up to mischief in the secluded and sheltered dunes ('What's in it for me?' 'Sand.') up on a high point from which he claimed that he could see his old man's house through his binoculars. (Scotland's a village, really; the first time I met Matthew he told me that he knew Oz's dad, Mac, having played against him once in a golf match.)

I've never asked, but I reckon that Ingrid must be about the same age as the formidable Dolores Fumado. Around the same height too, but that's as far as it goes. I wouldn't mind her figure and her blond hair is so natural that I wonder if she's ever been to a stylist in her life.

'Hello, Primavera,' she said warmly, as I slipped into the shop. 'I hear you've been dragooned into the wine fair.'

'She volunteered, Mum,' Ben protested.

She ignored him. 'Have you been to see that awful mayor?' she asked.

'Justine's not awful,' I told her. 'In fact, she isn't the problem either. It seems that the blocker is a local dinosaur called Planas, who seems to have an effective right of veto on the council.' I looked at Ben. 'What the hell have you done to upset him?' I asked him, in Spanish.

And that's when he blushed. I don't think Ingrid noticed, suddenly she was too busy studying the shop's range of specialist olive oils, but Matthew did. I could tell by his raised eyebrow; it was very expressive, and I knew I'd stumbled on something.

'You interested in one of those, Mum?' Ben asked, as blatant a change of subject as I've ever seen. 'Take one and try it if you like.' He broke off as two more customers came into the shop, and started speaking to them in passable French.

I went outside and said hello to Cher and Mustard, who were tethered to one of the bollards that keep cars out of the plaça. After ten minutes or so, the French customers made their choice and left, closely followed by Ingrid and Matthew, who winked as he waved me goodbye. I realised that his Spanish was better than I'd supposed.

'So what's the story?' I asked, as Ben emerged to take the dogs inside, out of the sun. 'How did you cross swords with this old bastard?'

'I've never met him,' he said, as I followed him.

'The mayor said I should ask you about him.'

'Justine did?' And then he grinned, reflectively. 'No, that doesn't really surprise me.'

'You didn't tell me that you knew Justine.'

'I don't, not really.'

'Come on, Ben, either you do or you don't.'

What's beyond sheepish? Goatish? I don't know, but if it's there, Mr Simmers was it, at that moment. 'I've only met her a couple of times,' he confessed, 'at parties: she doesn't have much time for a social life. It's Elena Michels I know better.'

'Elena?'

'Justine's sister.'

'Not the one who's married to Planas's son?'

'That's the only sister she has, and I can see where that might be where the problem lies.'

Scales fell from my eyes. Young, free and single: I should have guessed there would be a woman involved somewhere. 'Oh Jesus,' I heard myself exclaim, with an alarming hint of matronly disapproval, 'tell me you didn't . . .'

'Well, yes, but hey, there was nothing wrong with it, in anyone's eyes but old Planas's. It was before she and Angel were married. Elena and I had a thing.'

'A serious thing?'

'We thought it was . . . at least I did. We lived together for a while, but it didn't work out. I saw the writing on the wall, so I left.'

'I see. But you're history. Why's the old man so set against you?'

'He's like that. From what Angel told me he blames me for splitting him and Elena up.'

'But I thought you said . . .'

'I did, and they weren't. But they had been engaged. It's . . .' He broke off as a British couple in beach clothes came into the shop, looking to buy a bottle of water. As he served them, I took the dogs through to the back room, returning as I heard them leave. 'As I was saying,' he resumed, 'it's a long story. Angel and Elena were at school together, and they were a pair then. She went to university, and he went into his dad's furniture business, but they drifted on and got engaged.'

'Very conventional by today's standards,' I commented. 'Did they share a place? Or wouldn't Elena's mum have approved . . . or her dad, since he must have been alive then.'

'From what I've heard of him, Henri wouldn't have been

bothered. It was Angel's dad who'd have put the mockers on it.'

'Justine did say he's old school.'

'And the rest. Maybe he was the reason they split up. I never asked, but he could have been. All Elena told me was that she got cold feet. She told Angel that she didn't think she wanted to marry him. He's a gentleman . . . I know him; I like him . . . he said he understood, and they went their separate ways. They'd been apart for more than a year when she and I started seeing each other.'

'When did you know you had a problem with old man Planas?'

'Not fully until today. Elena's mother told me that he wasn't happy with what Elena had done, but that was all anyone ever said.'

'Why did you and she break up?'

He frowned. 'The kindest way I can put it is that she found she was wrong, and that she really had wanted to marry Angel all along. She never said as much, but I knew. When they did get back together, very soon after we split, I was the least surprised man in town.'

'And you bear no grudges?'

'Absolutely none. But Planas does, it seems, and he carries them a long way. What are we going to do about him, Primavera?'

'I'll talk to him. Maybe I'll buy some furniture from his shop, then get round to talking about the wine fair.'

'And if that doesn't work?'

'Then I'll make sure that everyone in St Martí, and L'Escala, gets to know what he's doing, and why. See if he gets elected then.'

'I don't think I'd like that; it would harm Angel and Elena.'

'Then I'll find another solution; fuck it, if we have to we'll hold the wine fair in my house. It's just about big enough. Way to go before that, though.' I smiled, as a thought struck me. 'You know what your real problem is, don't you?'

'What's that?'

'You picked the wrong sister.'

He pulled a sad clown face. 'I'd have had to join the queue.'

'What's she like? What's she got going for her? I mean, this is a very male town, yet she's a young woman and she's its mayor. Looks don't get you elected in a place like this.'

He scratched his stubbled chin. 'Justine gets results,' he replied, 'because she has the gift of making people do things for her, sometimes without even asking them, simply because they want to please her. Looks don't get you elected, no, but charisma does.'

'Does she have a partner?'

'Most of the single guys in this town, and a load of the married ones, I'll bet, fancy Justine Michels. And they're all wasting their time. There is a man somewhere, hidden away. I haven't a clue who he is, though; nobody has, not even Elena.'

'Pity we don't know. If we could tell him that Planas is giving his lady the mayor a hard time, he might sort him out.'

Six

'José-Luis Planas?' Gerard exclaimed, as he swallowed a mouthful of melted mozzarella on my front terrace. 'He of the furniture shop? Of course I know him . . . but not as a parishioner of St Martí. Senor Planas will be seen in the front row of the big church in L'Escala at the funerals of those he considers important, and at the marriages of those whose parents consider him important enough to invite. He will be there on saints' days, and on other occasions which he believes warrant his attention. But only in the big church; he hasn't set foot in mine, not since I've been here, at any rate. Senor Planas only acknowledges priests of his own generation. He's the sort who approaches God on his own terms, as an equal, and who frowns his disapproval at Jesus, as he would any young radical.' He reached for another slice, but Tom beat him to it: Primavera's pizza feasts always turn into a race when my son's at the table. 'Why do you ask?'

'I know the man in the furniture shop,' Tom said, as he slipped Charlie a piece of crust. I encourage him to join in adult conversation. I don't subscribe to the 'seen but not heard' school of motherhood; Dawn and I weren't raised that way, although my sister was more reticent than I was. 'Mum and I went there once, to buy my bed when we moved here. He's nice; he gave me a lollipop. And he's the same age as you.'

Gerard shook his head. 'You're thinking of his son, Angel. Now he is a parishioner . . . I assisted at his nuptial Mass in L'Escala. He married the mayor's sister; our church would never have been big enough for all the people who were invited. We had trouble seating them all even there. There wasn't a restaurant big enough for the wedding feast; they had to have it in a marquee.'

'It must have been hot in the church,' Tom mused, 'with all those people. It is even in our church in the summer.' I should explain here that I'm not conventionally religious. I have certain beliefs, but they don't include a God entity. (Gerard was okay about this from the off; he would never want me to pretend for his sake.) But I'm not about to impose anything on Tom. Our house adjoins the church . . . their origins go back to the same period, many centuries ago . . . and we hadn't been here long before he was in and out of the place, 'helping' as he put it. Now he's an altar boy . . . Gerard tried to tell me that 'altar server' is the new PC term; I told him that Tom is definitely a boy, so live with it . . . although he hasn't been baptised into the Catholic faith, and won't be, or into any other for that matter, until he feels old enough to make a choice for himself.

'It was,' the priest agreed, 'so hot that the bride's sister fainted, just as we reached the end of the Mass.'

'The bride's sister? Justine Michels? The mayor?'

'All three of the above; she passed right out.'

'Not very good for her public image,' I suggested.

'The congregation was standing at the time, only those at the front could see who it was. I picked her up and carried her into the registry; most people didn't even know it had happened. She recovered very quickly; fresh air, a glass of water and she was fine.' He paused. 'Senor Planas saw, of course. Angel was going to help, until he saw that I had the situation in hand, but the old man, he just stood there and stared at her, as if he was annoyed at the inconvenience. Afterwards, once we were outside the church, Dolores Fumado, Justine's mother, actually apologised to him.'

'What about the father? Was he there?'

'No, he had died a few months before that. In fact, the wedding had been postponed, out of respect. Both Planases, father and son, were pall-bearers at his funeral.' He paused, as if he was looking at the scene. 'And so was Justine. I remember, José-Luis wasn't pleased; I heard him mutter to the parish priest, my senior, that women these days seemed to have forgotten their place.' He beamed at me; Tom frowned as if he disapproved of something, but couldn't quite work out what. (Happily, some concepts are still beyond him.) 'Which brings me back to my question,' Gerard continued, taking advantage of the competition's preoccupation to nick a choice wedge of pizza. 'Why are you so interested in the old reactionary?'

Stage by stage, I told him of my meeting with Justine, and of the reasons for her inability to give the go-ahead for the venue for the wine fair. By the time I finished my story, his expression had gone from sunny to dark.

'The man can be that petty?' he growled. 'I know that as a priest I can't bless those who live together out of marriage, or who don't remain celibate before it, but I deplore vindictiveness. If Planas had been in the crowd that Jesus challenged to cast the first stone, then that would have been the end of the woman taken in adultery.' He was as annoyed as I'd ever seen him. 'Know what, Primavera,' he declared, 'I'm going to have a few words to say about him in church.'

'No, Gerard! Don't do that. It won't help Justine and it won't help Ben. Plus, it would probably piss off your senior priest and get you banished to Tavertet, or somewhere else in the back of beyond. I'll deal with this myself, the straightforward way: I'll tackle the old bastard face to face. I'll shame him into backing off. I promise you, I've squared up to tougher people than him.'

'Then I wish you luck, for you may find that there's no stronger armour than a man's sense of his own righteousness.' He broke off and stared at the empty plate on the table. 'Hey, what happened to the last three pieces?'

Tom laughed; Charlie looked guilty.

Seven

In the light of everything Gerard had told me, and of his warning, I decided on an oblique approach to the problem. I decided also that a hall table I had inherited when I bought the house was in need of a move to the garage, and so I headed for Mobles Planas, the problem's store halfway down Avinguda Ave Maria, L'Escala's main drag.

It's a big shop, warehouse-like, on two floors, with a range of furniture that had been drastically improved in the three years since my only other visit. Virtually all of the old dark, traditional stuff had been replaced by modern styles and modern materials; it seemed as if the business had gone from the nineteenth century to the twenty-first in a single bound. I guessed the reason, and so I wasn't surprised when it approached me, medium height, slim, dark haired, in light trousers and a striped open-necked shirt with long sleeves; pretty formal working gear by local standards, a sign of authority.

'Good afternoon, madam,' said Angel Planas, in English.

'And to you, sir,' I replied, in Catalan.

He smiled, in approval: a good sign, since I've met people,

invariably men, who pretend not to understand when I have the temerity to speak their language. 'How can I help you?' he asked.

I pointed to a Georgian repro semi-circular, three-legged wall table, one of the few pieces from the former stock that remained. I could see why, but my house is old, and it was quirky enough to fit in. 'That,' I told him. 'I think I'll have it.'

He nodded, checked the price label, then took out a calculator and hit some numbers. 'I can give you a twenty per cent discount that will take the price down to one hundred and forty euro,' he announced.

'Done.' I handed him my credit card.

'Do you want it delivered, Senora Blackstone?' he asked, as he entered the details into his reader, and handed it to me, to insert my pin.

'No, my Jeep's parked just outside; it'll fit on the platform.'

'I'll carry it out for you . . .' he paused, '. . . once we've discussed the other reason for your visit.'

So much for oblique, but I played it cute. 'Oh yes?'

'Justine told my wife about your call into her office, and about the problem that you and Ben have with his wine fair. You've come to ask me if I can twist my father's arm and get him to relent.'

'And to buy a very nice table, but yes, you're right.'

'I can cancel the sale if you like, for I'm not going to be able to help. My father and I haven't spoken in over a year. He has never been in our house.'

I looked around. 'But you manage his business.'

Angel shook his head. 'No. It's my business now, to my dad's great regret.'

'Does your father like anyone?'

He chuckled. 'Good question. Not really.'

'Then why does he keep on getting elected to the council?'

'Because he stands for certain values that he shares with the majority of older Catalans ... and maybe not only Catalans, maybe most Spanish people of his age. He was anti-Franco in his time, in his suppression of our identity, but he was right-wing nonetheless. He's against the European Union, against NATO, and against immigration. Foreign residents are anathema to him, just as most of his views are anathema to me.' He grinned. 'He'd never have given you the discount that locally born customers have always received. But he's not a fascist, and he's not a racist; he's a monarchist to the end, and he employs a Moroccan couple as his gardener and housekeeper.' The grin became a quick chuckle. 'OK, it's because they're cheap, but I know people who'd repatriate them all.'

'You sound fond of him.'

'He's my father. I am.'

'But you don't speak.'

'His choice. When Elena and Ben broke up and we got back together, he was furious. He told me that she was soiled, damaged goods. I laughed in his face. When I told him we were getting married, he exploded. He said he'd disinherit me; tried to throw me out of this shop. I told him, "You're

too late, old man. You've already made this business and
the property over to me." He said, in that case he'd never
set foot in it again, and walked out. He's been as good as his
word.'

'Yet he went to your wedding.'

'How did you know that?'

'Father Gerard told me.'

'Ah,' Angel murmured. 'But Gerard probably doesn't know
that it was his boss, the old priest, who insisted that he go. He
told him that L'Escala would never trust a man who would
boycott his own son's wedding Mass. Papa's very proud of his
position in the town; it's the only thing anyone could threaten
him with.'

'Then maybe I will.'

'It won't work. His voters don't care about an Englishman
holding a wine fair in St Martí, or anywhere else. They'd
support Papa if they knew what he was doing.'

'So you won't speak to him about this?'

'It would only make him more resolved. Let me tell
you something else about our wedding, something nobody
knows. As I understand it, in Britain the custom is for the
bride's father to pay for the wedding feast. We don't do that;
here each family invites and pays for their own guests, and
so do the couple. My father didn't invite anybody. So Elena
and I put him on our list. He came, didn't say a word to
anyone, and left as soon as he could. Two weeks later, after
the honeymoon, when I went back to the shop and sorted
through my mail, I found an envelope with cash in it, enough

to cover the cost of a single meal. I found out from the caterer that he'd asked him how much he had quoted per head. That's my father. You've never met anyone like him, when it comes to getting even.'

'Oh, but I have,' I said. 'And I was married to him.'

Eight

I asked Angel for his father's address, but he told me that there was no point in giving it to me, since I wouldn't get to see him there. He said that he had a video entry system on his gate, and that he'd never open it to a stranger . . . although, he added, undoubtedly he'd know who I was. It seemed that I was a hell of a lot better known in the town than I realised. That came as something of a shock, but maybe I was being naive, given my surname, and given the hornets' nest that Oz and I had disturbed during our final stay there.

My best plan, I was advised, was to run him to ground in one of his haunts, of which there were five: the town hall, where he had an office that he used occasionally, the restaurant in Hostal Miryam, where he ate most evenings, a bar in Carrer del Port ('Carrer' means 'street' in Catalan) that his grandfather had opened eighty years ago, another, on Avinguda Girona, that he had founded himself, and the estate agency that had been owned and run by Angel's mother, until her death.

I talked over the options with Ben, after I had unloaded my

new table, and moved its predecessor down to the garage beneath the house. Ingrid was looking after the shop while he and I, and Matthew Reid, walked the three dogs along the passage that links St Martí and L'Escala. I'm told that it used to be a dirt track, before millions were poured into the area to prepare for the arrival on the beach of the Olympic torch for the games of 1992, in Barcelona.

'What do you think, guys?' I asked. 'Where should I face up to the old lizard?'

'I think you should let me tackle him,' said Matthew, 'since he hates women . . . or at least he has no respect for them. Given the history, there's no way that Ben should do it, but he might be more responsive to a man-to-man chat.'

'Thanks for the offer,' I murmured, 'but I've never backed down from a man in my life.' *Not even from one who was holding a gun at the time*, I thought. 'I'm not about to start now.'

'Well,' he continued, 'you don't want to get yourself barred from the Miryam, since it's one of the best restaurants in town. Starting a barney in a Catalan bar might not be too clever either. That leaves the town hall or the estate agency.'

'I'd have to make an appointment in the town hall. I'm known there, since I more or less forced my way into Justine's office, so I couldn't use a false name, or anything like that.'

'The estate agency then,' Ben declared, before a frown crossed his face and his manner seemed to change. 'Unless . . .'

'Unless what?'

'Unless we forget the whole thing?'

Matthew took a deep breath, but said nothing. I took a deep breath, then said plenty. 'Are you saying that you'd fold this project because of the blind, stupid, antediluvian prejudice of a vicious old man? Is the village behind the wine fair? Yes it is. I know this because I've been talking to people myself. Everybody supports it. Are you going to let them down?'

'But . . .'

'How many wine producers have you signed up?'

'A dozen,' he admitted. 'As many as I can handle, all my targets, the best in Emporda.'

'And you're going to let them down too? Ben, why did you come up with the idea for the fair?'

'To promote the shop and make it known outside St Martí, to promote Empordan wines, and of course to make money.'

'Noble motives all, and worth standing up for. So don't even think about scrapping it. And even if you do . . .'

'What?'

'I won't. You brought me into the fair's organisation, you gave me a job and I'm going to do it. This is personal now: I will not let this fail. There are other venues.'

He frowned. 'Where?'

'My house was my original thought, but I've had a better idea. The car park beside the village. It's vast; I can rent as much land there as we'll need, for as long as we'll need it. And it's flat, so we can hire a big tent, as insurance against rain.'

'But all that will cost.'

'And I'll underwrite that, if it comes to it. But that's still second choice. The fair should be within the village walls, not beneath them, and it should be in Plaça Petita. It's public land, the people's land, the people want the event and they're fucking well going to have it, or my middle name isn't Eagle . . . and now you know that, I'll have to kill you both,' I added.

Matthew laughed, as he tugged on Mustard's lead, diverting his attention from a Dalmatian bitch. 'The snowball's rolling, Ben, and the further down the hill it goes, the bigger it's getting. Better off behind it than in front.' He looked down at me; he's quite a big bloke, six feet or so, and chunky with it. 'So it's the estate agency, Primavera?'

'Looks like it.' I frowned as a truth took hold. 'But I'll need to make an appointment there too, and if I'm as well known in L'Escala as people say I am . . .'

'However,' said Matthew, 'my son's been talking about buying an apartment out here. He's asked me to look around for him. If I call Planas's office, say he's been recommended as the best-connected agent in town and ask for a personal appointment, I'm sure I'll get it.'

'I want to see him myself,' I insisted.

'And you shall, Cinderella, you shall; you'll be coming with me.'

Nine

The estate agency was housed in a ground-floor office that had once been a bank, facing on to a small square where a fruit and vegetable market is held during most weekday mornings. Angel had told me that his father had moved the business from its original home and had been given permission by the town council ... now there was a surprise ... to demolish that building and redevelop the site as apartments.

The sign over the door read 'Immobiliària Ruiz', Angel's mother's name, I guessed, from what he had told me. It had been attached over the previous signage, which was predominately blue, a clash with the yellow of the lettering, and the logo of the former occupant was still visible on the smoked-glass frontage.

It had taken two days for Senor Planas to find a space in his crowded diary to see us. Even then, I wasn't certain that he'd be there. My fear was that he might have turned the appointment over to one of his sales staff.

'Let's go,' said Matthew, quietly. We crossed the sun-bathed square, picking our way through the stalls, before stopping briefly to study some of the homes for sale that were displayed in the window. I'd seen many of them elsewhere; there are around fifty agencies in L'Escala, and very few of them have exclusive selling rights over properties. I'd wondered how they could all hope to survive, until I'd learned that there's a loose cooperative agreement in place and that their standard commission rate is a whopping five per cent plus tax.

We stepped through the double doors and looked around. The place still looked like a bank; it was divided more or less in two by a massive counter, behind which I saw four desks. Three were occupied, one by a swarthy, tousle-haired, bespectacled man, in his early forties, I guessed, so way too young to be Planas, and the other two by women. The older of the pair looked up as we entered, and rose to greet us. She was in the same age group as her male colleague; her trouser suit, and the way her dark hair was swept back into a functional ponytail, gave her a briskly professional look.

'Senor Reid?' she began, in English; I might as well have been invisible.

Matthew nodded.

'You are here to see Senor Planas?'

'That's right; about property.'

'Very good. But there is a problem . . .'

Here we go, I thought.

'Senor Planas does not speak English. But we can get over that; I will translate between you.'

'That won't be necessary,' Matthew replied, nodding in my

direction. 'I anticipated that and brought my own interpreter. No offence, I hope, but this is business.'

She was narked, and she couldn't hide it completely behind her toothy smile, but she swallowed it. 'Of course,' she said. 'Senor Planas is in his office.' She pointed to a mahogany door to the left of the counter. 'If you'll wait a moment . . .'

We did, as she vanished through another exit at the back of the office. She was gone for more than her moment, but eventually, the entrance was opened and she reappeared, beckoning us into the inner sanctum.

The man seated behind the small, cheap desk was almost the same colour as the door. His skin was like leather, and looked as if it was folding off his face. I thought back to my crack about 'the old lizard' and reckoned that I'd been pretty close to the mark. He rose to his feet slowly, extending a surprisingly big hand as he approached Matthew: I say, 'approached Matthew', because again, it was as if I wasn't in the room. He was shorter than his son, but stockier, and there was a vibrancy to him. His eyes were red veined, but his gaze was sharp. It was hard to put an age to him, but I settled for somewhere between sixty-five and seventy.

'Senor,' he intoned, in a gravel voice, 'you are looking for property, I understand.' He spoke in Castellano.

'Indeed,' Matthew replied, 'and they say that you are the top man in this town.' He spoke Spanish too, slowly, as British people tend to, but passably, taking me by surprise.

The reptile face cracked into what might have been a smile. 'That's true. Most people who know L'Escala do say that. Tell me what type of property interests you, and I'll see if I can help.'

'Something old. Preferably not in L'Escala itself.' He was busking it; we hadn't researched at all, but at once, I sensed where he was going. 'I saw a house in St Martí d'Empúries that appeared to be unoccupied. That might interest me.'

'Tell me the street and I will find out if it is available.'

'Plaça Petita. It's next to the wine shop of my . . .' He stopped, stuck for the Spanish word.

'His stepson,' I said. 'You must know where it is, for you certainly know him.'

The thin veneer of amiability vanished in an instant. 'Pah!' he spat then lapsed into Catalan. 'This is a trick. I see you now; I see who you are. You are the woman who went to see our young lady mayor, to win her approval for this, this, this . . .' Veins stood out in his forehead and once more I could see red behind a tan, only this time it was the hue of rage rather than embarrassment. 'This presumptuous wine fair. That any Englishman should think to do such a thing.'

'But your opposition has nothing to do with Ben being English,' I told him, rocking him ever so slightly back on his heels by my fluency in his language. 'This is all about your ridiculous, feudal attitude to women.'

'Not to women,' he shouted, switching back to Castellano, 'to whores! This man took my son's girl and he made her a whore, and then he threw her back to him. I'd have killed him, but my son doesn't have the balls.'

'Just as you don't have the balls to argue with me in your own language,' I countered, quietly.

His eyes bulged. 'I know who you are, woman, and I know that if you support that English pup, then you are a whore also.'

I had to move quickly to block off Matthew as he moved towards him. The Spanish police take a dim view of physical assault, and Planas might well have had a few of the town cops on his payroll. I stood between them and stared deep into his bloodshot eyes. 'And you would know,' I hissed, 'since you are the son of one.'

His mouth opened, but he seemed to have run out of insults. For a moment I thought he was about to have a stroke . . . no kidding; I was a nurse once, remember . . . but it passed, and he seemed to sink into himself. 'Get out, get out,' he said. 'Your wine fair will never happen.'

'Ah, but it will,' I told him. 'That's taken care of. One way or another it will, even if you go on blocking Plaça Petita. But if you do, I'll promise you this. I will use my resources, and I have them, make no mistake, to make sure that everyone in St Martí, and in L'Escala, knows what you've done, and why. I'll put posters in the streets, I'll post an announcement on the regional website. I'll give the story to the Girona press. Your name will be shit, everywhere.'

He looked at me, and knew serious when he saw it. Then he shrugged. 'I'm an old man. I should care,' he sneered.

'You should,' I said. I turned to leave, ushering my companion in front of me, in case he decided to take a swing at him after all. 'Come on, Matthew.' I had gripped the handle when his voice came from behind me.

'Wait a moment.' His tone suggested that I got through to him, but not necessarily that he was beaten.

We stopped. 'Well?' I challenged. I could see him regrouping, regaining some bravado. I could see a crafty glint in his eyes.

'You want your little fair in your little village,' he murmured. 'You want me to give my approval, or you will try to ruin the reputation that I have built up through my long lifetime.' His back straightened, as he drew himself to his full height, only around five feet eight, but tall for a Catalan man of his age. 'Very well,' he announced. 'I will tell the mayor that should she wish to allow it, then for my part I consent. However . . .' he paused, '. . . this is public land, and just as the restaurants in Plaça Major pay ground rent to put their tables in the square, then you must pay a proper amount for using Plaça Petita.'

I knew that he was ready to fire his last bullet, so I invited it. 'And what would a proper amount be, for one day of preparation and three days of the fair?'

His right hand caressed his heavy jowls, as he made a show of considering my question. 'I would say . . . two million pesetas.'

Although the euro has been the official currency for nearly ten years, many Spanish people still think in pesetas and quote prices in the old units. I did a rough conversion in my head. The old swine was asking for just over twelve thousand euro, or if you prefer it in sterling, around nine and a half grand at the exchange rate then.

'Wouldn't it be for the mayor to determine a fair cost?' Matthew growled, having done the same mental arithmetic.

Old Planas laughed, and patted his right bum cheek, a crude gesture which I took to mean that he had the mayor in his back pocket, as well as the police.

It was my turn to shrug. 'OK,' I said, 'we'll pay that. I'll arrange to see Justine on Monday morning, to collect her signed permission. But I warn you now, if I find that the figure has gone up by even one peseta, then everything I promised will happen.'

His mouth fell open again, in surprise this time, not fury. He had no more to say as we left the stuffy little office.

We walked through the public area, and stepped back into the fruit market. I headed for my usual stall, to buy some peppers, onions, figs and nectarines, all on the shopping list that I had in the same place that Planas had claimed he kept the mayor.

Matthew followed. 'Primavera,' he muttered, leaning over me. 'We can't do that. Ben can't hope to cover that sort of overhead.'

'Ben doesn't have to,' I told him. 'I will.'

'But it's a hell of a lot of money.'

'Come on, man. You were in the PR business, weren't you? Have you never seen a pissing contest before?'

'Not one with a woman involved . . . and no, not even figuratively. Seriously, the fair isn't budgeted for something like that. Ben's talking about charging fifteen euro a ticket, to include six tastings. With that sort of ground rent, I reckon he'd need to sell three thousand to break even. He'll do well to shift a tenth of that. Ingrid and I, we can't let you do that.'

'Yes you can, Matthew.'

'Come on, you've got a kid to bring up. You can't be chucking away that sort of money.'

I smiled up at him. 'Actually I can. I don't like talking about my finances, but between you and me, the biggest mistake that old man made was in thinking that he could bully me financially. I can chuck twelve thousand euro into the pot without a second thought. When I was with Oz, we both made money. When we divorced, I did very well out of it, for he didn't want it to get messy. When he died, he left a trust fund for Tom that'll see him well through university, and beyond.'

'That's fine,' said Matthew, 'and it's very generous of you, but I still feel bad about it, and so will Ingrid, not to mention Ben.'

'Then don't mention it, to either of them.'

He looked at me, seriously. 'Primavera, if I've learned one thing in life, it's this: never keep secrets from your wife.'

I had to agree with him on that. Tom was three years old before his father ever knew he existed. That wasn't fair to either of them, and I'm ashamed of it now. 'No,' I agreed, 'but try to wait until all the tickets are sold. You might be surprised how many we shift. Truth is, I am careful, and I'm not given to chucking money down the drain. Maybe I have a secret weapon.'

'And do you?'

'Could be, but I'm keeping it to myself for now.' I sighed as

I started to make my fruit and veg choices. 'Life does get complicated, though. One thing about Oz; he had a way of slicing through problems.'

'Oh yes? And what would he have done in this situation? What would he have done about Planas?'

'If the old clown got him mad enough, he'd probably have had him taken out.'

Matthew laughed . . . but he couldn't see my face.

Ten

'Do you really believe that?' Gerard asked. I had just reached the end of a blow-by-blow account of the morning's events, over dinner in La Lluna, a restaurant in L'Escala that's as far off the tourist track as you can get . . . and that means, not very. More often than not, Tom would have been with us, but I'd wanted to talk to my friend on my own, and Ben had been happy to sit with him. Cher and Mustard had also been happy to sit with Charlie. About a year ago, Father Olivares, the senior parish priest and Gerard's immediate boss . . . although Gerard would counter that his immediate boss is God . . . attempted to give him a very gentle hint about the propriety of dining *à deux* with a divorced woman. He was told, pretty sharply, I suspect, that he was a priest, not a monk, therefore a member of an open society, and that the reverend father would have thought nothing of him dining *à deux* with a divorced man. (In other words, he told him to fuck off, but in clerical terms.)

'Yes, I do. Are you shocked, that I could love someone who's capable of such a thing?'

'I'm shocked,' he conceded. 'But not by that. I've been hearing confessions for long enough to know that love is blind, deaf, dumb, and has no sense of smell. Also I'm human, and as susceptible to rage as the next man. No, I'm shocked because I've seen a few of your late ex-husband's movies and wouldn't have suspected that he'd be capable of such a thing.'

I stared at him, astonished. 'You never told me you were a fan,' I exclaimed.

'I didn't like to,' he said, head bowed, but grinning.

'Well, I'm sorry to shatter your illusions, but not only was he capable, he did. The last night that he and I ever spent together, in New York, he told me everything about his life that I hadn't known before.'

Gerard sighed; I had shaken him. 'Did he ever confess these sins?' he asked.

'As in, to a priest? No chance; I was as close as he got to that, and we were hardly in the confessional at the time ... although I suspect that there may be as much truth told between the sheets as in your wee cabinet.'

'I wouldn't know about that ... but it could be that there is less omitted.' He shivered for a second. 'And you, Primavera,' he whispered. 'What are you capable of?'

I looked him in the eye again. 'Protecting the people I love, whatever it takes.'

'Does that include me?' he asked.

'Yes.'

'Then please promise me that you never will, not for me, that you'll always leave me to look after myself.'

'I'll make that promise when I can tell the future, but not before.'

We sat in silence for a while, sipping wine. (One of the great things about being out with a priest is that he always insists on driving, so you're never going to be stopped by the police.)

'Are you really going to pay this money?' He had moved on.

'Sure. I've said that I will.'

'But two million pesetas is a ridiculous amount. What if Justine refuses to sanction it?'

'She will. Planas went to see her this afternoon, and she called me as soon as he had left her office, to check that he wasn't lying in his teeth. When I told her he wasn't, she was livid. She told me that she wouldn't allow the council to be a party to blackmail. I told her that it was an agreement between the old man and me and that I was prepared to pay for his approval. She took a bit of persuading, but eventually she agreed to sign the permission.'

'I feel the same way as she does,' said Gerard. 'You are my sister, and I don't take kindly to seeing you being abused. As for calling you a whore, if he was a younger man, I would take off my collar and meet him after dark.'

'Father! Wash your mouth out and say a hundred Hail Marys, or whatever the going rate is.' I made light of it at the time, but I was taken aback by his smouldering anger. 'You never have done anything like that, have you?' I asked.

He looked into his glass. 'None of us is perfect, Primavera. A long time ago, but it was within my family . . . although that's no excuse.'

'Who did you fight with?' I asked. 'Your brother? Santiago?'

'No, no. Santi and I could never come to blows; we're too close. Primavera, I really don't want to talk about it.'

I took his hand, linking my fingers through his; maybe I expected him to flinch from the physical contact, but he didn't. 'You know, Gerard, I think the opposite's true. I believe that you'd love to talk about it, that you'd love to have someone to share your pain, other than a confessor. Well, that's what I'm here for.'

He gave my hand a quick squeeze, then released it. 'Not my brother,' he whispered. 'My father.'

'Why?'

'He was a harsh man, a cruel man; he was heavy handed with Santi and me when we were kids. All the time we were growing up, there were never words of encouragement, only complaint. We lived with it, and got out of there as soon as we could. I went to the seminary, Santi joined the Spanish air force. One time, I was given a weekend's leave, unexpectedly; I went home, and let myself into the house. As I did, I heard a scream, from not far away. I rushed through to the kitchen and found my mother, on the ground and bleeding from the mouth. He was standing over her, cursing her.' As he spoke he clenched his hands into fists. 'I yelled at him to stop, to leave her alone. He told me to go back to my novice's cell, although not in those exact words. I pulled him away from her, and he punched me. And then he laughed, and said, "Go on, Jesus, turn the other cheek." He stopped laughing when I hit him, when I knocked him across the room. Instead he roared like a bull, and launched himself at me. He was a big man, my father, a locksmith, with strong, heavy hands from his work. But I was full-grown, and I was more than a match for him. I threw him outside, into the small courtyard at the back of the house, and we had it out. I knocked him down half a dozen times, until finally he stayed there, cut above the eye and with blood and snot coming from his nose. I left him lying, went back inside and locked the door, locked him out of his own home, and tended to my mother. She told me that he'd been abusing her since the beginning of their marriage, Primavera, as he'd abused my brother and me, but she'd kept it from us. I told her that she'd be safe from now on. I packed some clothes for her, and took her to my aunt's house, close to the Alhambra, above Granada. Then I went back home to confront my father again. I had cooled down, and I wanted to talk to him, to try to understand why he had this thing in him that made him behave that way. But he was gone. I waited for him at the house, for two days, but he didn't come back. Before I left for the seminary I went to my local church, confessed what I had done, and received absolution. I also received my priest's promise that he would look after my mother, and ensure that she could live in safety once he returned.' He shook his head. 'But he never did, Primavera. He never came back. That's my last memory of him, seventeen years ago, lying where I left him in the yard, spitting out teeth. What a farewell between father and son, eh, my dear.'

'Is he still alive?'

'I have no idea. I've never tried to find out.'

'Has your brother?'

'Not that I know of. Santi doesn't know what happened. Mama and I let him think that the old man ran off with another woman; maybe he did. If so, may God have kept her safe.' He tried to smile, but didn't get halfway there. 'So, Primavera, my precious, what do you think of your perfect priest now?'

I wanted to hug him. I wanted to take him somewhere quiet and make him feel better, in any way I could. But that wasn't possible, so I turned his face towards me and I told him, 'I think he's only a man, and I've never met the perfect specimen yet. But I'm proud of him, for doing the right thing. After all, God's smitten a few foes in his time, hasn't he? And didn't JC lay into the money-changers in the temple? What would he have done if he'd caught Joseph hitting Mary? I don't think any the less of you; if anything, I admire you even more.'

He squeezed my hand again, and this time held on to it; we were in a corner, and his back was to the rest of the diners. 'Thanks. Your absolution means more to me than the other one. But I still don't feel cleansed. Because I know that when I fought him, it wasn't just for my mother. It was more than that, it was for Santi and me too, for all the thumpings he gave us when we were kids, for all the cruelty, and for the denial of all the love we should have had as his children.'

'He had it coming. Tell me, if it had been Santi who'd beaten the crap out of him, rather than you, would you have absolved him?'

'Totally.'

I raised his hand to my lips and kissed it, then set it down on the table 'Then do the same for yourself.'

Eleven

I went to church that Sunday. As I've said, I'm not an adherent, but something drew me to put on a skirt and a black scarf that also worked as a shawl and a head cover, and go next door. I took a place right at the back on one of the long wooden pews. They were not designed for comfort. 'They are all penitents' benches,' my father is fond of declaring. 'Church-going is not a social occasion; you can't win true believers with comfortable seats.'

You might think it was social for me, but you'd be wrong if you did. I was there to see my men at work. Even though my relationship with Gerard had defined limits, my feelings were proprietorial as I watched him conduct the service, and even more so as I looked at his white-robed assistant, my son the altar person. After the travails of the previous week, there was a . . . a niceness about it, a family feeling, that gave me a warm glow inside. Maybe I shouldn't have been there; once or twice I caught women in the congregation glancing at me over their shoulders. But I didn't feel that there was anything wrong about it, so I simply smiled at them, redirecting their attention to the main event.

I hadn't been first into the church, but I was first out. I went straight down to Can Coll, and found an outside table, taking a seat facing the way I had come, from which I could watch the worshippers emerge.

'What can I get you, Primavera?' asked Joaquim, the master of the café.

'Coffee Americano with a little milk, and a fizzy water, please.'

'And will Tom be joining you?'

'He will, once he's finished his tidying up duties and gone home to fetch the dog. But I'd better not make any choices for him.' I knew he'd want Fanta orange and a ham sandwich, but he always made a show of studying the menu.

I looked back towards the church. Gerard stood in the doorway, shaking hands with his people as they left, spirits lifted and ready to face the day. His fan club was out in force; quite a few, especially the ladies, paused for a word.

I hadn't realised that the mayor was there; she must have gone in before the sound of the bells had faded away, and been in one of the front rows. I had her labelled 'unconventional' in my mind, after seeing the way she dressed for the office, but her church-going outfit gave that notion the lie; black dress, black shoes, black lace around her shoulders. She was the last person to leave. It may be that she had been dealing with some of her own congregation inside. Whatever, she stopped beside Gerard, just as Tom emerged, no longer white robed but in shorts and T-shirt, trotted past them with a quick, 'So long,' and headed next door.

I watched as they spoke, neither glancing in my direction; their conversation didn't seem to be casual, for there were no smiles. I wondered whether they were discussing the wine fair, and Planas's extortion, then chided myself for such a self-centred thought. They were both important civic figures, dealing with many things, and ours wasn't the only game in town.

I'd been right, though. Justine saw me almost as soon as she and Gerard parted; she waved, and headed for me. My coffee and water arrived just as she did. She asked for the same, and took a seat at my table. 'Father Hernanz and I were talking about you. I came to church here today because I wanted to take another look at Plaça Petita. I've done that; I've even paced it out, to judge roughly how many square metres it is. Primavera, I'm not going to be complicit in this thing, and I'm not going to allow the council to be either. You will pay exactly the same rent per square metre, per day, as every other business in St Martí does, not a cent more, not a cent less. I'm taking a stand against Planas; I'm going to negotiate on my programme with the council's Green members, and deliver as much of it as I can.'

I stared at her. My day had just got even brighter. 'Are you sure?'

'Absolutely, and I apologise for ever even thinking about allowing that man to dictate to me.'

'Hey,' I said, just as Tom arrived, with Charlie on his short leash, 'I was going to pay him, remember. I was prepared to let him dictate to me as well.'

'No. You beat him. He quoted you a figure that he thought would be impossible for you, but you accepted it without batting an eyelash. He tried to bully you politically and he tried to bully you financially. You kicked his ass both times; you humiliated him privately and if the story ever comes out, he'll be humiliated publicly as well. People have supported him because he said he stands for the best of the old values, but they didn't include extortion.'

Tom had seated himself, and settled Charlie on the ground, as we spoke. He gazed at Justine, fascinated. I introduced her, formally: 'Senora Michels, the mayor of L'Escala.'

'Pleased to meet you,' he told her. 'What's extortion?'

She looked at me, batting the question to me. 'It can be many things,' I said, 'but in this case it means forcing someone to pay too much money for something.'

'And has someone done that to you?'

'They tried to, but they failed, because it was worth that amount of money to me, or would have been.'

He frowned, and in the instant, I saw a flash of his father in him. A quick shudder ran through me. 'Who was it?' he asked.

'A silly man, who'll know better next time. Now forget it. Do you want to see the menu?'

'Don't need to. I'd like a Fanta lemon and a chorizo sandwich.' My boy's tastes were evolving.

I invited Justine to stay with us for lunch. She and I were considering our options when a shadow fell across the table. I looked up, half expecting to see Gerard, but instead found Sub-inspector Alex Guinart, of the Mossos d'Esquadra, standing beside us. Alex is a good friend of mine . . . one of my rare official visits to the church in L'Escala was to stand as godmother to his daughter . . . but two things told me that his visit wasn't social. One was the fact that he was in uniform, and the second was the look on his face.

'I'm sorry to interrupt, Primavera,' he said, 'but I need to have a word with the mayor.'

She groaned. 'Town business on a Sunday, Alex?'

'Not of the usual kind,' he said, moving away with a nod of his head that indicated he wanted to speak in private.

'Sorry,' Justine murmured as she rose to follow him. 'Hopefully this won't take long.'

I watched them for a few seconds, as they walked up the hill towards Alex's police vehicle, a four-by-four, which he had parked in front of the church, then turned my attention back to the menu. A couple of minutes passed before the mayor returned, her expression sombre, and then some.

'Alex needs me to go somewhere. Given what's happened recently, I thought that you might want to come with us.'

I was surprised, but I was intrigued too. 'If you think so, and it's OK with Alex. How about Tom?'

She shook her head, firmly. By that time I wasn't smiling either.

'OK,' I said. I handed my son a fifty. 'Have your lunch, then either wait here till I get back, or pay for what we've had, then go down to Ben's shop and see if you can help out there.'

'Can I have an ice cream too?' Tom knows when he's in a good negotiating position.

'The biggest one they have, if you want.'

I spoke to Joaquim, to let him know what was happening . . . with him and Ben as minders, and with the added insurance of Charlie, who might be dumb but is loyal and can be formidable, Tom was in the safest hands possible . . . then headed towards Alex's vehicle, wondering what the hell could have happened to have him wearing his sternest cop face on a Sunday.

Twelve

On the way, I asked Alex where we were going, but he kept his eyes firmly on the road. Justine was no more communicative; her forehead was set in a deep frown.

We drove out of St Martí and back towards the main road. I assumed that he was taking us to L'Escala, but we were barely halfway to the junction where one of the tourist information centres is when he made a sharp left turn, on to a dirt track that I'd seen many times but never gone up, not even when I was running, or cycling, not even when Oz and I lived there in what I'm beginning to call 'the old days'. It has a name, but I'd never paid any attention to it, and that afternoon we were past it before I could read the sign. I still couldn't tell you what it's called.

I knew that there were houses up there, in the fields behind the ruins of the ancient Greco-Roman town, but I had never met anyone who lived there, so I knew nothing of them. The road rose gradually; the ground is quite high up there. I counted three houses as we passed, two on the left and one on the right, before Alex drew to a halt behind two other police vehicles and an ambulance. They were all lined up alongside a high stone wall, in which there was a double gate, partly open. I could just see the pitch of a roof from my raised position in the back seat of the car.

If the length of the wall was anything to go by, it enclosed a pretty substantial plot of land. 'Whose house is this, Alex?' I asked, as I stepped out of the cool of the vehicle, into the heat of the day.

'You'll see in a little while.' He led Justine and me through the gate into a garden that was mainly lawn to the front, apart from the swimming pool to the right. The house itself was splendid, as fine as any I'd seen in the area. It was two storey, stone built also, with a loggia over the entrance, and wooden shutters framing each of the small windows. Older Spanish houses were built to keep the sun out; now that there are things like air-con and heat-reflecting glass, the country's architects have been liberated.

We followed a paved path round the side. As we turned towards the back of the house, we stepped under a pagoda frame with a canvas cover that was set up to shade a small patio. I almost tripped over a chair, a solid wooden white-painted thing, but grabbed its leg to save myself, then trotted on to catch up with Alex.

As I looked around, I saw that the ground at the back sloped downwards, and that the stone wall enclosed the property completely, save for a gate at the back. Only the area of the garden along the length of the house was level, with a mixture of lawn and paving. It was defined by a small wall, of white cast concrete pillars, with plant pots set on top at regular intervals a few metres apart. A middle-aged man was sitting on the wall beside one of them, sweat forming dark patches under the armpits of his green uniform shirt. I recognised him. His name was Gomez and he was an intendant from the Mossos d'Esquadra criminal investigation branch.

He blinked when he saw me. 'Senora Blackstone,' he exclaimed. 'What connection have you with this?'

'The mayor suggested that she come,' Alex told him. 'And . . . well, she's the mayor, OK.'

'Connection with what?' I asked.

'Come and see.'

Gomez beckoned me forward. I approached him and as I did I could see over the wall, into the lower garden. Four crime-scene officers, in sterile tunics, were on their knees, searching the ground, square metre by square metre. Two paramedics stood off to one side, holding a stretcher, as if waiting to be called into action. At the foot of the steps that led down to the area, I saw a second uniformed officer: I had met him before too, Inspector Garcia, the intendant's more abrasive sidekick. He and I exchanged not very friendly glances; and then the smell hit me, that and the buzzing of what sounded like a thousand flies.

I stood against the pillared wall and looked down. Beneath me, maybe three metres below, there was a rockery, with cactus plants in the sandy soil, and in its centre, teeth bared as if he was snarling, glaring up at me as he had in his office, lay the unmistakably dead form of José-Luis Planas.

Justine came to stand beside me, and gasped in horror, even though she had been told what she had been brought to see. 'When was he found?' she asked Gomez.

'About two hours ago,' he replied, 'by his gardener, when he came in to check the watering system. Apparently it had been faulty for the last week or so.'

'He's been there for a while,' I said. 'You'd better move him pretty quick. I've seen this; I nursed in Africa for a while in a combat zone. Decomposition has a different timetable in the heat.'

'So how long would you say he's been here?' asked Garcia, who had climbed the stairway. 'Our medical examiner . . . he's gone back to his barbecue . . . says at least three days.'

'Then he's a fucking idiot . . . pardon my English. If he'd been here for three days in these hot weather conditions he'd be starting to go black; he might even have burst open. I'd say less than two days, that he died Friday night or Saturday morning.'

'And you know better than our doctor, do you?' he sneered. 'It's possible; his housekeeper comes in three days a week; her husband says that she was here on Friday, but that she has her own keys and often comes when he's not here. So he could have been lying here all that time and she might not have known. The husband, the gardener, he was last here on Wednesday.'

'In this instance, I do know better than your medic. I had a meeting with Senor Planas in his office . . .' I checked my watch; it showed 2 p.m., '. . . exactly two days and two hours ago.'

'And I had a visit from him in mine two hours after that,' Justine added. 'And I promise you he was alive when he left, frustrating as I may have found that.'

Alex winced. 'What happened?' I asked him.

'The doc reckons that he probably had a heart attack and fell over the wall. The back of his head's smashed in.'

'He fell backwards?'

'Seems that way. Accidental death.'

'Yes, Sub-inspector Guinart,' Gomez conceded. 'That's what we thought when you left to collect Senora Michels. But after you had gone, one of the technicians found this, grasped in his hand.' He reached into his pocket, took out a transparent evidence bag, and held it up.

All I could see was white plastic. 'What is it?' I murmured.

'According to Garcia, who says he knows these things, it's part of a priest's collar.'

Thirteen

Intendant Gomez said no more about his find. Instead he questioned Justine and me, courteously, about our recent difficulties with the late councillor. We told him how the situation had developed, how I had confronted Planas and how he had come up with his proposition.

'I wish you had come to me with this,' he declared, 'and made a formal complaint. I would have started an investigation at once.'

'And you'd have been tied in knots,' the mayor told him. 'That old man was as slippery as a shoal of eels.'

Gomez smiled. 'I'm the son of a fisherman,' he said. 'My father was a trawler skipper, and I used to go out with him. I'm used to eels.'

'Maybe not this one.'

'We'll never know now.'

He also asked me about Ben Simmers, and about his attitude to the demand for money. 'He knew nothing about it,' I told him. 'He left all that side of the organisation to me.' That seemed to satisfy him.

'And you were going to pay the money? Such a ridiculous amount?'

'It would have been worth it . . . and afterwards I'd still have let the world know about it. I'd made no vow of secrecy.'

That was all he asked us. Matthew Reid's name had never come up during our exchanges, and I saw no reason to volunteer it.

The interview had just finished, when we heard running footsteps behind us. Justine and I turned, just as Angel Planas appeared from the front of the house. 'Where is he?' he demanded, glaring at Gomez as he approached. Justine laid a hand on his shoulder, but he shrugged it off.

'I'm sorry, Angel,' she whispered, but he ignored her.

'Come on,' said Alex Guinart, to us. 'You're finished here. I'll take you home.'

'Why did you come for the mayor?' I asked him, as we walked towards his vehicle.

'Gomez asked me to,' he replied. 'When she told me about your trouble with the old guy, I thought it best to save some time by bringing you along.'

He said nothing more as we drove back. Justine sat in the back for a change, and I was in the front. We had almost reached the village when he glanced across to me. 'When did you last see Gerard?' he murmured, barely audible above the engine noise.

'Today, in church.'

'I don't mean that. I mean when did you last see him before that?' I frowned at him. 'For Christ's sake, Primavera,' he exclaimed, 'I'm not out to crack the case here. Gerard's my friend too. Sooner or later those two detectives are going to be visiting every priest in this area, and I'd rather know whatever there is to know before they do.'

'We had dinner together on Friday.'

'Where?'

'In La Lluna, near your office.'

'Did you tell him about your problem with Planas?'

'Yes, I did.'

'How did he react?'

'How do you think? You know him; he was angry.' I stopped short as I recalled his reaction to the story; that if Planas was a younger man, he might have taken off his collar . . .

I was afraid that Alex would press me, but he didn't. 'Yes,' he said, as we crested the road into St Martí, and he drew to a halt in front of the church, 'I can see he would have been. But you haven't answered my question.' He looked me in the eye. 'When did you see him last?'

'When we left La Lluna, he drove me back home; it would have been closer to one than midnight, for everything here was closed.'

'And?' He looked pained. 'Sorry, Primavera, I need to know.'

A lot of stuff went through my mind, very quickly. Going by what I'd seen of the body, from above and close to, as the paramedics had carried him past us, uncovered on their stretcher, I reckoned that he had lain in the open for all of Saturday, and Sunday, under cloudless skies and a blazing sun. Maybe he did have a heart attack and fall, while Gerard and I were having dinner. If he had, the autopsy would tell us, for sure. But maybe not. When he died, he'd been dressed in loose black trousers, a short-sleeved shirt and leather slippers, not the suit, tie and brogues that he'd worn for our meeting. He'd gone home and dressed for the evening. Maybe he was an early bedder, and he'd have been in pyjamas if he'd died after midnight. But I didn't buy that. No, I feared that when we knew the time of death, it wasn't going to help at all.

I almost said it: 'And . . . he came inside. We stayed in bed until around nine next morning, then we had breakfast, before he left around ten, through the garage down below, where he wouldn't be seen.'

It was on the tip of my tongue; it almost escaped, but just in time I realised that almost certainly it would destroy our friendship, our relationship, when he was asked to confirm it, as he would be. Also, I looked at Alex and remembered that I'd be lying to a man who trusted me enough to make me godmother to his child. And I thought of Tom. If it came to that point, Gomez and Garcia would be sure to want to interview him about his mother's bedtime habits; no way would I allow that.

'He dropped me off,' I finished, 'where we're parked right now, and then he drove off.'

'Where did he go?'

'Back to the priests' house in L'Escala.'

Alex sighed. 'Good.'

'You were expecting something different?'

'I wasn't expecting anything, I promise.' He paused. 'What

else?' he mused. 'Yes, how was he dressed? What was he wearing?'

'His usual off-duty gear. Denims, open-necked shirt and that sports jacket of his. You know the one, with the elbow patches.'

'Sure. Do him a favour, buy him a new one for Christmas, or his birthday, otherwise he'll wear that thing till it dies.'

I laughed with him, relieved that he hadn't asked me what colour the shirt was, or said anything that would have made me admit to what I'd seen sticking out of the breast pocket of the old jacket, the end of a white plastic clerical collar.

Fourteen

To my surprise Tom was still at the table in Can Coll, finishing up the biggest ice cream they have on offer – as I had allowed in my moment of weakness – accompanied by Ben, who had closed for his afternoon break, plus Charlie, Cher and Mustard. (By the way, before you get any ideas about Charlie and Cher, she's been fixed; so, for that matter, has Mustard, when he wasn't looking, although it hasn't affected his sense of smell.)

'Everything okay, Primavera?' the shopkeeper asked.

'Yes, but I'll tell you later.' He read the message in my eyes and let it drop.

My son didn't quiz me about what we had been doing. He simply handed me back the fifty unbidden . . . he knows that's too much money for him to carry normally . . . and told me that he and Ben were going to walk the dogs. Since I was long overdue lunch, I let them get on with it, and took over the table. Justine reckoned this was a good idea, and joined me.

Before we'd left, I'd made my mind up about what I was going to have, so I didn't need to consult anything before ordering omelette and chips, but I did add a jug of sangria to the order, plus some water, for instant rehydration.

As our waiter left to get things under way, I turned to the mayor. 'So,' I said, 'you've lost your majority on the council. Where does that leave you?'

She frowned. 'I've been thinking about that,' she admitted. 'I'll need to consult our lawyer, but I believe you're wrong. Planas was an independent, a one-man slate. Normally, when someone leaves the council, the party involved nominates the next person on their list of thirteen at the election, and that person takes over. In this case, there's nobody to nominate; logically, the vacancy will be unfilled. That means that we have only twelve councillors. My party and the combined opposition have six each. I'm the mayor, I have the casting vote, so, our majority is now absolute.'

'Hey presto,' I chuckled. 'But you realise that gives you a damn good motive for bumping him off. Hope you can tell Gomez where you were on Friday night and Saturday morning.'

She winced. 'I hope I don't have to.'

I winked at her. 'Oh yes?'

'It's that obvious?'

'Afraid so.'

'Shit.' She looked at me. 'Between us, yes?'

'Of course.'

'I wasn't in L'Escala. We spent the night in a hotel in Figueras. He's as busy as I am, and we meet up when it suits his schedule, and mine.'

'Not a local, then.'

'I didn't say that, but please don't ask me who he is.'

'Intriguing . . . but it's none of my business. The truth is, Justine, you're confiding in the right woman. I don't care how many secrets you have, I've still got more than you.'

Fifteen

I must admit I was curious, but I didn't try to ferret out the identity of Justine's mystery man. The only other detail she let slip was that they had been together for three years or thereabouts, meeting wherever they could but never in L'Escala. Her mother and her sister . . . as Ben had said . . . knew of his existence, but that was all.

'Are you ever going to settle down?'

'Maybe, when his career makes it simpler, and when I feel that I've given all I can to L'Escala. My profession, when I go back to it, will let me go anywhere.'

'What is that?'

'I'm an accountant.'

The rest of the probing over lunch went in the other direction. Most people I meet want to know, sooner or later, about my time with Oz, and even the sophisticated mayor was one of those. She asked me what he was really like, away from the glamour of his movie career. 'He used to fart in bed.' She wanted to know what had brought us to St Martí, the first time. 'We stopped for lunch . . . in this very café in fact . . . and bought an apartment.' She wondered why we hadn't stayed together. 'The first time, he left me for somebody he had always been with, really, yet should never have been with at all.' (That puzzled her, but it's part of the biography I'll never write, and there's only one other person alive who knows of it.) 'After she died, he went quietly crazy, became as unpredictable as me, and dangerous with it. We left each other, pretty quickly, but not before we'd made Tom. A while after that, he died.'

'It still hurts, doesn't it,' Justine murmured.

'Why do you say that?'

'You have tears in your eyes.'

I gave her my best nonchalant smile. 'For all you know they could be out of relief.'

'I don't think so.' She poured the last of the sangria. 'What about Gerard?' she asked abruptly. 'Should we tell him about Planas? Should we warn him? Should we tell him what Garcia found?'

'First of all,' I replied, 'I doubt we'll need to tell him. Angel will want a priest, to do whatever needs to be done in these circumstances. Even if he doesn't attend to it himself, he's bound to get to hear about it. As for warning him . . . leave that to me.'

She was happy with that. We finished lunch, then went our separate ways, she towards the car park, me back to the house.

One of the very few downsides about living in St Martí is the mobile phone signal, which varies from bad to very bad, and disappears entirely inside several of the old stone buildings.

When I stepped into the hall, and laid my phone on the new hall table, I realised that it had been switched off all day. I checked the landline, and saw that I had two voice messages. I pushed the replay button, put the handset to my ear, expecting to hear Gerard's voice . . . and almost dropped it again, as a deep, familiar accent reminded me of home.

'Primavera, this is the other grandpa speaking.' Mac Blackstone, Oz's dad; something wrong? Mary, Ellen, Harvey, one of the boys? And then he chuckled. 'Trust me to call when you're at church . . . or sprawled on the beach more like. Can you give me a ring when you pick this up? I've got an opportunity, but I'll need to know fast.'

'What the hell's this about?' I murmured, as I dialled Mac's number.

'What the hell's this about?' I asked, as he picked up my call.

'Puzzled you, did I?' He chuckled. 'Sorry to be mysterious, but you never know how long you have on these things. Do you fancy a visitor for a few days?'

'Depends who it is.'

'Me, woman. Who else?'

'Well, there's your wife, for a start.'

'Ah, but she's the reason. Mary's cousin's been ill; Isa, the one in Crieff. She's had a hysterectomy, and now they're discharging her from hospital, way too soon in my opinion. She's on her own, and she's going to need looking after, so Mary's going to stay with her for a week. I don't fancy any of that, so I've been thinking it might be nice to see my grandson and his mum. I've been looking around, and I can get a flight to Girona from Prestwick on Tuesday, for next to bugger all, going home next Monday. Would that be okay, or do you have other arrangements?'

I didn't take a second to decide; the cheery presence of Mac Blackstone was just what I needed, even if he wasn't quite the man he had been. 'Book it,' I told him.

'Are you sure?'

'Absolutely. Book it, then send me an email with your arrival time; I'll pick you up.'

'Not at all, I'll get a taxi.'

'You're not that rich; I'll pick you up. I won't tell Tom, though; he still likes surprises.' I remembered something. 'By the way, there's someone here who says he knows you; Matthew Reid, from East Lothian.'

'Is he, by God? In that case, I'd better bring the golf clubs.'

I ended the call and then went back to my voice messages. As I had expected, the second was from Gerard; timed less than an hour earlier. 'Primavera,' he said, his voice calm, 'I need you to call me. Something has happened. Use my mobile, as usual.' I'd always made a point of not calling him at the parish residence, for fear of embarrassing Father Olivares, the old priest.

I did as he asked. I could hear engine noise as he answered. 'Where are you?'

'I'm on my way back from Figueras. I had an office to perform, for Angel Planas.'

'I know what's happened,' I told him. 'In fact, I've seen what happened. Alex came for Justine, not long after you left, and I went with them.'

'You did? Angel didn't mention that when he called me.'

'Angel was upset at the time, as you'd expect. Gerard, I need to see you.'

'Of course. You must be upset too.'

'That's not why. Can you come here?'

'Yes. I'm only five minutes away.'

'Then I'll open the garage and wait for you there; drive straight in when you arrive.'

I left a note on the table for Tom, in case he came home and wondered where I was, then took the winding internal stair that leads down to the garage, where I opened the door with the remote. Gerard's five minutes were closer to ten, but eventually he arrived, parking between my Jeep and our bikes. As he climbed out of the car I saw that he was wearing a black short-sleeved shirt, with a flash of clerical white showing at the front of the buttoned collar. I closed the door and led him upstairs, and into the kitchen.

'This is a terrible thing,' he said, as I handed him a bottle of water from the fridge.

'You've seen the body, then? That's where you were?'

'Yes, I went to bless him.'

'When are they going to do the autopsy? Did anyone say?'

'That man Gomez, from Girona, was there. He said they hope it can be done this evening. I asked him why the haste; he said that they have to be absolutely certain about the cause of death.'

As he took a drink, I reached out and touched his collar. 'Take it off,' I told him. He looked at me, blankly. 'Please,' I added.

'As you wish.' He reached round to the back of his neck, fiddled around for a second or two, then flicked his fingers. The collar loosened and he drew it out; it was a complete circlet, nothing like the thing that Gomez had shown us.

'Is that the one you had on Friday night, in your jacket?' I asked, puzzled.

'Yes.' He folded it twice and slipped it into a pocket in his shirt.

'I thought you guys just wore a wee insert thingie.'

'Some do, but not us; we're traditionalists. Would you like to see my hair shirt also?' He smiled and reached for a button of his shirt. 'I don't think that would compromise us.'

I was flustered, didn't know what to do, or say. 'Bollocks,' I stammered, highly inappropriately. 'Stop it. I'm sorry, I was only wondering . . .'

He stared at me, then as if a penny had dropped he shook his head, and started to chuckle. 'And I can guess why,' he said. 'You went with Alex and Justine to Planas's house, because Gomez wanted to talk to you. When you were there, he showed you what he later showed me, and told you as he told me what his colleague had sworn it was. You know, Primavera my dear, we all accept that our Maker moves in mysterious ways, but the means by which He allowed an idiot like that man Garcia to become an inspector of the Mossos is beyond all comprehension. It seems that once upon a time he was in

Africa, and met a missionary who wore a short insert to his collar, to make it more bearable in the extreme heat. When he found that piece of plastic in Senor Planas's hand, he decided in his wisdom that the dead man had ripped it from the neck of an assailant. That is the theory he put to Gomez. However, when the intendant took a closer look, after you and Justine had left, he saw some faded writing on the material. What he thought he read was "Rev Rivularis". He admitted to me that he entertained the fleeting notion that this might have been the name of the owner, until his eye was caught by a pot on the top of the wall beneath which the body had been found, with a small, fairly recently, planted tree in it. Senor Gomez is gardener enough to know a Majesty palm when he sees one, and resourceful enough to do some very quick research, to discover that the botanical name of this genus is "Ravenea Rivularis", "Rav" for short. So the officially revised theory of the police is that as Planas fell over the wall, he grasped the palm in a vain attempt to pull himself back, and ripped the circular white plastic label from its trunk.'

I felt that the floor was crumbling away from beneath me. I had been afraid that . . . Christ I'd been a bigger idiot than Garcia. 'Gerard,' I mumbled, 'I'm . . .'

He stepped towards me, cupped my face in both of his hands and kissed me on the forehead. 'You were afraid. You feared that I might have given in to the baser instinct that I confessed to you, and that I might have gone to chastise Planas. You were afraid that I might have gone too far, and scared him to death. Or even pushed him over that wall.'

'No,' I protested. 'I'd never have thought that, not for a second.'

'Yet you did your best to protect me. I heard from Gomez that you told Alex that I had been with you all evening and into the next day, that I dropped you off and went home, as Father Olivares would have been able to confirm, if it had been necessary. He and I sat together for an hour, over a bottle of very fine garnaxa; my senior likes a liqueur before he retires.'

'I told him the truth.'

'I know, and I'm grateful.' He paused, and tilted my head up until he was looking into my eyes. 'Most of all I'm grateful that you did not try to give me a more personal alibi.'

'I thought about it. Sorry.'

'Don't be,' he said. 'I might have thought about it too, if the circumstances had been different and there had been no other way out. You never know how strong your will is, until it's tested.'

'I'd have backed you up, but it would have been a waste of time. Nobody would have believed us. You're not the type to two-time Jesus.'

Sixteen

Gerard had just gone when Tom returned. Remembering what I had promised Ben earlier, I called him and told him what had happened. He seemed genuinely shocked; if the fact that his problem had gone for good crossed his mind, he gave no hint of it. All I heard in his reaction was concern for Angel Planas.

That might have been all there was to it. Indeed I thought it was, for around twenty-four hours.

Tom and I had a small disagreement over dinner, when I told him he'd already had his ice cream allocation for the day, but otherwise we spent a quiet evening. There was a Spanish league football match on telly, Barcelona against Osasuna; Tom's a Barça fan, as are most of the kids around here. The local L'Escala team even plays in the same colours. It was a late kick-off, with a school day looming, but I didn't want two fights in one night so I let him stay up to watch it.

I had an eye on it too, but not too closely. My mind kept wandering back to the scene in Planas's garden, filling with the sight of the swollen, flyblown corpse of the detestable little man with whom I'd had such a bitter confrontation, less than a day before he died. I thought about Angel too, and the look on his face when he'd arrived in the garden. His father might have cut him out of his life, but clearly, the animosity hadn't been mutual. Just before half-time in the game I went into the kitchen, found his number in the telephone directory and called him.

I'd half expected his phone to be on answer mode, but he picked up. I told him who was calling, and how sorry I was.

'That's kind of you,' he said. 'I believe you mean that. I'm sorry also, for the trouble that my father caused you. I guess that will be resolved now.'

'It had been anyway; an accommodation had been reached.'

I heard him gasp, then laugh softly. 'You made my father compromise?' he exclaimed. 'I'm impressed. You must be a formidable woman. How did you do it?'

'We negotiated.'

'Ah, then there was money involved . . . or did you play cards for his approval?'

'He laid down a condition; I don't think he believed that I'd accept it, but I did.'

'My poor old papa; his face must have been a picture. No wonder he had a heart attack.'

I was surprised. 'You've had the autopsy result already?'

'No, but the police officer came to see us earlier this evening. He said that it was almost certainly the cause.'

'When will you hold the funeral? I'd like to attend.'

'I can't plan anything until the police release the body, but

I'm hoping for Wednesday morning, at the latest.' He chuckled. 'Do you want to make sure that he doesn't climb out of the coffin? I suspect that many of the mourners will be thinking that way.'

'I'll attend out of respect, nothing else; respect for you and your wife.'

'She may not go herself. I'm trying to persuade her, but the choice will be hers. She has every reason to stay away. I won't hold it against her if she does.' He took a breath. 'Senora, this problem you had with my father . . . nobody's going to hear of it, are they?'

'Not from me, I promise you.'

'That's good. It's my family name that he discredited, after all.'

'Then I'll do nothing to blacken it.'

I told him I'd see him at the funeral, and hung up. Then I remembered Mac's call. I went into the study, switched on my computer and went online as soon as it was booted up. (Tom has his own, but I supervise its use.) I had three emails waiting for me, one from my sister, one from my friend Shirley Gash, who was on a cruise from Dubai to Singapore, and as he'd promised, one from Mac. I left the others for later, and went straight to his. It confirmed that he'd be landing at Girona late afternoon on the following Tuesday, and ended, 'Remember, keep it a surprise for the wee man.' I smiled, thinking that he might be surprised himself when he saw how much the 'wee man' had stretched since his last visit, then closed down.

The teams were on their way out for the second half when I

went back to the television room. Barça were doing all right, but I couldn't summon up any real interest. My mind was full of thoughts of wine fairs . . . *'Maybe I should find one and visit it, to understand better what they were all about'* . . . of wet weather plans . . . *'Is this house really big enough to hold all those stands, or should I try to persuade the mayor to let us have the old foresters' house, on the other side of the church, as a back-stop in case it rains?'* . . . and inevitably, although I tried to push the awful image away, the scene in the garden of José-Luis Planas . . . *'After all that bloody drama, they've settled for the obvious. The old man was so pumped up by his battle with me, that his arteries seized up, he had a wobbler and he fell over the garden wall. And if that's so, Primavera, does that mean that you were responsible for his death?'*

'Not bloody likely,' I said aloud.

'What?' Tom asked.

'Nothing. Sorry, I was talking to myself.'

He shrugged, as if that was normal adult behaviour and turned back to the game, leaving me back in old Planas's garden, trying to put my finger on something about the scene that was not quite right.

Seventeen

Tom was as bright as the sun next morning, as usual. Late nights don't affect him at all. In truth I was the grumpy one, as I'd had a rough night, interrupted, unusually, by some pretty bad dreams from the recent and more distant past.

I didn't let him see that though, as I gave him breakfast, then waved him goodbye as he set out for school on his bike, along the car-free seafront passageway. One or two other kids live along the way, and by the time they get to the only proper road they have to cross . . . and that's supervised . . . they've formed a small peloton.

Once he'd gone, the niggly feeling came back. I fought it off by catching up on some housework; my usual Monday chores . . . changing the beds, laundering sheets and pillowcases, and doing the rest of the weekend's wash . . . then, when I was finished, slipping on a bikini, and going down to the beach to swim. That didn't last long, for there was a heavy swell coming in, probably the aftermath of a storm far out at sea. I went back home, stripped off my damp suit, and stretched out on the lounger on my private terrace, hoping that I might catch up on

some of my lost sleep, but someone was working on the renova-
tion of a house in the village, and the din of their machinery
put paid to any chance of that.

Finally, I gave up and settled for feeling like a pre-
menopausal hag for the rest of the day. I showered, dressed,
switched on my computer and cleared my mailbox, sending a
reply to Shirley that said in essence, 'Jealous as hell!' and one
to my sister in Los Angeles, that was an exchange of kid
information, and some forward planning. It's only when I
speak to Dawn, or email her, that I feel the lack of a man in my
life . . . in the fullest sense. Hers is great; even if he was an
ordinary Joe, a bus driver, a computer salesman, whatever, he'd
be great. The fact that Miles is one of the most famous men in
the entertainment industry is irrelevant . . . almost.

Once my box was clear, Charlie and I left the house and
went down to Ben's wine shop. (The 'Closed' sign had been up
all morning on the information booth, but there are very few
callers on Mondays in the low season.) I still had the best part
of two hours to kill before I was due at the town hall to collect
the signed permission, and it had occurred to me while tossing
on my lounger that now that the venue for the fair had been
tied up, we'd better get on with the minutiae. Ben was having
a quiet morning and so we were able to have a fairly productive
hour, doing some rough planning of the layout of the stalls in
the fairly confined square and working out what we were going
to need in terms of glassware, tables, covers, and parasols . . .
these would be essential to keep the sun off the stock. Ben also
called Mercé, the designer who was working with him on the

format of the tickets. She has a studio in the next street to the wine shop, so she was able to sit in on our impromptu conference and agree the last details.

'What about the print run?' I asked.

'I've got a decent price for three hundred,' Ben announced. 'Plus fifty posters.'

'Then the unit cost of a thousand, and a hundred and fifty posters will be much lower.'

'We'll never sell a thousand.'

'Don't you be so sure.' I turned to Mercé. 'Could you design an ad for the town council's web page, and for the tourist sites?'

'No problem. In fact, it already exists.'

'I've got a website too,' Ben explained, casually. 'It's called arrelsdelvi dot com. Mercé laid it out for me.'

'Now you tell me! Let's see it.'

I waited while he called it up on his laptop. It was fine, but no more than that, a simple one-page ad for the event that didn't go anywhere. 'Any thoughts?' he asked.

'Sure. It should explain what the punters get for their money, then we should list the producers who've agreed to appear, with links to their sites, and information on the wines that'll be available for tasting. It should market the event as the centrepiece of a visit for people who've never been before. There should be a page of information about St Martí itself, about the restaurants and the hotel and apartment accommodation available. And there should be information about us.'

'Us?'

'You, as founder and owner, Mercé as design consultant, and me as operations manager ... especially me, and this is what it's going to say about me: "St Martí resident and former wife of Oz Blackstone, sister of Dawn Phillips, and sister-in-law of Miles Grayson." All the big search engines have thousands upon thousands of entries every day from people looking for one or more of those names. When your site turns up among the hits, the event goes global.'

He looked interested, but cautious. 'Will it cost much?'

Mercé shook her head. 'No, and it can be done very quickly.'

'Then let's do it. Any more bright ideas, Primavera?'

'I'll see what I can come up with, after I've collected the permission from the town hall,' I told him. 'Got to go there now.'

I didn't expect to see Justine, but I was shown into her office when I arrived. She handed me an unsealed envelope. 'There it is,' she said, 'with a note of what the fee will be. I don't think it'll scare you too much.' I took a look; it didn't.

I told her about my conversation with Angel, the night before, but she'd known; in fact she'd been at his house when I'd called, with her sister. 'Elena's decided to go to the funeral,' she said, 'which is a big relief for me. If she'd stayed away, I'd have felt honour bound to do the same. But I'm mayor, and he was a council member; if I wasn't there it wouldn't look good to the people who don't know about the family difficulty, and very few do. Old Planas didn't talk about it, and neither did Angel.'

'Do they know yet when it's going to be?'

'No. I called Angel half an hour ago; he'd heard nothing from the police. They'd better get a move on. Already, tomorrow's out of the question; if they don't release the body soon, even Wednesday might be difficult.'

I left her and headed home, I just had time to get there before Tom, and to whip up something for lunch, specifically a long baguette stuffed with tuna and mayonnaise, followed by chunks of diced, fresh pineapple. Tom had more of the sandwich than I did; the boy could eat for Catalunya, or Scotland, or for any other country for which he might be qualified to compete. When I saw him off, for the second time that day, I felt a lot brighter than when he'd left in the morning. My burst of creativity down at Ben's had chased away my mood and, in addition, I was beginning to look forward to Mac's visit. I'd kept my promise and not dropped the slightest hint to Tom that Grandpa Blackstone was coming to visit. My plan was to find a pretext to drive him to school in the afternoon, rather than let him take his bike, then pick him up and head for the airport. If the flight was on time, we'd get there around the same time as he did.

I was smiling at the prospect as I programmed the dishwasher, when the door buzzer sounded. I checked the video screen in the kitchen, and saw Alex Guinart peering into the camera. There was someone else with him, another uniform, but I couldn't see who it was. I pressed the button that opens the gate, and went to the front door, to meet them.

As they approached through my small garden, it was

Intendant Gomez who took the lead, Alex a couple of deferen-
tial paces behind. 'Good afternoon,' I greeted them. 'You don't
usually travel together. Where's Inspector Garcia?' Given what
I'd learned from Gerard, my question was mischievous.

'He's in the office in Girona; we have a big caseload. I've
asked Sub-inspector Guinart to work with me on this matter.
After all, this is his town.' That was all Gomez volunteered. I
didn't press him; whatever the visit was about, his face said that
it was serious. Instead, I showed them into the television room,
just off the entrance hall.

'What brings you here?' I asked. 'Not that it isn't a pleasure
to see you, but . . .'

'We need to talk to you again. The autopsy on Senor Planas
has begun. It's not yet complete, but already things have
changed.'

'In what way?'

'He didn't have a heart attack.'

'Okay, he fell and landed on his head.'

'It's not as simple as that.'

I was waiting for him to continue . . . when I realised what
was wrong with my mental picture of Planas, dead in his
garden. 'He was lying on his back,' I exclaimed. 'He must have
fallen backwards over the wall to wind up that way. But Garcia
found the plastic in his right hand . . . incidentally, I know
what it was now; Father Gerard told me. If he'd reached out for
the Majesty palm to break his fall, and ripped off the label . . .
The pot was on the wrong side; he'd have grabbed it with his
left hand, not his right.'

'Hey,' said Alex, his eyes widening, 'that's true. And we hadn't got that far yet.'

'No,' Gomez agreed. 'But thanks for pointing it out. That takes our thinking forward; in fact, it helps our developing theory. The autopsy has been interrupted because our patholo- gist realised that he needed a second opinion, that of someone with more specific experience than he has. So we've called in someone from the university in Barcelona. She's an authority on blunt force injuries, and she's given evidence in criminal prosecutions all over Spain, and even in other countries.'

'Why do you need her?'

'To confirm our examiner's theory,' said Alex, '. . . if it's viable, that is. He's suggesting that Planas may not have died where he was found, or if he did, that he didn't sustain his injuries there. He reckons that he was attacked, hit hard enough to leave him dead or dying, and then thrown over the wall and down on to the rocks.'

'And the label?'

'Put in his hand to make it look like what we assumed it to be, a reflex reaction to a trip and a fall. The intendant and I have just been back to the house; he's sent the scene of crime technicians back in to take another look, across a wider area.'

'That's right,' Gomez confirmed, 'but already there are new possibilities to explore, and new questions to be answered. Think back to the scene, senora. Do you recall a patio with doors that opened on to it, from the house?'

I nodded. 'Yes, with a sort of pagoda structure over it. And a table. And chairs.'

'Indeed. And on the table there was?'

'I can't remember that.'

'A bottle. Faustino One, red, from La Rioja, a very fine wine. Beside it, a glass, half full, although there would have been a little evaporation between it being poured and being discovered. The bottle was empty, Senora Blackstone.' I frowned, wondering where he was going with this. I didn't have to wait long to find out. 'But Senor Planas didn't drink it all himself.'

'How do you know that?'

'From the contents of his stomach. One partly digested steak and French fries, consumed earlier that night in Hostal Miryam . . . where he had no wine, only a small bottle of water and a coffee . . . and forty-two centilitres of red wine. The bottle held seventy, the glass contained eleven, allowing for evaporation. Someone else had the other seventeen.'

'Maybe he drank the bottle over two nights,' I suggested.

'The corkscrew was on the table, with the cork still in it; it's logical that it had just been drawn. Left open, it would not have been drinkable on the second night. For sure, he had a companion, and after he was dead, that person cleaned the second glass and put it away, or simply took it when they left.'

'It's possible that person left before Planas was attacked.'

'And he was so tidy that he washed the second glass right away? Possible, but it's a tight timescale. Our examiner says that he died between midnight and four in the morning. He didn't leave Miryam until just after ten. The time on his bill, when it was printed out, was two minutes before. No. I believe he got home and had a caller, maybe someone he was expecting, maybe not, but someone he knew well enough to give a glass of damn fine wine. And I believe that caller smashed his head in, arranged things so that we stupid cops would buy it as an accident, then got to hell out of there.'

'Your second pathologist will be able to confirm this?'

'She'll be able to determine the exact shape of the fatal injuries, and tell us how much force was used.'

'Do you have any idea what the weapon might have been?'

'We found various substances in the wounds, dirt from the ground, stone chips and other debris. We plan to match everything against items in the rockery, as far as we can.'

'I hope you get a result. Now, much as I appreciate being told all this, why are you here? You haven't come for my advice.'

'No,' Alex agreed. 'We've come for a sample of your DNA.'

'Are you saying I'm a suspect?' I blurted out, indignantly.

'You did have an argument with the man,' Gomez pointed out. 'He tried to extort money from you.'

'Which I would have paid.'

The intendant smiled. 'I know. You're not a suspect, I promise, but you were at the scene. We're taking samples from everyone who was, police and paramedics too, so that we can identify any traces we find, and eliminate those who had business there.'

'Do you have a swab?' I asked.

He nodded and produced one, in a container, from a pocket in his tunic.

I took it from him and wiped the probe across the inside of my cheek, returning it with a sizeable saliva sample. 'There,' I said. 'Now let me warn you . . . if that winds up on a national database, there will be trouble. I am not a fan of Big Brother.'

Both he and Alex stared at me as if I was mad, and then I realised why. *Poor old Orwell*, I thought. *His greatest creation consigned to obscurity by a crap TV show.*

Eighteen

But did I really believe Gomez? Hard as I tried to get on with the rest of my day, that question kept interrupting it. After all, I did have a major argument with a murder victim a matter of hours before he attained that status. Had I been sweet-talked into volunteering a personal sample that no lawyer would have allowed Gomez to take without an order from the court? I thought of all the cops I've known over the years. In those circumstances Ricky Ross, when he was in Edinburgh CID, and even Mike Dylan, bless his imperfect soul, would have been all over me like a nasty skin condition. When I looked at the situation, dispassionately, even I would have had me down as a suspect.

After all, Gerard had dropped me off not long after midnight, at the very start of the four-hour period during which, the pathologist said, the guy had been killed. Ben Simmers had gone home as soon as I'd got back, leaving me alone with Tom, who was sound asleep. There was nobody to say that I hadn't crept out again, gone to Planas's place, talked myself past the entry system, had a glass of wine with the old shit, then bashed his head in. But, I asked myself, why would I have done that? The devil's advocate in me replied: the police could argue that I was saving myself twelve thousand euro. I might counter that, by my standards, that amount isn't worth the risk, even if I was the homicidal type, but . . . my father has a saying: 'There are two sorts of money. There is money, and there is *my* money, and one's attitude to each is completely different.' Christ, I had some sort of a motive, I had no alibi, and it was pretty much certain that they would find my DNA at the scene, somewhere. The problem with that was, given all those other factors . . . I couldn't think of a way of proving that I'd only been there once.

The way things stood, the only person in the world who knew for sure that I hadn't killed the guy was me. I won't say I was scared, but I felt a few butterflies. I called Gerard, for the comfort of hearing his voice as much as anything else, and told him about the change in the situation. I was surprised by the fact that he wasn't.

'Father Olivares grew up in L'Escala and he's known Planas since they were boys. He told me that he came from a long-lived family,' he explained. 'His father and his father before him, they both lasted into their nineties. As I understand it, José-Luis was only sixty-eight, and still danced a lively sardana with his cronies. When I told my colleague how he'd been found, he thought about it for a while then asked, "Did he fall or was he pushed?" Now we know, it seems.' He paused. 'This has upset you, hasn't it?'

'Yes, it has. I met the man, and hours later he was dead.'

'Then the police turn up on your doorstep.' He's a mind-reader.

'Yes!' I said, a little too loudly.

He laughed, gently. 'Primavera, don't be silly. This is a man who's spent his life upsetting people.'

I thought of Angel's comment. 'His son did say,' I admitted, 'that half the people at the funeral will be there to make sure he really is dead.'

'Exactly. Don't get yourself into a lather. If you want to safeguard your position, you could always hire a lawyer . . .'

'Gomez might read something into that. No, I won't be doing that unless it's necessary.'

'In that case, just relax. If they come back to you, let me know, otherwise . . .'

'Will do,' I promised. 'Here, are you doing anything on Wednesday evening?'

'Not that I know of at this moment. In my calling it's always possible that something may arise, but as it stands I'm clear.'

'Then would you like to come to my place, for supper? It'll be above suspicion: Tom's grandfather, Oz's dad, is coming to stay. You've never met him, but I'm sure you'll get on.'

'Fine, thanks. Is he Catholic?'

'No, he's the same as me. Baptised Protestant, but broad-minded. You've got something else in common though. You both see people at their most vulnerable and afraid. He's a dentist, or was, until he retired a few years back.'

He was laughing as he hung up. Gerard's laugh is soft, deep

and musical, not the braying kind that always strikes me as affected.

I had worked myself out of household tasks, and so I went outside and replaced the multilingual 'Closed' sign on the information booth with the one that reads 'Ring for attention'. Four people did: two British, one French, one German, with a variety of questions. I answered them all, sold two tickets for the cruise boat, and sent the German on his way with a map of the cycle routes across Emporda.

I was in the garden, reading *Fatal Last Words*, the latest Skinner novel . . . I'm a big fan . . . and waiting for Tom to get back from school, when the bell sounded again. I opened the door, stepped into the booth, and saw Alex Guinart standing on the other side of the wall. He was smiling, and I took that as a good sign.

'How can I help you, sir?' I asked. 'Tickets for the *carrilet*? A list of concerts in the church this summer? Contact numbers for local taxi services?'

'They're all on the noticeboard in our office. I've just had some good news, and I thought I'd share it with you. Hector Gomez couldn't say anything to me until he had confirmation from our HQ in Barcelona; he had the call half an hour ago, and I'm now officially an inspector. It means a transfer to Girona, to join his team: as his number two, in fact.'

I was dead chuffed for him. 'Alex, congratulations.'

'Yes, thanks. I'm pleased too, and so's Gloria, although it'll mean less-regular hours.'

'What about Garcia? Will you be working with him too?'

'No. He's been transferred to Tortosa.'

That was a new one on me. 'Where's that?' I asked.

Alex grinned. 'It's as far away from here as you can get without leaving Catalunya.'

I winced. 'You'd better behave yourself with Gomez.'

'Garcia had it coming. He isn't a good man. Hector made a point of never leaving him alone with a prisoner. I think he was biding his time; that nonsense with the piece of plastic gave him the chance to get rid of him. The guy was all ready to accuse Father Hernanz, after he heard about your argument with Planas, and since he knows that the two of you are . . .' He hesitated, as if he was taking care to choose the right word.

'Friends, Alex,' I told him, 'we're friends. Just as you and I are friends.'

He shook his head. 'No, Primavera; not as we are. Don't be so naive. You are a trusted friend of my family, and you stood for my daughter in church, beside Gloria and me. Gerard's a priest, a modern priest, I'll grant you, but he can't have a public friendship with an attractive single woman, who's around his own age, without tongues starting to wag.'

'Thanks for the compliment, but it's a private friendship,' I protested. 'There is nothing in the vows or even in the practice of his church that says that a priest can't have a private life. Our view is that we'd be wrong to keep our friendship a secret. Even old Olivares agrees with that, for he and Gerard had it out. Bottom line, we are friends, we are not intimate. We don't kiss, we don't cuddle, we don't fuck, all right?'

'Hey,' he laughed, 'don't get on my case. I know that, but people tend to apply their own values to others. When it comes to the likes of a guy like Garcia, it's fuel to him. He and Gerard have butted heads before too, and neither of them's the type to back down.'

'Are you saying I should just see him in church and leave it at that?'

Alex looked down, and shook his head. 'No. Like I said, you're a trusted friend. You know what's right and what's not. It's for Gerard to square the extent of your friendship with his duty as a priest, and to deal with the critics. But don't be too surprised if he also winds up in Tortosa one day, or in some other place far away. Father Olivares will be retiring soon. Even though he likes Gerard, when the bishop and the monsignor consider his replacement, your name might come up in the discussion.'

I hadn't thought that far ahead; if Gerard had, then it seemed that he'd made some sort of a decision. 'Fucking politicians,' I growled. 'They're more trouble than they're worth, wherever they are.'

'So it seems, in Planas's case, although it took a long time for someone to do something about it.'

'When does your expert get to work?'

'Tomorrow morning. Our first pathologist was right, I'm sure, but we have to report to the public prosecutor's office, so we need her confirmation of that. Meanwhile, the CSI people are doing the painstaking stuff along at the house.'

'Any suspects?' I asked, casually.

He grinned. 'Apart from you, you mean?'

'Stop it.'

'There's no chain of evidence so far. We have nothing to follow. All we can do is wait, to see what tomorrow may bring.'

Nineteen

Life is like a round of golf. If you drop a shot at one hole, you do your damnedest to get it back at the next, and it gives you real momentum when you do. So it is with days.

The sun woke me next morning, rising beautifully out of the sea and into a cloudless sky. You can't beat perfection. My moody Monday was a distant memory, and I could see a terrific Tuesday ahead.

Tom was in an upbeat mood too; I'd told him the night before that I'd be picking him up at five o'clock (a long day for the kids, but with long summer holidays as a compensation) and taking him on an errand. He'd quizzed me, but 'mystery tour' was all I would say. He was up by seven thirty and wanted to go for a swim before school, so we all did, he and I, and Charlie. You're not really supposed to take dogs on the beaches in the summer, unless they're designated, but at that time of the morning you can get away with it. Anyway, Charlie's good; he knows not to dump on the sand.

Once we'd finished breakfast I drove Tom to L'Escala, leaving Charlie in his garden kingdom, and parked outside the town's leisure complex. I watched Tom walk the last hundred metres or so, then took my gym bag inside. I was restless, and I knew why. I've always coped with my recent state well enough, but I'm a woman in my prime, and from time to time I get horny. So it was that morning. When you're celibate, and you get that way . . . well, I find that the best thing to do is to put on a pair of trainers and run like hell. I flashed my membership card at the entrance, changed, and went up to the fitness suite. It was busy, but there was a treadmill free. I switched it on, starting at a modest ten kilometres per hour, winding it up to twelve once I was warmed up. One of the nice things about our town gym is that there are no mirrors; people go there to exercise, not to admire their six-packs. Instead of looking at yourself sweating, as you pound out the distance, there's nice views of the pool below and of the clay tennis courts outside. That morning I saw only one swimmer, but the three courts were all in use, even though the sun had only reached one of them.

I'd done six kilometres of the ten I'd set for myself, when I was aware of a figure climbing on to the static bike next to me. 'Good morning, Senora Primavera,' said the newcomer. I glanced to the side and saw Angel Planas.

I was running smoothly; I can go faster than the pace I'd chosen, so I had the breath to reply. 'And to you,' I replied. He had spoken Spanish, as we had in our previous encounters, but I chose to reply in Catalan. 'I haven't seen you here before.'

He switched languages. 'Normally, I come during my

afternoon break, but I've closed the shop until after the funeral.'

'As a mark of respect?'

'Of course. It wouldn't have been seemly to do otherwise. Besides, my father may have been at odds with me, but . . .'

'He was still your dad. I understand. Has Gomez given you any indication about the funeral?'

He set himself a programme, and started to pedal slowly. 'He's told me that after the examination this morning, he will ask the public prosecutor for authority to release the body. Unless something unexpected comes up, that will happen tomorrow, so it will be on Thursday morning.'

'Doesn't give you much time to let people know.'

'We have a very good informal system for spreading the word. We put the details on notices in shop windows and on lamp posts, all through the old town. It works.'

'What about the other parts of L'Escala?'

Out of the corner of my eye, I caught a smile on his face. 'To my father, the modern areas barely existed.'

He set to pedalling, and I cranked up my speed a little, putting further discourse beyond either of us. I finished my programme with a sprint, then wound down for a couple of minutes, before stepping off the treadmill. As my heart rate settled back to normal I did some stretching exercises, until finally I reckoned I had burned off most of my raging hormones. I waved goodbye to Angel and went back to the changing room.

By the time I made it back to L'Escala, looking presentable

and fit for the day . . . I tend to use very little make-up, just Garnier sun cream as a base and a little lippie, and keep my hair shortish and spiky, the straight from the shower look . . . I had worked off breakfast and was fairly hungry. It was still well shy of eleven, but Meson del Conde's tables were out and ready for the day, so Charlie and I sat down and I asked Cisco for a cortado . . . a café solo with milk . . . a bottle of Vichy Catalan, a croissant and a dish of water for the dog.

I had just killed the coffee and was tucking into the crab-like roll when Ben Simmers came into the square, looking neither right nor left but heading straight for my house, his distinctive gait so brisk that it was almost a trot.

'Hey!' I called to him, between bites. 'If you're looking for me, try here.'

He spun round, saw me and came across to my table.

'Want a coffee?' I asked.

'No, no time.'

He seemed more than a little agitated. 'OK,' I said, 'quit acting like the white fucking rabbit and tell me what's up.'

'My mum,' he blurted out. 'She's down at the shop, and she's in a hell of a state. Can you come?'

'Of course.' I picked up the bottled water, stuffed the rest of the croissant into my mouth, tossed a ten on the table for Cisco, and followed him. Charlie wasn't best pleased, but he came too, perking up at once when he realised that he was going to see his pals.

Ingrid Reid was standing beside Ben's counter when I got there. As soon as I was inside, her son closed the door and flipped the sign round to read 'Shut' in three languages. I looked at her; her eyes were red, and she was chewing at her bottom lip.

'What is it?' I asked again.

'It's Matt,' she replied in a quiet, scared voice. 'He's been arrested.'

'What? When?'

'Half an hour ago. They arrived at the house, demanded to see him and told him, not asked, mind you, to come with them. He asked them what it was about, but they wouldn't tell him. I asked if I could come, but they said no.'

'Which police, Ingrid, the Mossos or the locals?'

'The Mossos; the serious ones.'

'Can you describe them?'

'Both dark-haired. The older one, the one who did the talking, he was in his early forties, I'd have said, quite bulky. The other one was younger and slimmer. He at least had the good grace to say "Sorry" to me as they took him away.'

She had described Gomez and Alex. 'What language did they speak?'

'Spanish. I understood some of it.'

'Did they tell you where they were taking him?'

'No.'

Ben stared at me. 'It has to be connected,' he murmured.

I nodded. 'Must be.'

'Connected with what?' Ingrid wailed.

'Planas.'

'Who?'

'The man Matthew and I went to see on Friday; José-Luis Planas.'

'Him? Matthew was livid when he got back from that meeting. He was muttering about going back down there to sort him out; Matt has a temper on him, you know.'

I let out a great, gasping breath. 'Jesus, Ingrid, don't ever say that to anyone else.'

'Why not?' she retorted, crossly. 'What's this man done that the police have arrested Matt?'

'You don't know?' Ben asked.

'No, we've hardly been out of the house since Saturday. Matt had a bit of a head in the morning. He went out with a pal on Friday night.'

'When did he get in, Mum?'

'God knows. I was asleep by that time. He confessed that they wound up in JoJo's bar. But forget about that. What about this man Planas?'

'He's dead, Ingrid,' I said, trying to sound as calm as possible. 'He was murdered.' I paused. 'Matt didn't go back to see him on Friday, did he?'

'No. I talked him down. He was still angry, though.'

'Too much information, Mum.'

She glared at him. 'Don't be silly.' Then the centivo dropped, and her mouth fell open with it. 'They don't think he . . . Oh my God, that's ridiculous.'

'Don't let's go that far,' I said. 'I know these people. They're formal, but they're very correct.'

'But what can we do? He's in there all alone. His Spanish is

OK, but he'll be vulnerable if they question him.' She looked at me, hopefully. 'Primavera, could you go and ask if you can translate for him?'

I sighed. 'I don't think they'd let me. I was in the room with him when he met Planas.' I thought about the situation. She was right, and I was kicking myself. He did need somebody in there, and I'd probably made it worse by neglecting to tell Gomez that he'd come with me to the Planas meeting. Through a detective's rheumy and jaundiced eye, I might be seen to have been covering up for him.

'Do you know any lawyers?' Ingrid asked.

'Not this kind,' I admitted, 'and anyway, he might not be entitled to one under Spanish law.' Then an idea hit me. 'But there is someone they'd have difficulty keeping out of there.'

Twenty

I was right; Gerard told me that when he presented himself, in uniform, at the Mossos office, asking to speak to Intendant Gomez, the desk officer was so taken aback that she didn't even think to ask why. Instead, she asked him to wait for a moment, disappeared through a door behind her, and returned a minute later with the detective.

But Gomez wasn't alone. Matthew Reid was with him, free to leave. Gerard asked no questions; he drove him straight to St Martí, where I'd told him that Ben, Ingrid and I would be waiting. His wife burst into tears as soon as she saw him; once she had calmed down I took them and Gerard up to my place, leaving Ben to reopen the shop. The square was busy as we walked through. I hoped he hadn't lost too much business.

As he sat on one of my kitchen chairs, Matthew seemed almost as bemused by the experience as Ingrid had been. I offered them a drink, but they both settled for coffee. 'First time in my life I've ever been arrested,' he muttered, as he took his from me, 'and it has to be here. And you know I'm still not entirely clear what it was about.'

Gerard leaned forward in his chair, forearms on his knees. 'What did they ask you?'

'The older one wanted to know why I'd been to see Planas on Friday. I told them that I've been looking around for property for my son.'

'Is that all?' I exclaimed.

'They didn't mention you, Primavera, and neither did I. That was what I said when I arranged the meeting, so I didn't lie.' He took a sip from his mug. 'Then the young one asked what we'd argued about. He said that one of Planas's staff, the guy, had told them he could hear the noise in the outer office, for all that the door's pretty thick. I told him that I'd taken exception to his manner.'

'You didn't tell them it was Planas and Primavera who had the argument?' asked Gerard.

'Why bring her into it?' he retorted.

'Because I am in it,' I sighed, 'because they already know I was there. Jesus ... sorry, Gerard ... you're as bad as me. I didn't tell them that you were there when I saw Planas. They'll think we're covering for each other ... they'll be right too ... and they'll wonder why.'

'The old bastard must have made a complaint against us, Primavera,' Matthew declared. 'Mind you,' he continued, 'that doesn't explain why they were so keen to know what I'd been doing on Friday night ... unless my mate and I got a bit outrageous and somebody made a separate complaint about that. They wanted to know everywhere I'd been; I told them that we'd started in Escalenc and wound up in JoJo's, then ...'

'We?'

'Mike Regan and me. He's a guy who used to be in the same business as me; he's in town on holiday and he looked me up.'

I thought it was time to lighten the mood. 'Two ex-PR consultants out on the piss,' I said. 'No wonder they took an interest in you.'

Matthew glanced at his wife, then shook his head. 'I was never in PR, Primavera; that's a cover story I use to avoid endless questions.'

'And for personal security,' Ingrid intervened.

'To an extent,' he agreed. 'I was a career soldier: I served for over thirty years in the Parachute Regiment, but that included a couple of spells on secondment to the SAS, during the Falklands War and at the height of the Irish trouble, then again during the first Gulf War. That's how I came to speak Spanish, much better than I ever let on, and Arabic. Those are the times I have to be careful about; not even Ben knows about it, so keep it to yourself, please.'

'I will, promise. Did the police ask you about your career?'

'No, they just looked at my passport, saw that it describes me as "retired", and seemed to be satisfied with that. I wish I'd had occasion to learn Catalan, though,' he mused. 'That's what they spoke between themselves, and I'm useless at that.'

'If they check up in Britain . . .'

'They won't find out anything about that side of my career. All they'll come up with is Brigadier Matthew Reid, retired.'

'DSO, MC,' Ingrid added, quietly.

'Pardon?' said Gerard.

'The Distinguished Service Order and the Military Cross,' I told him. 'They mean that our friend here's a retired hero.'

'Who should know better than to go out on the batter at his age,' Matthew muttered. His brow knitted into a frown. 'Nonetheless,' he declared, 'I reckon I'm beginning to get annoyed. Yes, I was a senior army officer and I've done nothing to warrant being taken from my house without a word of an excuse. I could have pulled rank on those guys, you know. Hell, I think I still might. Where's the force command based, Barcelona?'

'Yes, but before you head off there with all guns blazing, you'd better know the whole story.' I looked at my watch. 'People, I have to go and pick up my son from school. Gerard, maybe you could explain to Matthew exactly what Gomez and Alex are after.' I headed for the door that leads down to the garage. 'And once you've done that,' I said, as an afterthought, 'maybe you could take a look in the fridge and the larder and whip up some lunch for Tom, me and anyone else who fancies it.'

Twenty-one

Ingrid and Matthew had gone when Tom and I got back, so Gerard was fixing chicken salad for only three of us. He turned out to be pretty good in the kitchen.

We didn't talk about the morning's excitement until we'd eaten and Tom had gone to check his emails. Gerard told me that once he knew the whole story, Matthew's demeanour had changed. He'd become all business, and had gone through his movements on Friday night and Saturday morning, step by step. After Escalenc, he and Regan had indeed gone to JoJo's, as Ingrid had said. The proprietrix knows all her customers by name and keeps everybody's tab in a book; she wouldn't have noted down that they'd left at one thirty, but she'd remember it. The two old soldiers had walked back along the Passeig Maritim, until they'd reached the Hotel Nieves Mar, where Regan had said good night. But Matthew hadn't gone straight home; he had dropped into a night bar called La Taverna de la Anxova . . . yes, anchovies are everywhere in L'Escala . . . for a chat with the owner, and one last beer that had stretched out until after three o'clock. There had been one final witness to

129

his whereabouts. Ingrid had put their alarm on night set before going to bed, as he had insisted that she do. He had forgotten and had tripped it when he came in. He'd cancelled it before it could wake his wife, then waited by the phone for the inevitable call from the monitoring station. It came within a minute, and he'd given the code word that confirmed there was no problem.

Gerard told me that once he had worked out that he was covered, Matthew had made a decision: he had phoned the British Consulate General in Barcelona and had made an appointment for that afternoon with the vice-consul, to whom he intended to report the matter and to make a full, formal statement of his dealings with the late José-Luis Planas and his whereabouts at the time of his death. They'd left straight away.

'Did he tell you why the police let him go?'

'They didn't tell him either. All he said was that a woman officer came into the room and said something. Alex Guinart smiled and said something to Gomez. It was in Catalan, but your name was mentioned. Gomez laughed and said, in Spanish, "We'd better let him go then," turned to Matthew and told him that was all for now. Then he led him outside and handed him over to me.'

'He's a dark horse, isn't he?'

He looked at me, eyebrows raised. 'What?'

I'd forgotten the phrase doesn't translate directly into Spanish. 'He's got hidden depths,' I told him.

'Yes indeed. He disturbs me, Primavera. Men like him disturb me. Even before he'd told us anything about himself, I had a feeling about him. I sensed that he's a man who's seen much darkness, who's capable of great violence, and who's probably known it at some time in his life.'

'And you were right. You don't get those two medals for being company quartermaster; you earn them on the battle-field, with a gun in your hand, and bodies scattered around.'

'What is this SAS thing he spoke of?'

'British special forces; the kind who operate behind enemy lines, and take no prisoners. The Spanish military has its own, the Special Operations Group; it's modelled on ours.'

'How do you know about that?' he asked, sharply, taking me by surprise.

'I live here, I read newspapers. I have a son who's getting interested in big boy things.'

'I suppose. Sorry. As I say, I find such things distasteful.'

'In that case it's as well he's gone. You can avoid him in the future.'

'I couldn't do that; the man's in pain. He's seen things that he'll carry with him to the grave.'

So have I, I thought. But I wasn't telling any of that to Gerard.

'Maybe you should go back to see the police,' he said, suddenly.

'Why?'

'To make a full, formal statement, just as Matthew's going to do. Get your version of the meeting with Planas on the record.'

'Including the part where I had to step between him and Matthew?'

'Yes, he's in the clear, so why not?'

'Maybe I will. I'll call Alex and see if he'd like me to do that.'

'You should.'

'But only after I've taken Tom back to school. And that I must do now. So go on, back to whatever it is you do on a Tuesday . . . unless you want to man my information booth for an hour or so?'

He smiled, and touched his collar. 'Not in these clothes. Anyway, it's too much like a confessional.'

When I thought about it, I realised that there was something in what he'd said. Complete strangers have told me the most personal things in my box, on the basis of a few minutes' acquaintance.

I showed him to the door, then rounded up my son, who was finishing his reply to an email from his cousin Bruce in California. I could sense his growing excitement, in the car. 'Where are we going after school, Mum?' he demanded, just as we got there.

'Be patient,' I told him. 'That's a good virtue to acquire. You'll find out in a few hours.'

Back in St Martí, I thought again of Gerard's advice, and decided that he was right. I called Alex on his mobile. 'It's Primavera,' I said. 'Are you busy?'

He chuckled. 'I've known quieter times. Did the priest deliver your friend home safe? Imagine, you sending him along to rescue him.'

'I sent him along to translate, Alex . . . only I didn't send him, he volunteered.'

'Did he have a choice?' He laughed. 'His language skills wouldn't have been needed anyway. Senor Reid's Castellano is just about as good as mine.'

'Which is why you two spoke Catalan in front of him?'

'Exactly.'

'His story will check out, you know.'

'I know it will. I've already spoken to Jaume, in Taverna Anxova. Unless our first pathologist has got the time of death badly wrong, he couldn't have done it. Not that we ever thought he had. He's not the homicidal type.'

That's all you know, I thought. 'What about your second pathologist?' I asked

'Professor Perez is maybe the most thorough woman in Spain. She's insisted on performing the full autopsy for herself, from the beginning. We hope we'll have her report by the end of the day. If not . . .'

'Angel can't have the funeral on Thursday.'

'Exactly. Poor guy, it's not natural, having to wait so long.'

'Are you any closer to finding out who did it?'

'We thought we were, when Planas's office guy told us that Reid had visited him and they'd had what he called a violent argument. What we can't figure out is whether it was before you saw him or after.'

He still hadn't worked it out. 'Alex,' I explained. 'There was only one meeting. We saw Planas together. Matthew's appointment was just a way of getting me in there to tackle him about blocking the wine fair, out of spite against Ben.'

'Aw, Primavera,' he moaned. 'Why didn't you tell us this before?'

'I didn't think it was relevant.'

'Relevant? Primavera, I won't suggest that you didn't say anything because you were trying to protect him ... but Hector Gomez will. Your first thought was that he might have done it, wasn't it?'

'No,' I insisted.

I could tell he wasn't buying it, friend or not. 'Sure,' he drawled. 'It may concern you to know that he must have thought the same thing about you, since he said nothing about your being there.' He paused. 'He isn't right, is he?' he added with a soft chuckle.

'Alex!' Suddenly I was rattled again.

Twenty-two

I spent the rest of the afternoon in the garden . . . 'pottering', my mother used to call it, an inadequate description for the carefully organised vegetable crops she used to tend, and which my dad still does . . . uprooting every weed I could see and doing some dead-heading and judicious pruning. Charlie kept me company, but he was no help at all; afternoon is his siesta time, and he spent it dozing in his kennel. The information booth kept me busy too, with a regular flow of callers, until I closed it at four, to give myself time to make myself extra presentable for the trip to the airport.

I changed from shorts . . . my usual summer uniform . . . to a light cotton floral skirt, and a pale pink sleeveless shirt. For once, I put on a bra, thinking that it might not be seemly to bounce too much when meeting my former father-in-law. I also paid a bit more attention than usual to my hair and make-up. When I judged that I looked okay, I fed the dog . . . earlier than usual, but I didn't want him getting hungry and kicking up a fuss if Mac's plane was delayed . . . and headed for the school.

He jumped straight into the passenger seat, as I held the door open for him. 'I know what it is,' he announced, as he fastened his belt. 'My friend Alexia says I'm getting a new bike, because my old one's too small for me now.'

I hadn't expected that one, but Alexia had a point. Tom was getting bigger by the month, if not the day; also he was getting stronger and, being a boy, rougher on his bikes. But, he'd had his own computer for his birthday, and it was a long time to Christmas. 'No,' I said, as I put the car in Drive and moved off, 'it's not that.'

His face fell. 'Aw.' He paused. 'But can I?' he asked. 'I do need one; I can put all my feet on the ground when I'm in the saddle; and I can't make it go any higher.'

I'm not soft with him, honest, but buying a kid something he needs isn't spoiling him . . . and he probably did need something more heavy-duty. 'Okay,' I told him. 'But not today, that's not where we're going.'

He sat, contented, as I drove out of town, fiddling with the radio until he found Flaix FM, as we headed straight on, ignoring the Figueras slip road. 'Not the dress shop, then,' he murmured as we passed Camallera.

I grinned at him. 'No, but that wouldn't have been a very good surprise for you, would it?'

A little further on, we passed a girl, one of the regulars, sitting at the roadside on a white plastic chair. I don't think Tom believes any longer that she's waiting for a bus, but he hasn't quizzed me yet on what she might be doing. That's a conversation I'm putting off until the moment arises when I can't. He knows about the reproductive process . . . in a place with a sizeable dog population you can't avoid the subject . . . but I'd like to shield him from its commercial side for a little longer.

'El Corte Ingles?' he asked, hopefully, as I turned into the autopista pay station.

'No,' I replied, as I took the ticket.

'Barcelona?'

'No.'

He beamed. 'Then we're going to the airport.'

'No comment.'

He turned the volume up a little as I fed into the traffic, and I let him, for he knows that I don't like talking when I'm on that road. There are too many nutters about, guys who think they're Michael Schumacher but will probably wind up like Ayrton Senna; you have to check your mirrors regularly and carefully, and concentrate full-time.

I don't hang about myself, but it took me just under twenty-five minutes to reach the turn-off at junction eight. As I pulled into the pay station and handed the attendant my ticket and a ten-euro note, Tom dug me gently in the ribs. 'I was right, Mum.'

'Clever you,' I said, as I took my change.

'Where are we going?' he asked, more excited than I'd seen him in a while. 'Is Ben looking after Charlie?'

It's natural to want our kids to be perfect, or failing that, the best they can be, but, for me at least, there's a perverse satisfaction when Tom gets something wrong. It reminds me that he's a normal wee boy, like he should be, whatever high-flown hopes and dreams I may have for him.

I drove into the crowded car park, got lucky and found a space right away. I slung my capacious bag over my shoulder as we climbed out, patting it with my left hand as I locked up. 'And this is all the luggage we need, isn't that right? Change of pants for you, change of knickers for me, toothbrushes and passports. Come on then.'

I headed off for the terminal building, my son keeping pace with me. We walked through the departures entrance . . . I winced at the crowded concourse, and was glad that we weren't really checking in, then I turned left towards arrivals.

Girona Airport is very busy, and the airlines rely on rapid turnaround times to keep to their schedules. This means that occasionally a flight will arrive early. So it was that day with the plane from Prestwick. Mac Blackstone was standing in front of the baggage hall doorway, his case and his golf clubs loaded on to a trolley. Tom saw him before he saw us. 'Grandpa!' he yelled, and all of a sudden he was four or five again, breaking into a sprint and rushing towards him, jumping and being caught in Mac's bear-like grasp.

I let them have their hug-in for a minute or so, then moved up for one of my own. After we'd clinched, I stepped back and eyed him up and down. 'Not bad,' I said, and I meant it. I don't remember what age he is exactly, but he can't be short of seventy, he's had an emergency heart valve replacement, and he's lost his only son, so he's no longer the man I met thirteen years ago. Nevertheless, he's held himself together when he might have been forgiven for going into a decline. I could still see a sparkle in his eye, and although he was a little slimmer, he was still pretty solidly built.

'Thank you, my dear,' he replied. 'I could say the same about you, but it would be an understatement. Who's putting the bloom in your cheeks these days?'

'He is,' I told him, ruffling Tom's hair. 'He's all I need to get by.'

'Nearly a Marvin Gaye lyric,' he chuckled. (Mac has an encyclopaedic knowledge of sixties music; his heroes are Sam Cooke, Otis Redding and Marvin Gaye. 'Who's the odd man out?' he asked me once, then answered before I could . . . not that I knew. 'Otis. He died in a plane crash, the other two were shot dead.')

'Fine,' I grinned, 'but don't sing it.'

'Not even in the shower,' he promised.

His grandson looked around the concourse. 'Where's Grandma Mary?' he asked.

'Not coming this trip,' Mac replied, 'but she sends her love.'

I led the way back to the car park, and we loaded the Jeep, sticking his clubs through the split back seat. As we got moving, Tom unzipped the bag and took an admiring look. He and I play, but not very often in the heat of the summer. 'New Callaways,' Mac told him. 'At my age, I need all the help I can get. I get embarrassed these days when I play with your cousin Jonny; he hits it further than I can see, and that's only with his irons. He's doing very well at college in the States. I think your

Aunt Ellie had better get used to the idea that he's going to be a pro.'

'I'd like to be a pro,' his grandson exclaimed, then paused. 'That's if I'm not an actor, like my dad, or a manager, like my mum.'

'And what's your mum managing?' he asked.

'Ben's wine fair.'

Mac looked at me. 'Long story,' I told him. 'I'll fill you in later.'

Rather than go back up the autopista I took the quieter cross-country road, so that the two guys could talk along the way. And talk they did. Mac quizzed Tom about his school work, and his language skills . . . Mac speaks English, period . . . and was questioned in his turn about Scotland, about his cousins, Jonny and Colin, and of course about his dad. Every time Tom meets somebody who knew his father, he gets round to asking about him, and usually sooner rather than later. I don't mind; it gives me serious pangs of missing him from time to time, but it's his right to know, even if there are a few things I will always keep to myself.

We were just coming into Verges when Tom tapped me on the shoulder. 'Mum, I'm hungry. Where are we going to eat?'

I'd thought about that myself, and made arrangements. 'Esculapi. Outside, if it stays warm.'

'Can Gerard come?'

I must have reacted, for a broad grin spread across Mac's face. 'Oh aye?' he exclaimed. 'And who would Gerard be then? I thought there was another reason for your cheerful demeanour, young lady. You're like . . . like you used to be, and I'm pleased.'

'Then don't get too pleased, for Gerard is a friend of the family, no more, no less.'

'He's a priest,' Tom volunteered, 'and I help him in his church.'

If the old dentist had been a pipe smoker, he'd have bitten clean through the stem.

Twenty-three

I'd never even thought about inviting Gerard to join us on Mac's first night there, so for once I said 'No' to Tom . . . it's good for his soul. In fact he wasn't all that bothered; when he had time to give it a second thought, he realised that another presence at the table could only come between him and his grandpa.

The evening did stay warm, so, after Mac had installed himself in the guest suite and freshened up from his journey, I stuck to Plan A and chose one of the pizzeria's outside tables . . . close to a space heater, just in case. Maybe I should tell you, or remind you if you've been here, that Plaça Major in St Martí is a sloping square, bounded by the church, and my house, at its highest point and on the other three sides by old stone buildings, which house a total of five cafés, bars and restaurants. Three of them are seasonal, and closed in the winter months, but the other two stay open all year round, apart from a month or so, rarely overlapping, when their owners take their holidays, and carry out their annual maintenance.

Mac smiled contentedly as he settled into his chair, and looked around at the maze of tables. Little more than half of them were occupied, but that's not bad for a Tuesday at that time of year. All the parasols were deployed. As well as providing shade during the day, they hold the heat in the evening. 'God, you're lucky,' he exclaimed, his thick arms folded across a blue short-sleeved shirt that might as well have had M&S embroidered on the pocket. 'When I think of what I left in Scotland. It chucked it down all the way to the airport.'

'It rains here too, Grandpa,' Tom told him. It was almost a protest; he's very defensive of Catalunya and doesn't believe there's a single place on the planet that can improve on any aspect of its beaches, its food or its climate, good and bad. 'Last month we measured three centimetres on Mum's terrace in one night. There was thunder and lightning and everything.'

'Didn't it flood your mum's bedroom?'

'No, the terrace slopes and there's a hole in the wall for the water to get out.'

'So how did you know there was three centimetres? Did you measure them a millimetre at a time as the rain fell, with a tape?'

My son sighed at his grandfather's apparent stupidity. 'I've got a measuring box,' he said. 'Mum lets me keep it on her terrace because it's the best place. I've got a wind gauge too, fastened to the chimney.'

'Do you have to climb up there to read it?'

Tom laughed. 'No. I've got a weather station in my room, it tells me everything. It tells me about wind speed, how much rain we've had, what the temperature is, what the humidity is, what the weather's going to be like next. It's great, Grandpa. Uncle Miles gave me it for my birthday. When he was young he worked on a weather station in Australia. I might be a weather man when I grow up, if I'm not a golfer, or a manager . . . or an actor, or have a wine shop like Ben.'

'Yes . . .' Mac began, just as the tall Antonio approached, bearing menus. He asked if we wanted drinks. Grandpa Blackstone said he could murder a beer, I said I could put one out of its misery too, and Tom pushed his luck by asking for a glass of sangria. There's a non-alcoholic version that I make at home sometimes, but it's not found in bars, so he settled for a squeezed orange juice.

'As I was saying,' Mac resumed, 'who's Ben?' There was a raised eyebrow along with the question. Although they never say it straight out, I know that he and my dad would both like to see me with, shall we say, a man about the house. They don't realise that's something I'll never do just for the sake of it.

'Ben's your friend Matthew's stepson,' I told him. 'He's settled in St Martí, and he runs a wee wine shop just down the hill there. He's come up with an idea for a village wine fair; I'm involved with it, on the operational side.'

'What does "operational side" mean?'

'Helping to put all the bits together, sorting out town hall permissions, sales and marketing and stuff.'

'Hah,' he chuckled, 'the ubiquitous "stuff" meaning all the things that everyone's forgotten to do until the last minute. When's this event going to happen?'

Quintin Jardine

'September. All the producers are signed up for it; all that we need at any rate.'

'And you've got your permission sorted out?'

'Yes, after some serious roadblocks, but don't let's dwell on them.' I steered him away from the subject; Tom didn't know anything about it, and I didn't want him to, least of all about the death of Planas. I wasn't worried that he might learn at school; homicide isn't a playground topic in the third year of primary . . . well, not in L'Escala at any rate.

Antonio came back with the drinks and took our orders, one big tomato and mozzarella salad to be shared three ways, followed by steak for Mac, pinxo (kebab) for Tom, and spaghetti carbonara for me . . . I'd had a busy day, and found that my body was screaming 'Carbohydrates!'

'Where can I get hold of Matthew?' Mac asked me as he set his glass, minus half its original contents, down on the table.

'He and Ben's mum live on the other side of town,' I told him. 'They're in the phone book; I'll look him up and you can give him a call tomorrow.' I paused. 'He told me you two got to know each other through golf.'

'That's right; last summer. There was an inter-club competition for retired golfers, lower age limit fifty-five instead of sixty, to let in the suddenly redundant bankers that are filling the courses these days. Elie was drawn at home to Gullane and he and I wound up playing each other.' He smiled. 'I won, naturally, partly because Jonny caddied for me and made sure my club selections were spot on and partly because Matthew

146

played crap. He's good company, though; we got on and he invited me across to Gullane for a return match, with Jonny.'

'Did he talk much about himself, about his career and such?' I asked, innocently.

'He said he'd been in public relations, but we didn't dwell on our professional lives. If there's one profession that no normal person ever wants to talk about, it's mine. Be very suspicious of anyone who asks you questions about the detail of root canal work; they've got sadistic tendencies, for sure. Speaking of dentistry, how are my grandson's teeth?'

'Coming on fine; we had the gap-toothed smile over the winter.'

'The new ones certainly look straight. I'll take a look at them sometime . . . if he'll let me, that is.'

'For his Grandpa Mac, anything,' I assured him. 'How did your Gullane match finish up?' I asked.

'Matthew and I halved our game. Jonathan shot a sixty-six, off scratch, of course; never dropped a shot. When he drove the first green and just missed a putt for an eagle, the two of us realised that we might as well just talk among ourselves.'

'How is Jonny? I haven't seen him since he was a lad.'

'He's no lad now. Six foot two, golfer's shoulders, hands like mine,' he held up a great paw, 'and a look of his uncle about him.' Suddenly Mac's face darkened. 'After . . . after what happened,' he said quietly, 'given that it seems to be hereditary, Ellie and I both insisted that he and Colin had complete cardiac examinations. Jonny's all clear, but they want another look at Colin when he's finished growing.' He gave a very small sideways nod in Tom's direction, accompanied by a look that was an unspoken question. Tom was oblivious to the conversation; he had just received a text and was replying to it.

'Yes,' I said. 'I was still . . . away, at the time, but you know Susie.' For a troubled period in my life, Tom was raised by his father and his eventual widow, the former Susie Gantry. 'She didn't waste a second having him checked, along with her two. They're all absolutely normal, but they'll be monitored as they grow, to be sure.' A thought struck me, about Oz's sister. 'How about Ellie?'

Mac nodded. 'Clear,' he murmured, then sighed. 'You know, Primavera, I try not to think about it, but I can't help it. If Oz had had an examination like that after I had my valve malfunction . . .'

I laid a hand on his. 'You think I don't have the same thought? Do you think Susie doesn't? We've all got to live with it, and that's the bottom line.'

Happily, a young waiter appeared with our starter, and three plates, just at that moment, to break the mood. I shared the salad out, pretty much equally . . . try giving Tom a smaller portion than anyone else and see what happens. We must all have been even hungrier than we thought, for we demolished it in no time at all. The main courses weren't long in coming, though. I was just about to start on mine, when I saw Alex Guinart, out of uniform, ambling slowly into the square, pushing Marte, my goddaughter, in her chair, with Gloria, who's a real classic Andalusian beauty, by his side. Husband and wife both saw us, and waved to me, but didn't come to join us, opting instead for a table at Meson del Conde.

Mac didn't want a dessert, but Tom and I both voted for fresh pineapple; his kebab had been enormous, and I wasn't sure that he really was still hungry, but he slogged his way through it. Finally, though, he couldn't put off the evil hour any longer. 'Bed, kid,' I told him. 'School day tomorrow, and all that.'

'Aw, Mum!' He doesn't usually argue, but his grandpa doesn't arrive every day either.

'Come on,' said Mac, with a grin. 'She's saying my time's up too, you know. Us old guys and you young guys have to play by the same rules.'

That mollified him. I paid the bill and the three of us made to leave, but as we did, I spotted Alex waving to me, as if he wanted to talk. I tossed Mac the key and said I'd join him in a minute, if he fancied a drink on the sitting-room terrace. (That was a rhetorical invitation, folks.)

Alex and Gloria were at the coffee stage when I joined them. He asked me if I'd like one; I asked for a cortado, although I'd had one at Esculapi. I said 'Hello' to Gloria and made a fuss of Marte, who seemed pleased to see me even if she still can't say my name properly. 'Tia Prima' is as far as she gets . . . I'm an honorary auntie . . . and I suspect it's going to stay that way, by habit and repute, to use an old Scots legal phrase.

I asked Alex how things were going, in Catalan, as usual. 'Progressing,' he said. He surprised me by answering in English. Gloria doesn't speak it, not at all, and so I guessed that he must want to shield her from the darker side of his new job. 'Professor Perez gave us her findings this afternoon. She confirmed the original autopsy report, and more.'

'More? In what way?'

'She's not so convinced about the time of death; she reckons it could have been any time up to six o'clock, before the sun rose.' He must have seen my eyebrows rise, for he nodded. 'Yes,' he said, with a faint smile, 'that puts your friend Senor Reid back among the list of possibles, but from what I've heard of his state when he left the Anchovy Tavern, he would not have been able to find his . . . How you say? . . . his backside with both hands, far less go out again, find Planas's house and kill him. Also . . . Perez may be eminent, but I don't really think that the old man would have been in his garden in his day clothes at five or six in the morning. Especially as he must have been tired.'

'I dunno,' I countered. 'They say the older you get the less sleep you need.'

'I didn't mean that the hour had made him tired. He'd had sex not long before he died.'

'What?' I gasped, open mouthed. 'You're kidding me.'

He laughed, then said to Gloria, in Catalan, 'Finally, I have been able to surprise Primavera.'

She grinned back at him. 'Make sure you never surprise me like that.'

'Alex,' I said, 'exactly how eminent is this professor of yours? Could she be mistaken? You never mentioned this after the first autopsy.'

'The local pathologist missed it. In fact he didn't look for it. He's embarrassed now; he says that he was given the body of a man thought to have been killed by a fall, so it never occurred to him to look at his . . .' he paused, stuck for the English word, '. . . his *pene*.'

Gloria's eyes widened, then she smiled. 'Prick,' she chuckled. 'It's one of the only English words I know,' she told me, in Catalan. I didn't ask her how she had come to learn it. Neither did Alex, but I judged from a faraway look that came into his eyes for a moment that the subject might be raised later.

'Patricia Perez looks at everything,' he continued.

'Rather her than me, in this case. Does she know what sort of farmyard animal he'd been fucking?'

'Oh, it was a woman, no question of that. She found traces of body fluids on his . . .' He paused.

'If you'd like the proper English word, it's penis. There are several informal alternatives, apart from the one that Gloria knows.'

'Thank you . . . there, on his underpants and on his trousers.'

I couldn't help but laugh. 'Jesus, he was a real class act. He just unzipped himself and got on the job? What a knight in shining armour. I take it these samples are viable for DNA.'

'Yes. We're testing, but where we'll find a match . . . God alone knows that.'

I shuddered. 'Not with my sample, I promise you that. Does anyone know whether Planas had a lady friend?'

'That was one of the first questions we asked the people who knew him, including his son, his bank manager, the owner of Hostal Miryam, Justine Michels, and all the other people on the council. They all said the same thing, that he hasn't been seen with a lady since Angel's mother died six years ago. One or two of the older ones said that he wasn't seen with her all that often either. They would go to church together, but it was unusual for them to go anywhere else as a couple. She was a very quiet woman, apparently.'

'Did you ask Angel about her?'

'No. There was no reason.'

'I suppose not. So who do you reckon this woman was? A prostitute, a call girl?'

'That was Gomez's first thought. If she is, she won't be from L'Escala. The old goat would have been more discreet than to pick up a local. Maybe one of the clubs along the road to Figueras has been sending women out on house calls. We're going to check all of them tomorrow.'

'Then you'll be looking for someone who's gone missing.'

'You reckon?'

'Don't you? This woman, whoever she is, has to be your new prime suspect. Maybe he wouldn't pay her or tried to short change her . . .'

'That's our thinking,' Alex agreed.

'. . . she picked up a rock, or something similar . . . maybe she had a cosh in her bag . . . and hit him with it. She probably didn't mean to kill him, but when she realised she had, she did some quick thinking, dragged him to the wall and tossed him over to make it look like a fall. And after doing that, and getting rid of the second wine glass, she hung around? I don't think so.'

'I don't think so either. You have quite an imagination, Primavera; you see it much as we do. In fact the crime scene team found traces of blood on the grass, near the patio, and then again, in several other places, leading towards the wall. But you got the weapon wrong. Perez found something else that our man had missed: fine traces of wood and paint embedded in Planas's skull, where it was crushed. She says that there was only one blow, and that death was probably instantaneous. We're going back to the scene tomorrow, early, to see if we can find a match.'

'Whatever he was hit with, it did the job. Tell me, was there any money in his wallet? I assume that he had one.'

'Oh yes, he did, and there was four hundred and eight euro in it. He always paid his bills in cash, at Hostal Miryam and everywhere else. He didn't have any credit cards; no plastic at all.'

'Doesn't that argue against the prostitute theory?' I wondered, aloud.

'Not necessarily. If she was smart enough to fake the accident scenario, she'd have known that robbing him would have blown it. Besides, for all we know he could have had a thousand on him originally.'

'True,' I conceded. 'In any event, your lady killer is probably long gone from Spain by now.'

'I fear you may be right,' he conceded. 'But that isn't going to stop us looking for her.'

Twenty-four

Mac was waiting in the garden when I returned; the evening had cooled and he had put on a sweater. 'What would you like?' I asked him, as I led the way inside, and sent him up to the first-floor terrace, overlooking the square.

'A beer will do.'

I fetched a couple of bottles of Coronita from the fridge (they call it Corona in Mexico, where it's made, and just about everywhere else on the planet; it's my 'house' beer), stuck a wedge of lime in the neck of each and carried them upstairs. Grandpa Blackstone had settled himself into one of the chairs and was gazing down at the rapidly clearing cafés.

'You're doing a great job, Primavera,' he said, as I handed him his nightcap.

'Uh?' I grunted, as I lit a mozzy candle.

'With Tom.'

'He's due most of the credit.'

'Some of it, but you're setting the example, you're doing the raising. He's turning into a fine boy.' He smiled. 'I had a look at his teeth once he'd brushed them. He's got the same kink in his lower incisors that his father had, and his aunt still does. You could have it straightened by an orthodontist, indeed if you were American it would be automatic, but it's a very small imperfection. I never bothered with Oz or Ellie. It won't stop him having a killer smile when all his adult set are through.'

'That'll be good,' I murmured, 'as long as he smiles with his eyes at the same time.'

A frown seemed to settle on Mac's face in the candlelight. 'Are you saying that my son didn't?'

'He did when I first met him. I'll die thinking of the first time he smiled at me. Latterly, though, it wasn't always the case.'

'What changed him, d' you think?'

I sighed. 'Me probably.'

'Nah. You set him on the road to doing things he'd never dreamed of.'

'And came between him and Jan.'

'Sometimes monogamy isn't all it's cracked up to be.'

I had no response to that, and he wasn't about to elaborate, and so we sat in silence for a while, until he reached across and tapped me on the shoulder. 'Hey,' he began, and the grin was back, 'what about this Gerard then?'

'What about him?'

'Tom seems to like him.'

'Tom's one of his altar servers.'

'You're okay with that?'

'Absolutely. If you're looking for a role model for the son of a single mum, who better?'

'And for the single mother herself?'

I chuckled. 'Mac, think of him as the bloke next door, because that's what he is. You've been single, you know how these things really are.'

'Hah! Bad example, lass. In my case, Mary and I were creeping in and out of each other's houses late at night, until we went legit.'

'Well, there's no creeping done here!'

He nodded. 'Just as well.' He pointed with his beer bottle, down the square. Alex and Gloria had just left their table and he was steering Marte's buggy round the corner. 'That was a long conversation,' he remarked.

At times, Mac can be as subtle as a flying mallet, but I know that his curiosity isn't that of the prurient, but that of someone who really cares about me, almost as much as my own father does.

'See you,' I said, smiling. 'His name is Alex, his wife's called Gloria and I'm the baby's godmother, unlikely as that may seem. He's a cop, and he was giving me the lowdown on a case that is currently the talk of the steamie in this part of the world.'

'What happened? Has somebody been nicking the lead off the church roof?'

'No, someone's drawn a line under a prominent citizen. Alex is one of the investigators.'

'Jesus, homicide?'

I nodded.

'In a place like this?'

'We're not immune. I didn't mention it earlier, because Tom was around.'

I gave him a full rundown on the events leading up to Planas's death, and on what had happened afterwards.

'They thought Matthew did it?' he gasped.

'Let's just say that they entertained the possibility.'

'Ridiculous. The big fella's harmless. Plus, on the golf course he couldna' hit a cow on the arse with a shovel, so I doubt if he's capable of clubbing anyone over the head, unless the bloke stood very still and told him what to do. What about his stepson, this Ben lad? Surely he had a down on the dead man?'

'Ben's problems with him were over by that time, and he never knew about the money. Besides, he told me that Alex had been to see him and asked him where he was. Seems that he wasn't alone; he isn't saying who he was with, not to me, anyway, but he's not in the frame. As for Matthew, he can prove where he was at the time as well.'

'So the theory is that this righteous pillar of the community bought himself some nookie and then got hit over the head?'

'That's the current police thinking, yes.'

He looked at me. 'Do I get the impression you don't share their conviction?'

I frowned back at him. 'It seemed obvious at first, but . . . When I think about it, and I try to imagine the situation, like an old guy calling a discreet number on his mobile as if it's for a home delivery pizza: I can picture it, sure . . . but not with that particular old guy. When he and I had our set-to in his office and he called me a whore, there was real contempt in his voice when he said the word. He spat it out; the old bastard spat it all over me, in fact. He was saying that in his eyes a *puta* is the lowest of the low. So you see, I'm not sure I can see him soiling himself with one. I have a feeling that Alex and his boss can spend all day tomorrow checking the brothels between here and Figueras, or between here and Madrid for that matter, and they're going to come up empty handed.'

Twenty-five

I tried to forget about it. Really, I did. But it wouldn't go away. The vision of that odious man and his midnight assignation kept forcing itself between me and everything else I tried to do. And I had plenty on my plate next day, with our guest to look after. Tom dropped a hint about pulling a sickie from school, but I wasn't having any of that. The year end was approaching and that's a big time for the kids at every level, so I dug my heels in.

Once he had set off on his bike . . . with a promise from his grandpa that the two of them would go shopping for a new one at the weekend . . . I took Mac, and Charlie, for a stroll around the village, so that Mac could see it properly, before the holidaymakers and day trippers started to flock in. Yes, he'd been before, but there's always something you miss. For example there's the ruined building between the church and Esculapi; he'd never noticed that before. It has nothing resembling a roof, and it's overgrown, but lots of the outer walls are still there.

'Who owns it?' he asked.

'I've no idea,' I confessed. 'But somebody does, and if he ever gets the money together to rebuild it as it should be, then it'll complete the square.'

There are two or three spots like that left in St Martí, ruins with potential, you might say, and worth a bomb, even in their derelict state. I won't tell you how much I paid for our house, but it's appreciated mightily in value in the time we've owned it, and since it's very rare for an 'outsider' to be able to buy property within the village walls, it's not going to be affected by any credit crunch.

As we walked along Carrer del Pou towards Plaça Petita, Charlie ran on ahead, sniffing his mates, I guessed, and sure enough when we turned the corner there was Ben, in the process of opening his wine shop, despite the distractions of Cher and Mustard. As soon as I introduced them, Ben sparked. 'Ah,' he said, 'you know my stepfather, I believe.'

'That's right,' Mac confirmed. 'Does he know I'm here?' he asked.

'Not as far as I know. Why don't you call in on them? He'll be pleased to see you. Give him a call first mind; my mum doesn't like being caught unawares.' He scribbled an address and phone number on a scrap of paper from a pile on the shop counter. 'There you are. You know where it is, Primavera. It's just down the hill from Shirley Gash's house.'

'Thanks, I'll do that. If he's got over being picked up by the fuzz.'

'He has now. I spoke to Mum half an hour ago. She told me that he had a phone call this morning from the head of the force, the Director General himself, in person, apologising for . . .' He paused. 'How did he put it? . . . The embarrassment to which he was subjected.' He grinned. 'I suppose it's good to know that the good old British Consul still has some clout these days.'

I winced, even though I tried not to show it, as I wondered how much of that clout had made its way down the line, and round the ear of Intendant Gomez and my friend Alex.

Ben and I chatted for a few minutes about the fair, while Mac explored the stock displayed in stacked-up cubes. I told him that I'd sourced all the tables we were going to need, and the parasols. My next priority, I promised him, would be to go round our identified advance sales outlets, signing them up for the project. 'Justine's promised me that the tourist offices will stock them, and the town hall itself. I'll hit the hotels as soon as I can.'

'You're still confident we'll get advance sales?' He still had his doubts, clearly.

'Trust me. It's a certainty.' I was keeping my secret weapon to myself. Eventually I'd let him in on it, but I didn't want to go public too early.

Mac chose a couple of bottles, one red, one white, for dinner, he said; and an ecological cava, even though he had trouble working out why the maker had chosen to market a 'green' wine in a blue bottle. As we left the shop and climbed towards the square I saw that one of the church doors was open. It was possible that a florist was in there, setting up for a wedding, but I wasn't surprised when Gerard stepped out into the daylight. He must have seen us coming from inside.

He wasn't wearing his priest gear and as he approached us I saw that he had a day-old stubble on his chin. I'm sure Mac assumed that he was the handyman.

'How goes?' he said, in Catalan.

'Fine,' I replied, in the same language. 'This is my former father-in-law, Mac Blackstone. He's been dying to meet you; Tom's told him all about you.'

'Sir,' he exclaimed, in English. 'It's a pleasure to meet you.'

'Likewise,' said Mac, giving him that peculiar angled look he affects when he's greeting someone for the first time; it's as if he's trying to size up their teeth, 'even if you are trying to lure my grandson into the Catholic faith.'

'Which you don't share?' Gerard's expression grew cautious as he looked at the unknown quantity before him.

'Afraid not; the Church of Scotland may not be much of an outfit these days, but it's the only one I've got.' He grinned. 'I wouldn't force it on anyone else, though; I never did with my own kids.'

'And I won't try to persuade Tom,' Gerard promised. 'I'm pleased to have him help me with no conditions attached.'

Mac turned to me. 'And how about you, Primavera? You got any preconditions?'

Mischievous old bastard, I thought, but I put on my most gauche expression and replied, 'Me? None at all. My boy will find his own way through life; that's the way it should be.'

'Indeed. Since I got here,' he checked his watch, 'what, less than eighteen hours ago, he's talked about being an actor like his dad, a manager like his mum, a weatherman like his uncle, a golfer like his cousin Jonny, and a dentist like me. He's an impressionable lad, so what if he decides that what he most wants in life is to become a priest, like his friend Gerard? How would you feel about that?'

Honest to God . . . an appropriate expression? . . . I had not considered that scenario until that very moment. I was stuck for an answer. For a while, all I could do was frown. 'Well,' I began, eventually, 'I want him to be happy. But if I'm to be honest, and admit to a bit of selfishness, I suppose I do want to be a granny one day.' I could have been more specific; I could have said that I want my son to live a full life, in every way, including the sensual aspect, and that having done pretty well in that department, especially in my thirties, I felt sorry for anyone who'd missed out. Sure, I could have said that, but it would have been cruel to Gerard.

He bailed me out. 'I would not worry about that, Senor Blackstone,' he said. 'There's a requirement for the taking of holy orders, and Tom doesn't pass the test.'

'What's that?' I asked, ready to defend my boy against all charges.

'We're required to believe in God. Tom doesn't, and I don't expect he ever will.'

'How do you know that?'

He looked me in the eye. 'Simple, I asked him.'

'It's more than I've ever done,' I retorted. Quite out of the blue, I was angry. 'Don't you think you should have asked me before quizzing my son about his religious belief? He's only eight, Gerard! How can you expect him to have a mature view on the existence of bloody deities?'

'It's my job,' he shot back at me. 'I'm a diviner of faith in people. It's usual for me to begin a dialogue with those as young as Tom, to test their attitudes. His is already formed. If there was a God, he told me, he would not have let his father die. Now I agree that he isn't old enough to grasp the concept that life is full of misfortunes and imperfections, and that only God Himself is perfect, and I didn't try to explore that with him, but in my view he will be implacable. He will never be able to accept the existence of God.'

'Then why do you let him help you in church?' I snapped.

'Because he's very good at it.'

'You mean you're using him? Well, that's at an end.'

'Hey,' he snapped. Our voices were raised; I was aware, vaguely, that a few people were looking at us but I didn't give a damn. We were having a full-blown argument, our first ever. 'You don't believe in Him any more than Tom does, yet you were quite willing to stand in church alongside Alex Guinart and Gloria and promise to take responsibility for the religious upbringing of little Marte.'

I had moved closer to him; we were no more than two feet apart, eyeball to eyeball. 'I'm an adult,' I shouted. 'That was my choice and it was acceptable to Alex. Tom's a child, and you're letting him play a part, probably in the hope of winning him over to your team. But not any more you aren't. So bugger off!'

'Primavera,' Mac exclaimed, 'calm down. Listen, when Oz

was a kid he had a paper round, but that didn't mean he believed in Robert Maxwell.'

I stared at him; Gerard simply blinked and looked confused, having never heard of the notorious press baron or of his watery fate. 'What's that got to do with it?' I challenged.

'Fuck all,' he admitted cheerfully, 'but somebody's got to get between you two at this point.' He took me by the elbow, and I allowed him to steer me gently towards the house. 'Good to meet you, Gerard,' he said, over his shoulder, 'but you've got a lot to learn about coming between a tigress and her cub.'

Twenty-six

'That should squash the gossip,' I growled, bitterly.

We were sitting at the kitchen table, our hands wrapped round mugs of tea, which Mac had insisted on making. 'Nothing better than a cup of hot tea to cool you down.'

'You reckon?' I paused. 'An up and downer between me and the priest in front of half the village? Word will get around, bank on it.'

'But what will that word be? Honest to Christ, lass, watching you two, it really took me back. In all our marriage Flora and I never argued much, but when we did, they were belters. That's what you and young Gerard reminded me of out there, and I reckon that a few people will have similar thoughts.' He grinned. 'And before you ask, I always got the worst of it too.'

I had to smile. 'What did you fight about?'

'Mostly it was about our daughter. Ellen was a handful, even when she was Tom's age. She had a reputation as the toughest kid in the playground. One day a mother brought her lad into the surgery with a loosened back tooth. His jaw was swollen round it. When I asked him what had happened he said that a boy had hit him. "Don't tell lies," said his mum. "It wasn't a boy." No, it wasn't,' he laughed, 'it was our Ellie that did it. The idiot child had tried to force her to give him her apple.'

Knowing Ellie, I had no trouble believing the story. 'Did you ever argue about Oz?' I asked him.

He shook his head. 'Never had cause. Osbert was a paragon; well behaved, good at his lessons, and nobody ever tried to take his apple . . . any more than they will with his son.'

That was true, I realised. I'd never heard a whisper of Tom being in a scrap.

'What are you going to do about it?' Mac asked, quietly.

'About what?'

'Wee Tom, and the church.'

'I don't know,' I confessed. 'What would you do?'

'Nothing.' He paused. 'I must apologise to you, Primavera; it was me who kicked that argument off with that provocative question.'

'No, it was Gerard who caused it, with his to Tom.'

'Maybe, but I can see his side of the case. He's in the soul business; it's his job to see that everyone's in good shape, from an early age. And,' he pointed out, 'it's yours too, as a godmother.'

'Maybe I should resign then, for I'm not qualified.'

'I can't think of anyone who's better qualified. You've seen the pitfalls and you know how to avoid them.'

'So you're saying I should let Tom carry on helping Gerard?'

'I'm not sure you've got the right not to, if that's what the lad wants to do.'

'So should I go next door and eat humble pie?'

'Hell no! Arguments aren't best solved by one side giving in.'

'But what if Gerard says he can't be a server any more?'

'He won't do that. He's a good guy.'

'How do you know that? You've only just met him, and not in the best of circumstances.'

'Nonetheless, he is. Plus he would do anything for you and your son.' He drained his tea. 'Now,' he exclaimed, 'I must go and call Matthew Reid, to see if it's all right to pay them a visit.'

I stayed in the kitchen as he went to find a phone; for some reason the cordless that's usually there had been left in the TV room. I had just put our mugs in the dishwasher when he returned.

'Fixed up?' I asked.

He shook his head, frowning. 'No. I only caught them by a couple of minutes. Matthew said that he's so pissed off by the incident with the police that he and his wife have decided to go back to Scotland ahead of schedule. I said to him that after that apology from the top banana, I'd have thought it was all behind him, but he said it was best if he went, so as not to draw any more attention to himself.' He scratched his chin. 'I suspect that the thing's scared him more than he's prepared to admit. Who's going to pay undue attention to a retired PR man?'

'I can't imagine,' I said. 'I can't imagine at all.'

Twenty-seven

I could, of course, By going to the consulate, Matthew had done what any Brit should do in the circumstances, but he couldn't have foreseen the consequences. From the level at which the apology had been offered, I guessed that his military record had been disclosed to someone higher up the pecking order in the Catalan government than a mere chief of police, and that buttons had been pushed. Chances were that Gomez had been told who and what he had hauled into his nick, and that he had decided to get out of town before the locals started calling him 'Brigadier Reid', which would not have been good.

We were halfway through lunch when I was proved right. The phone rang; I answered to find Alex on the other end. 'What do you know about Ben's stepfather?' he asked.

'Enough,' I replied, 'but I was told in confidence. Is the intendant still smarting?'

'He's in a filthy mood, so I wouldn't let it slip any time soon that you could have warned us about the guy.'

'Honest, I didn't know myself until you'd put your feet in it. Honest.'

'I believe you.'

'How's the whore quest going?'

'Badly. I've visited most of the houses of horizontal refreshment in the area. None of them had ever heard of Planas, far less recognising him as a client. I've still got a few to interview, but I'm not hopeful of success. Gomez is insisting that I do it, though, even though we've checked the calls made from the old man's mobile and his landline, and can find nothing that links to any of these places.'

'What about the murder weapon?'

'Nothing on that yet . . . at least nothing that I've heard, having spent most of the morning interviewing madams.' He sighed. 'Ah well, back to the grind, so to speak.'

I smiled as I hung up, yet I was intrigued, too. Planas wasn't a whore-monger, but who had been deemed worthy enough to service him?

'What are we doing this afternoon?' Mac asked as I came back into the kitchen.

'What would you like to do? The world is your oyster; or anchovy, or mussel or clam, or whatever sea creature you prefer.'

In the end he settled for a round of golf, not on the big tracks of Pals or Emporda where you're going to take a minimum four hours to get round, but on the par three course at Gualta, which we could fit into the length of Tom's school afternoon. I'd have taken Charlie, but as I wasn't sure he'd be welcomed, I left him with Ben, and his two chums.

Mac still plays tidy golf, and I'm not bad, but for all that we found the little course more difficult than it looked, and each of us contributed a couple of balls to the water hazards before we were done. Afterwards, we had a cool drink in the bar before heading back to St Martí to pick up Charlie and to be in time for Tom getting home from school.

I was on my way up back from Ben's shop, with the dog trotting ahead of me when I saw a Mossos vehicle parked in front of my house; it hadn't been there when I'd stepped out of the gate five minutes before. My first guess was that Alex had stopped off to blag a coffee, after a weary day spent chasing whores, until I realised that the car was a saloon, and not the off-roader he usually drove.

Intendant Gomez was waiting in the garden when I let myself in; Mac was with him, but nothing was being said, not least because neither spoke the other's language to any significant degree. 'Good afternoon,' I greeted him, in Catalan. Mac looked bewildered, shrugged his shoulders and pointed to the front door, to indicate that he was going inside.

'Good afternoon to you, Primavera,' Gomez replied. I was surprised; he'd never been so familiar before.

'Yes, it is,' I continued, 'but now we've got that over with, why the visit?'

'It's a courtesy call, no more. I understand that Inspector Guinart let you in on the results of the second autopsy. I don't mind that at all. In fact, since it seems that you have friends with friends in high places . . .' there was more than a hint of irony in his tone, '. . . I thought I'd let you know the latest. Alex's tour of the clubs is over; it's left him a little disgusted, and us none the wiser . . . although we do have some potentially useful information about their client lists. However, we have determined the murder weapon.'

'Have you indeed? A wooden club, Alex said.'

'Not quite. It was a chair, from Senor Planas's patio set. It seems that he and his nocturnal visitor had some sort of a disagreement, he turned his back on her and she picked up the chair and swung it at him.'

'I see.' From what I remembered of the furniture in question, it had been solid enough to do the job. 'Alex also told me that you had DNA samples from Planas's clothing that would identify the woman. Any luck there?'

'Not yet. We've eliminated someone, though.' He laughed. 'Actually we've eliminated five people; two of our female officers, Senora Michels, you, of course, and Senor Planas's housekeeper.'

'Was she a suspect?' I asked.

'Potentially . . . and if not her, then her husband, the gardener. The lady was well paid by the dead man, and we wondered whether that might have covered more than the usual domestic services. They were our principal suspects, in fact, even before we knew of the sexual aspect; we've been questioning them since Sunday.'

'But now they're off the hook?'

'For the moment, although we haven't excluded them

completely. The son remains suspicious of them; he's never liked them much.'

'Angel? That reminds me. Do you know when the funeral will be?'

'Tomorrow,' Gomez replied, 'as he had hoped. It will be a burial. As you may know, cremation is becoming more popular in Spain, but you will appreciate that in the circumstances I couldn't allow that.'

'No, I can see why.'

He frowned. His small talk hadn't fooled me; I knew there was a specific reason for the visit so I wasn't surprised when he got round to it. 'Tell me,' he said, 'your friend, the gentleman we pulled in yesterday morning. During the meeting that you didn't discuss with us earlier, just how angry was he with Senor Planas?'

'Very, but it didn't come to anything.'

'Not then, but . . . You see, Primavera, the account of his whereabouts is so meticulous that it's almost as if it was planned in advance. Now, I have this new time frame that's been suggested. The thing is, I've been told very little about this man; I asked the boss when he called me, but he said that it was none of my business. That makes me imagine lots of things. Now I find that Senor Reid has left town, and that makes me imagine even more. I wonder whether there's any point in continuing with this investigation. From what you know of him, am I right?'

I thought about it, for a while; yes, Matthew could have gone out again, and yes, Planas might still have been up, sinking a bottle in celebration of having his ashes hauled. But against that, there was the inconsistency of the wine consumption, and there was something else. It would have been easy for me to have agreed with Gomez at that point, and there were times afterwards when I wished I'd done just that. But I didn't; instead I said, 'I don't think you are. From the little I know of his background, I'd be very surprised if he'd have needed to hit the guy with a chair. I reckon if he'd killed Planas, it really would have been written off as an accident.'

The intendant cursed, softly. 'Ah,' he murmured, 'what a pity. I really wish this thing would go away. For we've just had something else dumped in our laps.'

'What's that?'

'The mayor, Justine Michels, and her sister Elena, Angel Planas's wife; they've just reported their mother missing.'

Twenty-eight

Justine's mobile number was on the business card that she had given me on my second visit to the town hall, two days earlier, to pick up the permission for the wine fair. As I dialled it, I recalled that I'd been greeted in reception by a junior clerk, not by Dolores the Dragon herself.

Business hours were over, but wherever the mayor was there was plenty of background noise. 'It's Primavera. Are you able to speak?' I asked her.

'Yes. I'm at a gathering of our party group to discuss the agenda for this week's council meeting, but I haven't called it to order yet; we're still waiting for someone to turn up.' Her voice was strained, not that of the confident politician I'd met before.

'I've just heard about your mother. I had a visit from Gomez; he told me. What's happened?'

'We don't know.'

'How long's she been missing?'

'We don't know that either. On Sunday, after she heard what had happened, she told me that she felt she should be with

Elena. Even though things were as they were between Angel and his father, it had still come as a terrible shock. My sister's always been a little bit fragile . . . no, that's the wrong word . . . emotionally susceptible. I told her that was fine with me, and that she could come back to the town hall when she was ready. I thought no more about it. I was very busy on Monday and Tuesday, both days. It was only this afternoon that I got round to calling Elena, to see how she was, and to find out the time of the funeral. I asked her if Mother was still there, and she said, "What are you talking about?" She'd never been near her; she told me she hadn't seen her since last Friday.' Spanish people and Catalans always speak faster than Brits . . . I guess that's why I always have trouble following the in-flight English of Spanish cabin crew . . . and the further she got into her tale, the more Justine went at it rapid fire.

'Hey,' I exclaimed, 'slow down, calm down. When did you see her last?'

'I told you; on Sunday, when we agreed she should take time off work.'

'What did you do when you found out she wasn't where she was supposed to be?'

'I called her, of course,' she said impatiently, 'on her land line and on her mobile. No reply on either; in fact the mobile was switched off. I picked up Elena and we went to the house . . .'

'So you don't live with her?'

'No, I have a town house in Carrer del Mig; my father bought it, restored it and gave it to me. Mother still lives in our original family home, that was my grandparents', on the top of Puig Pedro. Elena and I went there, but there was no sign of her. Her car wasn't in the garage, everything inside was neat and tidy. But she's gone; she's vanished.'

'But are you sure she's missing? Justine, she's a grown woman and she's not in her dotage. Doesn't she ever do things on the spur of the moment?'

'My mother? No, never. As I told you, she's old L'Escala, very set in her ways. She'd probably never have been further away than Girona if it wasn't for my father. He made her go on holidays, took her to Belgium . . .'

Wow, I thought, but stayed silent.

'. . . to Paris, to London. She's hardly been out of town since he died.'

'How did she take his death? Has she been depressed since then? Do you think she might still be?'

'She dealt with it better than Elena and I did, to tell you the truth. My dad was a really nice man, a good father and a good husband, but he and my mother probably fell out of love years ago. I don't remember any great affection between them . . . you know what I mean, as there is between lovers.'

'What happened to him?' I asked.

'He died,' she replied, curtly. 'He just died.'

I moved on, quickly. 'Does she have family?'

'She has a brother, but I have no cousins. They're the last of the Fumado tribe around here. He hasn't seen her, and has no idea where she could have gone.'

'How about your father's people? Could she have gone there?'

'She barely knew them.'

'I thought you said that you had an uncle, your dad's brother.'

'Yes, Georges, but he lives in Brussels. My mother probably met him three times in her life, at her wedding, at Papa's funeral, and once when Elena and I were kids, when Papa took us to visit him.'

'So he's not part of the Belgian community here?'

'No, and never has been. Believe me, Primavera, Mother will not be with him. Something's happened to her.'

'But what makes you so certain?'

'I've checked with her hairdresser; she goes every morning, Monday to Friday, to have her hair arranged as you saw it when you met her; not Saturday, because it's too busy, or Sunday because it's closed, but every other day of the week, every other day of her life. My mother has her vanities, and her hair is the greatest of them. She hasn't been seen there since last Friday morning, and that tells me for certain that something is wrong.' She paused. 'That and one more thing: her make-up bag is missing. Wherever she goes, it goes.'

'I see.' A mystery indeed, I conceded; no wonder Gomez had been a little stressed. 'What did the police say when you and your sister went to see them?'

'Their first reaction was much the same as yours. The sergeant we spoke to said that she's neither a child nor an ancient, and that people have a perfect right to go off on trips without telling their families. I told her to go and fetch someone senior, and our friend the intendant appeared.

Eventually he took me seriously. As for having any theories, that's another matter.'

'Yes, he was pretty perplexed when he spoke to me. Did he update you on his investigation?'

She whistled. 'He did indeed. So the old pig had been entertaining a lady. Gomez did say that they had a suspect, but I got the impression, although I'm not sure why, that they're not moving heaven and earth to catch them. If that's true, then good; it'll give them more time to find my mother.' I heard a voice in the background, calling her name. 'At last,' she replied. 'Primavera, our latecomer has arrived, I have to go.'

Afterwards, when I thought about it, I found myself coming back to one thing that the mayor had said. *'I don't remember any great affection between them . . . you know what I mean, as there is between lovers.'*

Yes, I know what she meant; it's something I've longed for myself, from time to time. There had been a sadness in Justine's voice; she had known such tenderness herself, but I found myself wondering whether, for all she had said of her mystery man, she still did.

Twenty-nine

Gerard didn't turn up for supper that night. I wondered if he might be waiting for me to call him to tell him it was okay, but I wasn't about to do that. So Tom, Mac and I had another pleasant family evening, even if for much of it I did find myself hoping that the gate buzzer would ring, and it would be him, apologising for being late.

I had misgivings about going to the funeral of José-Luis Planas next morning, but in the end I kept my promise to his son. Maybe, since I had seen him in his final undignified pose, I felt the need to obliterate that as my last memory of a man I had known only briefly, or maybe I was just one of those cynics that Angel had said would be there only to make sure that he really was dead. Or maybe there was a deeper reason. The last funeral I had attended was that of my mother, five years before. When Oz died I was on another continent, and for various reasons I couldn't make it back for his. So I suppose it's possible that as I stood near the centre of the substantial congregation, I was looking at one coffin while my subconscious was seeing another.

Gerard was there of course, assisting Father Olivares. I made eye contact with him at one point, but didn't get as much as a flicker of recognition in return. *Oh dear,* I thought, *I've really burned some boats with him.*

Justine was there too, but not beside her sister; instead she was seated on the other side of the aisle in the centre of a group of twelve, the remaining members of the council either paying their respects or giving thanks for the political stability that the death had brought. She wore a simple black lace shawl over her head. (No, not a mantilla. That's held up by a comb.) It made me all the more aware of the lack of mine. I'd looked for it all over the house, but been unable to find it.

The requiem Mass dragged on, and on, as they do, before the old priest pronounced the benediction, shook hands with Angel and Elena, then stood to one side as the coffin was carried out to the waiting hearse with the couple following behind. Angel looked grave, his face pale, but his wife was hollow cheeked and her eyes were hidden behind wrap-around sunglasses.

As I filed out with the rest of the crowd, I saw that Angel was standing beside his limo; the door was open and Elena was inside, pressed into a corner, as far from the throng as she could force herself. I made my way towards him.

I held out a hand, formally. 'I'm sorry,' I murmured; I couldn't think of anything else to say.

'Thank you,' he responded. He seemed strange, friendly enough, but slightly distant; not unnatural, I supposed, for a man who was burying his father.

'Has there been any news of Elena's mother?' I asked, although her absence was a pretty fair indicator that there had been nothing positive.

He shook his head. 'No. Nor do there seem to have been any new developments in the investigation into my father's murder. The Mossos have not been at their most impressive,' he added bitterly. 'Justine has instructed them to inform her of everything they have, but all they can give her are suspicions that I for one cannot credit.'

That puzzled me. 'What do you mean?' I asked.

'Nothing,' he replied. 'Nothing you need worry about. I shouldn't have said anything at all.' He broke off as the undertaker approached, to tell him that they were ready to go, then turned back to me. 'Listen, we are having a small reception in the terrace restaurant of Meson del Conde this evening, for my father's council colleagues and for those people in the town who knew him best. It's at seven; please join us.' He slid into the big black car beside his wife, and closed the door before I had a chance to tell him that I was cooking for Mac and Tom that evening.

Thirty

'Of course it's all right with me, woman,' Mac exclaimed. 'D'you think I've never made the tea before? You go to this wake, or whatever the hell it is, and I'll allow my grandson to crush me at the video game of his choice.'

'If you're sure,' I told him. 'If I don't go now that I've been invited, it'll look as if I'm snubbing them. It's not that I'm looking forward to it . . . it'll be weird . . . but Angel needs support.'

With the go-ahead given, I decided that I'd better dress up for the occasion. I showered, shampooed, and gave myself a good going over with the Gillette Venus (confession: I've taken to shaving it all off in the summer; it's cooler) before coating myself in a very expensive moisturiser that my sister recommended to me, and coaxing my hair into its most sophisticated presentation, rather than its quick and easy format. When all that was done I chose a light, below-the-knee, plum-coloured satin dress with a halter neck, and matching shoes. And that was all; yes, I often go commando, but I never tell anyone. My shawl would have set it off perfectly; I had

189

another look around for it, but still couldn't find the damn thing, so I settled for the shoulder bag in the same material, that I'd bought with the dress.

Mac whistled when I came downstairs. 'Are you sure this is a funeral reception?' he asked. Even Tom looked a wee bit surprised.

I was mildly embarrassed. 'Yes,' I retorted, defending myself. 'You don't know the way the women dress here; they do glam pretty well. I'm not going over there looking like a country mouse. And besides, I don't often have the chance to get jazzed up.' This was true. I'd always dressed conservatively whenever Gerard and I went out to eat, to avoid provoking the gossips even more. 'I'll be back in a couple of hours, I expect.' I pointed at my son. 'Do not wait up for me, young man.'

I made my way outside and down the square, towards Meson del Conde; I drew a few looks as I went, but didn't return any of them. The terrace restaurant isn't quite as described. It's a glass-walled, air-conditioned extension to the main building, with its own entrance. Angel was standing just inside the doorway. He was still wearing his dark funeral suit but the black tie was gone and his shirt was open at the neck. We shook hands, and he thanked me for coming. 'Is Elena here?' I asked.

'No, she's too upset . . . over her mother,' he added, not that I thought there would be another reason, given that her very attendance at his father's send-off had been a toss-up.

As I stepped inside, a waiter offered me a glass of something pink with bubbles in it; Perelada rosada cava, I suspected, a little frivolous for the occasion but never mind. I took one, and scanned the room for a familiar face. As I'd expected, all the women were dressed to the nines. L'Escala is a competitive place in some surprising ways; I've learned to play that game, and I'm not accustomed to losing at anything, other than love.

'Good evening, senora.' The voice came from my left. I looked around and saw, to my surprise, the little figure of Father Olivares approaching. No cava for him, his hand clutched a glass of what looked like a dark garnaxa.

'And to you,' I replied.

'I am pleased to see you here,' he said. 'Angel has told me of your difficulty with José-Luis. It shows a kindness of spirit that you have put that aside and come to pay your respects.'

'I'm here for Angel and his wife,' I told him.

'I appreciate that, but the same principle applies.' He paused, then glanced up at me. 'If you're looking for my young colleague, he's not coming.'

'I wasn't, but thank you for telling me.'

'He was invited,' the old priest continued, 'but he declined. He won't tell me why, but he's upset about something. In fact he was sharp with me when I asked him about it. You don't know what might be troubling him, do you?'

'I might,' I admitted. 'We had a disagreement; a rather public disagreement.'

'I thought it might be something like that. And of course, you're both powerful, proud and stubborn personalities, and neither is in a mood to apologise.'

'I can only speak for myself; I have no idea what he's

thinking.' I frowned at him. 'Are you getting round to warning me off, Father?'

'No, no I'm not,' he said, quickly. 'After some initial reservations, I've come to approve of your friendship. It's good for a priest, especially a young, modern priest, to have a private circle, of people who are not necessarily of our church, and if it includes single ladies like yourself, I have no problem with that. However, there can be volatility within such groups, arguments, and they can bring out the worst in anyone. I have a great regard for Father Hernanz; I admit it, he's my protégé. But I can see his faults; there's a fire in him and as with all fires, if it's fanned it can burn out of control. I don't want that to happen. So, my dear, it might be for the best if you and he were to avoid each other for a while, until things have cooled and you are able to discuss your differences calmly and rationally.'

'Would that include me keeping my son away from the church?'

'Who would that penalise?'

'Only Tom.'

'Then of course you shouldn't. Gerard won't turn him away, I promise you, or treat him any differently.'

I smiled at him. 'Okay,' I promised, 'I'll do what you ask and let time take care of it. Thank you, Father Olivares,' I added. 'I think I'd like to have you as a friend too.'

'You have, my dear.'

For a moment, I was on the verge of leaning forward and kissing him on the cheek, but I reckoned that some of the older women in the room might have burned me at the stake if I'd done that, so I restrained myself. Instead, I moved on towards Justine who was standing with two of the men who'd been with her in the front row at the church. She was poshed up too, in a tight-fitting black silk dress that came close to making me feel frumpy. She detached herself from her group and joined me at a table where a *pica pica* buffet had been set out.

'Any news of your mother?' I began. As I spoke I saw Alex Guinart on the far side of the room, standing half a pace behind Gomez; he was looking in our direction, with a small frown on his face. I guessed that he knew what we were discussing.

'Nothing. The police have even checked with my uncle in Belgium; I told them it was useless, and it was.' She laid her glass on the table and picked up a plate. I followed suit and together we chose from the dishes on offer; a wide selection, prawns, quail's eggs fried on circles of bread, feta cheese cubed, meatballs, olives, and a few things that even I had never seen before. 'I don't know what to do, Primavera; I've never felt so helpless. Elena, she's a complete wreck; the doctor's had to give her a sedative.'

'She'll turn up,' I reassured her, inanely, for I had no greater reason for optimism than anyone else. I picked up my glass and drained it as we ate. One of the waiters saw that I was empty and came across with a refill; the quail's eggs were loaded with salt, so to save him a return trip, I took two. 'What about Angel's dad?' I asked her. 'Has Gomez told you anything about that?'

'Yes,' she replied, but her tone had changed, become more hesitant. 'But he insisted that it was in confidence, so . . .'

'It's okay,' I said at once. 'Forget I asked. Anyway,' I added, 'I suspect that I know what his current thinking is.'

She gave me a curious look, but said nothing more than, 'Mmm.'

We ate some more then went back to the table, where new, more substantial, hot dishes were waiting for us. I found that I was out of cava again, so I picked up a glass of red something. That was rather nice too; it was familiar, reminded me of one I'd had from Ben, even though I probably shouldn't have been drinking it with *fidua*.

I was beginning to get the impression that Justine had had a few also, especially when she looked me in the eye and said, 'Okay, tell me about you and the priest. I know I was told no, but, let's hear it from you. Are you or not?'

'Not,' I replied firmly. 'Why, do you have ambitions?'

'Ouch. Even if I did, I couldn't. I'm the mayor, remember. But . . . would you like to? Come on, secretly.'

'You wouldn't tell me your secrets a minute ago, so why should I tell you mine? But it's still no. He's a pal, that's all.' (Even though, at that moment, he wasn't.)

'Don't believe you.'

'Honest,' I tried to insist.

She'd have pressed me further, maybe asked me if the thought had ever crossed my mind, but we were both distracted by the sound of a mobile. We followed it, to see Gomez reaching for his pocket. He pressed the phone to his ear. As he listened, his face seemed to darken, and he glanced towards Justine. He ended the call, quickly, spoke briefly to Alex, then headed for the mayor, but she was already moving towards him. He spoke to her quickly, earnestly, and I saw her hand go to her mouth, then he and Alex turned and made for the exit.

I stepped up to Justine's shoulder. 'What is it?' I whispered.

'They've found my mother's car; in some woods beside the main road, opposite Ventallo, where nobody lives. It's a shell, burned out.'

'And . . .' I gasped.

'No. She wasn't in it, thank God.' She put a hand on my arm. 'Primavera, I have to go, to be with my sister.'

'Of course.'

She went in the same direction as the two cops, through the whispering crowd, ignoring everyone who spoke to her. As she did, I felt the room begin to wobble, very slightly, or maybe it was me. Maybe it was the news, maybe it was the cava, maybe I'd lost a week somewhere and it was the time of the month, but I knew my evening was over. I thanked Angel . . . he was still by the door, frowning as if he didn't know what to do for the best . . . and made my way unsteadily home.

Thirty-one

When I woke up next morning, I felt fine. My memory of the latter part of the evening was hazy, but with a little effort I recalled announcing that I was going to bed and Mac saying that was fine and that he was going to see if Ben was still open, and if so, he was going to drag him off for a beer.

I swung my feet out of bed and planted them on the floor . . . right in the centre of my satin party dress, which lay in a perfect circle exactly where I'd let it drop and stepped out of it. I winced, and hoped that I hadn't destroyed it, but it looked okay when I fastened it to a hanger, no food, wine or other embarrassing stains.

I checked my watch; seven fifty, too late to go for a swim and be back in time to make breakfast, so I settled for a quick shower instead, dressed in my usual daywear and headed downstairs. I beat Tom by five minutes . . . he's a self-starter these days . . . and in that time his oranges were freshly squeezed, his Coco Pops and my Special K were in their bowls, ready for the milk, and the coffee percolator was on the stove alongside a pan in which three eggs were beginning the short journey to being soft boiled.

Of Mac, there was no sign. I sneaked a look into the garden, and into the kennel. Of Charlie there was no sign either, and so I guessed that one had taken the other for a walk. With our dog, it's sometimes difficult to tell who's in charge.

They still hadn't come back when Tom headed off to school on his soon-to-be-replaced bike, but a burst of furious barking, in a familiar canine voice, told me that they weren't far off. Charlie was still giving it plenty when the garden gate opened and he burst in, pulling on his leash.

'I don't know what the hell's up with this dog,' Mac exclaimed. 'We were just going past your garage when he stopped in his tracks and started barking at the door alongside it. He wouldn't come when I told him; finally I had to put the lead on him and drag him away. What is that down there anyway?'

'It's mine,' I told him. 'Go through to the kitchen and pour yourself some coffee. I'll go down and take a look.' I headed for the door that opens on to the stairs and trotted down to the garage.

As I've told you, my house is very old, but clearly, my garage isn't, not in relative terms, given that cars have only been around for a hundred years or so. It's big, and could hold at least three vehicles, although it doesn't. The rear part is cut into the rock on which the house stands, and the rest is built out from that. The oldest man in the village is over ninety; he told me that his father told him, that when he was a boy, a hundred and twenty years ago, the back of my garage was a dwelling in its own right, and that a family lived there . . . the cave dwellers, they were called. Alongside it, there was, and still is, a *trustero*, an outhouse, entirely self contained, that he believed was used as a privy by the nineteenth-century occupants. It's possible that it might have been; the floor's mainly stone, but there's a concrete slab right at the back that might be covering what could have been a limepit, a makeshift chemical toilet. Today, I use it as a storeroom, for logs mostly, for the wood-burning stove in the main living room. That's what Charlie had gone off at, and I couldn't figure out why, for he goes past it every day without a murmur.

I opened the up-and-over garage with the remote, grabbed the big old store key from its hook and stepped outside. The wooden door was scratched, by Charlie's hard claws, I guessed. I'd half a mind to dock the cost of the paint out of his next bag of dog food. I slid the key into the lock, turned it and pushed the door open.

There's no light in the cupboard and it's at least twenty feet deep, so I couldn't see very clearly, not straight away anyway. There was a tall pile of logs near the door; I stepped past it to see what was beyond. As soon as I did I knew what had scared my big tough softie of a Labrador. We had a visitor, a woman. She was seated, on some more logs, leaning against the back wall, and she was staring straight at me, sticking her tongue out at me as if a game had been played and I had lost. As I looked back at her, I knew that, somehow, she was right too.

It was Dolores Fumado, Justine's mother, Elena's mother. Her normally immaculate hair resembled a caricature of the

Beijing Olympic stadium, and her face was streaked with days-old make-up. I didn't have to touch her to know that she was dead, and I didn't have to go any closer to know how she'd died. Something was knotted tight around her neck, something black: my clever, all-purpose, missing shawl.

I'm not usually a screamer, under any circumstances, but I came close then. I backed out of there faster than Jackie Kennedy crawled out of that car in Dallas, pulled the door shut and locked it, stepped back into the garage and pressed the remote closer. I didn't even think to look around me, to check that nobody had been watching.

I leaned against the wall, panting, feeling the thumping of my heart, trying to retain a degree of self-control, fighting against the sheer blind panic that threatened to overwhelm me. The best way to do that is to put your mind to work, and so I made myself analyse what I had seen, and tried to fit answers to some obvious questions.

How long had she been there?

Only a matter of hours, I told myself. Charlie went past the storeroom every day; he'd been set off by an unfamiliar scent, one his doggie brain told him instinctively was wrong. Tom had taken him out as soon as he'd got back from school the day before. Which meant that: she must have been dumped in there during the night. And in turn, that since the store is directly below my bedroom terrace ... quite a few metres below, I'll grant you, but below it ... even though I'd left the patio door slightly open, as I often do when it's warm and out of the peak mosquito season, I'd slept right through it.

How long had she been dead?

Only one way to find out. I picked up a torch and went back outside. It was still way too early for beach-goers, so I was able to slip back into the storeroom unseen. This time I went right up to the body and touched it, taking care not to shine the torch on her face. I wasn't brave enough to look into those eyes. She was cold, but, I judged, still above the ambient temperature of her windowless crypt, which only ever feels the early morning sun. I took her hand and lifted her arm. I sensed stiffening, but rigor mortis was still well short of complete. I thought back to my classes during my nursing studies, when they taught us the facts of death. 'Six to twelve hours to completion,' I murmured. Semi-educated guess; she'd either been killed there, where she sat, or just before she was dumped. I had to assume the latter; Dolores was a sturdy woman and I couldn't imagine her going in there like a lamb to the slaughter. She'd have fought, raised hell probably, raised every sleeper in the village. But not me, not Mac, not Tom.

But why had she been killed?

Yes, why? She must have been kidnapped at some time on Sunday, some time after telling Justine that she was going to look after the fragile Elena, not long after the discovery of the body of José-Luis Planas. That one was beyond me; I hadn't the faintest, and I knew that I could have sat there all day without coming close to an answer.

What should I do about it?

Call the police, silly bitch. Call them right now. Only, hold on for a minute . . . She'd been put there, on my property, for a reason. Again, I'd no idea what that might be, but I knew one thing for sure: I couldn't come up with a single answer that was good for me. So, proceed with caution, senora. In any other situation, my first thought would have been to call Alex Guinart, my friendly face within the Mossos. But some things precluded friendship and this was one of them.

'Primavera! Is everything okay?'

Mac's voice sounded too close for comfort. I bolted out of the storeroom and locked the door, just before he appeared from the garage entrance.

'It's okay,' I assured him. 'Panic over. A squirrel got in there somehow or other and died.' It was the best lie I could come up with at short notice.

He frowned. 'How the hell did it manage that? That door looks pretty solid.'

'How should I know?' I blustered. 'How should I know how long it's been there? Does the word "hibernation" mean anything to you?'

'It's May.'

'Then it must have overslept.'

He shook his head. 'This bloody place,' he chuckled. 'I guess everything moves at its own pace. Gimme the key and I'll get rid of it for you.'

'Bugger off,' I retorted. 'Do you think I'm too timid to clear away a dead rodent? Get back upstairs and make yourself some breakfast while I bag it and chuck it in a bin.'

'Yes, boss,' he said, chastened, doing what he was told and disappearing back into the garage, leaving me with the idle considerations of where I could possibly find a bag big enough to contain what was in the store, or a bin big enough to take it.

In the end, I could only think of one thing to do. I took my mobile from my pocket and punched in a number I knew off by heart.

'Good morning, Primavera,' he greeted me. His tone was neutral, perfectly pitched between cold and friendly. 'If you're calling to ask whether Tom can come to church on Sunday, the answer is, of course he can. Or are you going to disappoint me by saying that you're not going to allow it?'

'Gerard, I'm sorry,' I exclaimed, and in the instant I realised that I was. I'd blown up in his face for no good reason, other than that possibly I was trying to make the point to Mac that I wasn't some sort of clerical groupie. 'I didn't mean all that stuff. Where are you?'

'I'm in L'Escala.'

'Can you come here, now? I'm downstairs, in the garage.'

He sighed. 'In truth I was coming anyway. Ten minutes.'

I was puzzled by what he'd said, but I didn't dwell on it. As I waited for him, I realised that my mouth was as dry as a lizard's . . . whatever the driest part of a lizard might be. I have a small drinks fridge in the garage; I took out a bottle of water and sat on the wall looking out to sea, trying not to feel scared by what had happened and was still happening.

Gerard must have left a layer of rubber on the road, for only seven minutes had gone by before his old white Fiat crested the hill. I beckoned to him; he drove down and swung into the garage, and I followed him inside. 'Primavera,' he said, as he climbed out of the car, but he didn't get any further before I hugged him tight, pressing my unfettered breasts into his chest so hard that they hurt. He didn't resist, just wrapped his muscular arms around me.

'I think I'm in trouble,' I whispered.

'I know you are,' he said, as finally we separated. He held me at arm's length and looked into my eyes. 'I had a visit from Alex Guinart early this morning, in church. I heard his confession, but when it was over he told me something else. He said that he and Gomez are going to detain a suspect this morning . . .'

I guessed what was coming. 'Me?'

'Yes.'

'But why?'

'They've examined the chair that hit Planas over the head and cracked it open. They found a palm print on it and they were able to extract a DNA sample from it. It's a perfect match for yours. There were no other prints on the chair other than one of Planas's at the top, where he'd probably dragged it to move it.'

I thought back to Sunday afternoon, and I remembered something: tripping, falling and grabbing hold of the leg of a chair, that chair. I told him. 'Did anyone see you?' he asked.

'I doubt it. I think that Alex and Justine were both ahead of me; neither of them would have noticed.'

'Still,' said Gerard, sounding optimistic for the first time, 'it's plausible, and it will be for them to prove that couldn't have happened.'

'Maybe not,' I sighed. 'Go next door and see what's in my storeroom.' I handed him the key and the torch.

He was gone for two minutes; when he returned his face was grim. 'When did you . . .'

'Twenty minutes ago.'

'Oh my.' His eyelashes flickered.

'Are you going to ask me if I did it?'

'I know you didn't, so why should I?'

'But how do you know?'

'Because I . . .' he barked, then stopped himself. 'Primavera, if you're going to tell me I'm wrong, then please let me hear your confession as a priest, so that I can never be called to give evidence against you. If not, then just accept my support.' I smiled helplessly at him, and nodded. 'You have to get out of here,' he continued. 'Alex Guinart told me what he did outside the confession box. I reckon he did so on purpose, guessing that I'd pass it on to you. He doesn't believe that you killed Planas any more than I do, and he wants you to clear off so that he can sort it out, and so that Gomez and the public prosecutor don't settle on you as the easy answer. If you get caught up in the criminal system here, you can be inside for a couple of years before you even come to trial, and if you are there, they won't be looking for anyone else. Alex has put his job on the line for you, so don't let him down. Is there somewhere you can go now, to hide, where you won't be found?'

I thought about that, and the first question I asked was, *Did I want to?* If I ran, who knows how long it would be for, and who knows who'd look after Tom. No answer to the first, but to the second, he was upstairs, Mac. If I stood my ground . . . did I fancy my eight-year-old seeing me in the nick? Last time I was inside, I'd barred all my close family from visiting me. 'I have a key for Shirley's house,' I told him. 'I could hang out there for a while.'

'Then do so. I'll come to see you there tonight, and we'll see about getting you further away. Don't think about it. You have to hurry.'

He didn't have to tell me that. 'I have to see Mac,' I said. 'Wait here.'

I ran upstairs, heading straight for my room on the top floor; by the time I got there I was panting. I grabbed some clothes, almost at random, and some other essentials, girlie stuff like make-up, facial wipes, and such, and rammed them into a haversack. Finished, I went back down to the kitchen. Mac was there, wolfing a slice of toast.

I looked him in the eye and handed him the key to the store. 'In ten minutes,' I told him, 'I want you to open that door again. When you've seen what's there, do what has to be done.' I gave him a quick hug. 'You're right, Mac, I'm a magnet for bother; trust me again, please, and look after my boy.'

He stared at me. I could still feel his eyes on my back as I left the room.

There's a safe in the garage as well as the fridge. It's built into the wall, it can't be drilled out and it's pretty much impregnable; not even the legendary Johnny Ramensky could have cracked it. Ever since my trouble a few years back, I've made a point of keeping an emergency stash of money, near at hand. I had four thousand euro in there, cash, and I took the lot. I also had a brand new taser weapon, but I left that where it was.

I took my bike from its place against the wall . . . I could hardly have taken the Jeep, could I?

I stepped up to Gerard, and for the first time in my life, I kissed him, woman to man. Again, he didn't flinch. 'Thanks, love,' I whispered. 'It isn't just Alex who's putting his job on the line, is it?' He said nothing in reply, but I knew. 'We both have to leave,' I told him. 'You first. Come to Shirley's back gate, after dark; I'll leave it open.'

He nodded, climbed into his car and drove away. I counted to ten, then slipped on my haversack, straddled my mountain bike, and swung it out of the garage. I pressed the remote closer, chucked it back under the door as it began to swing down, and pedalled out of Dodge, or in this case St Martí d'Empúries, as fast as my legs could pump.

Thirty-two

Quite a chunk of my sensual history is tied up with Shirley Gash's garden; I haven't had all that many sexual partners, but two of my encounters have taken place there. Enough said about them, though.

Still, I had lots on my mind as I sat in the summer house and waited for night to fall. I'd made sure that nobody had seen me slip into the house and the garden isn't overlooked by any of the neighbours, so I felt secure, or as secure as I was entitled to feel in the circumstances. Shit, I was an old hand at the game. I'd been a fugitive before ... or, to be accurate, I'd believed that I was. This time, though, it was for real. I was as innocent as I'd ever been in my life, but the Mossos d'Esquadra were after me, and they are not people you want on your trail.

The palm print on the chair: I had an answer for that, and I was pretty sure that a good lawyer would keep me out of jail, if only that was all they had on me. But it wasn't; there was something nasty in my woodshed, and that wasn't deniable. Planas killed. Then Justine's mum kidnapped; done away with. I assumed that there had to be a connection, but I had no idea what it was. I had even less of an idea as to why anyone would choose to plant her body on me. I had . . .

I had nothing. I was sitting uninvited in my absent friend's home, with four thousand euro, a change of knickers and no idea of what I was going to do next. I couldn't stay there for ever, I knew that sooner or later they were going to get round all my friends, and that would include calling on Shirley. When they found the house empty . . . they'd be over the wall, for sure. Even with Alex running blockers for me, and I doubted if he'd do that again, not after the latest development, I reckoned I had a day's grace, no more. My imagination grew more bizarre by the minute. Did they use bloodhounds in Spain? I wondered.

I was puzzled, I was scared, I was uncertain, I was missing my boy, all the more because I was afraid to call him to explain that I had to go away for a while. I had to assume that there would be a tap on my home phone and that they'd be monitoring my mobile as well. The one thing I wasn't, was hungry. I'd raided Shirley's freezer, microwaved a lasagne from her stock, and washed it down with a bottle of fizzy water.

I'd found something else too. Shirley has a great mane of hair; she's very proud of it, and in recent years she's taken to changing colours and styles all the time. Occasionally she'll go blond, but usually she prefers a darker shade. She prefers DIY and often I'll help her, so I knew where to search. It didn't take me long to find what I was after, a box of her preference of the moment, a deep chestnut colour. I had plenty of time, so I took great care, and after an hour or so . . . I wasn't unrecognisable, but anyone who'd been told to look out for a blonde was going to give me a miss.

I knew I was going to need more than a change of hair colour, though. Men on the run have a great advantage, over a few days they can grow facial hair as a disguise, or if they had some to begin with, over a few minutes they can take it off. Us girls, we're stuck.

It seemed to take ages for the darkness to fall. I spent the time wondering where I was going to go. Air travel was out, and probably trains as well. For a while I considered following Matthew Reid's example and heading for the British Consulate in Barcelona. I gave up on that notion fairly quickly, however; his innocence had been demonstrable, while to a neutral eye, indeed to any sensible eye, mine was questionable. There was also the consideration that as soon as the consular staff ran a check on my background, they'd come up with my criminal conviction. I wasn't a retired brigadier with dangerous secrets to protect. I was an ex-con and no reputations would be risked on my behalf. Plus, Avinguda Diagonal was a long way off on a bike. Hard as I thought about it, I could come up with no better solution than to cycle up into the mountains and hide out in a rented apartment or on a campsite in the hope that . . .

In the hope that what? That whoever had decided to set me up, and had made such a good job of it, would have a crisis of conscience and confess?

'Let's face it, girl,' I murmured as the big swimming pool reflected the first of the moonlight, 'you're fucked.'

A second or two later, I heard a creak; there's a heavy iron gate at the back of Shirley's property, and it needs a touch of oil. I shrank back into the summer house and waited, not quite certain who was coming, hoping that Gerard hadn't fallen victim to a crisis of conscience himself, or been followed by Gomez and Alex.

He was alone, though; I shouldn't have doubted his trust in me or his caution in making sure there was nobody on his tail. Puig Sec, the area where Shirley lives, is very quiet, even in the summer and so it's easy to spot a following vehicle. I could see him from my hiding place as he walked up to the poolside; thick chested, narrow waisted, in T-shirt and jeans, his soft leather moccasins making not a sound. He carried a bag, over his shoulder.

'Hey,' I called out, stepping out of the shadows. He turned towards me and for the first time in more than twelve hours, I felt something other than despair. 'Thanks for coming.'

He grinned as he walked towards me. 'I said I would, didn't I?'

'What's been happening?' I asked him.

'What do you think? The mayor's mother has been found murdered. When Senor Blackstone called it in, all hell was let loose in L'Escala. The police . . . all the police; the Mossos, the municipals, even the Guardia Civil . . . stopped and searched every car heading out of town for five hours afterwards, looking for you. Eventually they stopped; they now believe that you'd left the area already.'

'Have they put out a description?'

'Yes, but that's all. They don't have a photograph of you on record, and when Gomez asked Senor Blackstone for one, he refused him.' He paused. 'Do you have your passport on you?'

'Yes.'

'Then give it to me, and your credit cards; you won't be able to use them anyway, and you don't want to be found with anything that identifies you.' He grinned. 'I like the new hair, by the way.'

'I don't,' I growled. I dug my passport and cards out of my haversack and handed them over. 'Alex has pictures of me,' I told him, 'taken after Marte's christening.'

He nodded. 'And Gloria told him what would happen if he gave one to Gomez . . . or rather what wouldn't happen, for the foreseeable future.'

That gave me my first laugh of the day. 'How did they handle Mac?' I asked.

'Politely. He told them that he hadn't seen you since last night.'

'What about Tom?' I asked him, anxiously. 'Did they question Tom?'

'We wouldn't let them, his grandfather and me. They were content for Mac to ask him when he had seen you last, then tell them. He said that you'd given him his breakfast, and that everything had been as usual.'

'You said Mac and you. They questioned you?'

'Of course they did . . . or at least Gomez did; I think he now feels that Alex is too close.'

'You mean he's kicking him off the investigation?'

'No. But he's doing all the interviews himself.'

'What did you say to him, Gerard?'

'I told him that we'd had a very public argument on Wednesday morning and that I hadn't seen you since.'

I stared at him. 'You lied for me?'

He nodded. 'Yes, shocking, isn't it?' And then he chuckled. 'Come on, what was I going to say? That the last time I saw you, you were pedalling towards Puig Sec? Primavera, my dear, if I thought for one second that you killed Planas and Dolores Fumado, I would have handed you over to Gomez this morning, but I know you didn't. So I'll protect you, and I can square that with my conscience. If, eventually, others take a different view, I'll deal with that.'

'You're a darlin' man,' I told him. 'One thing I must ask you though: the police have my DNA all over the chair that Planas was hit with, and Dolores was found in my shed, so how do you know, for sure, that I didn't do it?'

'Simple,' he replied. 'I believe in you, in the same way that I believe in God. I have faith in you. What's the definition of faith? Belief, devotion and trust despite the absence of any logical proof.'

I felt my heart melt, and my eyes mist over. 'And I believe in you too,' I told him. 'But I have plenty of proof. You give it to me simply by being here. I wish I could just stay with you, and let you protect me.' I grinned up at him. 'You couldn't give me sanctuary in the church, could you?'

'I wish I could, but the sanitary arrangements are pretty basic; you'd give yourself up to Gomez within a couple of days, just for a shower. Plus, it would provoke the sort of confrontation between church and state that each of those institutions is desperate to avoid.'

I knew that was true, and as I thought about it, I realised something else, the gravity of Gerard's own situation, and what he was risking personally, for me. Defrocking, disgrace, arrest; they were all possibilities, and I had put him in harm's way. 'Go,' I said, suddenly and earnestly. 'Get out of here. You're crazy to have anything to do with me, and I'm wicked to have asked you for help.'

'No. I'm proud that you did. I'll go all right, but only when you're safely on your way. When you're gone, we'll keep in touch and I'll let you know what's happening here.'

'Do you know what the police thinking is, Gerard? What connection do they see between the two deaths? Or do they see any? Do they think I've just been picking off people I don't like?'

'They believe there is a link, but I don't think they know what it is. Alex has to be careful what he says to me now, but he told me when Gomez was out of earshot that they're not reaching any conclusions until they've got the results of an autopsy and, he said, of other forensic tests.'

'There's one big hole in their case, isn't there? Why the hell would I kidnap Dolores? Why would I want to harm her? Why would I burn her car? Justine spoke to her mother on Sunday, after Planas's body had been found. If the two deaths are linked, why would I snatch her so much later, after I'd killed Planas?'

'I asked Alex those same questions. Justine spoke to her mother by telephone; the thinking is that you had her by then and that she was forced to make that call, to give you time to decide what to do with her. They assume that you burned her car to destroy any evidence that you'd been in it, after you'd taken it where you thought it wouldn't be found, for a while at least. When it was, they believe you went back home and killed her; you were seen to leave the reception just after they did.'

'But why would I have done it?'

'That, they don't know ... or if they have a theory, Alex hasn't told me.'

'But even if I had a reason, how would I have done all this? Dolores was a sturdy woman.'

'Gomez found your taser weapon in your open safe; he reckons you threatened her with it. Anyone who didn't know the difference would take it for a real firearm, and someone who did wouldn't want to be shot by it. Or, he thinks, maybe you did shoot her with it, to subdue her.'

I whistled. 'If you were talking about someone else, I'd believe she did it. I'm helpless, Gerard.'

'No, you're not; you have me on your side, and I suspect that you also have Alex.'

That alarmed me. 'Please make sure he doesn't risk anything for me; it's bad enough having one of you in jeopardy. Two, I couldn't take.'

'Don't worry; he's being professional. What I have to make sure is that Gomez isn't using him, having him feed me information in the hope that I'll pass it to you and flush you out.'

'Then don't; don't pass anything to me. That would be as big a risk for you as me . . . bigger, for I'm done already.'

He put his hands on my shoulders. 'Primavera, I'm not going to abandon you. I have this all thought out.' He reached into his bag, produced two mobile phones, one red, one blue, handed the red one to me, and put the other in his pocket. 'These are new, pay as you go; untraceable. I bought them this afternoon, in Figueras where nobody knows me, in two different shops. I was dressed like this, so no one will remember a priest. Your charger's in the bag. There's a car parked outside with a full tank. Nobody will spot that either; it's my spare, an old banger of a Suzuki that I keep in a garage in case my Fiat should give up on me.'

'But where do I go?'

'You go to Granada, by a route that I've planned for you, one that doesn't involve autopistas where you might be recognised at the toll booths.' He held up the bag. 'There's an address written down in here, a road map, a street map to get you there, and a key to get you in. It's my old family home, my private bolthole, and nobody will follow you there. You'll be safe; it's in the Albacin, and there you'll be anonymous, just another tourist.'

'For how long?' I whispered.

'For as long as it takes. Don't worry, Mac will look after Tom; I've already made sure of that. His wife will come here, if necessary. You didn't kill these people, Primavera, but somebody did. I'm not going to rest until that person's been found, and you're in the clear.'

His certainty made me feel stronger, but I couldn't shake all my doubts, all my fears. 'But what if that person can't be found, Gerard? What if it's somebody from Planas's past, or Dolores's, someone you and I have never heard of, and they're gone already?'

He drew me to him and pressed his forehead against mine. 'Return my faith as you say you do, Primavera; I'll make you safe, and I will keep you safe. That's my most solemn promise, and I won't break it. And there's something else; we are not alone. Now, you really must get on the road.'

It was nice to know that God was with us, but at that time I could only deal with the immediate practicalities. 'How can I be sure I won't be stopped at the first roundabout?' I asked.

'You can't, so avoid them all. There's a track, opposite the football ground; if you follow that it will take you all the way to Sobrestany. From there you can get to Ulla, and on to Verges; you'll be in the clear by then.' He handed me the bag. I took a look inside, found all the things he had mentioned, plus a couple of bottles of water and what looked like sandwiches, wrapped in silver foil. 'On your way now. I'll take your bike back to L'Escala and hide it in my garage. Call me on the mobile when you get to Granada; the unlock code is four zeroes and the number of mine is in the memory of yours. But remember, call only me, no one else. You can't even send Tom a text or you'll risk being traced. That'll be the hardest part, I know, but you have to deal with it.'

I retrieved my mountain bike from the summer house, we walked to the back gate, and stepped outside. The street was deserted and the only vehicle in it was a small, battered four-by-four; looking at it I realised that it would take another act of faith to accept that it could get me to Granada.

'The key's in the ignition,' Gerard told me. He took my hand, put it to his lips and kissed it. 'God bless you,' he whispered. 'It may be that when your troubles are over, our troubles will begin.'

Thirty-three

I found the track that Gerard had described; it was rough and even in the rattletrap I was driving I had to go cautiously in the dark, for you can find potholes on those dirt roads that an elephant could hide in. It took me to the hamlet they call Sobrestany, though, and from there I was able to plot my way out of the area without tripping over any junctions at which the police were likely to be waiting.

It took me almost an hour to reach the trunk road south, but when I did, it was quiet and I was able to pick up some speed. I followed it as far as Girona Airport, where I switched to the trunk road that goes to Vic.

Gerard's route had been well planned. It took me inland, then south, through Manresa and beyond, skirting Llieda. For some reason I felt safer once I knew I was out of Catalunya, and off the patch of the Mossos d'Esquadra. I drove on through the night, but it's a thousand kilometres from L'Escala to Granada and eventually there came a time when I couldn't go any further. Fuel was becoming an issue too. I'd topped up once already in a small town garage

221

but the petrol gauge wasn't the most accurate I'd ever seen.

I stopped in a parking area near a place called Vilastar and put my head down for a couple of hours. Once I judged that the tiny town would be properly awake, I found a *gasolinera*, filled up the tank, and then went exploring until I came across a small hostel, where I took a room. I almost dropped myself in it by speaking Catalan as I checked in, but remembered where I was at the last minute and switched to my most polished Castellano, explaining the odd time of my arrival by saying that my car had broken down further on up the road and it had taken me the best part of the night to get moving again. The owner bought that story without question, and showed me to a room with a comfortable bed and a nice en-suite shower room, for which I paid cash, in advance. I spent most of the day asleep, until early evening, when I judged it safe to chance a meal in the small restaurant. I had decided that I was going to travel during the hours of darkness, and so just after nine, I left my key on the counter and got back on the road.

I'd been worried that I might find the night humidity a problem the further south I went, but I hadn't reckoned for the fact that much of the route was high above sea level. As it happened, the Suzuki's heating system was well knackered, so keeping warm was my main difficulty. Eventually I decided to grin and bear it, letting the cold help me by keeping me focused. All the same, I was happy when the sun rose on that Sunday morning, and happier still when the road grew wider, almost to autopista standard, and the signs told me that I was almost in Granada.

I stopped for coffee and a croissant in a roadhouse, having first checked that there were no television cameras in evidence. The last thing I wanted was to have driven all that way only to be fingered by CCTV. As I ate, I dug out the address that Gerard had written down for me and found it on his street map. As he'd said, it was in the heart of an area called the Albacin, on the other side of a river from the Alhambra.

The city was bigger than I had expected, and the traffic much heavier. I was also surprised by its modernity; I'd been expecting it to be ancient, and heavily Moorish, but what I found as I entered were shopping centres, a science park and a conference centre, all very twenty-first century. Eventually, though, I found myself on something called the Grand Via de Colon . . . for an Italian, Columbus gets a lot of exposure in Spain . . . and as I reached its end, and turned into the Street of the Catholic Kings, I had my first real view of the Alhambra and of the way in which it dominates the city, perched on its great rock.

I followed Gerard's instructions to the letter, even though they took me along a crazy wee road running alongside the river, about a car and a half wide, where I had to take turns with tourist pedestrians for much of the way. Eventually it opened out on to something called the Paseo de los Tristes, 'the passageway of the sad'. It looked pretty cheerful to me, with bars and restaurants on my left as I drove along, serving tables on the other side of the street, all of them with an unobstructed view of the Alhambra.

I turned left at the end, then took another left at the top of a steep hill, then a right, then a left until I began to feel dizzy, and for the first time, lost. The road narrowed all the time, but I kept an eye out for the sign that marked the end of the journey, and finally, there it was, rising up ahead of me . . . Cuesta de los Cabras, Hill of the Goats, and rarely was a road better named.

It was a dead end, and Gerard's house was almost at the end; stone built and painted white, with a tiled roof. There was nothing to say that I couldn't park there, and so I did. I gave the red-hot bonnet of the Suzuki a pat of thanks as I climbed out and dug the key out of the bag.

The place was dark as I stepped inside. There was no entrance hall; I found myself in a big room; it was mercifully cool, for the shutters were closed. I gave myself time to let my eyes adjust, until I could see where everything was; heavy wooden table with four chairs to my left, with two doors beyond, two central heating radiators (Gerard had told me that it gets cold in Granada in the winter), two chairs to my right on either side of a fireplace, big plasma television in the corner . . . not that rustic then . . . and patio doors facing me, locked from the inside. I sniffed; for an unoccupied house the place smelled fresh. I supposed that he must employ a housekeeper, or perhaps his aunt was still alive and looked in on the place.

I went across to the twin doors, turned the key in the lock and opened them. The shutters were secured by small bolts top and bottom. I unfastened them, pushed them open, and stepped outside on to a tiled terrace . . . to find myself staring directly across at the full width of the Alhambra Palace, a huge structure that seemed to go on and on. It was the first time I'd been able to take a proper look at it. I gasped; I'd never seen anything quite like it.

Once I'd stopped gawping I looked around. A flight of steps led down to a garden area. I frowned as I saw it, and imagined Gerard, enraged, and beating the crap out of his brute of a father. I stepped back inside, to banish the vision as much as anything else, and explored the rest of the house. There was a kitchen off the living room, but it wasn't what I'd expected. The units and the lighting were modern, there was a gas combi boiler on the wall, the range cooker was as impressive as mine and a large American fridge freezer stood in a corner. I took a look inside. There were two unopened cartons of UHT milk in the fridge, and half a dozen tins of San Miguel, but nothing else. The freezer was well stocked though, with peas, broccoli, pizzas, fish, chicken, vacuum-sealed pork fillets, butter, and three round sliced loaves. I'd gone shopping in Carrefour with Gerard once and this was exactly the sort of stuff that he'd bought, the sort of food he wolfed down when we were out or when he ate at my place. He went away on leave once a year. 'On retreat,' he said, and I'd never asked him where, but it seemed that now I knew.

As I thought of him, I remembered my promise to call him when I arrived. I went back out on to the patio, switched on the mobile he'd given me, unlocked it, then called the lone number that was programmed into its memory. An overly friendly Spanish lady told me that the phone I was dialling was switched off, but invited me to leave a message. As she spoke I checked my watch. Five minutes past twelve, Sunday, idiot; he'd be in church.

'Hi,' I said, after the beep, 'it's me and I'm in your lovely house. When I think of the other place I could be right now, it makes me realise how lucky I am to have you looking after me. I'm tired, but I'm not going to sleep until you've called me back.'

I checked the charge on the phone; it was full. I put it in my pocket and went back inside, to resume my exploration. The second door of the living area led to a stairway and down to a lower floor, with two bedrooms, one of them en suite, with a door that led into the garden, and a second bathroom, with a full-sized bath and shower above. Like the kitchen, the bedroom furniture was contemporary. I got nosy and looked in the wardrobes. The one in the second bedroom was empty, but there were clothes hung in the other, jeans, a pretty respectable suit, a couple of shirts and two jackets, one winter weight; again, Gerard-style gear.

I didn't look anywhere else; I had a sudden feeling that I was invading his privacy. Instead I went into the bathroom . . . not his, the other one . . . relieved myself, and ran a bath. As it filled, I searched for towels and soap, and was first time lucky when I found them in the unit that housed the basin, white fluffy cotton and Dove cream, plus, unexpectedly, foam crystals. I was about to shut the door when my eye caught something else, a box, tucked away behind a couple of aerosols and a bottle of Nivea sun cream. I took it out; it had been opened, it bore a dealer's stamp on the end flap, 'Farmacia

Xaloc', and all but two of its original contents were gone. I blinked, hard, as if it would look different on second inspection. But it didn't. 'Oh no,' I moaned, out loud. What the hell would a priest be doing with Tampax? Personally, nothing, but . . .

Thirty-four

As I lay soaking, I made myself think logically. I knew that there was, or had been an aunt. Aunts beget cousins. Gerard had a cousin, a female cousin around his own age or younger who has a key for the family home and who uses it occasionally, but who's been told to keep clear for now. That was it. And if it wasn't? If his annual retreat involved him getting his leg over a nice Andalusian girl, what business is it of yours, Primavera Blackstone, you who have made it very clear to him that your interest is in his companionship, and not in his body? None at all. If he can square it with God, he can shag who he likes, for you are definitely not interested in such transactions any more.

When the mobile rang I had managed to put my find in perspective. I'd fixed on the cousin theory as the likeliest. But still, it's unsettling to suspect that your idol's feet might be even a wee bit crumbly. 'You made it,' he said. 'Are you comfortable?'

'Couldn't be more so, although you might be upset if you could see me.'

'Why?' He sounded puzzled.

'Because I'm naked, lolling in your guest bath, blowing bubbles all around the room.'

'In that case the bubbles will preserve your modesty.'

'That's why I'm blowing them away. Does this phone shoot video? If it does I might send you some footage.'

'Primavera, please. Have you been drinking?'

'No. I'm just feeling crazy, that's all.'

'Understandable.'

'Was Tom at church?' I asked him, to break my mood.

'Yes, he was. He was very good, as usual. Mac came to see him at work; he said he was very impressed.'

'Him in a Catholic church? He'll have to report that to his minister when he gets home. The roof didn't fall in, did it?'

He laughed; at once I felt better, and sorry for winding him up. No, those tampons couldn't have had anything to do with him. 'It's stood solid for a few hundred years,' he said. 'I think it will take more than one heretic to bring it down.'

'How's my boy?' I whispered.

'He's okay. Mac told him that something had happened, and that you had to go away for a few days. But there are whispers around town, and I'd rather he didn't hear them. Mac and I have spoken about this and since there's so little time left in the term, we wonder whether it might be better keeping him off school.'

'That's vetoed,' I told him firmly. 'If you do that you'll have to confiscate his mobile too, for his pals are always sending him texts. I'm innocent; if he goes into seclusion it'll make me look guilty. I know his teachers; they'll look out for him. And I know his friends too; they're good kids.'

'Very well, if you say so.'

'You say there's talk in town. Does that mean they've released my mug shot?'

'No, and this is interesting. They haven't released your name either. All they're saying is that they have a suspect and that a hunt is under way.'

'Uh? Why would they want to keep my identity confidential?'

'You can thank your connections to famous people, or so Alex tells me. Public prosecutor's orders, he says. He's terrified that if word gets out that Dawn Phillips's sister, Miles Grayson's sister-in-law, Oz Blackstone's former wife is a murder suspect, and that the police have let her get away, the story will become global, and his job will be on the line.'

My sister, I thought. We usually speak online at weekends. 'Does Dawn know?'

'Maybe,' he replied. 'That will depend on your father. Mac felt that he was honour bound to advise him of what had happened. It's for him to decide whether to tell her.'

That would be a tricky one for Dad, I reckoned. Our Kid can be a bit of a flake. The last thing I wanted was her air-dropping into St Martí in a flood of celebrity.

'We've got to get this sorted, Gerard,' I exclaimed. 'I'd rather be here than banged up, don't get me wrong, but I'm feeling isolated, exposed, and it's got nothing to do with having no clothes on.'

'Don't feel that way. I told you, you're being watched over.'

'That's nice of God,' I retorted, 'but I'd rather He was looking over Hector Gomez's shoulder and pointing him in the direction of who really did those murders.' He laughed and started to say something else, but I talked right over him. 'Have there been any other developments that you know of, any results from the Dolores autopsy?'

'Alex told me that they've established that she was killed early on Friday morning. They found fibres from the shawl that strangled her . . .'

'My shawl,' I interposed.

'. . . in her mouth, and believe that it was used to gag her while she was held captive. They say she'd have been pretty weak by the time she died; she'd been starved for a week.' He hesitated, in the manner of someone who has nothing good to tell. 'They found something else too, in the storeroom: a bag containing her make-up pouch, a wine glass, with her fingerprints on it, and traces of red wine.'

'Eh?' There are times when my brain works pretty fast; instantly I knew where this was going, and a bizarre picture formed in my mind. 'That's clever,' I exclaimed, 'really fucking clever. The next thing you're going to tell me is that they've identified the wine and it's Faustino One.'

'How did you guess that?'

'Because that's their case, that's the link that would tie me to both victims, and give me a motive for killing Dolores. Sex, Gerard, sex; you're never too old. This is what the police and the prosecutor will say. Are you ready for it?'

'Let me hear it.'

'Okay, it reads like this. José-Luis and Dolores were having it off on the quiet; when he got back from the Miryam, he had a visit from her. Gomez will say that Planas had just given her one and zipped up, and she'd gone into the house to, freshen up, let's say, when I arrived, with the intention of saving myself twelve thousand euro. I'd just clobbered him with the chair when she came out of the house, taking me by surprise, for I didn't know she was there. I subdued her, rigged the scene to make it look like an accident, took the glass to eliminate any trace of her having been there, and took her away in her car. I hid her at my place, gagged and bound till I figured out what to do with her, then dumped and burned her motor. When I heard at the old man's wake that the car had been found, I decided that the time had come to kill her, and, when I had a chance, to put her body somewhere it would never be found, maybe under the flagstone in the storeroom itself, in what I reckon was once a limepit. But I got unlucky, they'll say; first I left a print on the chair, and second, Charlie smelled her, once she was dead, and raised the alarm. My love,' I used the term without thinking, 'even you would convict me on the basis of that evidence.'

He was silent for a while. 'No,' he replied, eventually, 'I wouldn't . . . faith overcomes all doubts.' I felt a renewed burst of guilt at my suspicion over those feminine items. 'I understand your scenario, though, and you're right, that's how Gomez, and even Alex will see it.'

'So what can I do?'

'Stay where you are, be patient, and wait. Nobody is that clever; there's something wrong with the picture and in time we'll see it.'

'Okay,' I agreed. 'Any other orders, sir?'

'Yes. Get out of that bath; it must be cold by now . . . plus, the bubbles must have disappeared and it's starting to disturb me.'

Thirty-five

I chose the second bedroom. It wouldn't have felt right to have slept in Gerard's bed. The divan was made up, with a fitted sheet and another, loose, on top, all that was needed there in the summer. Too much, in fact, for I found when I woke at half past six, after about five hours' sleep, that I'd kicked it off.

I dressed, then tidied up, took the few clothes I had left from my haversack and put them away in a small chest of drawers beside the door. When I was done I took the stuff I had worn on the journey up to the kitchen and put the lot into a washer-dryer that was plumbed in near the sink, with a dishwasher on the other side. I looked in the cupboard between them and found detergent and liquid capsules. There was no manual, but the controls were self-explanatory, the kind that even a man would find easy to work out.

I programmed the machine, and then turned my attention to the fact that I was starving. I could have raided the freezer, but I felt that I'd run up a big enough tab with my benefactor, so I decided to be brave and go out. There was another consideration . . . I couldn't find any booze in the place apart from the San Miguel, and I don't like San Miguel.

I decided to head down to the Paseo de los Tristes; it had looked friendly, the sort of place where the police wouldn't need to hang around, so I was sure I could chance it. I had no problem finding it, although I'd reached Goats' Hill by a circuitous route. All I had to do was head for the Alhambra, and I'd be bound to get there.

The streets in the Albacin are narrow, many of them too narrow for cars, but it's hardly a maze. Even so, I missed my way, and came out at the foot of a flight of steps, in the middle of the narrow street where I'd played tig with pedestrians, beside a building with a sign that announced an old Arab thermal bathhouse . . . a thousand years old, to be approximate. I went inside, on impulse. I'd been to Andalusia before, but not exactly as a tourist, so I'd had few Moorish experiences. The baths aren't operational any more . . . and anyway, I'd just had one . . . but the building looked as if it was seeing its second millennium. There were no windows, just star-shaped holes in the roof and walls that provided both light and ventilation. In Scotland, a place like that would be turned into a pub in the wink of an eye.

I didn't stay long but joined the crowd outside as it weaved its way in the direction that I wanted to go. When I got there, I was lucky; the first two groups of tables I passed were fully occupied, but I managed to find one opposite the third café. It had a French name, but an Italian menu . . . that's Spain for you. I went for cured ham and bread as a starter, then tagliatelle with a pesto sauce, plus a bottle of Chianti, and some still water. From my table I could see that the kitchen was small, so I anticipated that I might have a wait before the food arrived, but the wine came by return, so I wasn't bothered.

As a bonus, I was sitting in the shadow of the Alhambra . . . not literally; the sun was heading west by that time . . . being entertained by three buskers with guitars and a very nice way with the works of Lennon and McCartney and Eric Clapton. I felt . . . looking back, it's hard to explain what I felt, but there I was, accused of murder, separated from everyone I loved, yet I was exhilarated, and in that moment, utterly perversely, I was able to be completely honest with myself and to face the truth about myself; that although I had chosen the ideal environment in which to raise my son, I couldn't just settle for that.

There were things I was missing; I had known excitement in the past, and I had thrived on it, but since Oz's death I had run away from anything that smelled of personal fulfilment, other than Tom. I'd become diminished, and I knew of someone who would not have approved of that at all. 'Okay,' I whispered to him. 'I'll find myself again.' And as a very first step in that process, I knew that I was going to break a promise. But what the hell; it was one that I'd been finding it hard to keep anyway.

Thirty-six

The food when it came was pretty good; the buskers were . . . funny thing, but the more Chianti I drank, the better they got. When one of them came round the tables flogging their CD I bought it before I'd even asked the price. When I found that it was only ten euro, I bought three, the extras intended for Gerard and Mac.

It was dark when I left the pavement café. During the evening a couple of guys had tried to hit on me; it was good for morale, and happily neither of them had taken it badly when I'd made it clear they were wasting their time. I found Goats' Hill more easily than I'd found the Paseo earlier; it turned out that it was more or less in a straight line up a passage that began directly across the road from where I'd been sitting.

The streets of the Albacin are poorly illuminated, but there was enough light in the moon to show me the way to my temporary home. When I got in, I watched a little telly . . . Gerard had CNN in English as well as Spanish, and BBC World Service, but that's crap so I didn't stay on it for long . . .

until I decided that taking a shower then going back to sleep was a good idea, and did both.

I had left the bedroom shutter open, just a crack, but it was enough to wake me when the sun rose high enough to hit it. I felt refreshed, and hungry again, so I slipped on a knee-length T-shirt . . . nightshirt, really . . . and trotted upstairs. I dug out a couple of slices of bread from one of the loaves in the freezer . . . I had transferred the butter to the fridge the night before . . . stuck them in the toaster and pressed the lever down. Rather than wait for it to pop, I filled the electric kettle, from a five-litre flagon of drinking water that I'd found beside the detergent, and set it to work.

It was just coming to the boil, and I had just finished buttering the toast, when I heard a loud thump on the front door. My heart vaulted into my mouth; a slice of breakfast stopped halfway there. I froze, not knowing what to do, and so in effect doing nothing. Which was not what the people at the door wanted. Another bang, and a shout. 'Open. Police!'

'Oh my God,' I said, aloud, reverting to my native language in my moment of crisis. 'How the fuck . . .' What options were open to me? Go back downstairs and get away through the garden? But was there an exit that way? I didn't know. Try and wait them out? They didn't sound like the types who'd go away before they battered the door down. Open the door and take what was coming?

The way I saw it I didn't have a choice. I walked through to the living room, shouting, 'I'm coming, be patient,' in Spanish, then throwing the door open. Two officers stood there, in

uniform, big guys, looking belligerent, guns on their hips . . .
on their hips but not in their hands, I registered. 'Yes?' I barked
at them, deciding that it was better to attack than flutter my
eyelashes.

They didn't take kindly to that; some cops don't. One put
his hand on the butt of his pistol; the other one snapped, 'That
your car outside? That ancient little blue thing?'

'Not exactly,' I replied.

'What the hell does that mean?' the pig . . . that is not meant
to be the insulting noun often applied to police officers; this
guy was a male chauvinist, impure and very simple . . .
sneered.

As he spoke, I thought I heard a sound behind me, the
sound of a door opening.

'It means it's mine,' said a deep, familiar voice. 'So tell me
what your fucking problem is and leave my girlfriend alone.'

He walked past me, dressed in jeans and a khaki shirt that
I'd never seen before, his wide shoulders filling the narrow
doorway as he squared up to the two cops. They backed off
straight away. Able to look at them more calmly, I saw that they
were from the city force, and not of the considerably more
authoritative Guardia Civil. 'You shouldn't be parked there,'
the non-pig explained.

'It's my house. Am I blocking anyone's way?' He stepped out
into the street, forcing them to move away from the door.

'No, but . . .'

'No, but nothing; I've been parking there for years. You ask
Jorge Lavorante; he'll tell you that.'

Both cops seemed to flinch at the name. 'One of your tyres is nearly bald,' Porky chipped in, as if he was determined to get out of there with some sort of a result.

'Thanks for pointing it out. I'll replace it today.' He kept moving, ushering them towards the Suzuki. 'Let me show you the papers and insurance documents for the car; they're in the glove box, and they're all valid.'

'We'll take your word for it,' said the kosher cop.

'Thanks. Now if there's nothing else you want to bother us about, my breakfast has a greater call on me than you guys.'

Piggy gave him a look, but not for long; he followed his mate to the patrol vehicle and they reversed it out of there.

He turned and came back towards me. I was standing just inside the doorway, stunned, speechless. I'd spoken to him less than a day before, and he'd said nothing about flying down to L'Escala. 'Sorry for the surprise,' he said, smiling. He needed a shave. I'd never seen his full eight o'clock shadow before; it looked good on him. 'I got in very late. I guessed you'd be asleep, so I was very careful not to wake you when I came downstairs.'

As I looked at him, I remembered my thoughts in the Paseo de los Tristes, and the resolutions I'd made. 'Maybe I wouldn't have minded if you had,' I murmured.

His eyes widened as he looked at me. I'd taken him aback.

'Gerard,' I began, 'I can't bottle things up any longer; and I sense that you can't either. We have to talk, you and I.'

And then he laughed; he put his head back and roared with laughter. I felt the heat rush to my face.

'He didn't tell you,' he chuckled. 'The innocent, unworldly idiot didn't tell you.'

'I'm sorry,' I exclaimed, truly bewildered. 'Who didn't tell me what? Gerard, for . . .'

'I'm not Gerard,' he said. 'I'm Santiago, Santi, his brother. His twin brother.'

It's funny, but looking back, as soon as he said it, I knew; I saw all the little differences, the hair cut slightly shorter, the signet ring on his right hand, the Breitling watch on his left wrist, not the Tissot that was all Gerard would allow me to buy him the Christmas before, when I'd suggested a Tag Heuer or a Mont Blanc, the small, healing scar on his forehead, and most of all, the difference in the way he looked at me.

'You're right,' I told him, softly. 'He didn't tell me, not that you're identical. But now I think of it, he did warn me that you'd be here. He said we were not alone, and that I was being looked after. Gerard being what he is, I assumed that he was talking about God.'

'My brother might be a priest, but he's more practical than that. He's hands on when he has to be,' he smiled again, 'although not in the way that's often meant.'

'So this is actually your house?' I ventured.

'No, it's not; it's Gerard's. He's half an hour older than me, and so when our mother died he inherited, naturally, under Spanish law. He offered me half . . . in fact he offered me it all . . . but if I'd accepted he'd have had nothing. Anyway, I didn't need it. I'm an airline pilot; I'm rolling in money. I have an apartment in Madrid.'

'But this house has been modernised. Gerard can't have done that.'

'No, I did it. I use the place a lot; I come here on holiday, and if I have a stopover in Malaga. He hasn't been here for years; he has no idea what I've done to it.' He smiled. 'The car is mine though. I left it with him the last time I saw him, in L'Escala.'

'You've been to L'Escala?'

'Only twice. And we didn't go out; not far, anyway. It would have confused the parishioners, we decided.'

'Are you married?'

He blinked, not sure why I'd asked. 'No; I have a girlfriend in Madrid, but she's cabin crew with another airline, so our meetings are unpredictable.'

'Sorry to be so inquisitive. It's just . . .' I explained what I'd found in the bathroom.

'When I come here on stopover,' he said, 'I usually bring my co-pilot. One of them's a woman.' Then the implications hit him, and he laughed. 'But you didn't know about me. So you thought . . . Gerard? No, never.' He stopped and his eyebrows rose. 'Unless you and he . . .'

'Gerard?' I replied to the unfinished question. 'And me? No, never.' I almost added, 'More's the pity,' but I didn't feel that I knew Santi well enough.

Thirty-seven

I called Gerard on the mobile as soon as I went back downstairs. Breakfast was abandoned when I realised that I was talking with a stranger while clad in a long T-shirt and nothing else.

I told him of my heart-stopping visit from Pinky and Porky, and of my nick of time rescue by his doppelgänger brother. 'You should have warned me, Gerard,' I complained. 'Have you any idea of the way I felt when he walked into that room and took on those two cops? I honestly believed it was you, that you'd climbed on a plane and come down to . . .' I paused. 'Even when he said that he'd got in late and had been careful not to wake me,' I continued, 'I thought he was you.'

'I imagine that could have been embarrassing.' He sounded apologetic.

'Could have been?' I squawked. 'Could have been? Bloody well was.'

'You didn't do anything . . . inappropriate, did you?'

'Certainly not!'

I thought I heard a sigh of relief. 'I'm sorry,' he said. 'I was going to tell you all about Santi, before you left from Shirley's, but you talked across me and I was anxious for you to be on your way, so the chance never came up again.'

'Did you know he was coming here?'

'I sent him an email from a café in Figueras, telling him that I had a friend who was in trouble and that I was sending her down to Granada for a while. I asked him to keep an eye on you, if he could, even if it was only from a distance like me. Last night, after we'd spoken, I had a reply from him saying that he'd adjusted his schedule and was taking some time off. I didn't expect him to arrive so soon, though.'

'I'm glad that he did. I don't know how I'd have handled those two cops if he hadn't walked in and taken over.' I recalled a detail. 'Who's Jorge Lavorante, by the way? Santi mentioned the name to them and it seemed to impress them.'

'It would have; he's a tough guy. Jorge's a captain in the municipal police. We were at school with him.'

'I bet you were tough guys too, you and Santi. They were backing off him even before he mentioned Lavorante. And you: you've got a temper on you; you can't deny it.'

'We could handle ourselves,' Gerard admitted. 'With the old man we had we'd no choice but to grow up tough.' His voice was sad.

'Never mind,' I said, 'you grew up nice with it as well.'

'That was down to our mother.' He stopped, abruptly. 'I have to go. If I have the chance I'll speak to Alex later today, to see if there have been any developments. I'll try to call you this evening.'

'Can you look in on Tom?'

'Of course. I treat the boy like my own son, Primavera; you must realise that, surely.'

It had occurred to me, but it was nice to hear him say so.

I had another shower, and dressed properly for the day, before going upstairs to rejoin Santi. He was still in the kitchen, but he'd clearly been out shopping, for he was working on a mushroom omelette in a big frying pan, and a fresh baguette lay on the counter. There was coffee on the hob too, in one of those old-fashioned percolators that beats a filter every time, and fruit in a bowl on the kitchen table.

I offered to help, but there was nothing for me to do, other than set the table for two, and watch him as he flipped the omelette over and finished it off.

'You make a damn good breakfast,' I told him, as we ate.

'I enjoy cooking,' he replied. 'Given my line of work, most of my waking up is done in hotels. I could list the breakfast menus in most of the Sheratons, Marriotts and Hiltons in North America and the Far East. Appetising they may be, but it's volume food and you can have too much of it. There are few things I like more than working in my own kitchen . . . or in this case my brother's . . . after sleeping in my own bed.'

'I can understand that,' I conceded. 'I've been a nomad for quite a bit of my life, and I've eaten a few institutional breakfasts too.'

'What sort of institution?'

'The kind where they lock you in at night.'

He whistled. 'Is that the sort of trouble you're in now?'

'Potentially, but I didn't do it.'

'I know. Gerard told me that you've been wrongly accused of something. But that was all; he made a point of not telling me more than that.'

I smiled at that one. 'On the evidence, the accusation's justified. But the evidence has been fixed, planted, fabricated. Gerard's sent me down here to hide out, while he does his best to get to the bottom of it.'

'So you have God on your side,' he murmured. 'What's your name?' he asked suddenly, throwing me off balance in the process. 'My brother has never been one for filling in every small detail.'

'Primavera Blackstone,' I replied. 'My house is next door, literally, to Gerard's church.'

'That big old house?'

'You've seen it?'

'Four years ago, just after Gerard was posted there, the first time I went to visit him; he drove me around, but we never got out of the car. Very imposing. You live there on your own?'

'With my son.'

'No . . . ?'

'His father is dead. It's Mrs Blackstone, by the way; that's the name I choose to go by. Tom uses the Spanish form at school, adding on the mother's surname, so on the class roll he's Tom Blackstone Phillips.'

I caught his frown, and knew what was coming. 'That's an unusual name,' he commented. 'I go to the movies a lot, between flights . . .' He paused.

I nodded. 'It was him,' I said, and filled him in on my connections with the rich and famous, alive and dead. I couldn't tell whether he was impressed or not. It barely registered with Gerard when I told him.

I moved on, to fill the silence as much as anything else. 'One of the few things your brother told me about you is that when he went into the church, you went into the air force.'

'Yes. Our upbringing wasn't . . . what should I say . . . wasn't ideal. We both had to get out; otherwise we might have wound up like our father, heavy-handed bullies. I wanted Gerard to join the military like me, full-time, but his experiences sent him in another direction.'

'Were you surprised by his choice?'

'Not in the circumstances.'

'What circumstances? The thing with your father?' He nodded. 'I thought that happened after he'd gone to the seminary, that he came home and found him beating your mother.'

Santi sighed. 'So that's the official version, is it? That's how he explains it. For a priest, my brother can be indelicate with the truth, even if it's for the best of motives.'

'That's something I've learned for myself, Santi, but what do you mean by it?'

He picked up the percolator and refilled his cup; the coffee must have been almost cold by then, but he didn't seem to notice as he sipped it. 'For all his many faults, our father never laid a hand on our mother in his life; on us, yes, and he abused her verbally, all the time, but she had brothers, and that thought may have restrained him. He was an awful man, though, hateful. We put up with it at home, and I suppose we took it out on others outside, for nobody messed with us, not even Jorge Lavorante. But our mother's influence kept us more or less straight. She made sure we went to church; there was a good old parish priest, and he taught us proper values. Gerard, in particular, came under his influence.'

He put his cup down, picked up an apple from the fruit bowl, and bit a chunk out of it. 'When I was nineteen, I applied to join the air force as a regular, rather than simply do national service. Gerard didn't know what to do as a career, so he did his nine months in the marines, then came home to decide his future. While he was away . . . not far, only in Cartagena . . . he met a girl. Her name was Irena, nice kid, very churchy, like he was. When he came back, they got engaged, and she moved to Granada, to live with an uncle and aunt, down in the modern city, near Federico Garcia Lorca's house. Gerard got a couple of jobs, as a labourer during the day and as a bar bouncer in the evening.'

'A bouncer?' I exclaimed.

'Gerard never had to bounce anyone. He had a gift for turning away trouble. Anyway, he had a night off once, and he and Irena were going out. He was to go home from work to change, she was to meet him, and they were heading off from there. Unfortunately . . . Irena arrived early. Our father was there. Mother was visiting our aunt, her sister. The old man was drunk. To cut to the chase, he raped her; he dragged her downstairs and raped her. Gerard walked in and heard her screaming. He threw the old man out into the back yard and he beat the living shit out of him. He'd have killed him too, for sure, but for a piece of luck that he believes to this day was divine. I was given a forty-eight-hour pass, for some spurious achievement or other. I arrived just in time to haul him off, something that only I could have done, I reckon. I dragged him inside, leaving an unconscious heap behind us. We took care of Irena, got her covered up, and that helped to distract Gerard. It didn't calm her, though. She was bleeding and she was hysterical. He carried her upstairs and I called an ambulance. Gerard said that he was going for Jorge Lavorante. Knowing Jorge, that could have been to have the old man arrested or to finish him off, but neither came about, for Irena screamed, "No police, no police." She wouldn't make a complaint, not then, or afterwards, in hospital when they'd sedated her and stitched her up. I wouldn't let Gerard go back to the garden. I went down myself, with no clear idea of what I'd do when I got there. But I had no decision to make, for the old bastard was gone. He never came back.'

'What about your mother?'

'We told her nothing about what had happened. After a while she assumed that he had simply left her, and she was happy.'

'And what about Irena, and Gerard?'

'She went back to Cartagena. He talked about going to bring her back, but he never did. Instead he went back to church, to our old friend the priest, and a few months later went to the seminary. A little while after that, I tried to trace

Irena. When I did, I found that she'd committed suicide, a couple of years after the rape.'

'Does Gerard know?'

'Yes.' He shuddered, as if to shake off the horror, then stood up. I felt pretty numb myself. I could understand why Gerard had no desire to go home.

'Come on,' he said, briskly. 'That's enough family history for a while. What would you like to do?'

I looked at him; blankly, I suspect. 'Do?' I repeated.

'Yes, do. You're in Granada; far away from your trouble. You don't need to hide away here. Let me show you around.'

And that's what he did. He stilled all my nerves and protestations with his calmness, and led me out into the day, my personal tour guide. We walked back down to the Paseo, then back along the riverside road until it opened out into the Plaza Nuevo, through which I had driven around twenty-four hours earlier. It was Monday, and so it was noticeably quieter, as we strolled down towards a blue booth on the shady side of the street. There were a few people before us in the queue, but it cleared fairly quickly. Santi had a quick conversation with the attendant and came away with two white tickets. 'These are the bono turistica,' he told me, 'the best value in Granada. They'll let us into all the monuments, including the Alhambra. We'll go there this afternoon, but they also get us a ride on the tour bus, so let's find it.'

The stop turned out to be next to the cathedral, beside some steps where gypsy women were selling sprigs of lucky white heather and telling fortunes with it. Normally I don't go for such stuff, but that day of all days, I couldn't resist. It's probably the most expensive heather I ever bought, but the show made it worth it. The woman seized my hand and stared at the palm, which had half the number of lines, I reckon, that there were on her brown forehead, knitted with concentration as it was.

'I see happiness and sadness,' she announced, 'both in the past and yet to come. I see fine children …' *Hold on*, I thought, *I'm forty-two; the plural's unlikely now.* '… and grandchildren to come.'

'How about the immediate future?' I asked her.

She peered once more, and a funny thing happened; she squeezed her eyes shut and seemed to go into a trance. 'I see death,' she moaned, 'but not yours. It is the father who dies.' My blood ran cold. 'I see difficult times, but you come through them. I see evil, I see a fall, I see tears, I see separation. The father,' she repeated, 'the father. He dies.'

And then she fainted; she folded up and fell to the ground. I had to yank my hand free to avoid being pulled over. Two other Roma women came across and bent over her; one was grinning. *An act*, I thought. *Sucker*.

'That looked pretty dramatic,' said Santi, as I rejoined him at the bus stop.

'All bullshit,' I told him.

'Don't you mean cowshit, in this case?'

'I suppose. Here, you can have this.' I handed him the sprig of heather; he pushed its stalk through an unused buttonhole in his shirt, just as the open-topped tour bus pulled up at the stop.

We took seats upstairs, right at the front; there were audio guides available, but with Santi as a commentator, I didn't need one. He began as soon as we pulled away, explaining where we were, place by place. The tour began by taking us out of the city and up towards the Alhambra. It was a clear day, and so we had a fine view of the Sierra Nevada, the mountain range that's one of the great surprises of southern Spain. Think Spain, think Pyrenees; that's how it is for most people, but the Snowy Mountains are more dominant, and those who do such things tell me that the skiing and snow-boarding are more reliable there than in the north. Santi was a skier, as it turned out; he had taken it up once he could afford it, but in his youth and Gerard's it had been a luxury scorned by their father.

He knew just about everything there was to know about the city and its history, ancient and modern, from the expulsion of the Moors . . . 'In case you haven't noticed,' he joked as the bus passed a gaggle of young mothers, all with heads covered, 'they've found their way back' . . . and the death of the poet Lorca during the Spanish Civil War. 'Granada Airport is named after him,' he told me. 'One thing I've noticed in my job is the number of airports named after people who've been shot. Think about it; apart from him, there's JFK, La Guardia, also in New York, John Lennon in Liverpool, Abraham Lincoln in Illinois, Ronald Reagan in Washington . . . although he survived . . . and Charles de Gaulle.'

'De Gaulle wasn't assassinated,' I pointed out.

'Only because of incredible luck. So many people tried to shoot him, he deserves to be on the list.'

254

I laughed. In truth I was grateful for the distraction, because for all that I was interested in what he was telling me, my mind kept drifting back to the gypsy woman and what she had said. I've always convinced myself that fortune telling, be it centred on palmistry, tea leaves, tarot cards or anything else, is based on probability, and on intelligent guesswork. But her insistent use of the word 'father' had lodged itself in my brain. Did she mean my dad? That was possible; most of us outlive our fathers and the way she had put it, that's where she was most likely to have been taking me. But had she meant Tom's father? I wear a wedding ring, so it was a fair chance that I was a mother. I was alone, for she hadn't noticed Santi, I was sure. Yes, another good guess. But . . . the thought that wouldn't go away, however hard I pushed it, what if there was something in the whole claptrap nonsense? What if she'd meant Father Gerard?

The bus tour ended where it had begun, but we stayed on board until it arrived at the Alhambra for the second time. Santi explained that the greatest benefit of the bono turistica lies in the fact that it includes an advance booking time for the Alhambra, or specifically, for entry to the Nazrene Palaces, the heart of the place, and it lets you bypass the regular ticket queue, which can be enormous.

By the time we got to the main concourse, breakfast had worn off; we grabbed sandwiches and beer before Santi led me into the Alcazabar, the castellated fort that was the earliest construction on the great rock.

There's a lot I could tell you about the Alhambra, but I'll restrict myself to three things: one, although the place as a whole is vast, the Nazrene Palaces are smaller than I'd expected; two, there is a very fine art collection in the Carlos Five palace; and three, it has the finest public toilets in all of Spain. After three hours we'd visited the lot, and were ready to leave. I'd have taken the bus, but Santi promised me that it would have been a nightmare, so we settled for a taxi, back to Goats' Hill, or as close to it as the driver could take us.

'Put your feet up for a while,' said Santi, as we stepped back indoors. 'I'm going to see what's in my mailbox.'

'Do you have a computer here?' I asked.

He shook his head. 'No. I have an iPhone; for my job, it's best.'

He left to get on with it, and I went outside, on to the patio. The sun was still high, so I unrolled the awning that was fixed above the doors. As I settled myself into a chair, I couldn't help wondering what state my email must have reached, and from that to those people who were likely to have sent me messages. As I scrolled down my mental contacts list, I paused at a name, and found myself wondering why I hadn't thought of him before.

As I did, it suddenly occurred to me that the old Primavera wouldn't be hiding out waiting for her luck to take a turn for the better; the old Primavera would be doing all she could to make that happen. Fond as I was of Gerard . . . oh hell, much as I loved him . . . I'd allowed him to take me so far under his wing that I hadn't bothered to look out. First chance I had, I promised myself, that was going to change.

Thirty-eight

That was for later, though; I didn't want to ask Santi if I could use his tricky wee phone, and I didn't want to try to access the internet on mine, because it was my point of contact with home, and I didn't want to risk running out of credit. So I kicked off my shoes, wiggled my toes in the sunshine, and sat for a couple of hours, trying to be patient.

When Santi reappeared, he had changed into a white shirt and what appeared to be the trousers of the suit I had seen in the wardrobe. 'I've booked us a table for dinner,' he said.

Immediately, I thought of my wardrobe, the ill-considered selection of garments that I had rammed into my haversack. 'Where?' I asked, cautiously. 'Nowhere too posh, I hope.'

'I believe it calls itself avant garde. That embraces all things.'

I had a skirt, hanging in the bedroom, a shirt that I still hadn't worn, and a belt, but . . . 'Please tell me you have an iron,' I ventured.

'Of course,' he laughed. 'I'm what they call a new man.'

I found it, and an ironing board, in a cupboard off the kitchen. An hour and a half later, after a shower, and a little pampering with the scraps of make-up I had brought with me, I was ready. I had found some shampoo in the bathroom cabinet, and a hair dryer. Maybe they belonged to the co-pilot too: I didn't care; the shampoo was L'Oreal Professional (I'm worth it) and the dryer worked. While I was putting the finishing touches to my still unfamiliar chestnut hair, I took a good look at my roots. They weren't too bad, but another treatment was going to be needed in the next couple of days.

Our bono passes entitled us to a few rides on public buses, as well as to the tourist trip. Santi said that we'd be quicker taking one of those into town than waiting for a taxi in the Albacin, and so we did just that. It took quite a while, but eventually we got off at a big junction, outside a very posh ice-cream shop. We walked down a busy shopping thoroughfare called Calle Recogidas, the street of the harvests, but not very far before Santi announced, 'We're here.'

Our destination turned out to be a five-star hotel called Palacio de los Patos, that's Ducks' Palace to you, although the first things I saw as we approached the entrance were two white marble swans, in something that looked like a long basin. I guessed that whoever had done the décor had decided that *patos* were too downmarket for five stars and had gone for *cisnes* instead. We passed them by, Santi leading the way, turned a corner and trotted down a few steps to arrive at a restaurant called Senzone. We were fairly early by Spanish standards, but there were a few diners already at their tables; I glanced at the women and felt decidedly underdressed.

The maître d' was actually a maîtress, a very efficient lady who greeted Santi as 'Captain Hernanz' and showed us to a table beside a small green pool with twin fountains. She gave us each menus and handed Santi the wine list, but he asked her for a bottle of Segura Viudas Lamit Brut Rosado. All I knew about that was that it was going to be cava, and pink, but when it arrived and I tasted it, I was seriously impressed. I made a mental note to check whether Ben Simmers stocked it, and if not, to ask him to find me a case.

'So you're a captain,' I said, as we studied the menu.

'That's my title.'

'How long have you been flying commercially?'

'For ten years now. I qualified as a military pilot when I was twenty-one. I flew Hornet fighters, although only ever in training exercises, I'm happy to say. When I was twenty-six, they made me what you would call a squadron leader, but I was transferred to transport planes, mostly great turbo-prop brutes like the Hercules and C 295, but also the Boeing 707; we had three of those in my time. They were used for transport and aerial refuelling.'

'That must have been exciting.'

'Nah, it was boring; fighters are where you want to be. I tried to get back there, but there were no openings at my rank, so after three years, I resigned my commission, and found a job as a commercial pilot. Fact is, I was lucky; some airlines have a certain resistance to military pilots . . . they see them as risk-takers . . . but it was my experience of flying those Boeing 707s that got me in. I was a co-pilot for a couple of years, then I made the jump into the top seat.'

'What do you fly?'

'The Airbus 340, on long-haul routes; my last trip was to Los Angeles.'

'My sister lives there.'

'I know; I'll be flying her, and her family in September, LAX to Barajas; first class, naturally. When they do our schedule, sometimes they give us a heads up on VIPs booked on our flights.'

I shuddered. 'They're coming to visit Tom and me. I hope I'll be around to entertain them.'

'Is there a chance that you won't?' He paused. 'I'm not prying; I don't want to know any more than you've told me already. Indeed, let's forget that you even told me that much. I can't know any details for my own security. You're a friend of my brother the priest, that's all. He's insistent that I should always be able to deny knowledge of your situation.'

'Understood. But to answer your question, there's no chance. I'm going to sort this thing out, and get back home as soon as I can.'

A waiter arrived at that moment, putting an end to the discussion. We made our choices from the nouvelle menu, and Santi chose a bottle of Pesquera Reserva from the list, to go with the steak that we had chosen as our main course.

As we ate, he told me of his work, and of the places he'd seen. Some of them I've visited myself, and others are still on my 'One day' list, including India, but it'll be a while before I can get round to that. He asked me about my parents; he seemed fascinated by the sort of people who could have produced Dawn and me. I told him that Mum was no longer with us, and hadn't been for five years, but that Dad was soldiering on, filling his days by carving ever more elaborate chess sets, selling the originals for a small fortune and, more recently, giving reproduction rights to specific models to one of Britain's biggest retail chains. 'If anyone else called him eccentric,' I said, 'I'd be on them like a rockfall . . . but the truth is, he is. How about your father?' I asked him, just a little hesitantly. 'You told me Gerard inherited the house when your mother died. Does that mean that he's dead too?'

'No, it doesn't, for the house was always my mother's, so he had no claim on it.' He frowned. 'He is, though, at least I believe he is. About twelve years ago, when I was still in the military, I decided that it would be best if I knew where he was, if only to make sure that he could never come back to give my mother a hard time. So I asked Jorge Lavorante to try to trace him. It wasn't difficult; he'd got into trouble in Cadiz, got into a brawl and wound up in court. Jorge checked and found that he was still there.'

'So you know he died there?'

'No, not for sure. As I said, I believe,' he leaned on the word, 'he died there, that's all.'

'Why?'

'Irena wouldn't make a complaint against him, yet in the end he was responsible for her death, and for ruining my brother's life. That sat badly with me, so . . .' He frowned into his wine glass, then turned to look me in the eye. 'There was nothing the police could do about him, so I took other measures. Irena's uncle, the one she lived with when she came from Cartagena to be with Gerard . . . let's just say he was a lot less legal than he should have been. I went to see him and I gave him the old man's address. "Thank you very much," he said. "I appreciate that." Although I never made any further inquiries, I'm not in any doubt about the outcome.'

'Does anyone else know about this?' I asked him quietly.

'You're the first person I've ever told, and you'll be the last. I've only shared it with you because I know I can trust you never to pass it on to my brother . . . not as long as I'm alive, at any rate.'

'If that's what you want, I'll promise and I'll keep my word. But don't you think he has a right to know about this? He must wonder himself what happened to him.'

'That truth won't help him. Plus, if I told him he might never speak to me again.'

Maybe you don't know your brother as well as you believe, I thought. *I reckon he'd give you absolution.*

Thirty-nine

I kept the mobile switched on all the time we were out, even though the battery was getting low, but there was no call from Gerard. I was tempted to ring him, but it was pretty late by the time Santi and I made it home, so I decided against it, switched off and put it on charge overnight.

I slept later next morning; Santi was up before me, and when I went upstairs, there were a couple of glasses of freshly squeezed orange juice on the table, alongside two plates, each with a monster slice of watermelon, and a bowl for the seeds. Tom and I both love watermelon, for the fun of eating it as much as for the freshness and the taste.

'I have to shop,' I told him, once we had finished it, and the toast that followed.

'Sure,' he replied. 'I'll take you down to the city.'

I shook my head. 'No, Santi; I said I have to shop. Me, personally, for women's things.' I tugged my hair. 'For example, I don't want this reverting to blond. And I've got hardly any make-up; at my age I can't go without it altogether.' There was also the matter of a new Gillette Venus; I was beginning to look like a gooseberry, and getting itchy with it. 'I saw enough yesterday to know where to go. I'll be back by lunchtime; maybe we can do some of the other monuments this afternoon.'

He was fine with that, so I set out on my own, down to the Paseo then along towards the main shopping drag, behind a square called Plaza Bib-Ramblas, which seemed to be the local flower market. I found the stuff I needed without difficulty, including the same brand and tint of hair dye that I had used at Shirley's. I bought two, in the optimistic hope that I wouldn't need the second one, and could replace hers without her ever knowing.

I was shopping for sensible underwear in a department store, trying on a bra in a fitting room, in fact, when the mobile sounded in my bag. I snatched at it. 'Gerard.'

'Primavera.'

'Surprise me; give me some good news.'

'It's raining, and the earth needs it. Other than that, I have nothing to offer. Alex has been as helpful as he can, but it's not good. Your theory has proved to be correct. The police tests have shown that Senor Planas had relations with Senora Fumado just before he died.' He sounded pained by the idea. 'Their conclusion is as you said it would be. I told Alex that was ridiculous, but he said that it was where the evidence pointed and that he couldn't ignore it. The public prosecutor is satisfied; he says they needn't look any further.'

'But they must. There has to be evidence that shows somebody else was there. They can't just stop looking for it.'

'They're not going to look for it, Primavera. They're sticking with what they've got. The prosecutor is going to ask a judge to issue a warrant for your arrest, tomorrow, Alex reckoned, at the latest.' He sighed. 'He's guessing that we're in touch. He said last night that if he was in your shoes, and had your resources, he'd adopt a new identity and disappear. I hate to say it, but he may be right; as you've told me, you've done it before.'

I was shaken. 'Are you giving up on me, Gerard?' I asked, tersely.

'No!' he protested. 'I'm trying to keep you safe.'

I'd wounded him; instantly I was sorry. 'I know,' I sighed, 'but I don't think that your way's working. I'm going to try something different, from here. You don't need to know about it, though. Give me a couple of days; I should know by then whether it's paid off.'

'And if it doesn't?'

'Then I'm coming home.'

'You can't. If you're convicted of double murder you'll go to jail for thirty years.'

'I didn't do it; I won't be convicted.'

'That's not what Gomez thinks; it's not what Alex fears. You can't come back, Primavera.' He sounded desperate.

'Then only one thing will keep me away. You bring Tom to me, and the three of us will disappear together. You're right; I've done it before, and I have the means to do it again.'

'Primavera . . .'

'If it comes to it, that's what I want. Will you do it?'

'I'll bring Tom to you. The rest . . .'

'If you bring Tom, you'll be walking away from your career. Gerard, I might not be Irena, but . . .'

I heard his intake of breath. 'He told you.'

'Yes. The whole story.'

'And what do you think of me now? I'd have killed my own father, but for Santi arriving when he did.'

'If the man had tried to rape me, I'd have killed him myself, no mercy, no second thoughts.' I pulled myself up, sharply. 'Which is probably not what you want to hear from a murder suspect, but it's true nonetheless. I'm glad Santi stopped you, but for your sake, not for your father's.'

'Try your other way, Primavera,' he sighed. 'Try it and let's hope it works. If not, then we'll see.'

Forty

I'd been a lot more confident with Gerard than I really felt. It's much more difficult to disappear into thin air than most people imagine. I'd been able to do it before more by luck than judgement; I was no expert. To make it work for three people would take money; I have plenty, but accessing it would be difficult.

I knew that I'd do it, or try to, if it became unavoidable, but before we got to that stage, there was Plan B.

During my time with Oz, I met a man. His name is Mark Kravitz and he runs a very discreet business that he describes as a security consultancy. That covers a variety of services; some are pretty secret, others involve high-level contacts in places of influence. He has worked for Oz on occasion, and in the recent past, when I had need of him, I'd been able to turn to him for help. My fingers were crossed that I could again.

I finished my shopping, then retraced my steps, until I found an internet shop that I'd noticed earlier. I'd been going to make the contact anyway, but my discussion with Gerard had concentrated my mind on it. I went into the shop, bought an hour's time, and settled into the booth that was furthest away from the door. I'd planned to send Mark an email, but as soon as I switched on the terminal, I came up lucky. I saw that it was loaded with Skype, that clever internet tool that lets you eyeball friends and family around the world; that's how Dawn and I keep in touch. (We've tried to get Dad into the way of it, but we're wasting our time.)

I was pretty sure that Mark would be there as I slipped on the headset that was plugged into the computer. He has MS, and is having increasing motor difficulties, so he rarely leaves his home-office. I opened the software, keyed in his contact details and pressed the green button. It didn't ring for long before he answered and his face appeared on the monitor screen. He was in his wheelchair, thinner than the last time we'd spoken, and his hair was a little greyer, but the old light still burned in his eyes.

'Primavera, what a nice surprise,' he exclaimed; then he frowned. 'What have you done to your hair?' he asked. 'And where the hell are you?'

'I've decided on a change of colour,' I told him, 'and I'm away from home.' I looked around to check that there was nobody within listening range, for at least half the voices I'd heard that morning had been speaking English, most of it with an American accent. When I felt secure, I explained why. I told him everything, every last detail.

'Mmm,' he murmured, when I had finished. 'You don't get into small trouble, do you? I bet you've never tripped over a step and skinned your knee, or picked up half a dozen parking tickets in a fortnight. No, with you it's always grand scale stuff, like that business last year with your cousin.'

I had to admit that there was something in what he said. I've survived an air crash where others did not, been duped by one of the cleverest con men ever to have worked a scam, but I've never picked up even one parking ticket, let alone half a dozen in a fortnight. And no, I don't remember ever falling and skinning my knee, not even as a child.

'You say the police are happy with the evidence?' he continued.

'Yes, and it points to me.'

'But you didn't do it, so they must have missed something.'

'Not necessarily. It could be that whoever killed these people didn't leave a trace.'

'Everybody leaves a trace, Primavera; miscarriages of justice come about because investigators stop looking when they've found enough to satisfy them, and to fit a particular theory.'

'Why would anyone want to frame me, Mark?'

'From what you say I don't think they did; not at the outset. I think they killed this Planas man, and kidnapped the woman. The police thinking has to be right in that respect; they didn't expect her to be there. You seem to have been a convenient fall . . . person.'

'You keep saying "they". The police are prepared to believe that I did it all on my own.'

'That's another weakness in their case against you. It's possible, but bloody difficult. The dead woman; was she weak?'

'Anything but, from what I saw of her.'

'Well, there you are. You can handle yourself, Primavera, but you're not a giant. Probability says to me that you couldn't have done all that by yourself. Put it this way; if I was contracted to do a job like that . . . not that I handle such work, of course,' he added, hastily, '. . . I'd send three people, two to do the wet work, and one to get them there, keep a lookout and get them away again. I wouldn't be sending a lone woman.' I saw him frown. 'No, there's something about this that stinks.'

'Tell me about it; I'm at the really smelly end.'

'And who put you there?' He frowned. 'When did you become a suspect? I mean when did they even begin to consider you a possibility?'

'I suppose it would be when they identified the murder weapon and found my DNA on it.'

'Exactly. And when was the woman killed and planted in your cellar, or whatever it is?'

'Friday morning.'

'Exactly. After the link to you had been established.'

'And after Dolores's car had been found . . .'

'. . . confirming that she hadn't run off, but had been abducted, forcing the hand of her kidnappers, making them realise they had to get rid of her there and then.'

'Right.' I knew where he was going and I didn't like it.

'They killed her with your scarf and they chose your place to dump the body. Why would they do that?'

'Because they knew by that time that I had handled the chair, and that the police were about to ask me why.'

Over a thousand miles away, by flying crow, he nodded. 'That's it. The police set you up, or helped.'

'No,' I protested. 'One of the investigating officers . . . he's just about my best friend. I can't believe that.'

'One of . . .' Mark repeated. 'But not the only.'

'I know Hector Gomez too.'

'How well?'

'Not that well, but . . .'

'Look, it needn't have been either of them; leaks rarely come from the most obvious point.'

'It doesn't help me, though.'

'It gives me somewhere to start.' He gazed into his webcam, and through it, into my eyes. 'Primavera, I want you to give me an hour. Go away, do something, then come back to where you are and get back online. With luck, I'll have come up with something.'

'What are you going to do?'

'What many people do these days when they're up against it. I'm going to phone a friend.'

Forty-one

I still had plenty of cash left, but I had bought all my essentials and anyway, shopping for frills wasn't really on my agenda, even if I did find myself looking longingly at an iPod Touch that looked just like Santi's clever phone.

Rather than wander for the rest of the hour I went into a place that I'd noticed earlier, a busy café called the Alhambra . . . there's imagination for you. There's a delicacy, a confection, in the south of Spain in particular, called churros. Imagine something that looks like a doughnut, only lighter, in strips rather than circles, and deep-fried. I'd never tried them before, and since I doubted whether they'd be on the menu at Barcelona women's prison, I thought I'd better. I looked around and saw that most of the people were eating them dipped in hot chocolate, and so I went along with that. My waiter brought me a great pile of the things, so many that I suspected that he'd assumed I was waiting for some- one to join me. It was heavy stuff, and may have accounted for the fact that many of the other customers were on the chubby side. I managed two, then had the hot chocolate replaced with a straight café con leche, more to my taste.

It took me the rest of the hour to munch my way through what I decided would be a once in a lifetime experience. I paid the bill, and went back to my internet shop. The booth I'd used earlier was occupied, but I found another that was almost as far away from the door, and with nobody on either side.

Mark Kravitz came on line instantly when I called him up. 'Hiya,' he said, then seemed to peer at me. 'Is that chocolate on your top lip?' he asked. There's a small box on the screen in Skype in which you can see your own image. I checked and it was; I wiped it off, hurriedly.

'How did your phone call go?'

He smiled. 'Every bit as well as I expected and more.'

'Are you going to tell me who you rang?'

The smile stretched; I'd never seen him look so amused. 'The Home Office. Top floor.'

I saw my image stare at him. 'Justin Mayfield? The Home Secretary?'

'That's the man.'

A year and a half ago, when I'd got into the situation with my cousin, Frank McGowan, to which Mark had alluded earlier, it had led the three of us to cross the path of one of the British government's rising stars, a friend of Frank. It had also left Mr Kravitz and me in possession of some information that could have turned Mayfield into a black hole overnight and had him banished to the furthest known point of the political universe. We hadn't used it; Mayfield had been stupid rather than criminal and we didn't see any point in terminating his career when there was a chance that he might actually be good at the job to which he'd just been appointed. I'd been keeping a distant eye on British politics, and that's how it seemed to have turned out. Word was that all doors were open to him. 'You're not thinking of . . .'

'Hey,' he exclaimed. 'I didn't threaten him, not at all. I told him that I'd been contacted by a British subject who was being stitched up in a murder investigation on the basis of leaked information and a crime scene investigation that would be a pure fucking joke, if its failings weren't so serious. He was appalled; then I told him who was on the wrong end of the business. I didn't have to mention last year; he'd have done something anyway. For you he'll push it all the way.'

'What's he going to do?'

'He's done it. He phoned his opposite number in Spain, and got him to agree to a specialist forensic team from Scotland Yard being flown over, "to assist the local investigation" as he put it, by examining the crime scene, and all the other evidence. He called me back fifteen minutes ago, to tell me they're on the way.'

'Won't the crime scenes be compromised by now?'

'Yes, but not hopelessly. Justin's established that the house and garden have been under guard since the man's death was found to be murder, and there's a new security lock on your storeroom. There's every prospect of finding something.'

'But if they don't, am I not deeper in it?'

'Justin says no; he's vouched for you personally with the Spanish, and he says he's got something else up his sleeve.'

'Does that mean I can go home now?'

'No, not yet. He said to give the Scotland Yard people a couple of days. They have three scenes to examine, remember.'

On screen, I saw myself look puzzled. 'What's the third?'

'The car; the Dolores woman didn't leave it there, or set it on fire. But don't worry; the Home Secy's well on your side. Almost the first thing he asked me when I mentioned your name was how you were doing.'

'What did you tell him?'

'I told him that you were festering away as an Earth mother out in Spain, casting around for things to do.'

'Why did you tell him that?'

'Because it's true,' he declared. 'You're bored out of your skull; that's what I see every time we speak on this device. The voluntary information office you told me about, and showed me a picture of; what's that other than a desperate attempt to keep yourself busy?'

'It's my contribution to the community; that and my involvement with the wine fair that kicked all this business off.'

'You'd make a better contribution by getting a proper job.'

'I've got one,' I said stubbornly. 'I'm an Earth mother, remember.'

'Sure, and when you're fifty, and Tom's an independent young adult, what will you be then?'

'Happy that he's independent.'

'And bored and lonely.'

'Maybe not lonely,' I murmured.

He shrugged. 'Okay, so you find a man, and you move on

from being a mother to being a Spanish housewife. That's not you, Primavera . . . and you know who'd have been the first to tell you so, if he was still around. He'd tell you to go out there and get your life back.'

My vision grew blurred; I blinked to clear it. 'But the part I want back the most, I can't have.'

'So move on; that's what he'd say, like I'm saying.'

'Where I live now, he loved it too.'

'I didn't say move house. Get a life, Primavera, get a life.'

I scowled at him. He was helping me, but at the same time, he was telling me things I didn't want to hear, not from anyone else, at any rate. 'If you come up with any ideas about how I might do that,' I growled, 'be sure to pass them on.'

'I will,' he said, 'I will. Call me back on Thursday; hopefully I'll have good news by then, on all fronts.'

Forty-two

I was later than I'd anticipated when I got back to Goats' Hill. I'd meant to use my bono turistica and jump on a bus, but when it came to it I wasn't sure which route to take, so I grabbed a taxi instead and got him to take me as near as he could.

I apologised as soon as I stepped inside, in case Santi had been worried about me, but he hadn't; and anyway, the bags I was carrying told some sort of a story. He had been shopping himself and had made lunch, a salad consisting of curly pasta . . . it has a name but I can never remember it . . . hard-boiled eggs, quartered, chopped black olives, capers and smoked salmon, all tossed in what looked like Thousand Island dressing, but had a bit more zing to it. I was still digesting churros, but I wasn't going to tell him that. I sat down and I tucked in.

I was glad that I did; it was fantastic. 'Do you ever think about doing this for a living?' I asked him.

He smiled, pleased by the compliment. 'Maybe, one day, it might be possible. I don't want to be flying airbuses forever; my airline will let me go on till I'm sixty, but fifty's my personal retirement date. After that I'll look at other options.'

'What about your girlfriend?' I asked. 'Is that serious? Might you do something together?'

'Oh, it's serious, but where it will go? I can't see two years ahead with her, far less eleven.'

It was well after three by the time we'd finished eating, and I'd tidied up . . . that consisted of loading everything into the dishwasher . . . *lavavajillas*, in Spanish: lovely word, it means exactly the same thing as the English version, but looks so much nicer. We still had four days to go on the tourist pass, and plenty to see, so when we were ready we walked down into the city, slowly and in the shadows, for it was hot, heading for the cathedral. The heather sellers were out in force again, but I passed them by. My internet sessions with Mark had left me with a warm feeling, one that I didn't want to put at risk from another round of Romany histrionics.

Granada's cathedral isn't as big as that of its Andalusian neighbour Sevilla . . . that's the biggest in the world, they say, since St Peter's in Rome isn't actually a cathedral . . . but it's pretty chunky nonetheless, and beautiful inside. Once again, Santi guided me round, explaining the history, and the meaning of each of the nine stained-glass windows. As we sat in the centre of the aisle, beneath the enormous twin banks of organ pipes, the thought occurred that it would be nice to come back with Gerard, to hear his take on it. I fancied he might have been less impressed than his brother. He'd said to me more than once that he felt slightly uncomfortable when he was confronted by the wealth of his church, and in that ornate building there were great riches on open display.

That was it for the day, as far as sightseeing was concerned. I was able to concentrate on the cathedral, but as soon as we were outside my mind headed back home. It was early evening: I wondered how long it would take the London team to reach St Martí.

As it happened, the word got there before the reality. Santi and I were sitting in a pavement bar in Plaza Nueva, contemplating a litre jar of sangria that had just been delivered to our table, trying to guess from our first taste what was in it, apart from ice, when my mobile sounded. 'Gerard,' I said as I took the call, 'say hello to your twin.'

I handed the phone to Santi. They exchanged very few words before he passed it back. 'Sounds agitated,' he whispered.

'What have you done?' Gerard asked.

'You might call it direct action,' I replied. 'What's happened?'

'I've just had a visit from Alex. He told me that they've all been chucked off the case, him, Gomez, everyone. There's a team on its way from Barcelona, senior officers, to take over. And he said something else, a story he'd been told by his boss, that some specialists are coming over from London, at the request of Madrid, to re-examine Planas's house and your storeroom.'

'Are they indeed?' I said. 'Poor Alex; I hope he isn't too upset.'

'Very far from it. Given your involvement, he's relieved to be having no more to do with it. Gomez isn't though; he sees it as a personal and professional slur.'

'Maybe if he'd been a bit more professional, it wouldn't have happened.'

'Primavera, did you have anything to do with this?'

I chuckled. 'Gerard, do you think I can make a phone call to Madrid and this sort of thing happens?'

'My dear, I would put nothing past you. Is this going to work in your favour?'

'It can't make it any worse, but yes, I believe it will.'

'I'll pray for it.'

I laughed again. 'You mean you haven't been?'

'Of course I have. Morning, noon and night.'

'Then maybe they're being answered.'

'So God's hand is in this, not yours?'

'Not unless he's in a wheelchair.'

'Pardon?'

'Never mind. I hope I'll be able to tell you all about it very soon.'

'Let's hope so, and not on a slow boat to Morocco. Don't tell Santiago, though, not yet; he still needs to be totally innocent of all knowledge of this business.'

'Don't worry,' I promised. 'I won't let any harm come to either of you.'

Forty-three

Mark Kravitz had asked me to sit tight for a couple of days, but I wasn't sure I could manage that; I was too pumped up, and I was missing Tom too much. I knew one thing, though, knew it for certain. For me even to contemplate disappearing had been a sign of weakness, and I had rediscovered my courage. No way was I running; I was innocent and I was going home, to proclaim it if necessary.

I thought all this through that evening as night fell and as Santi and I were eating, again, in yet another restaurant that he knew, along the Camino del Sacromonte, a fairly short walk from Goats' Hill. I did something else too; I sent Tom a text from my illicit mobile. I suppose it was possible that the police might have been able to trace me, if they were monitoring his phone, but since that was a pay and go type too . . . not even I would be crazy enough to give an eight year old a contract phone . . . I doubted that they could. All it said was, 'Hello son, miss you, love Mum,' but as soon as I had sent it I felt tons better.

He'd have been in bed by that time, so he must have had it

beside him, switched on just in case. The reply came through inside a minute, in what passes these days for English: 'Miss u 2. Where r u?'

I smiled as I flashed back, 'Secret mission. C u soon.'

Our main courses arrived as I finished. Santi had insisted that we eat Andalusian, so we had begun with pescadíto frito, a mix of deep-fried fish that's as far away from a haddock supper as you're ever going to get, and we were moving on to la tortilla sacromonte. He insisted that we had that because that's where we were, but he refused to tell me the ingredients. Afterwards, when I bothered to look them up, I was glad that he hadn't, for it was fantastic, and, modern woman though I am, I would not have gone knowingly for anything that involved lamb's brains and bull's testicles. (A guy did call me a ball-breaker once, but I doubt if he meant it literally.)

For once, I wasn't drinking alcohol; I'd stuck to fizzy water and he was on Cruz Campo beer. We'd had a little white wine for lunch and the afternoon sangria had pushed me up to my self-imposed daily limit. (I've never believed all that arbitrary crap about weekly intake that the 'experts' feed us. I know what my body can and can't take, and I make sure that I don't push it to the edge too often, and hardly ever beyond it.) Apart from that, I had an additional reason to lay off. What had begun as an idea at the back of my mind had turned into a firm intention.

'What did you think?' Santi asked, as I finished.

I complimented him on his choice. 'There have to be Andalusian restaurants in L'Escala,' I added. 'We have everything else. I must find one and give it a try.'

'Gerard will know,' he said. 'He'll also know if it's any good, just by looking at the menu.' He gazed at me. 'You reckon you'll be back soon, do you?'

'I can't hang around here forever,' I told him. 'Neither can you, for that matter. When do you have to be back?'

'I have a flight out of Madrid Barajas to LAX on Friday,' he admitted. 'That means I have to leave Thursday at the latest.'

'Do you have a flight home booked?'

He smiled. 'Don't have to do that. I can turn up at Lorca Airport and get on any flight. If it's full, I'll use a crew seat.'

There was nothing in what he said or how he looked, but I had a feeling that he'd rather be back home sooner than later. I said nothing to him, but right then, my mind was made up.

I didn't have coffee; I was tired from my hectic day and didn't want anything to get in the way of a good night's sleep. I went to bed as soon as I got in, after I'd explored the menu of my temporary phone and found out how to set its alarm. It trembled on the bedside table at seven sharp, but I was up by then. I don't know about you, but every time I set an alarm I'm always awake before it rings. I'd refreshed my dye job before we went out to Sacromonte, so all I needed was a quick shower, brush of teeth, and I was ready. I packed my bags, more carefully than I had a few days before, and climbed the stairs. If Santi had been there, I'd have said a proper 'So long and thanks for everything', but there was neither sight nor sound of him, so I took the notepad on the kitchen work surface and scribbled him a note that said much the same thing.

I suppose I should have asked him if it would be all right for me to take the Suzuki . . . bearing in mind that it was his, and not Gerard's . . . but that didn't occur to me until I was well on the road, until long after I'd reversed back down Goats' Hill until I had room to turn, then driven carefully out of the Albacin and out of the city of Granada.

I hadn't told Santi, but I was going home. I wasn't pissing about on N roads and C roads either. I didn't have a map, since the one that Gerard had given me had only covered his route, but I knew that Autopista Seven runs all the way up the coast and that it was probably going to be the shortest route and certainly the quickest, so that's where I headed with my chestnut hair and my wrap-around sunglasses, looking for Murcia as a first step.

The little Suzuki wasn't made for motorway driving. In addition, it was very hot and its ancient air-conditioning system had its limitations, so I had to make quite a few stops to let both the car and me cool down. I'd never intended to make it back in one day; I'd hoped I might have got as far as Barcelona, but reality kicked in and in the end I was happy to settle for reaching as far north as Valencia. (I had considered Benidorm as a possible stopping-off point, but not for any more than a couple of seconds.)

I came off the motorway and made my way into the city centre looking for somewhere to spend the night. Eventually I settled on the Hotel Villareal, three star with a handy car park. If they'd insisted on ID I'd have turned and walked out, but I told the receptionist that I'd left my passport in the car, and when I paid cash in advance, any worries she might have had faded away.

The hotel didn't have a formal restaurant, but I wanted to go out anyway. These days there are two things in the world that you can find simply by turning a corner in any city. One is a Starbucks and the other is a sign advertising internet access. I had to walk a little further than usual, but still I came up lucky in Valencia; I found both in the same place, and it was quiet. I bought myself a tall filter, Colombian, with a little milk, and chose one of the four unused computers, pleased to see that it too had a camera and a headset, undoubtedly so that little Annabelle from Anywhere, Indiana, could let her mom back home see that she was safe in Valencia, Spain.

I booted up and Skyped Mark Kravitz. He wasn't in the wheelchair, but in a leather swivel, so I guessed that he must be having a good day with the MS, or as good as they've become for him. 'Where are you now?' he asked.

I told him.

'I said to give it a couple of days,' he reminded me.

'I know, but I thought I might as well spend them travelling. Have you heard any more from our well-placed friend?'

He nodded. 'Two things. The first is that the Scotland Yard people have found several more DNA traces on the sites they're examining, and preliminary tests show that one in particular is common to all three. Good news? It's not yours. Bad news? Well, not all that bad, but it doesn't rule you out completely. They could suggest that you had an accomplice. However, if they do, they'll run into a problem.

The second message I've had from our friend is that he's pulled a string or two in the Foreign Office. They've been getting grief from the Scottish Nationalist government in Edinburgh because there's nobody in our embassy set-up with responsibility for looking after Scottish interests in Spain, and in Catalunya in particular. So a special counsellor has just been appointed.'

In my own wee box on screen, I saw my mouth open. 'Are you going to tell me who it is?' I asked.

'Do I need to? It's you.'

'Can he do that? Without my agreement?'

'Are you going to refuse?'

'What do I gain from it, apart from a job I never asked for?'

'Diplomatic immunity, Primavera. It means that you're untouchable by the Spanish police without the consent of our government.'

'So I'm an honorary consul or some such?'

'No. They only have limited immunity. Your appointment makes you a diplomatic agent; suppose you as much as parked your car in the wrong place and it got towed, they'd have to bring it back.'

'How long will it last?'

'Until you resign, or they fire you for incompetence. It's a real job. I told you yesterday that you should get a life. Well, this is it.'

'But what do I do?'

'That's to be defined by the Foreign Office, after the Scottish First Minister's put his two groats' worth in. But broadly, you'll represent Scotland in Spain. They're not talking full-time, not yet; two days a week, salary pro rata.'

'But it's a scam.'

'No it's not. How often do I have to say it? It's for real. Yes, there is a potential downside: if the Spanish authorities insist on charging you with murder, you'll still be tried. But in London, not in Spain, under the British system. The Crown Prosecution Service would need to be satisfied that there's a case to answer, and from what I know of the CPS they'll need a hell of a lot more proof against you than the Spanish had, even before the Met team got involved.'

I stared at him and at the small image of myself. 'I'm going to need some time to get my head round this,' I said. 'There's so much to consider. I'm not moving out of L'Escala.'

'Why should you? You'll have travel and other expenses; you can hire a live-in housekeeper to look after Tom when you're away. Primavera, I could recruit somebody for you. There are female ex-soldiers out there just now, with Afghan and Iraqi experience, looking for civilian jobs.'

He was so earnest that I laughed. 'One step at a time, Mark,' I protested. 'Let me get home first, and let the police catch whoever set me up. When that's done I'll decide all the rest. It's nice to be immune, I'll grant you. But I want to be seen to be innocent as well, beyond the shadow of even the most *un*reasonable doubt.'

Forty-four

Given my new and entirely unexpected status, I had a moment of wishing that I'd booked into a five-star hotel, but the Hotel Villareal suited me fine for that one night. I did a little more shopping while I was out, a nice loose white top that I reckoned would be cool on the road next day, and a box of those items that I'd found in Gerard's bathroom cabinet and which I expected to need myself by Friday at the very latest. As I paid the pharmacist's assistant, I felt a surge of guilt as my first, involuntary, suspicions came back to me. Maybe I'd tell him when I got home, for a laugh, but I was sure we'd have other, serious, things to talk about. During my crisis, my real feelings had been revealed, and maybe his too . . .

What had he said? '*It may be that when your troubles are over, our troubles will begin.*'

The white top wasn't needed next morning. It had poured during the night and Thursday promised to be much cooler than the week had been until then. In fact, it rained again mid-morning when I was close to Tarragona, so hard that I had to come off the road for a while, since the Suzuki's wiper blades were even less use than its air conditioning, and since the detachable hard-top wasn't too well sealed.

Thanks to that it was well into the afternoon by the time I reached and passed Girona Airport. I gave some thought to going straight to the school and surprising Tom by picking him up, but I decided that our reunion would be better at home, since one of us was going to cry, and I doubted that it would be him. So instead, I pulled in at a picnic area and called my landline number, in the hope that Mac would be in.

He was, and he must have been carrying the cordless phone, so quickly did he answer. 'Aw Jesus, lass,' he exclaimed. 'Am I glad to hear your voice! Where are you?'

'I'm on my way home.'

'Can you?'

'Yes. I may not be completely in the clear, but I'm safe from arrest.'

'I've been hearing things,' he said, 'about the investigation. Tom made me take him to Can Coll last night, and the guy there was saying something about a team from London being flown in. I asked him who made that happen, but he said that he hadn't a clue. Apart from that there hasn't been a lot of talk that I've heard, although I'm sure there's been some behind my back.' He paused. 'They searched the house, of course; on Friday.'

I'd expected that. 'Messy?'

'No, they were tidy; your friend Alex was there and he made sure that everything was put back in its place. Apart from your computer, that is. They took that away; brought it back this morning though. I was surprised by that; I thought they'd keep it longer. The man Gomez was going to take Tom's computer too, but Gerard asked to see the court order that would let him, and he backed off.' He chuckled. 'He's a tough guy, your priest; if it came to the bit, he doesn't look like he'd take any prisoners. I'm pleased that he's on your side. I take it he helped you get away?'

'Not over the phone, Mac,' I warned, 'not even now.'

'No, maybe not,' he conceded, 'but it's obvious that's what Gomez thinks. There was real antagonism between them; he didn't come right out and accuse him, but it was written all over his face.'

'It doesn't matter what Gomez thinks. He's back in Girona counting paperclips.'

'Is he indeed? Is that connected with the guys from London arriving?'

'Yup.'

'And you know about it?' I could hear him pondering. 'Has your brother-in-law been leaning on people?'

'Hopefully, he still doesn't have a clue about it. Anyway he's in America; there isn't anyone he could lean on even if he wanted to. No, there's somebody else who believes in me and reckoned that he owed me a favour.'

'If he can do that for you,' he growled, 'keep him in mind the next time I need one. When will you be back?'

'Half an hour; open the garage door for me and make sure there's a space clear.'

'You on wheels?' He sounded surprised.

'Yes, and I want to keep them out of sight; I don't want anyone asking how I came by them.'

I ended the call and got back on the road. As I passed over Viladamat and approached the St Martí junction, my last fear was that the Mossos might be waiting here as they do from time to time as a matter of routine, but it was clear, as was the big roundabout outside the village. I took the short route up to the garage. Mac had opened the door as I asked; I swung in carefully, just in case there was something in my way.

I'd barely applied the handbrake before the door started to close, and before Tom stepped out from behind the Jeep. I jumped out of the Suzuki and he jumped at me; I hugged him for about a minute, until he got too heavy for me to hold up any longer, and I had to set him back on his feet. I'd been right about the tears too.

'Mission accomplished,' I told him, wiping them away. 'No more unexplained absences, I promise.'

'It's all right, Mum,' he said. 'I've had fun with Grandpa Blackstone.' I wasn't quite sure how to take that until he looked up at me, smiled, and added, 'But Charlie and I are both glad you're back.' He looked back over his shoulder, to something that leaned against the wall, something that hadn't been there when I'd left. 'Do you like my new bike?'

I surely did. It was nearly as big as mine, with thick, rugged tyres, strong off-road suspension, and what looked like around twenty gears. The saddle was set right down, so there was plenty of room for growth. 'I hope you said a proper thank you,' I told him.

'You mean in English?' he asked, ingenuously.

'In every one of your four languages.'

I let him lead the way upstairs to the kitchen, where Mac was waiting. It was his turn to hug me. He had a Coronita in each hand, and he gave one to me. 'I thought you might appreciate this,' he said.

'And the one after it,' I admitted, killing half of it in a single slug. 'But first . . .' I headed for the stairs and for my bedroom. As soon as I had closed the door behind me I stripped off my clothes and stepped under the shower. I left it cool, short of lukewarm even, and stayed in there for a good ten minutes, shampooing my hair three or four times in the hope of at least toning down the chestnut. Neither Tom nor Mac had mentioned my new colour, but I'd had as much of it as I wanted. I knew I couldn't wash it out, but I promised myself that as soon as I could I'd find something as close to my natural shade as I could, repair the damage and then let it grow out.

But I wasn't simply washing my hair, or washing off the sweat and grime of the journey. I felt that I was cleansing myself of the whole experience, and that when I emerged from the shower, I'd be the woman I'd been a couple of weeks before, the Primavera who'd never heard of José-Luis Planas, or of Dolores Fumado.

That's not how it turned out; I couldn't erase the memory of the angry little man in his office, or of the swelling corpse on the rocks beneath the wall, or of the bulging-eyed, purple-faced woman sitting on the logs at the end of my storeroom. I don't believe I ever will. I couldn't escape my desire for a conclusion either. Whoever had put Dolores there had tried to frame me for both murders. I had to know who it was, and I had to know that he was out of the picture, for my own peace of mind, and possibly for my safety and that of my son.

I had to steer clear of the continuing investigation, though. I'd caused some very thick strings to be pulled, ropes almost, and one of them had tightened around the neck of Hector Gomez, maybe choking off his career in the process. In truth, I hadn't wanted that to happen. He was a straight cop, even if he had been misguided about me. And I certainly hadn't wanted any misfortune to come Alex Guinart's way. His flow of information to Gerard had shown that he was on my side, not that I'd ever needed proof of that.

What I did need was to see him, as soon as possible, as soon as it could be arranged, but after I'd contacted Gerard. He was my top priority; I hadn't heard from him since leaving Granada, and that had surprised me. As soon as I'd towelled off, blow-dried my hair, and dressed in something pale green, light, airy and cotton, I dug the mobile out of my bag . . . and replaced it straight away.

I might be more or less in the clear, but Gerard wasn't. He'd planned the escape of someone the police wanted to arrest for murder, and he'd lied about it afterwards. His guilt didn't disappear with my innocence. That phone was evidence against him, and the sooner it was at the bottom of the Mediterranean, or somewhere just as inaccessible, the better it would be for him. As a first step I opened it, took out the SIM card, held it up by a corner, and set it on fire with a Zippo that

I keep in my room for lighting mosquito candles on the terrace.

Once I'd flushed the ashes down the toilet, I picked up the landline phone and called his regular mobile number. It rang six times then switched me on to voicemail. 'It's me,' I told him. 'Plan B worked, you'll be pleased to hear. I'm back at the house, and I'd like to see you as soon as you can make it. Or I'll come to you if you'd rather.'

However, that didn't satisfy me; as I've said, I'd always made a point of not calling him at the residence, unless it was absolutely necessary, but this was one of those times. Voicemail again; this time the announcement wasn't spoken by a gushing female Movistar voice, but by Father Olivares. I didn't leave a message.

Instead I went downstairs, for my second beer, and to see my lovely boy again. He was in the computer room, knocking hell out of his lovely grandpa at a realistically violent game that seemed to have appeared in my absence. 'Nice bike, Mac,' I said. 'Not so sure about that, though. There are age categories for those things.'

'This is eight and over, Mum,' Tom exclaimed. 'Anyway, I'm nearly nine.' To a kid, eight years and one day old counts as nearly nine. Soon he'd be nearly ten.

'Something came for you this afternoon,' Mac announced. 'Sorry, I forgot to tell you earlier. It arrived by courier; extra special delivery, all the way from London, with a big red stamp saying diplomatic mail. I'd to sign for it.' He walked through to the hall, returned with a brown A4 envelope, and handed it to me. 'Go on,' he insisted, 'open it. It took me all my time not to do it myself.'

I tried to open it neatly, but that's difficult when you're gripped by curiosity and the envelope has been taped shut. In the end I made a small hole in the wrong end, widened it with a finger and ripped it open. The contents slid out into my hand; five documents. The first was a letter, addressed to me. It was on the crested notepaper of the Foreign and Commonwealth Office; it advised me that Her Majesty the Queen had that day been pleased to appoint me a special counsellor attached to her embassy in Madrid with immediate effect, and it was signed by someone called Joseph O'Regan, MP, Minister of State and Minister for Europe. The second was another letter, on slightly less majestic notepaper, but still with the FCO crest. It had come from one John Dale, a deputy secretary in the diplomatic section; it welcomed me to the team, told me what my pro rata salary would be . . . that made me blink . . . asked me to make contact with the ambassador in Madrid at the earliest opportunity, and to call him to arrange what he called 'familiarisation' meetings in London and Edinburgh. The third was a note on the rights, privileges and responsibility of diplomats, the fourth was a form for completion and return to the human resources department, and the fifth was a declaration, for my signature, accepting that I was bound by the terms of the Official Secrets Act.

I handed them to Mac, one by one, as I read them. 'Jesus, Primavera,' he whispered, as he read, 'what's this?'

'You could call it my stay out of jail card,' I told him. 'On the other hand you could call it a major job opportunity.'

'Congratulations, girl. Did you apply for this?'

'No, it was offered.'

'Convenient timing. You really do have friends in high places if they can do that for you.'

I smiled at him. 'Looks that way, doesn't it.'

'We'll have to start calling you "Ma'am", Tom and me.'

' "Mum" will be fine, thank you. And now she's going off to think about feeding her boys.'

'Don't bother; I'll take us out. After all, you've got a new job to celebrate.'

I shook my head. 'I'd rather not. I want to keep my head down for a bit; tomorrow I'll let the new investigating team know I'm back, but tonight I'm staying in.'

There was one more thing I had to do; I picked up the cordless phone from my desk . . . Mac must have taken to carrying it with him everywhere . . . went through to the first-floor living room, and dialled my father's number. He doesn't have voicemail; if he's working on a piece when the phone rings, he'll always take a few seconds to finish what he's doing before he answers, so when he tried the service it was always cutting in before he got there. I waited for the usual ten rings or so, before he picked up. 'David Phillips,' he announced. Dawn bought him a phone with number recognition, so my name would have been displayed, but that makes no difference; it's how he always answers.

'Dad, it's me.'

'So I see. Where are you?'

'I'm calling from home, Dad; that's why your screen's telling you it's me.'

'Ahh,' he exclaimed, as if I'd just switched on a light and he could see clearly, 'that's how it works, is it.' The age of information technology is still waiting for my old man to catch up with it. So, for that matter, are the Iron and Bronze Ages. He's a Wooden Age man, and that's where he'll always live. 'Mac called to tell me you've been in one of your scrapes again. It's all sorted now, is it?'

'Yes; as far as my involvement's concerned at least. I'm sorry I didn't contact you myself, but I wasn't able to. I hope you didn't worry too much.'

'Primavera, once upon a time you had us all thinking you were dead, for the best part of a year, and then you popped up again. After that experience, I can switch off worry where you're concerned. I never had any doubt that you'd take care of whatever it was.'

'Did you tell Dawn?' I asked.

He has a lovely soft chuckle that's always made me feel warm. 'My dear, most people who know me are free to believe that I'm slightly round the bend, but it upsets me if they imagine I'm stupid with it. Of course I did not tell your sister; that would have been unspeakably cruel.'

'Dad, she has a right to know about family problems; she has to learn how to handle crises maturely.'

'She never will; she's a throwback to my mother. She was as excitable as a wasp's byke poked with a stick. No, I meant that it would have been cruel to Miles. He'd have had to handle the flak; I like my son-in-law far too much to do that to him. Anyway, what would have been the point? You're fine, as I always knew you would be.'

'I love you, Dad. Come and see us soon, yes?'

'Book me a flight, give me the usual notice, and I'll be there.'

'Will do.' That's our usual arrangement. Dad wouldn't know how to go about booking his own travel, so Dawn and I do it for him. 'See you in a month or so, then.'

I was smiling as I ended the call, standing in the doorway that opens from the living room on to the patio; smiling at the thought of him, but also at my home village. There had been times during the week gone by when I'd been at my lowest, when I'd feared that I'd never see it again. Had I panicked? Hell no, I'd missed arrest by minutes, and as Gerard had warned, once inside the Spanish judicial system, escape is pretty much impossible. And he should know, I thought; but for his brother's intervention all those years ago, it might have swallowed him. Thinking of him, I called him again, on both numbers, but had the same response on each. I stepped on to the terrace far enough for me to see the front of the church, but there was no sign of activity there, and his car wasn't in its usual slot in the parking area to my right.

I was about to step back inside when my name was called, from the square. I recognised the voice. I turned and walked to the patio railing. 'Hello, Alex,' I replied. He was out of uniform, looking up at me; he was frowning, and I don't suppose I was beaming at him.

'Fancy a drink?' he asked.

'Sure, as long as I can come back home afterwards.'

He smiled, and the ice was broken. When I joined him at a table in front of Meson del Conde, having told Mac where I was going, there was a lime-wedged Coronita waiting for me. I was glad I hadn't got round to the second one I'd promised myself earlier. 'When did you get back?' His voice was quiet, conversational.

'About an hour ago.'

'Going to tell me where you were?'

'Do you need to know?'

'No.'

'Best I don't then.'

'Yes, I suppose. It's none of my business anyway; Hector and I have been taken off the investigation. But can I assume that you know that, since you're home again?'

'Yes, I knew about it. I'm sorry if it's affected you career-wise, Alex.'

'It hasn't; I'm the new boy in Girona, remember. The bosses in Barcelona have barely heard of me. For Hector it's not so good; they've told him that he ran a shoddy investigation, that he made a few facts fit a convenient suspect and that he quit far too early.'

I shrugged as I pushed the lime down into the neck of the bottle. 'I can't disagree with any of that,' I admitted.

'Maybe not, but it wasn't all his fault. He reports to the public prosecutor; he's an ambitious guy, on the lookout for quick results and high-profile cases. He saw both in you, so he told Hector to arrest you, purely on the basis of your palm print on that chair, even before Dolores's body was found in your *trustero*. I tried to stall him, and I succeeded for a day or so. You must have noticed that he didn't come over to talk to you at Angel's funeral reception. It would have been too awkward; that was why. After Friday morning, though . . . I shouldn't say this, but I'm glad you got away. I'm not going to put you in an awkward place by asking you how, for I can guess anyway.' He paused. 'As for Hector, yes, he's in the doghouse for now, but Madrid has crapped on the public prosecutor. The right people know what happened, so it won't harm him long term.'

'If you get the chance, tell him I'm sorry.'

'Why should you be? You're the one who was being set up, and we're the guys who fell for it.'

'I'm still sorry that he's in trouble. I didn't mean for that to happen.'

He stared at me. 'How could you have made it happen?' His eyes widened even more as it dawned on him. 'It was your government, wasn't it? You did like Senor Reid, you got to your consulate and made a complaint of false accusation. Then you hid somewhere while they put it right, or they hid you. That's the story, isn't it?'

'It was my government,' I conceded, 'but that's not exactly how it happened. Don't ask me any more about that either, Alex, for I really can't tell you.'

'Whatever, I'm glad it's worked out. You know I did what I could to help, don't you?' he added. 'Even after you'd gone.'

I smiled at him. 'If by answering "yes" I'm not going to

incriminate anyone, then yes. If I am, then I don't know what you're talking about.'

He nodded, and smiled.

'What else do you hear?' I asked him. 'I might be on solid ground again, but I've still got an interest in this. I'm as keen to solve this mystery as you guys are.'

'I don't hear much, Primavera, not any more. The new team, the guys from Barcelona, they've been told not to speak to Hector and me. Mostly they're sticking to that, but I did my recruit training with one of them; he's been telling me stuff.'

'About DNA, linking all three crime scenes?'

'How the hell did you know about that?' he exclaimed. 'Or that they were looking at three scenes now? Mother of God, Primavera, who are you?'

'I'm your daughter's fairy godmother, that's all. So what's your friend been saying?'

'They've identified a common DNA pattern from each of the three locations; only one, but the new prosecutor reckons it's grounds for action. They're ready to make an arrest, so it looks as if pretty soon you're going to know who it is that's had it in for you. As for me, I have no idea. That's as far as my pal would go; he said that it was more than his career was worth to tell me anything else.'

'I can wait,' I said, unashamedly vindictive, 'but when I find out I'm going to savour the moment. This character would have seen me go down for the rest of my life; I hope he doesn't forget that as he contemplates his.'

Forty-five

I took Tom to school next morning; it was the end of term and he was hyper, so I judged it best not to let him take his new bike, in case he got carried away and started doing tricks on it. He was curious about the Suzuki in the garage; I told him the simple truth, that I'd been using it while I was away, and that seemed to satisfy him.

Since it was right next door I went to the gym after I'd dropped him off, and put myself through a fairly strenuous workout, partly to sweat off the extra kilo that I'd acquired with all that eating in Santi's Granada haunts. I thought of him as I ran; chances were he was halfway across the Atlantic, bound for Los Angeles in his flying bus.

I thought of his brother too: I'd heard nothing from him and had called him again before I'd left the house, with no more success than the day before. I thought of what had been said at Shirley's; we'd both been very emotional, but I knew that I'd stepped across the invisible barrier that I'd put between us. I thought of what I'd said on the phone in Granada, about the last resort, and of how he'd reacted. The more I thought about it, the more I came to realise that was why his mobile was switched off. He knew that our old relationship had been compromised, at the very least, and that next time we spoke I was going to have some very personal questions to put to him . . . all the more personal now that I knew about Irena. There was a relationship with a woman in his past. Had he been put off for life by its horrible conclusion, or did he feel at least some of what I felt for him? I had to hear his answer, and strangely, I was scared by the prospect . . . whatever he might say. If he turned me down . . . it would be the end even of what we'd had. If he said, 'Yes, I do love you and want you' . . . Jesus, that might be even tougher to handle. He might insist that we leave St Martí. Would I do that for him? I'd have to; my sacrifice would have to match his.

My musing came to an end as my treadmill programme ran out. I did some stretching exercises to warm down, then changed and headed back to the village. I had things to do. There was Mac for a start; he'd stayed on for days longer than he'd planned, but the previous evening I'd managed to book him on to a flight from Girona to Stansted that would link up with another to Edinburgh and get him home in time for dinner. I had to have him there for eleven fifteen, then be back to collect Tom at lunchtime.

And then there was my new, unlooked-for, job. I'd gone to sleep asking myself whether I wanted it, and woken up realising that I did. I fancied the challenge, I needed to be stimulated intellectually and I liked the thought of what it involved, being an informal sub-ambassador for Scotland in

Spain. Hell, I thought, if I'd seen it advertised I probably would have applied for it. Could I manage that and a new situation with Gerard at the same time? Sure I could; maybe I wouldn't have to recruit one of Mark's soldier girl housekeepers. *Mental note: never use the word 'nanny' to Tom.*

For all the upheaval and unexpected responsibility, Mac looked to have enjoyed his break. He was the colour of well-oiled teak, and looked rested ... perhaps because he hadn't played all the golf that he'd anticipated. I hoped that Mary would approve of the state in which he was being returned. I saw him off to the departures gate, after making him promise that they'd both come back for the wine fair in September.

I'd been so busy that I was on my way back to L'Escala before I got round to thinking about what Alex Guinart had said the night before about the likelihood of an arrest. I was intrigued to know who it would be, but from everything I'd heard of Planas, I guessed it was likely to be someone I'd never heard of, someone with a grudge big enough to kill over, ruthless enough to take care of Dolores when she got in the way, and smart enough to set me up to take the rap after he'd picked up some inside dope from the police. This was Catalunya, after all; much as I love it, the place is full of people who meet those requirements, even if they are heavily outnumbered by the good. No point in speculating, though, I told myself, as I headed back to the school.

It was out for the summer, as Alice Cooper has been insisting since I was about four years old, a half-day, and so I took my son for lunch to celebrate. We took the Jeep home, picked up Charlie and walked along to the Hostal Ampurias, a white-painted hotel near the Greco-Roman ruins, sitting almost on top of a beautiful little bay. When Tom cycles to school he goes past it. He asked for a Catalan salad to start . . . he likes his meat, and that's what it is . . . while I settled for wild green asparagus. (It grows all over L'Escala, but only the old-timers know where to find it, and it's hard to spot.) As we ate I told him that I had a job, one that might take me out of town for a couple of days at a time.

'Can I come?' he asked.

'When you're not at school, if it's convenient, and I don't think you'd be bored. Other times, there'll be somebody to look after you.'

'Can Gerard look after me?'

'Gerard has his own job.'

Tom frowned. 'Somebody at school said he'd left.'

I felt a tremor in my chest. 'What?' I gasped.

'One of the girls said her mother saw him leaving, and that he isn't going to be our priest any more.'

I snatched my phone from my bag and called Gerard's mobile again; again that purring voicemail message, 'At this moment . . .' I found Alex's number and pressed the green key.

'Primavera,' he said, quietly, before I had a chance to speak, knowing my number off by heart and recognising it. 'I'm in the office. It's very busy and very noisy, so I can't really speak. However, I can guess what you're calling about and the answer's "yes". I'm sorry, but it's true.'

'That might be the answer, Alex,' I hissed, leaning away from

Tom so that he couldn't hear me, 'but what's the fucking question?'

'You don't know. God, the rumour is all over town. The man they've arrested, for both murders. It's Father Gerard.'

Forty-six

I couldn't tell Tom, of course. Equally I couldn't keep my panic from showing on my face.

'What's wrong, Mum?' he asked.

I pulled myself together. 'Nothing.'

'There is,' he insisted, stubbornly, 'you look as if you've had a fright.'

'It's nothing,' I repeated, with a hint of a warning not to push it in my voice. 'Something's happened that I didn't expect, that's all. Nothing to do with you, young man, so mind your own.'

'Yes, Mum.' He sighed as kids do when they want you to know they see through you but they're indulging you anyway. Happily his spaghetti bolognaise arrived just at that moment, to distract him. He's less messy when he eats it than he used to be, but he still has to concentrate to make sure he doesn't wind up wearing some of it. Me? I had a piece of sole, and nothing else. That extra kilo, remember.

When we got back home he asked if I'd go to the beach with him. It was a little windy, but I took a sun lounger and sat under a mushroom-shaped parasol, watching him in the water, but thinking at the same time. Finally, because I could come up with nothing else to do, I rang the residence again. This time Father Olivares answered in person. I wondered whether he'd want to speak to me, but he actually seemed pleased that I'd called. The old chap was as distressed as I was, but he didn't have to hide the fact from anyone.

'This is madness,' I said to him. 'Do you know what's possessed them?'

'Or is it him who's possessed?' he countered. 'They said when they came to arrest him that they have clear evidence.'

'You were there when he was taken away?'

'Yes. It was people I didn't know. They came to our house in uniform and with guns, and asked for him. They said that they had very clear evidence that linked him with both murders. At first, he seemed amused. He laughed at them and told them that they were making it up, but they said that they could prove with science that he had been at José-Luis's house, at the place where Dolores Fumado was found, and in her car. They could prove it, categorically, they insisted. They said that he would be charged with murder and with attempting to implicate you, by putting the poor woman's body in your house, to be found.'

'How did he react to that?'

'He said to them, "You can actually prove that?" and they replied, "Absolutely." With that his attitude changed. "Then do so," he said, "for I'll be saying nothing." So they took him away, to Girona, in a closed van. But before he left, he did say one more thing, to me, very quietly. He asked me to say to you,

Primavera, that he was sorry, but he could do nothing else. He admitted it, my dear. I am so sorry. I know what you have come to feel for him, and I'd begun to suspect that he had the same regard for you. But no, it seems that he's betrayed us all.'

I don't think I've ever heard such despair as that which sounded in the old man's voice. For a moment, I found myself accepting what he was saying . . . until I told him, 'No! I will not believe that, never. I don't care what they say, there is another explanation. A week ago, those people, or others like them, claimed to have proof that I committed these crimes. Gerard didn't believe it then, as I don't believe it now. I'm going to get him out of this.'

'But if their evidence is as strong as they say . . .'

'Let's see what a lawyer thinks of it. Will the church appoint someone to act for him?'

'My dear, the church is not used to having its priests accused of murder. There isn't a precedent for this. It will need to be considered.'

I could hear the mills of God grinding, exceedingly slowly. 'We don't have time for that. Father, you've been here for a long time. Who's the best advocate in this area?'

'From what I've heard, that would be Josep Villamas. He has an office in Figueras, and he's very well known in the courts. He lives in L'Escala; he's a member of my congregation.'

'Can you give me a number for him? I'd look it up myself, but I'm on the beach with my son.'

'I think so. Give me a moment.' I waited, listening to a rustling of paper in the background. 'Yes,' he said finally, then gave me two numbers, one local, the other, by its prefix, the office in Figueras. I keyed both into the memory of my phone. 'Thanks, Father. I'm going to call him right now and instruct him.'

'He'll be expensive,' the old man warned. 'We priests are poor men, and there's no guarantee that the bishop will agree to meet the cost, whatever the temptation to which Gerard may have succumbed.'

'Cost isn't an issue,' I told him. 'When I have something positive to tell you, I'll let you know. You'll be at home, yes.'

'Yes.' He paused. 'Apart from this evening, and tomorrow, of course.'

'What happens then?'

'Dolores Fumado's funeral is tomorrow morning. It's at eleven.'

'I didn't know.'

'The body is being released to Justine and Elena this morning; it will be received into the church this evening.'

'Then let's hope we can put this nonsense to bed in time for Gerard to assist you at the requiem Mass.'

'You are one of life's optimists, my dear.'

'I wasn't a week ago; that's something else I owe to him.'

He wished me good luck, but he still sounded low.

Tom wanted me to come into the water with him, but I told him I wasn't swimming that day. He knows that sometimes I don't, and he never asks why. Instead I called the Figueras number. A woman answered, in Catalan. I gave her my name and asked if I could speak to her boss. I expected her to ask me what I wanted, but she put me straight through.

I got down to business. No time for pleasantries; with lawyers the clock is always ticking. 'Senor Villamas, I want to instruct you to undertake the defence of my friend Gerard Hernanz. He was arrested early this morning, and is being charged with two murders.'

'And with fabricating evidence against you, Senora Blackstone,' the advocate added, in a deep rolling voice; he sounded as Morgan Freeman would if he spoke Catalan. (Maybe old Morgan does: I don't know.)

'So you've heard what's happened?'

'Yes, I was told a few hours ago. When I learned of it I went straight to Girona, and offered my services to Father Hernanz. I know the man. He's heard my confession, often. I like him very much, and I could not credit what I'd been told. He refused to see me; a policeman came to tell me that he'd said he didn't want a lawyer, and that if one was appointed by the court, he'd refuse to cooperate with him. To be frank, I didn't believe the officer, and I told him as much. I threatened to go straight to the court to demand access. He went away and returned a few minutes later with a handwritten note from Father Hernanz confirming what he had said the first time. And more; the message said that if I was asked to act for someone else in this matter . . . I suspect that he meant you . . . it would serve no purpose. He said that if the police have evidence against him, they can present it. He'll let God defend him, and judge him.'

'Does God have a law degree?' I exploded. 'Does he have

much experience on the Bench? I'm sorry, Senor Villamas,' I added at once. 'I'm not getting at you. It's just that he's so . . .'

'Resigned, I'm afraid,' the lawyer said. 'He seems to be accepting his guilt.'

'Well, I won't,' I declared.

'You may have no choice. After I'd left the police officer, I spoke to the prosecutor. I know the man; he's very experienced, very capable and he's in no doubt that he'll secure a conviction. I'm sorry, I wish I could help, but other than appearing as a character witness when it comes to sentencing, there's nothing I can do.'

What the hell is he thinking about? He was all that I could think about, as I lay on the lounger, propped up on my elbows, keeping an eye on Tom as he tried to catch a cresting wave with his mini surfboard. The whole thing was fantastic. Why would Gerard want to kill Planas? What possible reason could he have? *The man had called you a whore, and you told him that over dinner.* So what? Is that a reason to kill a man? *What did he do when Irena was attacked?* That was years ago, and it was rape, a far different thing. *Unless, in his eyes, it was an insult he couldn't tolerate.* 'Rubbish, Primavera,' I said aloud. And then I remembered anew what he'd said in La Lluna and I shuddered.

'As for calling you a whore, if he was a younger man, I would take off my collar and meet him after dark.'

Had he decided that Planas wasn't that old after all? 'Stop it!' I called out, so loudly that a woman three mushrooms along turned and looked, to see what was happening. I fixed her with a glare, and she went back to her book. I wouldn't believe it, I told myself, I couldn't believe it; but so much seemed to fit.

For once in my life I could not think of a single thing to do. I needed someone else's input, but whose? Santi. Of course, Santi. He'd come up with something. But then I saw the snags. I didn't have a contact number for him. I didn't know where he was, but given the time it takes to fly from Barajas to LAX, I was pretty sure he'd be nowhere in Spain. I didn't know for sure what airline he was with. I'd assumed that it was Iberia, but I couldn't be certain, for he hadn't mentioned it. Even if it was, I'd have been surprised if they had put me in touch with him, at least until they'd checked me out. I could try, and I would, but I held out no great hopes. Only one man could put me in touch with him quickly, and he was locked up in Girona.

I'd had enough of the beach. I was restless, plus, the wind was getting stronger by the minute. I called to Tom that it was time to go and feed Charlie . . . that always works faster than simply, 'Time to go, Tom' . . . rolled up my towel and stuffed it away in my bag.

The dog was pleased to see us, although he wasn't fed until I'd made Tom stand under the cold shower in a corner of the garden to get rid of the considerable amount of beach that he'd brought back with him, then towel off before he went inside to fill Charlie's bowl. He was halfway through his evening ration . . . That meant he'd been at it for less than half a minute. Have you ever seen a Labrador eat? . . . when I heard the phone ring in the hall. I was sand-free myself by this time so I stepped indoors and picked it up.

'Senora Blackstone?' A man's voice.

'Yes.'

'My name is Comisari Nino Valdes,' he said. 'I am now in charge of the investigation into the deaths of Senor Planas and Senora Fumado.' *A commissioner*, I registered. *They have brought in the big guns.* 'I don't know if you are aware, but we have a man in custody in respect of the two crimes.'

'Yes,' I snapped. 'I am aware of it, and I'm quite certain that it's the wrong man.'

'That's not what he says, senora. I am quite confident that we have a case, and I'm happy to explain it to you. It would be helpful to us if you would agree to be interviewed, purely as a witness, you understand. I know,' he continued, smoothly, 'that given your recently conferred status I can't compel you to do this, but I would appreciate your cooperation.'

I was on the point of telling him that I wasn't interested in helping him, only Gerard, but stopped myself. I'd be in control in any interview, and I'd volunteer nothing that would be of harm to him. 'Okay,' I said.

'Excellent. When can I visit you?'

'You can't; I'll come to you. I'd prefer it that way.' I checked my watch; it was half past five. 'You're in Girona, yes?'

'That's right.'

'I can be there for six thirty.'

'I'm sorry, I have another appointment this evening. There's no need to rush; no one's going anywhere. Let's make it two o'clock tomorrow afternoon. Will that be convenient?'

'Yes, of course.'

'That's good. I'll be waiting for you. I appreciate this.'

I hope you're as pleased when we're done, I thought, *you smug bastard*.

Forty-seven

I did my best not to think about what had happened, until I actually had to. I went into the computer room . . . I'd have to start thinking of it as my office . . . and picked up my envelope from the FCO. I did what I'd been asked to do, beginning with a call to the ambassador in Madrid. She had gone for the night, so I said I'd try again on Monday morning. Then I rang John Dale, the man who seemed to be my point of contact; we were still in normal office hours, according to British Summer Time.

I'd expected a civil service mandarin type, somebody with a plummy accent, honed at Eton and Oxbridge; instead I found myself speaking to a bloke from Bradford, who'd made no attempt to lose his. Progress, I supposed.

'Mrs Blackstone,' he exclaimed, 'good to hear from you. I was told not to expect a call until next week.'

'Primavera, please. Who told you that?'

'Joe O'Regan, my man upstairs; he got it from the Foreign Secretary, his man.'

'Was my appointment as big a surprise to you as it was to me?'

'Yes and no. I wasn't anticipating anything in Spain, but there have been quite a few appointments like yours lately around the world, special counsellors with specific briefs. It's been the practice of this government since they've been in office. If the Tories had done it they'd have called it "Jobs for the boys and girls", but to this lot it's "Bringing in a breath of fresh air", which you sound like, if you don't mind me saying so.'

I didn't mind at all, as I told him. 'If your man upstairs got it from his man, who did he get it from?'

'From what I gather it was Mayfield, the Home Secretary. Am I close to the mark?'

'Think Francis Urquhart.'

'Uh?'

'Novel and TV series, *House of Cards*, by Michael Dobbs. "You may say so, but I couldn't possibly comment." That's the Urquhart character's great line.'

'Ah,' he exclaimed, 'that's where it comes from, is it? Before my time, I'm afraid.'

'Thanks, John,' I said cheerfully.

'Oops.'

I let him off the hook, although I did register that the guy was probably younger than me, for all his high rank. 'That's all right; they repeat it on nostalgia TV every so often. Tell me,' I went on, 'in the event that what you gather is true, how would the Home Secretary manage to pull off something like that in the Foreign Office?'

'Well,' he replied, stretching out the word as if he was

framing a diplomatic reply, 'word is there's going to be a revolution soon. Our guy is very ambitious, and if he's to succeed to the big chair, he's going to need the younger group on his side . . . especially Mayfield.'

'I see. I must start to read the UK media on a daily basis.'

'Yes, but read the lot. The *Guardian*'s facing three ways at once, as usual, but *The Times* and the *Telegraph* both subscribe to another theory, that our guy is a little too ambitious to be trusted, and that when he does kick off the upheaval, the party will get behind someone who's shown a bit more loyalty, and who's just as smart.'

'Justin?'

'Ah, you're on first-name terms,' he chuckled.

'I've met the man twice,' I told him, firmly.

'Then you must have impressed him. Now, when can you come to London? Next week too soon?'

'A little. I'll have to make arrangements for my son, and in addition I'm involved in a situation here that's going to take a couple of days to resolve.'

In the end we agreed that I'd report to the Foreign Office one week from the following Tuesday, 10 a.m. 'What's the dress code?' I asked.

'Pinstripe suit, blue shirt, white collar,' he replied, 'or jeans and a T-shirt saying "Welcome to Spain" if you prefer. Whatever's your norm. But no jewellery of a religious nature; we're not allowed to show or imply favouritism.'

'You are joking, aren't you?'

'Fortunately, yes.'

I'm going to like John Dale, I thought as I hung up. But what to do about Tom? Was I really prepared to be a working mum? *Yes*, I told myself, *and the answer's simple: get Gerard out of jail, and he can look after him.*

I kept that thought with me through the evening, even after I'd called Father Olivares and been depressed by his pessimism over Gerard's prospects, especially when I told him that he'd rejected Josep Villamas's offer of representation. 'He is accepting his situation, my dear,' the old cleric sighed. 'If that is the case, then perhaps we should also.'

'I'll never do that,' I insisted. 'Father, do you know how to get in touch with Santiago Hernanz, Gerard's brother?'

'I'm afraid not. I was away on both his visits to L'Escala, so I've never met him, and Gerard rarely speaks of him.'

That was true enough, I had to concede.

I found relief from one problem by concentrating on another. Should I go to Dolores Fumado's funeral? After all, I'd met the woman as often as I'd met Justin Mayfield, and on one of those occasions she'd been dead. Still, Justine had been pretty square with me. On balance I decided that non-attendance might be seen as a snub, so next morning I dug out a black dress, left Tom with Ben Simmers, in charge of the dogs, and drove into L'Escala. Parking wasn't a problem; there's an official area behind the church. In the winter it's free, so it's full, but in the summer you have to pay, so it's half-empty; the locals don't use it then, on principle, even though it only costs a few cents. See Catalans; see money?

I bought a new shawl in a shop at the top of the hill, not

because I wanted one, but to comply with convention. It wasn't as nice as my old one, but the police still had that, and anyway, going to a funeral wearing the murder weapon would have set a new standard in political incorrectness.

As I had at Planas's send-off, I tried to make myself invisible in the middle of the congregation, but I could only find a seat at the end of a row, right on the aisle. Hah! If the ghost of John Paul II had appeared at the altar to conduct the Mass he wouldn't have attracted much more attention than I did. For all the discretion that the police had shown in bandying my name around when I was on the run, I must still have been the talk of every hairdressing salon in L'Escala . . . and believe me, that's a lot of shampoo and set; anyone parachuted into the town and asked to name its main industries on the basis of a quick walk round would probably say anchovies second, hairdressing top of the list.

Just about every head in the place turned to look at me, and a buzz of conversation started. It was only stilled when the mayor, her sister, looking more ghostly than ever, and Angel entered the church and walked slowly up the aisle; they were followed by two other men, of an older generation. Justine stopped beside me. She put her hand on my arm, kissed me on the cheek and said, in a voice loud enough to carry for several rows in every direction, 'Thank you for coming, Primavera. I know you've had an ordeal too.'

That took care of the chattering classes, I'm happy to say. I was forgotten as the Mass progressed. It didn't seem to last as long as the previous one had . . . Father Olivares was acting alone; that may have accounted for it . . . before we were making our way outside, into the square with the vast palm tree, full of noisy birds, in the centre. I would have left straight away, but Justine came across to me. She'd been talking to the two older men, but detached herself. One of them, the taller of the two, moved on to talk to Angel, but the other followed her with his eyes, until they settled on me. 'My uncles,' she explained. 'My parents' brothers. What have you heard?' she asked me quietly.

'Nothing that I believe,' I told her. 'I'm going to Girona this afternoon to see the new head honcho. He wants to interview me.' I stopped, and reminded myself that I was talking to a woman who'd just lost her mother in terrible circumstances. 'But how are you? I haven't had a chance to tell you how sorry I am.'

'I'm as shocked and disbelieving as everyone else in this town,' she replied. 'The man you're going to see, he visited me last night. Primavera, I'm like you. There are things I find it almost impossible to accept. When Gomez told me you were a suspect, I laughed at him. I was ready to laugh at the man Valdes too, but after he'd spoken to me . . . I still find it hard to conceive of such a thing, but . . . You go see him; maybe you'll spot a flaw in his argument. My God, I hope you do.'

I followed the cortège to the cemetery on the edge of town. They bury their dead differently in Spain, not in the ground as a rule . . . for much of the year you'd need to use explosives to dig a grave . . . but in a space in a wall, a vertical mausoleum, which is then sealed. I watched Justine's mother's sad little box being slid into hers, then slid off quietly myself and headed for Girona. I'd looked up the address of the Mossos headquarters. It's in a street called Vista Alegre, near the river that flows through the city. I didn't know it, but my satnav took me straight there.

Commissioner Valdes was ready for me, in a utilitarian office with one-way windows and cream-painted walls, a tall slim man with a high forehead and black hair that was cut fairly long. He reminded me very much of John Cazale, the actor who played Fredo Corleone in *The Godfather* series. I suspected that he'd adopted the hairstyle after seeing the movies. I wondered whether he'd made a special trip, or whether he always worked Saturdays. That was unlikely, I decided, for someone of his rank; I didn't know whether to be flattered, or worried. 'What do you want to discuss?' I asked him, bluntly.

'Why did you run after you found Dolores Fumado's body?' he retorted, as if to show he was better at bluntness than I was.

'Because I was scared. I'd had a tip that my DNA had been found on the murder weapon; when I found Dolores dead in my wood store I flipped.'

'Who told you that you should go?'

'In those circumstances, do you think I needed telling? If it had happened to you, Commissioner, you'd have been out of there like Speedy Gonzalez.'

A gleam in Valdes' eyes suggested that he might not have liked being compared to the fastest mouse in all Mayheeco, but he let it pass. 'One never knows how one will react until such a thing happens,' he conceded. 'And in your case, Senora Blackstone, you may as well have vanished into a mouse hole. For there was no trace of you to be found when Intendant Gomez put out a call for your apprehension and arrest. You must have had help; there's no question. Nor is there any question in my mind that the person who helped you was Father Hernanz.'

I shrugged. 'What makes you think that?' I asked, casually.

'I'm helped by the fact that we found your passport, your credit cards and a bicycle, later identified by Inspector Guinart as yours, in a garage in L'Escala, rented by Father Hernanz. We searched it on Thursday evening, before his arrest. Now why would he have those?'

'Maybe I left them at his residence,' I suggested, 'and asked him to keep them for me.'

Valdes laughed. 'When you started to run, I can't see you dropping anything off. He made you leave them behind when he sent you off, with your dyed hair. No point in changing colour if you were carrying documents that identified you.' I didn't see any point in commenting on that, since he'd got it dead right. 'Do you know what I thought when I found those things, senora?' He picked up an envelope and tossed it across the desk. 'They're all in there, by the way. You can have them back.'

I picked it up. 'Thank you. No, what did you think?'

'I thought you were dead, I honestly did. I thought that your friend the priest had killed you too, and that we'd find charred remains of you in the boiler below the church. I thought I was going to have to tell your little boy that his mother was gone. I was afraid, senora; afraid I was going to have to do that.' Valdes frowned, and I saw that he was serious. 'Even when I went to arrest him, I thought that was the case. It was only later that morning when I asked Guinart to identify your bike that he told me, no, that you had come back. Do you still want to deny that he helped you?'

'I'll choose to say nothing, if that's all right with you.'

'Fine, for it doesn't matter to us. It should matter to you, though, for it was all part of the set-up.' He stood up. 'Before we go any further,' he said, 'I'd like you to come with me. There's someone I'd like you to talk to.'

For a moment I thought he was going to take me to see Gerard, down in the cells or wherever they were keeping him, but all he did was lead me into the room next door. It was bigger than his, with several desks; most of them empty, but one, near a window, was occupied by a man in civilian clothes. Even seated he looked big, and when he turned towards me, he looked ugly as well, a touch of Frankenstein's monster in his thick gnarled eyebrows.

'Let me introduce you,' said Valdes. 'Senora Blackstone, meet Captain Jorge Lavorante, of the Granada city police. He's a contemporary of Gerard Hernanz; they were at school together, in fact. He has a story that I believe you have to hear.'

I had a terrible feeling that I knew what it was, but I held on to my poker face as I took the seat that the commissioner offered.

Lavorante's voice turned out to be as soft as he was hard,

with an attractive Andalusian lisp. 'A long time ago, back in the city,' he began, 'I was a new kid on the force, when we got a call. It was from a house up on Cuesta de los Cabras, where the Hernanz family lived, from one of their neighbours, scared. She said that someone was being killed up there. I got sent to the scene by my sergeant, on my own. On my own, lady, d' you hear that? Why? Because Gerard Hernanz and his old man were involved, and none of my brave colleagues wanted any part of them. Plus they knew I knew Gerard, and that if anyone could calm things down, I could.'

'You make him sound like a monster.'

Lavorante shook his head. 'I make him sound like the toughest man in Granada, for that's what he was. You know he was a pub bouncer when he was a kid, after he got out of the marines?'

I nodded, defiantly.

The big cop ignored me. 'Nobody fucked with him, apart from one time. I got the story afterwards, from the other doorman. There was one guy wouldn't take a telling. He was rude and abusive. Gerard's girl was there at the time, and the idiot called her a whore. He was still semi-conscious when they got him to hospital, yet Gerard only hit him once. He was a gypsy, and later three of his family came to the bar looking for revenge, the knife-carrying kind. Like I say, Gerard had been in the marines by then, and he had learned all sorts of close-combat skills. He took the blade off the biggest of them so fast he didn't even see it, put him in an armlock, and held it to this throat. Then he told them very quietly that their brother had been way out of order, and that it would be a pity if someone had to die because of a stupid little shit like him. "Put like that," one of the gypsies said, "we can't argue." They all shook hands with him and went off into the night.'

I didn't realise it, but I was trembling as he told his story. 'Senora,' said Valdes, 'would you like a glass of water?'

I realised that I would. Once I'd drunk it, the Andalusian carried on. 'So there I am, up at the Hernanz house. The neighbour had said that the trouble was in the garden so I went in the back way, through a little gate. It was all quiet, not a sound. Then I saw Gerard's old man. He was lying there, covered in blood, and when I say he was out of it, I thought he was dead, till I took a closer look at him, and found a pulse. I could hear voices inside, Gerard's and his brother. Santi was all right, the more sociable of the two, but he was as formidable as Gerard. No way was I handling one of them, let alone two, and besides, they were my friends, so I picked their father up, carried him out of there over my shoulder, and took him to hospital. We were there when the boys brought Gerard's girlfriend in. They didn't see him, or me, and I made sure it stayed that way, but I found out from the staff that the girl had been raped. I also heard that she'd refused, point blank, to call the police. The old man was starting to come round by that time. He'd a fractured skull, they reckoned, and maybe his upper jaw too, but they said he wasn't going to die. "Oh no?" I told them. So I got him out of there, again, put him back in my car and drove him all the way to Cordoba, and left him at the hospital there. I also told him that if he ever came back to

Granada, I'd fucking kill him myself. Trust me, he believed that.'

I listened to the rest of the story, although I knew it all. Irena's leaving, and Gerard's decision to save his life, as Lavorante put it, by entering the priesthood. 'I never did find out what happened to the old man after that,' he concluded. *Ah well, I was one up on him there.*

'Now you've heard that,' said Valdes quietly, 'there's something else I want you to listen to.'

He led me back to his office, produced a minidisc recorder, and put it on the desk. He peered at a dial as if he was setting it up, then pressed Play.

'Do you love Senora Blackstone, Father,' I heard him ask, 'in the way a man loves a woman, that is?'

I heard a sigh. 'Just once,' a disembodied Gerard said, 'I'll answer your question, although I wouldn't if she was here. Yes, I do.'

'I thought so. In that case, I'm going to put a proposition to you, the same one I'm going to put to the court. Two weeks ago, exactly, the lady had an argument with José-Luis Planas in his office, during which he called her a whore, loudly enough for it to be heard by people outside. I've spoken to the lady who managed the business for him; she told me this. Eighteen years ago, in Granada, you knocked a man unconscious and were prepared to kill his brothers when such an insult was aimed at the last woman you loved. When she was attacked by your father, you beat him almost to death. That isn't part of my proposition, by the way; that is witnessed fact. In this case, what

I believe is that you went to Senor Planas's home on the night of his insult to Senora Blackstone; you left the residence after Father Olivares had retired to bed. He let you in, you hit the man with a chair and you killed him. The London forensic team are very good, much better than our people, I have to admit; eventually they found a hair on the murder weapon. The DNA they took from it matches a sample you gave Intendant Gomez for elimination purposes, in Figueras when you went to the morgue to perform the final offices on the man you'd killed. But that night, at the house, you didn't know you'd find Dolores Fumado there. Her relationship with Planas was very much their secret. You dealt with it; you made the scene look as if an accident had occurred, you abducted the lady, and you imprisoned her. You drove her car into the countryside, and you burned it. But not well enough, for you also left a DNA trace on a corner of the driver's door, more hair and some skin, as if you'd bumped your head. So what to do with Dolores? You didn't know, until . . . A few days later, you learned that Gomez's team had found Primavera's palm print on the chair, and you conceived a very bold plan. You killed Dolores, with a shawl belonging to Senora Blackstone. We believe that either she left it in your car on that Friday night, or that you stole it from her, possibly on the Sunday afternoon in St Martí.'

Of course, I thought, *I wore it to church*.

'You put the body in her storeroom. Careless, Father, you left your DNA there again.'

Of course he did, I sent him in there to look.

'When she found it, and called you, as you knew she would, you told her she must leave. You actually framed the woman you love for two murders that you had committed, and then you persuaded her to confirm her own guilt by escaping.'

There was a pause in the recording. 'But why would you do this?' it continued. 'What possible reason could you have had? Let me tell you. You planned to disappear too; you planned to take her son and to join her in hiding, letting her be condemned as a murderess in her absence, but freeing you to spend the rest of your life with the woman you love. Brilliant, flawless . . . or it should have been. You underestimated her resourcefulness, and her ability to prove her own innocence.'

'Something I will never do again,' said Gerard, quietly.

'So that's it?' Valdes asked him. 'You admit it?'

'You're a very smart man, Comisari,' he replied, with a soft chuckle that caused me physical pain as I listened to it, 'to have figured all that out. You put it on paper and I'll sign it; as you said, it's brilliant.'

The commissioner switched off the recording. 'So you see, senora,' he sighed.

I stared at him, that John Cazale lookalike, and as my eyes filled with tears, I knew that he'd done to me what Fredo did to Michael in *Godfather Two*. He'd broken my heart.

Forty-eight

I asked Valdes if I could speak to Gerard. He told me that he had no personal objection, provided that there was a guard present for my security, since I was now a potential witness against him, but that 'the prisoner' . . . how I hated it when he used that word . . . had made it clear that he did not want to see anyone.

I asked him if he would contact Santi, but he replied that the prisoner had expressly forbidden him from contacting his brother. 'He says that he will not allow his situation to compromise his career. He has that right, senora; I have to respect it.'

There was nothing that I could do but leave. I sat outside in the car park for a while, not wanting to drive until I had pulled myself together and was able to concentrate on the road. The last thing I needed was to hit a kid, or get hit myself, through lack of attention.

I was stunned. I'd gone in there telling myself that nothing would ever make me believe that Gerard was guilty, only to hear him admit it. I called Mac, on my mobile. He had been in on it, so he had a right to know. I told him where I was, and what had just happened.

He was as stunned as I was. 'He set you up?' he repeated. 'He did that to you?'

'I don't think he set out that way, but when he heard that I was implicated, he saw a way to get himself clear and to get us what we both wanted, each other. I'm in no doubt that if I had been caught he'd have come forward and confessed.'

'You reckon?' he growled. 'You're too good to people, Primavera, that's your problem. You trust too much.'

'I haven't always. This time I really thought I could. Luck of the devil, eh. Oh Mac, why do I always fuck up? I get close to someone then I do something daft, or he dies, or goes to the bad. I'm a fucking carrier of disaster; they should lock me up like one of those typhoid women and chuck away the key.'

'Aye, and who'd look after your boy then? Don't beat yourself up over the imperfections of others. You were far more loyal to my son than he ever was to you, and as for this fellow, seems to me you're lucky you didn't get any closer to him.' He took a deep breath. 'Look, would you like me to come back out there, me and Mary? We could look after the wee man while you get stuck into this new job of yours.'

'Thanks, Mac, but I'm not even sure I'll go ahead with that.'

'Hey,' he exclaimed, 'you'll get me angry in a minute. There's every reason why you should. This guy's kicked you right in the self-esteem. You've been given this opportunity because people think you're worth it. If you walk away from it, you'll be letting them down, Tom down, me down, yourself . . .

Ach shit, Primavera, you're going ahead as planned, you're going to let Father Gerard take his coffee and you're going to wash him out of your hair along with that bloody dye. So, do you want us to come out?'

I considered his offer; then I turned it down. 'It's good of you, but if I'm going to do what you say, I'd best begin by standing on my own two feet.'

'That's more like it. Keep in touch, though.'

'I promise.'

I was ready for the road; Mac had put some backbone into me. I found my way out of Girona and took the quickest way home, via the short hop up the autopista from junction six to five. I got home just as Tom was getting to the fretting stage, fed up with the dogs and worrying about me. I bought a case of Riogenc from Ben, partly as a thank you and partly because I was running low on pink wine, and took Tom and Charlie home.

The dog had barely settled into his kennel before Tom planted himself in front of me, looked me square in the eye, and asked, solemnly, 'Mum, what's wrong with Gerard?' He didn't add, 'And don't fob me off with some crap story about him going away to another parish.' He let his expression do that for him.

'He's with the police, son,' I replied. 'He's in trouble.'

'I heard someone saying he's killed people.'

'That's what the police say too.'

He looked at me scornfully, dry eyed. 'Gerard wouldn't do that. You don't believe them, do you?'

'He's admitted it, Tom. He's confessed to it; I heard him say so, on a recording.'

'But has he told you that he did it? Has he told YOU?' He shouted the last word.

'No, he wouldn't see me.'

'He wouldn't see you because he knew he couldn't tell you a lie.'

He's a tough little monkey, but he was getting close to tears. I drew him to me, and pressed his face into my chest. 'Tom, my love, you don't tell a lie that's going to put you in prison for thirty years. I'm sorry.'

'No!' he shouted, then twisted out of my grasp and ran into the house. I didn't follow him; since he was about three he hasn't liked anyone seeing him cry, not even me. I'm not keen on it myself, so I went indoors too.

After a while, I changed out of my black dress, into denim shorts and a red shirt. I hung the dress up, tossed my new shawl into the box where I keep odds and ends like that, and went down to what I was going to have to think of as my office. I had it to myself, so I booted up my computer and Skyped Mark Kravitz.

'What's the matter?' he asked, immediately. Christ, did I look that bad? A glance at my box onscreen showed me that I did.

I told him the story. 'Jesus, Primavera,' he murmured into his mike, 'what a length to go to. Wouldn't you have shagged him if he'd just asked?'

'Not on the side,' I replied, 'not while he was still a priest.'

'The police case is rock solid, is it?'

'Rock solid and with a signed confession. I spoke to a cop who knew him back in Granada; this guy's supposed to be the hardest man in town, but he didn't think so himself, when the Hernanz brothers were lads. Gerard was, plus he has a history of violence when his women are insulted, or abused.'

'Indeed?' He looked at me. 'So what are you going to do now?'

'Look after my boy; he's broken-hearted. Then . . .' As I looked at him, I had an idea. 'I've been told to get on with my life, so next week I'm coming to London to meet a man at the FCO. How do you fancy having an office junior for a couple of days; nearly nine, and big for his age?'

'That would be great. Why don't you both stay here?'

'No, Mark, I wouldn't impose that much. We'll get a hotel; the FCO are paying for it, and I can't remember the last time I was on expenses.'

Tom came into the room just as we finished our conversation. I wondered if he'd been listening, and immediately felt ashamed of myself; he doesn't have a sneaky bone in his body. 'We're going to London,' I told him. Normally a piece of news like that would have set him hollering, but all he did was shrug.

'Do I have to?' he asked.

'Afraid so, buddy. I have to go, and I'd like your company.'

'Okay then.' He looked at me as he switched on his computer. 'Can I visit Gerard before then?'

'He's in custody, Tom. You wouldn't like it.'

'Maybe not, but I'd like to see him. Please, Mum.'

'It's not my decision, son. The police would have to agree, and Gerard would have to agree himself. But if it's what you want, I'll ask the commissioner, I promise. It probably won't be before Monday, though.'

'Can I go to the church tomorrow? I suppose Father Olivares will be saying Mass; I've helped him before when Gerard's been away.'

'Of course you can. I'm sure he'll welcome your assistance too.'

I was reading through the diplomatic service house rules when the phone rang. I saw Alex Guinart's home number displayed.

'How are you doing?' he asked. 'Commissioner Valdes called me after you'd gone. He's concerned about you. He might sound like an asshole from time to time, but he's actually not such a bad guy. He's been going out of his way not to upset Hector.'

'How do you think I'm doing? I'm gutted.'

'How's Tom?'

'In denial; that's as good a description as any.'

'Do the two of you have any plans for tonight?'

'Huh,' I grunted. 'Put it this way. We're not going dancing.'

'In that case, come and eat with Gloria and Marte and me. We're going up to St Martí this evening. Since it's Saturday, we thought we'd try the other pizzeria, about eight thirty.'

I came close to turning him down, for I knew I'd be lousy

company. Then I thought of Tom; I had to do something to break his mood. 'Fine,' I said. 'I'll ask them to keep us a table.'

'The other pizzeria' is actually the second business of Meson del Conde; it opens during the summer months, when you could put out as many tables as the village can hold and they'd all be occupied. (I suspect the café owners would do that, but their kitchens could never keep up.) I took care of it there and then, or rather I delegated the task, asking Tom to run across and make the booking.

Suddenly, I was tired. The events of the day caught up with me; I told Tom, yes, he could watch cricket on television . . . if it's sport he'll watch it . . . then went upstairs to my private terrace off my bedroom, stripped off, and stretched out on my lounger. I'd probably have slept through till next morning if Tom hadn't wakened me. I dreamed, of course; about Granada, about Gerard . . . Or was it Santi? I can't be sure now . . . about Tom, on a rock, shouting, 'Mum.'

His voice drifted from the dream into my consciousness. 'Mum,' he called from the doorway, for what was probably the third or fourth time. A couple of years ago, he'd just have prodded me awake, but he's beginning to understand the concept of privacy, and so he feels slightly awkward about seeing his mother naked. 'Wake up, it's eight o'clock and the table's . . .'

I sat up and nodded, bleary eyed. 'Thanks, Tom. I'll shower and come down. You get yourself ready.'

He looked at me askance; he does askance well. 'I am ready,' he said. He was too; he'd changed into cargo pants and an

Aussie T-shirt that Uncle Miles had given him, with Shane Warne's face, larger than life, on the front . . . or is Shane's head really that big?

I thought about glamming up, but decided against it for two reasons: one, I suspected that Gloria wouldn't, and two, I couldn't be arsed. So I washed, blew my hair dry, making a mental memo to buy a tint to kill the chestnut, and put on the shirt and shorts that I'd picked earlier, with a blast of Chanel No. 5 as my one concession to femininity.

We got to the table five minutes early; Alex and Gloria arrived ten minutes late. No Marte, though; the wee soul was cutting back teeth, and had been fractious, so they'd left her with Gloria's mum.

'Did Valdes play you the tape?' Alex asked, quietly, once we were settled in.

'Enough of it. Have you heard it?'

'I was in the room, Primavera. Valdes wanted me there, someone you would trust, so that there could be no doubt about everything being above board. I was there when he interviewed the big ugly Andalusian as well. The Gerard he described was one I've never met, but that guy Lavorante is not the sort to talk himself down, so when he said that he'd never have dreamed of crossing him, I believed him.'

'Me too. Santi told me as much.'

'Santi? Who the hell's Santi?'

'Gerard's brother.'

'Ah. The guy didn't mention his name. You've met him?'

'That's where I was, Alex, it's where I ran to; Gerard's house in Granada. He'd arranged for Santi to be there to look after me.'

'Should you tell me this, Primavera?' he asked, frowning.

'It doesn't make any difference now. Valdes knows anyway; he may not be certain where I went, but he knows that Gerard helped me get away, and if he was interested in finding out where he sent me, it wouldn't take him long. But it's not relevant.'

'I don't suppose it . . .' He stopped in mid-sentence as a waiter arrived to take our food orders. Alex and I hadn't even looked at the menu, so we let the other two go first. I realised that I was hungry; I'd done a big salad for Tom and Ben before I'd left for the funeral, but with everything that had happened afterwards, I'd forgotten to eat lunch myself. I chose a simple pasta starter, then a Four Seasons pizza, with still and fizzy water for the table, a bottle of the ever-reliable Vina Sol, and fresh orange juice for junior. He was beginning to look a bit brighter, but he still wasn't his usual self.

None of us were, for that matter. Conversations at the tourist tables buzzed on oblivious, but the thing . . . I couldn't think of another word to describe it . . . that had happened hung over ours like our own personal cloud.

'You know,' Alex continued, still speaking quietly, so that Tom, who was locked on to his hand-held PlayStation, couldn't overhear, 'most of the time I love my job. What I do, I right wrongs; I investigate crimes and I bring the people who commit them to account. That gives me satisfaction, big time; I feel that I've given something back to the community that raised me, and it pleases me. But every so often I get involved in something and I hate myself for it. Like this business. There are no winners, only losers. Two people we knew are dead. Okay, Planas wasn't a nice man, and Dolores was known around town as "The mouth of L'Escala", but they had a right to life. And who killed them? One of the most popular men in town, a friend of many of us, and now we've lost him too. Sitting in that office today, listening to him confess to everything that Valdes put to him, watching him put his signature on it . . . Primavera, that was one of the saddest moments of my life.'

'And mine.'

'I feel lousy about it, because I don't remember ever misjudging anyone so much. I should have been angry with him when they took him away to the cells, but I found that I could only be angry with myself, for being duped.'

'Are you sure?' I asked. 'Could it be that you were angry with yourself because you're part of the machine that caused his downfall?'

He shook his head. 'No, because we didn't; he brought it on himself. This isn't Jesus Christ we're dealing with here. This is a man from Andalusia with a record of extreme violence in his youth, who managed to run away from what he is by entering the church, but who couldn't keep his other side at bay forever. He fooled us all.'

'So he was a bad priest?'

'No, and that's the damnable thing. He was a great priest; he and Olivares, they're the best team we've ever had in this town, in my lifetime. I can't imagine how the old man's taking it.'

'How do you think? You saw, he got through the funeral Mass today, but he's devastated.'

'And you, Primavera, how are you taking it? I can see that Tom's hurt, but can you deal with it?'

'Chum, I can deal with anything. Tom's hurt, but not the way you are, because you feel let down. He's hurt because he sees a great injustice being done. But he hasn't heard the tape, he didn't hear Gerard confess. The thing I'll find hardest to deal with is the thought that if he did it, it was because of me.'

'You're still saying "if", I notice.'

'Yes, because a part of me's like Tom, refusing to believe. I love that man, Alex, and I have faith in him. It's very hard for me to accept that I've misplaced that faith, and for all the apparent facts of the matter, I don't think I ever will, not completely.'

'And he loves you. We've both heard him say so. We've both heard him acknowledge the truth of Valdes's brilliant deduction. He saw a way of having you, he took a chance . . . and he lost. Now he's willing to pay the price.' He frowned. 'Maybe I can see nobility in that. Many crimes are about greed, many are about hate; these seem to have been about love, anger yes, but anger fuelled by love.'

I shook my head. 'I'm sorry; you can't argue that about Dolores. She was in the way; that was why she died. That wasn't rage, it was cruelty. Didn't the autopsy show that from the time she was captured to the time she was killed, she was starved? That's the part that's out of kilter. Even if everything else is true, that's what disturbs me the most. It's what makes me think that maybe I didn't really know the man at all.'

'I'm afraid that none of us did,' he murmured, as our starters arrived.

I was glad of the break; in truth, the discussion was tearing me apart. I don't think I've ever been as happy to see a plate of linguine Napolitano. We changed the subject as we ate, not least because Tom was back with us. Gloria asked him what he was going to do during the school holidays.

'I'm going to London,' he told her. 'With Mum. Next week. It's about her new job.'

'New job?' she exclaimed, puzzled. Alex said nothing, which more or less confirmed my assumption that he'd heard of it already, although he'd never raised the subject.

'I've been appointed to the staff of the British Embassy,' I explained, 'on a part-time basis. It has to do with representing Scotland in Spain. It was a big surprise; someone in London put me up for it.'

'Congratulations. It doesn't mean you'll be leaving us, does it?' she asked, anxiously. 'We'd all miss you, especially Marte.'

'Don't worry,' I assured her. 'We're not going anywhere. They've still got to tell me exactly what I'll be doing, but I suspect that a lot of it will be in Barcelona. I'll still be around to keep an eye on my goddaughter.'

'What about me?'

I looked at Tom, surprised by his direct question; but he was in that sort of mood, slightly rebellious. It wasn't the moment I'd have chosen, but the issue couldn't be dodged. 'I think we're going to employ somebody, full-time, to look after the house,' I announced.

'Like Ethel?' He fixed me with an unblinking stare. It was a loaded question. Ethel Reid looks after Janet and wee Jonathan, his half-siblings, Oz's kids by Susie Gantry; she's very efficient, very nice, but she's Mary Poppins, no messing. That is not what Tom wanted to hear.

'No,' I replied, meeting his gaze with a wink. 'A lady, yes, but more like Conrad.'

Conrad Kent was recruited by Oz and Susie as property manager or some such, but actually he's a minder. He still works for Susie at her place in Monaco, even though she has a new man, of whom I know very little, so far. Conrad is half Jamaican, half Welsh, ex-military, and Tom is one of his biggest fans.

He said nothing, but when he nodded, I knew I'd scored.

The main courses arrived. They do a damn good Four Seasons there; the artichokes are always the best. Mine kept me quiet for the best part of fifteen minutes. I let Alex and Gloria do most of the damage to the Vina Sol; nothing against it, but I wasn't in the mood.

Perhaps I should have had a glass, to shake off my moroseness . . . or how about my morosity? (I know the word isn't in the dictionary, but maybe it should be.) We were at the coffee stage when Alex and I drifted back into our funk. 'How long will the court proceedings take?' I asked him, quietly.

'No idea. Our courts work in varying degrees of slowness. The prosecution will present its case, even if Gerard chooses not to defend it. They'll proceed when they're ready, not before. If Gerard had a lawyer . . . and at the moment, he's refused all offers . . . he could apply for habeas corpus, but he wouldn't get it, not against the evidence. I don't know the new prosecutor, how quickly he works. The previous one, the one who leaned on Hector, he was no ball of fire . . . but of course he's out of the picture now. He has to be.'

Something in his tone made me ask 'Why?'

'Because he's Javier Fumado, Dolores's brother. He was at the funeral today; the small man, with Justine and Elena's Belgian uncle. He could hardly prosecute the killer of his own sister.'

'Maybe that's why he frowned at me after the service,' I said. 'I wondered about that.' I paused, for thought. 'Earlier, you said there are no losers in this. When you think about it, of course there are. There's Angel Planas; even if the old man had threatened to disinherit him, he's still lost his father.'

'I suppose,' Alex conceded, 'although that was an empty threat. Spanish law won't let you disinherit your eldest son.'

'Whatever,' I said dismissively. 'Then there's Justine and Elena; they've lost their mother, poor girls.'

'True, and it's doubly hard for them. Our parents are supposed to die in their beds, not violently, as they lost both of theirs.'

'What do you mean?'

He stared at me. 'Didn't you know? The father, Henri Michels, he was out walking, was taken ill and fell off a cliff path. It was a long way down. He was killed.'

I blinked, twice, hard, and saw myself back in Granada with the mad fortune teller. What was it she'd said?

'*I see evil, I see a fall, I see tears, I see separation. The father, the father. He dies.*'

Well, I thought. *Is that not as weird as a bottle of potato crisps?*

Forty-nine

I didn't sleep very well that night. It had nothing to do with my snooze in the afternoon, or with my lack of interest in the white wine. No, I was still thinking of the nutty white heather lady, trying to recall the rest of the stuff she'd come out with.

'*I see difficult times, but you come through them.*' That had been the woman's other prophecy. I took some heart from that.

After all, she'd been right about the tears, she'd been right about the separation; most of all she'd been right about the evil. On top of all that she'd been right about a father dying in a fall, Henri Michels, Justine's dad, Elena's dad ... Dolores Fumado's husband.

Hard as I tried, I couldn't get that out of my head. In fact, it had taken such a grip of me that as soon as Tom, Charlie and I had breakfasted, I called Alex.

'Henri Michels,' I said. 'Tell me again what happened.'

'He was found at the bottom of a cliff,' he replied, patiently, 'in the area between the marina and Illa Mateu, the bay at the foot of the hill the Brits call the Garbinell. They did an autopsy on him; it showed that he'd had a heart attack.'

'What did he die from? The MI?' (Myocardial infarction, the posh name for a coronary; my nursing vocabulary's still there, I just don't use it very often.)

'No, he died from multiple injuries, more or less instantly.'

'So he could have had the heart attack on the way down?'

'Jesus, Primavera, I suppose, but . . . It was an accident, and not the first up there. It's a dangerous place.'

'Was it investigated?'

'Of course, and that was the finding.'

'Were you involved? "You" as in the Mossos?'

'Initially, but the public prosecutor's office took it over. Because it was the mayor's father, they said, and we were happy to hand it over, to let them sign off on it.'

Somewhere I sensed ducks forming into a row. 'Who in the prosecutor's office?' I asked.

'Javier Fumado.'

'And now we find out that the widow, his sister, has been making the two-backed beast with José-Luis Planas. Alex! Be a cop; trust your nose.'

He sighed. 'I'll grant you that's of interest . . . but only,' he added, 'in respect of Henri Michels' death. It has nothing to do with the current situation.'

'Maybe it hasn't, but you'll never know that for sure until it's investigated. Are you up for it?'

'I suppose.'

'Could we get into Planas's house, to have a look at his papers? He was a councillor and he had various business interests; he must have been an organised man, and he must have kept a diary of sorts.'

'Yes, easily; technically it's still a crime scene. But Primavera, what's with the "we"?'

'Humour me. There's a fortune teller's reputation riding on this.'

Fifty

Alex was nervous about it, but since Valdes had gone back to Barcelona, taking Gerard with him to the long-term remand wing in the prison, and since technically what we were doing had nothing to do with the commissioner's investigation, he went along with my brazen proposal, and he took me along with him. He picked Tom and me up after church. Father Olivares had been subdued. He had not referred to Gerard, or the reason for his absence; he had simply conducted the Mass, and preached no sermon. Tom had been sombre too, but he had performed his duties admirably, earning a pat on the head and a smile from the old man when he was finished.

We parked at the front gate; it wasn't a secret mission, since Alex had signed the keys to the place out of the Mossos's L'Escala office. We left Tom in the car, with plenty of water and his PlayStation, and went inside. I have to admit that once we had opened some shutters to let the light in I really liked Planas's villa. His housekeeper had been doing a good job; yes, there was a film of dust, since she hadn't been in for a couple of weeks, but the place still smelled of furniture polish, the floor and wall tiles were spotless and shiny, and the bathrooms were immaculate, apart from a facecloth that had been tossed into a bin in the downstairs toilet and lay there, dried out and crumpled. Remembering the traces the scientists had found on Planas's person and clothing, I made a fair guess about its last use.

'Does Angel inherit all of this?' I asked as we looked around. 'You said his old man couldn't have cut him off if he tried.'

'At least half,' he replied. 'We won't know about the rest until the will's published.'

'Hypocritical old bastard, wasn't he? The fuss he made about Ben and Elena, the grudge he carried against the guy, and all the time he was porking her mother on the quiet.'

'He was Spanish,' said Alex, as if no other explanation was needed. He opened a door, on the first floor. 'Hey, this is it; this must have been his office.'

Unlike the rest of the place the room looked as if a woman had never set foot in it. I found myself thinking back to *The Godfather* again, not to poor old Fredo this time, but to that dimly lit, smoky study, where Don Corleone himself held court and took tribute. There was a big twin-pedestal desk, made of a dark wood that had grown even darker with age, with carved features that marked it out as a valuable piece, a high-backed leather-upholstered chair behind it that looked as if three generations of Planases might have left their marks on it, and two single Chesterfields that fitted my mind picture of a classic London gentlemen's club. There was a small sideboard against one wall, with a decanter sat on top, surrounded by four brandy goblets, and a cigar box beside it.

Alex moved behind the desk and began opening doors and drawers. 'Shit,' he whispered. 'Look at this.' He reached into the drawer that would have been at Planas's right hand and produced a revolver, with a barrel that looked to be around six inches long.

'I thought those were illegal here,' I said.

'They are, without a permit … and I don't recall him having one.'

'It didn't do him much good.'

'No, but it shows the kind of man he was; not to be taken lightly. Like Gerard.'

'Don't.' I shuddered. 'What else have you found there?'

He squatted beside the desk, rifling through its contents. 'Personal accounts, tax papers, bills, bank books,' he listed; then his face broke into a smile. 'And diaries,' he added, 'old-fashioned page per day diaries. Going back five years. You told me to trust my nose, Primavera; I'll trust yours from now on.' He took them from their shelf in the left pedestal, and laid them on the desk. 'Should we start at the beginning?'

'Eventually, but for now, let's go back just two years, to when Henri Michels was killed. Can you remember the date?'

'I looked it up in the office, among our incident reports; the body was found on the twenty-eighth of May, a Monday. It was called in at eight twelve by a fisherman; he was out checking his pots near Saltpax rock when he spotted the body at the foot of the cliff. But there was an earlier note from the municipal police, timed at eleven thirty the night before, letting us know that Dolores had reported that her husband hadn't come back from a walk.'

'It was a long walk to where he died, since they lived in the old town.'

'They didn't, not then; they had a house in Carrer Muga, up in Puig Sec, not far from your friend Shirley's place. Henri bought the land . . . oh, must be seven, eight years ago now . . . and built the house himself.'

'I thought he sold carpets.'

'So he did, when he came to Spain. But like a lot of people here he went into property development in the boom years, and made a lot of money. Dolores sold the house right after he died, and went back to her old family home. Nobody was surprised; to someone from an old L'Escala family, moving to Puig Sec's like moving to L'Estartit, or Begur.'

'So she couldn't have been too happy, living up there?'

'Well,' he began, 'as a police officer I don't like to go on rumour . . .'

I laughed at that. 'Bollocks! The cops I've known all told me that gossip is where it starts. You keep your ears open, you hear what's being said, you investigate and you find out whether it's true or not.'

Alex smiled. 'That's crime; I'm talking domestic here. My mother-in-law said the other night she heard that Dolores was furious when Henri built that house. When he bought the land she assumed that it was for a project for sale, but he told her that he'd always wanted a view of the sea and the mountains and that they were moving in.'

'That's interesting.'

'What is?'

'The time frame. Henri bought the land seven or eight years ago; let's say it took him a year or so to build the house. They must have moved in around six years ago.'

'Yes, that would be right. So?'

'So, that was when Planas's wife died. Does your mother-in-law recall what went wrong with her?'

'As a matter of fact, she does; she says that she had breast cancer. She fought it for a while, but eventually she lost.' He glanced at me. 'You're suggesting that maybe Henri Michels had good reason to move his wife a little distance away?'

'I'm floating the idea, that's all. Let's see what the diaries tell us.'

Alex nodded and selected one from the pile. 'Two years ago,' he announced, then flipped it open. He frowned as he looked through the first few pages.

'What's up?'

'It's only appointments, council meetings, various business dates.'

'Too much to hope for, that he kept a daily journal. See what you can find, though.'

'Okay, be patient.' He thumbed his way to a particular page, then made his way back, day by day. He was halfway through turning one more when he paused. 'Hey,' he said, 'take a look at this. Wednesday, May the twenty-third. He's had a busy day, three meetings with clients in the estate agency, two council committees, and a session with Angel in the furniture shop. There's no room left on the page, but look what's written in the margin.'

He held it up for me, pointing at a note in a neat, clear hand; I read aloud. 'H M, El Burro, 8:30. H M being Henri Michels?'

'Let's suppose that it was.' His forehead wrinkled. 'But El Burro? Why the hell would they meet there?'

'What's wrong with it?'

'Everything. It's closed now; it went broke before the public health people could shut it down. It was a dirty little Brit bar up in Riells de Dalt. Planas was a patron of the Miryam, and Henri Michels drank in El Golf Isobel; they weren't the sort of guys who'd have been seen dead in El Burro.'

'So they met somewhere they wouldn't be recognised. Who do you think set it up?'

He scratched his chin. 'Michels built some houses on a plot not far from there. I doubt if Planas had even heard of the place. I'd say Henri.'

'And the agenda . . . I wonder who set that?' I took the diary from him and looked at the next page; again, business meetings, council meetings, but nothing else. I flicked on to the next; more estate agency stuff, but at the foot of the page, the last entry read, 'F. Rhodas, P-S. 2:00.' I showed it to Alex. 'Who's this F, d' you think?'

'I'd only be guessing,' he said. 'But from that I'm pretty sure I know where they were meeting. There's a restaurant named

Rhodas, in a place called Palau Saverdera. I know it quite well; once a year a few friends and I, all Mossos, have dinner there. It's famous for its lamb. Let me make a call.'

He wandered across to the window, mobile in hand. 'Hey, Chico,' I heard him say after a while, 'it's Alex Guinart. Yes, I know it's Sunday and I know you're busy, and you know I'm a cop so listen to me, okay.' Then he lowered his voice a little and I couldn't hear what he was saying any more, until finally, he laughed. 'Good customer?' he exclaimed. 'Well, chum, if I were you I'd go out and find another to take his place, for you won't be seeing him again, or her for that matter.' He ended the call and turned to face me. 'I just described Planas and Dolores to my friend Chico, the owner. He says they've been customers there for as long as he can remember, and he goes back twelve years; they went there for lunch, last Friday of every month. But the weird thing is he didn't know their names . . . although he did say he overheard him calling her "Flora" a couple of times. The table was a standing reservation, and Planas always paid cash.'

'Ask your mother-in-law if Dolores had a nickname when she was younger, and see if she says it was "Flora". Bet?'

'There's no danger of me taking that one on. But I wasn't finished. My pal told me a story about them. Their regular lunch date, a couple of years ago, May, he reckons, they were mid-meal and a guy walked in, big guy, white hair; he went right up to their table, shouting at them, something about having warned him, but Planas being too fucking arrogant to listen. Spoke Catalan, but with a foreign accent. Planas stood up, and the man decked him, grabbed the woman by the arm and hauled her out of there. Chico offered to call us, but Planas told him not to.'

'And two days later Henri Michels had a heart attack and fell over a cliff?'

'And one month later, Planas and Dolores were back there, and it was as if the whole thing had never happened.'

I whistled. 'That's what I call a result. What does the diary say,' I asked, 'about the night Michels died?'

He looked up that page. 'Nothing. No appointments. No alibi.'

'What do we do next?'

'You take your son back home,' he said. 'I call Hector Gomez and tell him what we've found here. Then he and I might decide to have a word with the guy who was so keen to write off Michels' death as a suicide.'

'If you do,' I asked, 'can I come?'

He stared at me, in disbelief.

Fifty-one

There wasn't a cat's chance of that, and I knew it; still, I persuaded Alex to make his call from my house, so that I could be on hand to defend him if the intendant blew a gasket over our search of the Planas place, and threatened to send him on night patrol in the no-go areas of Barcelona . . . and there are some, trust me on that.

But Gomez took the news calmly; I know this for sure because we used the office phone, which has a hands-free facility, and so I could hear him. 'You know, Alex,' he said, when the story was told, 'I always thought the Michels investigation was irregular. I was going to take it on myself, but Javier Fumado brushed me off. His angle was that it was a family tragedy and should be handled quietly for the sake of his sister, and his nieces. I fell for it too. Christ, if I had known this stuff about Planas . . .'

'There's no evidence that Fumado knew either,' I pointed out.

'You're right, Primavera, there isn't. But it's come to light now, and it's put the power in my hands. Thanks to you two, I can walk into his office tomorrow with this new evidence about Dolores and reopen the investigation.'

'Even though both she and Planas are dead?'

'Henri Michels doesn't know that, though. If his death wasn't accidental, and wasn't caused by a heart attack, he deserves justice. This too,' he added. 'I've never liked that little bastard Fumado and I've never trusted him. Over the years he's taken a few decisions against prosecution that have struck me as odd. So we'll pay him a visit.' He paused, and then he surprised me, totally. 'Would you like to come, Primavera? You've earned it, I reckon. If it wasn't for you we'd never have established that Michels knew about this triangle. And there's a second reason: you being there will unsettle him, make him uncertain.'

'But how will you explain me?'

'I'll tell him that our regular secretary's on vacation and that we've taken you on as a temp. You take the note of the meeting.'

'I don't know shorthand,' I said, lamely. (I had to use the English word.)

'What's shorthand?' he replied. 'You know how to switch on a recorder, don't you? Come to Girona, tomorrow morning, ten. We'll go to his office from there.'

'How do you know he'll be there?'

'I have an appointment with him already, to discuss another case. He'll find that the agenda's been changed.'

As it happened, Tom had an appointment of his own next morning. One of Ben's neighbours was running a summer sailing school for kids, and I'd enrolled him. I dropped him off at the marina, in front of Café Navili, with instructions to meet me when the session finished, at two o'clock, at a restaurant called La Clota, just around the corner, then I headed off for Girona.

My mood was far different from what it had been two days before. I was still worried about Gerard, of course, deeply worried, but I felt that at least I was doing something. It might not have had anything to do with the two murders of which he was accused . . . okay, Primavera; to which he'd confessed . . . but then again. It was a can of worms, and if our visit to the public prosecutor's office tipped it up and sent them crawling all over his desk, who knew where they might take us?

I'd even taken my own recorder with me for the meeting, but Gomez gave me a small minidisc machine, like the one . . . maybe the same one, for all I knew . . . that Valdes had used to let me hear Gerard's confession. He said that it was better if I was seen to be using official issue, for the sake of propriety. That made me smile.

The office of the public prosecutor isn't far from the Mossos building. The morning was dry and not too hot, so the three of us walked there. His secretary was at her post in the main reception area when we arrived. I expected Gomez to wait to be shown in, but he simply said, 'Meeting with your boss,' and headed for an unmarked door behind her, with Alex and me trailing along behind. The woman, mid-twenties, white shirt, tight grey skirt, enhanced blonde . . . another reminder to do something about my chestnut hair . . . rose to her feet, open mouthed, but we were past her before she could say a word.

Javier Fumado stayed in his seat as the intendant stepped unannounced into his office. He looked mildly annoyed, and more so as his gaze took in Alex. When it got to me it reached angry, and bewildered.

'What is this, Gomez?' he exclaimed. 'What has Guinart got to do with the Iniesta investigation . . . and what the hell is this woman doing here?'

'Iniesta can wait. We're here to talk about something else. As for the lady,' he stressed the word, 'she's working for me while my regular clerk is on vacation.'

'And she can leave right now!' Fumado snapped. He was an unpleasant little man, with a sharp face, pointy enough to have played a villain in *Wind in the Willows*.

Gomez shook his head. 'She stays. We may need to take a formal statement later; that's her job.'

'Statement? From whom?'

'From you, Javier.'

'What the hell are you talking about?'

'We're here to reopen the investigation into the death of Henri Michels.'

'That file is closed.'

'Wrong. It was closed; now it's open again. We have new evidence in the case, and so I need to look at your records.'

'It's been two years, man!'

'So?'

'It was misfortune, that's all; Henri was in poor health, he went on a walk that was too strenuous for him, had a heart seizure and fell to his death.'

'Henri Michels was as strong as an ox,' Alex Guinart intervened. 'I worked out with him in the gym in Riells about a month before he died. He was bench-pressing his age in kilograms, fifteen repetitions at a time; as you'll know, he was sixty-four years old. When he'd finished that, he did ten kilometres on the exercise bicycle.'

'The file, please, Javier,' said Gomez.

The public prosecutor locked eyes with him. I thought he was going to refuse, but he blinked first. 'Okay,' he said, with a huge sigh. 'I'll get it.' He made to rise.

'No,' said the intendant, briskly, 'we'll do that. I need be sure that all of it arrives. Inspector, please.'

'What the hell . . .' Fumado exclaimed, but Gomez cut him off.

'When were you first aware that your sister was in an adulterous relationship with José-Luis Planas?'

The little man frowned. 'When I received the lab comparison between samples taken from her body and from his,' he replied.

'Not before?'

'No.'

'Then why didn't you question my use of the word "adulterous"? Dolores and Planas were both single.'

'A simple oversight.'

'You're a very precise man with words, Javier. Now, would you like to have another shot at answering my question as it was originally put?' He paused, and looked at me. 'Primavera, we've reached the point at which this interview should be recorded. If you would, please.'

I produced the machine he had given me, switched it on, checked that the battery had plenty of life in it, inserted a disc and pressed 'Record'. As I set it on the desk between the two men, I felt strangely proud to be playing an active part, however small, and even if I was under orders to keep my mouth shut.

Formally, as he had done once with me across the table, Gomez stated his name for the tape, then added mine and Fumado's. Just as he finished, Alex came back into the room carrying a slim folder, and so he completed the set.

'So, Senor Fumado,' he continued, then repeated his question, word for word. Alex paid no attention; he sat beside me, with the file on his knees, going through it page by page.

'I may have been aware of it,' the prosecutor admitted.

'May have?' the intendant laughed. 'Your sister was fucking a pillar of the L'Escala community. That's not something you would have forgotten. You either knew or you didn't.'

'Very well, I knew.'

'From when?'

'From fifteen years ago. That's when it started.'

'How did you come to learn of it?'

'From Dolores; she told me about it. She said that she and Henri had . . . fallen out of love, was how she put it. She said that she would leave him for José-Luis if he asked her. I told her flat out that he never would, for he was very aware of what he saw as his position in the town. Maybe things have changed now, but back then . . . you'll know as well as I, Gomez . . . different standards applied. A man could do what he liked, and as long as it was not admitted, it would be overlooked, but a woman would always be a whore. I said also that if she was thinking of divorcing Henri, she should do it anyway. He was not a man to be cuckolded, I told her. She should be very careful.'

'But she ignored your advice?'

'Most of it, but not the part about discretion.'

'Did Henri ever mention it to you? Did he ever voice any suspicions?'

'No.'

'Are you sure?'

'Well . . . Henri was a big man, good looking, with an ego to match. It would have taken a lot for him to even consider that Dolores might be playing away. But he did once say something that made alarm bells ring with me. He told me that he'd found an envelope in the house . . . nothing in it, just an envelope . . . that was addressed to Flora; no surname, just Flora. "Wonder who the hell Flora is?" he said. But I knew.'

'It was your sister's nickname, when she was younger.' Fumado nodded. 'He must have had a feeling that something wasn't right, though, when he moved house? When it was likely that Planas's wife was going to die.'

The prosecutor looked at him blankly. 'That had nothing to do with it, as far as I know.'

'But he did find out,' the intendant said. 'We know for sure that he did. We have a witness who says that he found them together. Two days before that, he and Planas had a meeting in a backwoods bar. We reckon that Henri confronted him and warned him off. We know that he followed them to a restaurant across in Palau Saverdera, knocked Planas flat on his back, and took Dolores away with him. Two days after that he had his supposed heart attack and went over the edge. Did you know about that incident, Javier? Did your sister tell you about it?'

The little man shook his head, vigorously.

'Are you certain?' I knew that the question was fully loaded. If he had been aware of the fight, then he'd have been duty bound to investigate, or pass the case to another prosecutor. 'I need you to answer, for the recording.'

'No, she did not,' he declared.

'Did she call you on the night that Henri died?'

'Yes. She rang me quite late, to tell me that he had gone for a walk on the cliffs and hadn't come back. She was worried about him.'

'How late?'

'I can't be sure, but it was some time after ten.'

'That's late?'

'For some.'

'Not for Henri. Inspector Guinart did some asking around yesterday. It seems he was a regular in a bar on the crest of Avinguda Montgo. He dropped in there often, after he'd been on the cliff walk; never left much before twelve. But on this night, of all nights,' he went on, 'your sister was worried, so what did you tell her to do?'

'To call the police,' he replied at once. 'Sure, I knew he was probably in a bar somewhere,' to my ear that was too glib, too quick to grab hold of what Gomez had told him, 'but it was late and I couldn't be bothered.'

'I'm sure,' said the intendant. 'One last question; when did you first learn that Henri was dead?'

'When you told me.'

'And that was the same time as you advised me you would handle the investigation yourself, out of consideration for your sister, although you knew that she'd been cheating on the dead man for fifteen years.'

'I . . .' Fumado spluttered.

'A simple yes or no, please, for the record.'

'Yes!'

'Thank you.' Gomez reached across, stopped the machine. I checked the last few seconds on the disc to make sure that it was in order. When I was satisfied, I put it away in my bag. Our leader rose to his feet; Alex and I followed suit.

'Hey,' Fumado yelped, holding out a hand, 'my file, please.'

'It's our file for the moment,' Alex told him.

'It can't leave this office,' the little man protested.

'You can come with it, if you wish,' said Gomez, ominously. There was no reply. We headed for the door.

'What's in it?' the intendant asked, as soon as we were out in the open.

'Not as much as there should be,' Alex replied. 'There's a note of the original police call, a couple of pretty poor photos of the body where it landed, there's the post-mortem report, and there's a statement from Dolores. That's it; almost. No interview with Planas, or with any witnesses. No public appeal for sightings of Michels either. These were all things we'd do automatically. Fumado must have been shitting himself until he got the post-mortem report and saw the reference to a heart attack. As soon as he saw that, he wound the investigation up as quickly as he could, only . . . the report isn't original.'

'How come?' I asked.

'The autopsy was done in Figueras, as normal. The pathologist sent his findings as an attachment to an email. It was printed out in the public prosecutor's office, which means it could have been edited.'

'Then let's find out whether it was,' said Gomez. 'Find the pathologist who opened up Michels and get hold of his original report, for comparison. Then call our best contact in Telefonica; Inez Medel, as I recall. Ask her to go back two years and to check all the calls made from the number registered to Henri Michels, on May the twenty-seventh, then to go a week forward and see how many calls were made to the same number, either from Javier Fumado's home phone or from the prosecutor's office.'

Alex nodded. 'Now do you want to know what else was in the file . . . by mistake, I am pretty certain?'

'Out with it,' I exclaimed, forgetting my place in the hierarchy.

'There's a note of a call made by a lady, Senora Hernandez, to our office in L'Escala on May thirtieth, two days after the body was found and passed on by them to Fumado, in

372

accordance with his instruction. She said that she had information for the police. Her address is in Carrer Muga, same as Henri and Dolores, and although the house has a name and not a number, I'm pretty sure she was their immediate neighbour. The note is there, but there's no sign of any statement. Either our friend didn't follow it up, or he didn't like what he heard.'

'We better go see her,' Gomez declared, 'and hope her memory's still good.' Then he looked at me. Before I even had a chance to open my mouth, he said, 'No!'

Fifty-two

Tom's first day at sailing school overran by quite a bit, and so it was almost three before we sat down to our light lunch. Happily, that's not a problem at La Clota; it's an all-day restaurant during the summer months. After we'd eaten, I had coffee and let him run through his morning. Actually he walked through it, step by step, knot by knot, tack by tack; the more he talked, the more I saw him as Johnny Depp, in his Jack Sparrow costume.

It was gone four by the time we climbed into the Jeep to go home, and I was hoping that Charlie hadn't out-stayed his welcome with Ben. Still, a glance in the mirror as we pulled away, a glimpse of that Godawful hair, persuaded me that there was time for one last call, and so I stopped at the new Farmacia in Avinguda Girona and ploughed through its stock of hair tints, until I found the one that seemed to be most like I usually look.

I needn't have worried about the dog; Tom found him happy with his pals, and his presence seemed to make Cher and Mustard less demanding of Ben. It was the quietest time of the working day in St Martí, so I expected him to be alone when I walked into the shop, but he wasn't. A blonde woman was sitting on a high stool beside the counter: Elena Fumado. She didn't look pretty; there were black circles under her eyes, and her face was lined. It struck me that she must have been crying over her mum for ten days.

'You two don't really know each other, do you?' said Ben.

We both shook our heads. 'We've met in the furniture shop,' I told him, 'and seen each other at a couple of funerals, but you're right. Hello, Elena, it's good to be formally introduced.'

'Yes,' she agreed.

'I'm sorry about your mother; truly I am.'

'You found her, didn't you?'

I wasn't ready to admit to that, so I stuck to the official version, which had a semblance of truth about it. 'My father-in-law did . . . my former father-in-law, I should say. He was walking Charlie and he barked at the storeroom door.'

'And now our priest's in prison.' She paused. 'Justine told me he's guilty. That's true?'

'He's confessed to both murders, that's true.'

'You don't believe him?'

'I'm finding it difficult,' I admitted. 'I've heard him admit it on tape, and I've learned a lot of stuff about what he was like when he was young, in Granada. Yet I'm still finding it difficult. I don't care what he was like then, I know him as he is now, and I can't come to terms with him having done something as awful as this . . . or done anything awful, for that matter. Be honest with me, Elena, you must know Gerard . . .'

'Yes,' she interposed, 'when Ben and I were together, I went to church here. I know him; he's a good priest.'

'And a good man. Can you accept this?'

'Not easily . . . but I suppose I have to. He's declared his own guilt, and the forensic evidence is absolute.'

There are no absolutes in humanity, I thought, and as I did so I felt a faintly uncomfortable wriggling, somewhere at the back of my mind.

'In a way I'm glad it's him,' Elena continued.

My frown was so quick and strong I thought I'd pulled a muscle in my forehead. 'You're glad?' I repeated.

She stared at the floor, avoiding my glare.

'Tell her, love,' said Ben quietly. 'Tell her what you've just told me.'

I looked at her for long, silent seconds as she studied the wooden flooring. 'The night José-Luis died,' she whispered, 'Angel wasn't with me. He told me that he was going to a trade association dinner in S'Agaro, and that he was going to stay overnight, since it would be a late finish, and there would be drinking. I know I shouldn't have, but with the bad blood between Angel and his father over me . . . after his body was found, and after we learned that it wasn't an accident, I checked with the hotel. There was no dinner and he didn't stay there. I've been afraid, so yes, when at first they thought you had done it, Primavera, I was relieved, I admit it. When you were cleared, my fear returned, then when Father Gerard was arrested . . .'

'I see.' She was able to return my gaze. 'Anyone but the man

377

you love. I understand that. I've been there myself . . . and I'm not talking about Gerard. But,' I added, 'you know what you've got to do, don't you?'

'Go to the police.'

'Hell no!' I exclaimed. 'You do that and you're suggesting that Angel murdered his father and your mother. I don't know the guy very well, but I don't believe that. You go to the Mossos, they clear him, then what? Do you reckon he'd ever forgive you? No, you go straight home or to the shop, wherever he is, you pin him to the nearest wall, and better still grab him by the balls, with intent, and make him tell you where he was that night.'

She looked at me, with a new respect, and a faint smile. 'Grab him by the balls?'

'With intent, remember. He has to look in your eyes and know that you're very, very serious. Also,' I added, 'since, wherever he was, he's unlikely to have been visiting his sick nun aunt in her convent, chopping and handling a few fresh chillies before you do the deed wouldn't be inappropriate either.'

'God, you're hard,' she whispered.

'No, dear, just experienced.'

Ben said nothing; he just sat there, looking terrified.

'Go on,' I said. 'Do it; and remember to call in at the fruit and veg shop on the way home.'

'I will,' she promised, 'but I don't have to rush. It's Monday, so our shop's closed; Angel's running my sister to the train station in Girona. She's off somewhere on council business. She told me where but I can't remember.'

She kissed Ben lightly, chastely, and left. I thanked him for looking after Charlie . . . Tom was herding the three dogs on Plaça Petita . . . bought some anchovies and a wheel of a very nice sheep's cheese, then headed for home.

I thought about Elena's situation. I couldn't see Angel as a killer, but clearly the guy had been playing away-games. It was interesting that she'd gone to Ben to pour out her misery; I filed that fact away for future attention.

It was gone five thirty when we got home. Normally, Tom could outrun the Duracell bunny, but his morning on the Mediterranean had left him yawning. If I'd told him to go for a snooze, there would have been rebellion, for boys don't do that during the day, not when they're nearly nine, so instead I asked if he'd like to lie and read on my terrace, while I fixed my hair. That's a bit of a treat for him, so he jumped at the offer, and headed out there with his choice of the moment. I make a point of buying him children's books in all his languages . . . Catalan's a bit difficult, but the range on offer is improving. His choice that day was *Harry Potter and the Philosopher's Stone*, in French. (No offence, JK, but I'm trying to keep him to one book a year, appropriate to his age.) I left him to it; when I checked on him five minutes later he was asleep on the lounger.

I sat in a cane chair beside him, looking at him, and thinking over my day, in particular the meeting with Javier Fumado. I wondered how the guys were getting on with Senora Hernandez . . . they had established that she still lived at that address . . . and whether what she had to tell them would prove so important that it should have been in the file, or so trivial that it wasn't worth the paper.

I knew that Alex or Hector would tell me either way, when they were good and ready, so I put it out of my mind and forced myself back to the real world, the one filled with ordinary humdrum tasks, like returning your hair to a more acceptable colour than the one you chose when you were on the run from the police. I went into my bathroom, stripped off, got under the shower and went about my task, very carefully since I wanted to make sure that every last chestnut strand was eliminated. It might be difficult for someone who is not a woman to understand that applying a hair tint is a complicated business; but then again, in this day and age, it might not. It took me the best part of an hour, but when I was finished, I was happy. In fact, I was more than happy. The shade was virtually the way I am naturally, without the sun-bleaching, and with the added bonus that I couldn't see a single one of those silver strands that have been intruding more and more over the last few years.

'Yes,' I said aloud, as I finished dressing, 'you'll do, girl.' I decided that I would buy a stock of the stuff; not that I would use it all the time, just to keep for the occasional morale boost and against the day when, God forbid . . . although he rarely does, from what I've seen in my lifetime . . . silver would move into the majority.

I picked up the discarded box so that I could make a note of the shade reference number. It was on the back at the foot. I copied it on to the notepad I keep beside the bedroom charger for the cordless phone, and as I did so, I saw something else.

It's a funny thing, one of L'Escala's peculiarities, that in the town, we only see the big green cross outside, and we tend not to think of *farmacias* as having names, other than that of the street in which they're situated, be it Avinguda Riells, or Ave Maria.

I'd bought the dye in the *farmacia* in Avinguda Girona; that's all it was to me. But when I looked at that box, and saw the stockist's name stamped on the back, I knew in that single moment exactly where the mayor of L'Escala was going on her business trip, I knew that I'd been away from my original profession for too long, and I knew that, once again, the police had got everything fundamentally wrong.

Worst of all, though, I had a terrible feeling that I knew what Justine Michels had gone to do.

Fifty-three

I was still staring at that box when Tom called to me from the terrace, book in hand, bright eyed. I hadn't expected him to sleep for more than fifteen minutes; that does the job for him during the day. 'The phone rang when you were in the shower, Mum. It was Alex; he asked if you would call him back.'

I was going to call him anyway, but first I went down to the office, went online and made some arrangements. It was only when I was ready that I picked up the phone and keyed in his mobile number.

'Primavera,' he answered, sounding on the triumphant side of cheerful, 'an update for you. Hector and I have interviewed Senora Imelda Hernandez. She was very pleased to see us, as it happened. She did make a statement two years ago, but only after she got fed up waiting for someone to call her and decided to go to Girona herself. She spoke to the public prosecutor, personally, although . . . and this is very important . . . she didn't know that he was Dolores's brother. In fact she didn't know that until we told her.'

He was so excited, I decided that my news could wait. 'What did she have to say?' I asked.

'She told us that on the night Henri died, there was shouting from the house next door, an argument, both of them yelling. Then the door slammed. Imelda Hernandez has a big round living-room window; she can see a lot from it, without being seen herself, and I reckon she looks out frequently. That night she saw Henri leave; she watched him turn into Carrer Pinedes, then round into Manol, and finally into the road that leads to the woods and beyond, to the cliff walk. But before he'd got that far, Dolores had left the house too. She took the same route, but she didn't go into the woods, not straight away. She waited, until a car pulled up, and a man got out. Imelda was too far away to identify him, but she said that he was not tall, but quite solidly built, with dark hair. Together, this man and Dolores followed Henri into the woods. That was as much as she saw, but it's what she told Fumado. That's what's important to us.'

'So you've got him?'

'Yes, beyond any doubt, because there's more. I've seen the original autopsy report. While it says that Henri suffered a heart attack, it adds that there's no way of determining that it was the cause of his fall. As you said at the very start, it could have happened when he was on his way down to the rocks. That qualification has been removed from the report that's on the file. In addition to that we know that Dolores Fumado called her brother at home at nine fifteen, not after ten as he said. My bet is that she told him straight out that she and Henri had had a fight and that when he was out walking, she'd shoved him off a cliff, and then said, "What are you going to do about it, Javier?" Yes, he's well sewn up. You're a clever lady, Primavera.'

'What happens now?'

'Tomorrow, we're going to see Chico at Restaurant Rhodas, to take a formal statement from him. Once that's done we go to the senior public prosecutor, and lay what we've got before him. Fumado's going to jail; we picked him up as he was leaving his office. Hector says thanks; we owe you one.'

I contradicted him. 'You owe me several, and I'm going to collect. First, you should go back to Imelda and ask her if she's told her story to anyone else. If so, when and to whom? Second, I want you to pull every string you've got to check all of Justine Michels' communications over the last few days . . .'

'Justine?' he exclaimed.

'Yes . . . from her home, from her mobile and from the town hall; all the calls she's made and received, texts sent and received, everything you can trace. If you can get into her personal email, that would be even better. Third, can Gomez do all the rest of the stuff on his own, and can Gloria look after Tom? I am going somewhere tomorrow, with or without you, but I really would like you to come.'

He whistled. 'Are you sure that's all? Christ, Primavera . . . what's this for, who's this for?'

'It's for Gerard,' I told him, 'and it may be about saving two lives.'

Fifty-four

I picked him up very early next morning and dropped Tom off; all three of us had an overnight bag. There wasn't much said as I drove south; Alex seemed to be still half asleep, and I never have anything to say to anyone before eight, save my son . . . not that I have anyone else looking for conversation. I had the radio on, for traffic information, but eventually Alex broke the silence.

'Imelda Hernandez grew impatient waiting for something to happen,' he announced. 'Prosecution can take a long time in this country. She knows that, but nearly two years after the event, she began to suspect the truth, that her evidence had been ignored. She tried to contact Javier Fumado, several times, but she was ignored. Eventually, she was so frustrated that she went to someone else. She went to see the mayor.'

'Yesss,' I hissed, 'that fits absolutely. To stir the family pot, no doubt.'

'No. Thing is, Senora Hernandez isn't from L'Escala. She moved here five years ago from Valladolid, after her husband died. She lives up on the hill and she hardly ever goes into the old town. She doesn't know who's who, so when she told Justine her story, that her neighbour and a mystery man had pushed her husband off a cliff, she had no idea that she was talking to Henri's daughter.'

'Indeed,' I whispered. 'When did this happen?'

'About six weeks ago.'

'And after that she followed them; she established their patterns, the time of their meetings, and when she was ready she acted.' I frowned, as a thought occurred to me. *I wonder if she had her suspicions. Was that why she kept Dolores close, in the town hall?* 'The London CSI team found Justine's DNA at the scene, I bet.'

'Sure, and discounted it, because I'd taken her there, on Hector's orders.' He twisted in his seat to look at me. 'Primavera, what are you saying?' he asked.

'You know what I'm saying: that Dolores wasn't an innocent victim; she was as much a target as Planas.'

'You're telling me that Justine Michels murdered her own mother?'

'Exactly. She took revenge for her father; killed Planas, kidnapped Dolores . . . she even covered herself by saying that they'd spoken on the following Sunday . . . starved her for a week, and when the moment was right, she throttled her.'

'I don't believe you,' he whispered.

'Yet you believed that I did it. Don't deny it, you did, or you were prepared to, on the evidence.' My mind flashed back to that Sunday, re-ran the movie. 'She must have seen me,' I said. 'She must have seen me slip and grab that chair. She saw me leave a palm print on it, on the thing that she knew was the murder weapon. And then there was my shawl,' I exclaimed.

'What about it?'

'When you drove us to Planas's house, I sat in the back. I remember now; I was wearing it then. Alex, you've got a cop's memory. Was I wearing it in the garden?'

He closed his eyes as he thought back. 'I don't recall that you were,' he said, eventually.

'I don't think I could have been, or when I slipped it would have fallen off, and I'd have noticed it. I reckon it must have dropped off my shoulders in your car. But when you took us back to the village, I sat in the front and Justine went in the back. That's when she took it, for sure.'

Alex threw his head back, and let out a deep breath. 'And do you know what? She had me keep her informed of every step of the investigation. I told her the lot, including the fact that we'd found your DNA on the chair, and that we were going to have to talk to you about it, probably on the following Monday. But I told her also that we weren't taking it seriously, that not even Hector at his most zealous could see you as a killer, not over a sum of money that would hardly buy new tyres for your Jeep.'

'When did you tell her this?'

'At Planas's funeral, outside in the square.'

'That figures. My assumption was that she might have decided to get rid of Dolores on the spur of the moment, because her car had been found, but now I can see that she was already planning it when she came to the reception in Meson.'

'Maybe, but putting the body into your store, that was a huge risk, was it not?'

'Not after Justine drugged me. She put something in my wine glass, Alex, when I wasn't looking. All of a sudden I was out of it; I left not long after you and Gomez, and I remember virtually bugger all after that till next morning, when Charlie got spooked and I found the body.'

'You did? Not Tom's grandfather?'

'Mac never saw the body, or knew it was there, until after Gerard and I had both gone. No, I found it, like an idiot I panicked, and Gerard got me out of there. Justine must really have thought she had me stitched up. She was right too, for a few days.'

'Justine and Gerard,' he murmured. 'Now he's taking the fall for her. She must have seduced him.'

'A nice old-fashioned term, Alex. Ben says that she can make people do things for her, simply because they want to please her. Yes, I suppose you could call that seduction.'

We drove down the autopista in renewed silence for a while after that, each of us with plenty on our minds. We were driving into Barcelona Airport when I remembered favour number two. 'How did you get on with tracing Justine's communications?' I asked.

'It's under way,' he replied. 'If and when our people come up with something, I'll hear about it.' He looked at me, as I drove into the multi-storey car park. 'Are you going to tell me where we're going now?'

'Malaga.'

'Why the fuck are we going to Malaga?' he asked, bewildered.

'You'll find out when we get there.'

Fifty-five

What he found out was that Malaga wasn't our ultimate destination. As soon as we emerged from the baggage hall I headed straight for the Hertz counter. (Sure, Avis may try harder, but they still haven't caught up with Number One.)

We were driving out of the airport when he asked again. 'Where? Please.'

He was starting to sound pathetic, so I gave him a clue. 'Remember that big cop you had in your office last week?'

'Captain Lavorante?'

'Yes. You might want to give him a call, since we're going to be on his patch.'

'Granada? But why?'

'Because that's where Justine Michels is headed.'

'How can you possibly know that?'

'She left a box of tampons in Gerard's house, with the stamp of Farmacia Xaloc on them. I found them when I was there, but I didn't make the connection till last night, when I saw the same name on something I'd bought. We shop in the same place.'

'Oh dear,' he sighed, 'so he and she . . . They really were . . . You must be very disappointed, Primavera.'

I laughed. 'Men stopped disappointing me a long time ago. They always live down to my expectations.'

'You're taking it well.' He frowned. 'She'll have a pretty good start on us,' he observed.

'Not much. Angel took her to Girona station; given the time that he did, I reckon she was catching the sleeper from Barcelona. It doesn't get into Granada until just before nine.'

'So what do we do when we get there? Go to Gerard's house and grab her, I suppose. But why the hell's she going there?'

'Maybe she isn't going to the house. Go on, make your call.'

Most people would have used directory inquiries. Alex didn't; he simply called One One Two, the emergency number, identified himself and asked the operator to connect him with Captain Jorge Lavorante of the Granada Municipal Police. I switched off from the conversation, much of which was in police speak. When it was over, he turned to me and said that Lavorante had suggested that we go to his office.

'Did you agree?'

'Yes, but I didn't say when.'

I had asked for a car with a navigation system. It was telling me that we weren't all that far from the city, although I could see that for myself, when Alex's phone rang. He flipped it open. 'Yes?'

This time I did tune in. 'Yes? Well done. Only one? Yes, do that please, right now.' He closed the phone and looked across at me once more. 'There's a number, a mobile number, that Justine's called a lot. It's a top-up card and we don't have a clue who's on the other end. She called it last on Saturday morning, had a call back on Sunday, then yesterday morning she sent a text.' The phone sounded again as he spoke; he flipped it open. 'My star at Telefonica can access it; she's forwarding it to me.' He pressed a button. 'And here it is now. "*Torre de la Vela, ten thirty, tomorrow night.*" That's it; that's all she says. What the hell does that mean?'

'It means they're meeting in the Alhambra tonight; that's where Torre de la Vela is.'

'How will they get in? It isn't open at night.'

'Who told you that? There's a guided tour of the place every night, after dark, when it's floodlit.'

'So who's she meeting? It can't be Gerard; he's locked up in Barcelona. Do you know?'

'I suspect she knows we're on to her, or figures that it's only a matter of time. This meeting is all to do with her escape plan.'

'So what do we do in the meantime, once we get to Granada?'

'First we check into the very nice, very large hotel that I've booked us into.'

'What if Justine's there as well?'

'She won't be. I'm ninety per cent certain that I know where she'll be staying. Once we're settled in, I suggest that to avoid any chance of the two of us being spotted, even in a city with a few hundred thousand visitors, we go and spend the day with our friend Lavorante. Oh yes, and we'd better get tickets for the night tour.'

Alex grinned at me. 'You're a diamond, Primavera, but you're flawed, thank God. We don't need tickets; we're the police.'

Fifty-six

'You're looking for a woman.' Lavorante laughed across his coffee table. 'You've come to the right place, Inspector Guinart. Would you like gypsy, Arab, Chinese, South American, African, or, of course, East European? All available in Granada, and very reasonably priced. Or you could have German, or Scandinavian, or even French; they're here too, if rather more expensive.' He looked at me from under the Boris Karloff eyebrows. 'But not British, senora,' he added. 'Not that I know of, anyway.'

'That's comforting.' I took a card from my bag, wrote a name on the back and handed it to him. 'If you call this place,' I said, 'you might find that the one we're after is registered. She's none of the above, by the way; she's Spanish.'

'Discreet, mind,' Alex warned.

Lavorante spread his arms wide. 'Do I look like the unsubtle type?'

He went to the desk, in his surprisingly spacious and elegant office, picked up the phone and made the call. 'You're right,' he grunted as he came back to us. 'She's there and she's in her room.'

'We could check to see whether she's bought a ticket for the tour through the hotel,' Alex suggested.

'We could,' I agreed, 'but we know she's going there anyway, plus, I suspect that she'll have bought privately.'

'So,' he said checking his watch, 'we stay here for another five, six hours.'

'It would be just like the thing for us to go for a coffee and sit at the next table to Justine, suppose she decides to go out for some fresh air. There's no reason why she shouldn't either.'

'You don't need to lock yourselves in,' our host told us. 'I'll take you somewhere damn few tourists will go, especially a lady on her own. A couple of hours and we'll head off. Meantime . . . enjoy my city.' He took a DVD from a pile on the table, stuck it into a player and switched it on. It was an elaborate story of the history of Granada; even I found it fascinating, and I'd already had the unofficial guided tour. It ended with a section on the Alhambra, useful advance information for Alex.

When it was over, Lavorante told us to go with him; we slid into a patrol car and he murmured an instruction in the driver's ear. He nodded, and headed for the Albacin, then up past the road that leads to Goats' Hill, and beyond, higher still. 'Are those caves?' I asked Lavorante, as we drew to a halt.

'They sure are,' he said. 'Pick us up here at nine,' he told the driver. 'These are the caves of Sacromonte, where the gypsies live and where you will see the best flamenco in the world. Come on.' He led us into what I'd thought was a dwelling; it turned out to be a small theatre, with tables set below a stage.

A woman came towards us, dressed in pure Romany style. 'Big Jorge!' she bellowed. 'Good to see you again.'

'Can we eat?' he asked.

'Of course. And drink.'

'Maybe but not too much. We have something to do later.'

'What do you want?' she asked. 'The tortilla?'

By that time I knew what was in it; I declined, with a show of regretful thanks, and settled for a ridiculous amount of jabugo ham, with tomato bread and hard manchego cheese. We washed it down with a carafe of red wine and then another. Alex and I were abstemious, but it occurred to me that if Big Jorge was having a quiet night, I wouldn't like to see him on a bender.

And they danced for us; three girls, two men, with three guitarists playing behind them and singing the sort of songs that makes it worth learning Spanish just to understand them.

When Lavorante looked at his watch and nodded to us that it was time, I didn't want to leave. But I remembered what we were there for. I reached for my money clip in my bag, but the big man shook his head. 'These people are friends of mine; don't offend them.'

Outside, night had all but fallen. Our driver was waiting, as ordered. To take us down one hill and then up another, the one on which the Alhambra stands. By the time we got there, it was just short of ten, and buses were starting to arrive at the top of the rise above the entrance. We went straight there; Lavorante badged the guy on the gate and he let us in.

'Over here,' the cop said, leading us into the one dark corner of the square, in front of the great ramparts of the Alcazabar, the citadel. Even in the gloom I was afraid that his bulk would give us away, but he seemed to have the gift of making himself smaller, for as the visitors began to arrive, not one of them looked in our direction.

There were more than I'd expected, enough for someone to hide in their midst, if she was worried about being spotted. But she wasn't.

Alex saw her first, bringing up the rear of a group of about thirty. He nudged me and pointed. Lavorante whistled softly in the darkness. 'Hey,' he whispered, 'a looker and no mistake. What's she done, this lovely woman?'

'Murdered her mother and her mother's lover, after she found out that they killed her father.'

'In L'Escala? But this is the thing that Gerard did. You heard yourself, he said so.'

'Now that I think about it very carefully, Jorge, he didn't say any such thing. All he did was acknowledge the so-called brilliance of Valdes's theory, and said that he would sign his name to it. Actually, he admitted nothing.'

We waited until the group was inside and followed them, moving slowly, keeping to the shadows in case Justine should glance behind her. We followed the stone path that leads to the courtyard of the citadel, slowly, for the guides were taking their time, but eventually it opened out, into a big rectangular space.

'Here,' said Lavorante. We followed him and stood behind a yellow floodlight, against a wall, completely invisible even to someone who was daft enough to stare straight at it. We watched Justine as she slipped into the shadows also, looking about herself, as the parties made their way round, back towards the way they had come, and on to the next stage of the tour. I checked my watch; it was just luminous enough: ten thirty.

She began to move, not worried about concealment any more, stepping out of the shadows and on to the path that led to the great square battlements of the highest point in the city, the watchtower of Granada.

We hung back until she had reached the enclosed stairway that leads to the very top, and vanished from our sight, before we followed, moving quickly along the path, and as silently as we could. Lavorante never made a sound. He led the way up the stairs, I followed and Alex brought up the rear. We were in no hurry, for there's no other way out.

The soft light flooded the square summit of La Torre de la Vela as we reached the last of the steps. The captain stood aside, to let Alex and me go ahead.

He'd slipped in ahead of her. I'd seen him, but I'd said nothing; it was enough that Alex and Jorge were looking for Justine. They were standing in the corner to our left, against the ramparts with an inadequate, incongruous little rail on top, beyond the bell tower, at least thirty metres away, and maybe more, but we could see them clearly. They were kissing, and I do not mean once on each cheek, Spanish style. His hands were by his side, and her left arm was wound around his neck, her palm on his shoulder. Her right hand, though, was moving up slowly, from his waist. We watched as it stopped, fingers splayed, in the very centre of his chest.

She'd have pushed him then, I know it for sure, over the edge and down to his death, if I hadn't shouted when I did.

'Justine!'

She broke away from him and spun round, staring at us as we stepped out from the doorway and into the light.

He looked at us too . . . no, he looked directly at me . . . but in a different way, with a serene resignation that I'd never seen before.

'Gerard?' a bemused Alex murmured beside me.

'Santi!' I screamed, for I knew what he was going to do.

He smiled at me, the lovely man, then leaned backwards over that useless rail, and disappeared, making not a sound as he plunged into darkness.

Fifty-seven

We all stared at Justine, and she stood looking back at us, regaining her composure with every second.

'Primavera,' Alex whispered, 'what . . .'

I was shivering with horror at what had just happened. At least thirty seconds must have passed before I was able to speak. 'You didn't know they were twins, did you?' I said at last. 'Nobody on your team did, and Jorge here never mentioned it. As for me, it took me too long to work it out. Gerard and Santi were monozygotic; identical twin brothers. That means, Alex, that they were born with identical DNA. It wasn't Gerard's you found, it was his brother's; Gerard knew that right away, and he confessed to protect him. He even forbade Valdes from contacting Santi, to stop him finding out and making the connection.'

'And was he protecting her too?'

'I don't know, but I suspect that he was, if only because he didn't think he had a choice. Santi only came to L'Escala a couple of times; he and Justine must have met on one of those visits. The priest's identical brother, the airline pilot with pads in Madrid and Granada: I'll bet he was a trophy to her. Just like Angel Planas is.'

'Angel?'

'Yes. When Elena was with Ben, Justine took his scalp, so to speak. Remember the story about her fainting during her sister's wedding? That wasn't because of the heat, it was because she was pregnant. By him, by Santi? She'll never say, but Angel believed it was his. She had a termination in a clinic in Barcelona, she made Angel pay for it, and the poor guy's been under her control ever since.

'He called me yesterday evening and told me all of it, after his wife had given him a real grilling about where he was on the night his father was killed. He'd spun her a story about a business conference, but he was really with Justine, on her insistence, in the Hotel Bon Retorn in Figueras. To be her alibi, if necessary, I guess. Only she wasn't with him all night. She drugged him, probably with the same stuff she used on me, then slipped out to kill Planas and kidnap her mother; he woke up when she climbed back into bed, once Santi had taken Dolores to wherever they kept her, till Justine was ready to get rid of her.

'Santi was a really nice guy, you know; he had everything going for him. He must have been completely besotted to have done what he did for her. I don't believe he killed anyone. I'm sure Justine did that, but he helped her to set up the accident scene and to get Dolores out of there, then later to plant her at my place. Yet she was going to dispose of him too, as you've just seen.'

'You knew him,' Lavorante said, more a statement than a question.

'Yes. Gerard asked him to go to Granada and look after me. Ironic, isn't it?' I thought about our time together. 'And yet I never felt threatened by him. I should have guessed much earlier about the twin thing, but it never occurred to me for a moment, because Santi was so nice.'

'Yeah,' the big cop whispered. 'He was all that.'

'I'm surprised he let you leave,' Alex murmured.

I hadn't considered that point. 'I didn't tell him I was going,' I replied. Maybe if I had, he might not have been so nice . . . I banished the thought.

'How did they get into the place?' he pondered. 'It's still clear that the old man was taken by surprise.'

'I don't know,' I admitted. 'But I'll make a guess. Santi and Gerard's father was a locksmith. There's a back gate in Planas's garden wall, and if you check, I'll bet you find that it's been picked, just as the lock on my store was opened without a key.'

'All of that. Why?' Lavorante asked. Justine was walking towards us, her dark hair falling around her shoulders, her eyes shining. She had gathered herself together completely. Indeed, it was more than that; an aura of triumph seemed to embrace her.

'Because she worshipped her father,' I told him. 'I could see it in her eyes the first time we met, and every time she spoke about him after that.'

She stopped, a few feet away, and looked directly at me, as

calm as anyone I've ever seen. 'I'll give you that much,' she said. 'I worshipped my papa.' Then she looked at Alex, with a sneering smile. 'Now go ahead and prove the rest of it.'

Fifty-eight

They couldn't. They didn't even have enough evidence for Captain Lavorante to be able to hold her that night, or to detain her at all. She walked out of the Alhambra, went back to the Palacio de los Patos, and checked out next morning. We found out later that she took a taxi to Granada-Jaen Airport, and flew to Madrid; I'm sure she had a key to Santi's apartment. She never came back to L'Escala and nobody's seen her since that night. Through a lawyer, she sold her town house in Carrer del Mig, and her mother's place, which she'd inherited automatically, as the older child. Elena didn't get a cent.

Two months ago, Angel Planas skipped town. He left to open the shop one morning and when Elena went there to join him, she found a note. It told her only that he was leaving, and had instructed his solicitor to make the business and their house over to her. He'd already disposed of the rest of his father's property. So I guess Justine wasn't blackmailing him after all . . . or she really is that good at manipulating people.

Elena has what she has but she's alone now. Maybe she'll

wind up back with Ben. I don't know, but I hope so. Somebody deserves a happy ending out of all of this.

Gerard didn't come back either. He went home to Granada as soon as he was released from prison, the day after Santi died, to take care of his funeral. It may turn out to be one of the great regrets of my life that I flew home next morning without thinking about that. If I'd stayed, if I'd been there when he arrived, maybe lots of things would be different now.

But then again . . .

I had a letter from him a few days later.

My dearest Primavera

I'm sure that you will have heard me say this once before, on a recording, and I'll admit it again. I love you. But I loved my brother too, and I loved Irena, and look what happened to them, so I hope you'll understand that I'm more than a little afraid to expose you to the same danger.

There is also the fact that I still love God, although for the first time since I made my vows to him, he has a rival. I have many things to discover. Do I still have my vocation? Am I the poison to people that I fear I might be? Can I learn to love myself, as well as to love others? For at this moment I do not.

To find the answers to these questions, or as many as I can, I have taken leave from the priesthood. I'm going to enter a Benedictine monastery in Limerick in Ireland, for the next two years according to my present plan.

There's a boys' school attached, and I'm going to teach Spanish.

I ask you to do something that you may find difficult, but maybe not, maybe it'll be easy for you. Please don't visit me there or try to contact me. Get on with your life, look after your fine boy, and let me work things out for myself. I have a weakness for you, and if I saw you it would probably overcome me, just as that woman overcame my poor brother. May God forgive me for introducing them the first time he came to L'Escala, for I'll never forgive myself.

My love again, to you and Tom,

Yours ever,

Gerard

It took me a couple of boxes of Kleenex to get through that one, I'll tell you.

I took his advice. I'm getting on with my life. I still have the falling dream every so often, but by and large I'm all right. I've settled into my job with the embassy, and I'm doing a fair bit of travelling, thanks to a lady called Catriona O'Riordan, once of the Royal Green Jackets, would you believe, and latterly a sub-lieutenant in the Rifle Regiment. She looks after the house, she looks after Tom and she even helps me run my silly, self-indulgent information booth; plus she makes me feel secure.

The wine fair happened, and was it ever a success. We sold two thousand tickets, the most we reckoned the venue could handle. Sales were sluggish at first, until finally, I used my secret weapon, my brother-in-law Miles Grayson. Like many famous Aussies, Miles has his own wine label, and it's an expanding business. His latest acquisition is a small but high-quality producer, not far from the town of Cadaques, and one of the exhibitors at the fair. He'd never heard of it until I pointed him in its direction, but once he'd looked at the books and tasted the product he was hooked. When I announced that he would be on-site for all three days of the fair, the tickets went in the blink of a bloodshot eye.

Tom's handling Gerard's absence. I showed him the letter. He didn't shed a single tear. Far from it; he smiled, gave it back to me and said, 'He'll be back.'

'Son,' I began, but he let me get no further.

'Read it again. That's what it says.'

I've tried, but I can't share his certainty, his faith, I suppose. He's nearer nine than ever now, and still acting as an altar server for Father Olivares, sometimes in the big church in L'Escala. The old man's set aside any thought of retirement; I suspect that he's keeping the seat warm for someone . . . just as I am, I suppose.

I've decided that I will give him at least one of his two years. After that, if he hasn't returned, I'll either declare myself open for suitable invitations, or I'll say, 'Bugger this for a game of Benedictines!' and head for Limerick.

Until then . . .